PRAISE FOR *LOVE G*

"Holy smokes, I loved, loved, loved this. . . .
put it down. I recommend it highly."

—Abernathy Peterson, librarian, Kentuck

"With his experience as a forensic psychiatrist, Dr.
readers inside the mind of a man that is dangerous,
point, brilliant, persistent and definitely diabolical
yers, judges, doctors and an entire courtroom. Once
pens a novel that far surpasses many others and is ri
Lescroart, Daniel Silva, James Patterson and Phillip M

—Fran Lewis, Host, *Book Discussion*

"Excellent! Well written with strong characters and an interesting story line."

—Joanne Carrero, educator, Puerto Rican Family Institute

"A good read. I could not put it down!"

—Sybil Huffman, librarian

"A fast-paced, exciting mystery sure to hold readers' attention."

—Rosemary Smith, librarian, Williams Library, Regional School Unit, Maine

PRAISE FOR *MAD DOG HOUSE*

"I stayed up all night to read *Mad Dog House*. I didn't plan on it, but when I got into it, I couldn't put it down. It was fantastic, riveting, suspenseful, twisting, loving, horrific—and I'll never go into the restaurant business, ever. I just kept reading faster and faster to find out the ending."

—Martin West, film and television actor and filmmaker

"The characters in *Mad Dog House* are compellingly real. It was a great read!"

—Ann Chernow, artist and writer

"In Mark Rubinstein's *Mad Dog House*, the characters—all well-developed and dripping with authenticity—propel the novel along with style and edge-of-your-seat excitement. Word of caution: be prepared for an all-night, page-turning read where you will emerge exhilarated and begging for more. Rubinstein, a master at his game, introduces us to a world of glitz, glam, sex, and intrigue. Slip into a chilled martini and settle in for a literary ride you won't soon forget."

—Judith Marks-White, author of *Seducing Harry* and *Bachelor Degree*

"Thank you for the great adventure . . . made me feel like a participant. I could not put the darn thing down."

—Rose Buzzutto, RN

"The characters are well-drawn, the dialog is real and not stilted . . . and the action is well-paced.

—*Rochelle's Reviews*

"A gripping, harrowing, and provocative psychological thriller, featuring a plot packed with action and intrigue, staggering and brutal twists, and deeply disturbing possibilities . . . the author . . . has a gift for delivering gut-punching surprises while raising unsettling questions about the basic nature of human nature and the inescapable hold of the past. The ending is a real shocker!"

—Mysia Haight, www.pressreleasepundit.com

Love Gone Mad

Other Books by Mark Rubinstein

Fiction

Mad Dog House (Thunder Lake Press)

Nonfiction

The First Encounter: The Beginnings in Psychotherapy
with Dr. William Console and Dr. Richard C. Simons (Jason Aronson)

The Complete Book of Cosmetic Surgery
with Dr. Dennis P. Cirillo (Simon & Schuster)

New Choices: The Latest Options in Treating Breast Cancer
with Dr. Dennis P. Cirillo (Dodd Mead)

Heartplan: A Complete Program for Total Fitness of Heart & Mind
with Dr. David L. Copen (McGraw-Hill)

The Growing Years: The New York Hospital-Cornell Medical Center Guide to Your Child's Emotional Development (Atheneum)

A Novel

MARK RUBINSTEIN

Thunder Lake Press

Thunder Lake Press
25602 Alicia Parkway #512
Laguna Hills, CA 92653
www.thunderlakepress.com

Ordering Information
Quantity sales. Special discounts are available on quantity purchases by corporations, associations, and others. For details, contact the "Special Sales Department" at the address above.

Orders by US trade bookstores and wholesalers. Please contact BCH: (800) 431-1579 or visit www.bookch.com for details.

Printed in the United States of America

Cataloging-in-Publication
Rubinstein, Mark, 1942-
Love gone mad : a novel / Mark Rubinstein. -- 1st ed.
p. cm.
ISBN 978-0-9856268-6-0
1. Psychological fiction. 2. Suspense fiction.
I. Title.
PS3618.U3L68 2013
813'.6 QBI13-600077

Author photo by Philip W. Kaufman

First Edition

17 16 15 14 13 10 9 8 7 6 5 4 3 2 1

For Joshua, Vernon, and both Ediths

Part I

One

Adrian Douglas heads for the operating room doors. He glances back at the argon beam coagulator, the hydraulic operating table, and brilliant OR lights. As sterile as the filtered air and gleaming instruments may be, the place is a thing of ineffable beauty. It signifies a kind of artistry, one he's spent years mastering. Adrian thinks this after every successful surgery, and for the moment, the OR is the best thing in his life. He knows it's good to be alive and in the life-saving business.

The patient had been dying—his heart barely able to pump blood. They had cracked open his chest, bypassed the clogged coronary arteries, and closed up in near-record time.

A stitch in time . . .

"Great job, Adrian," Fred Bailey, the assistant surgeon, calls across the room.

"Thanks, Fred. Thanks, everyone. Fabulous work, guys," Adrian says, snapping off his surgical gloves.

"Hey, Adrian," Dottie, the chief OR nurse, calls.

"Yeah?"

"Chalk another one up for the good guys."

Though her face is masked, Adrian sees the shine in her eyes. And he hears the smile in her voice.

Still wearing surgical scrubs, Adrian dons his windbreaker and New Balance running shoes and then takes the elevator to the hospital's main floor. He leaves through the emergency room. It's a balmy night in early September, and a brisk breeze whips up the ambulance ramp, which is illuminated by sodium vapor lights. Though he's been on his feet since six this morning, he feels invigorated with the postsurgical high he loves and doesn't want to make the lonely drive back to his cottage in Simpson.

Looking up at the hospital facade, Adrian tells himself he's glad he left ground zero of the medical universe—Yale-New Haven Hospital—and took the job at Eastport General. He's in on the ground floor of an exciting new heart surgery program. At Yale, he'd be just another guppy darting about an aquarium of sharks cannibalizing one another.

None of that political bullshit for me. Not anymore.

It's nearly midnight as Adrian crosses Fairfield Avenue. He passes a row of shuttered stores—a Kinko's, a Wendy's, and a Starbucks that's closing for the evening; Adrian realizes that no barista will serve up a steaming latte, Frappuccino, or foamed macchiato at this hour. It's time to go more downscale, and besides, a little alcohol would be better than some caffeine-laced brew. So he heads for King's Corner, a watering hole two blocks away. He's grown absurdly fond of this dated pub with its beer-stained mahogany bar, neon Schlitz signs, potted snake plants, and 1950s-style, CD-filled Wurlitzer jukebox. It's so retro, it reminds Adrian of the old Irish bars in Manhattan he'd frequented as a medical student.

Entering the place, Adrian hears the first lines of Led Zeppelin's "Stairway to Heaven." The acoustic guitar sends out a mournful melody; it's joined by the soulful recorder. Then comes the plaintive vocal by lead singer Robert Plant.

The place is dimly lit and smells of malt—actually, stale beer. And there's the faint odor of piss, or, Adrian wonders briefly, is it sweat? No matter. It's familiar, comfortable. A muted cathode-ray television on a shelf casts an aqueous hue over the place as the

Red Sox play the Yankees—it must be extra innings to be running this late. Swivel-top, vinyl-covered stools line the length of the bar, like soldiers at attention before an iron-pipe foot rail. There's a vintage tin ceiling. The dim seediness seems welcoming after hours in a brightly lit OR with its modular orbital lighting and antiseptic tile walls.

Vinnie, the thirty-something bartender, turns to him, his face creasing into a smile. "How ya doin' Adrian?"

"Good, Vinnie. You?"

"Can't complain."

"How're the wife and kids?"

"They keep me workin'," Vinnie says, and shakes his head.

Vinnie has a flattened nose and rough-hewn features and always sports a thick stubble of beard. He looks like a guy who's seen his share of barroom brawls. He wears faded jeans and a tight-fitting, sleeveless T-shirt. His bloated biceps are covered with a riotous array of tattoos.

"Bottle of Bud, Adrian?"

"Right on, Vin," he says as the music in a minor key hits its ethereal stride.

Adrian and Vinnie usually talk about the Red Sox. As a former college baseball player, Adrian loves the game.

"Score's tied . . . five apiece," Vinnie says, setting the bottle on the bar.

A smoky vapor rises from the open top.

Adrian puts the bottle to his lips, takes a gulp, and feels the cold effervescence at the back of his throat. After a long day in the OR, the beer's warmth mushrooms through his belly and rises to his chest. It's followed by a deliciously light buzz. Adrian feels his muscles loosen.

"That's damned good music, Vinnie," he says.

"Adrian—my *man*," Vinnie calls. "Nobody loves Led Zeppelin like we do." Vinnie moves down the bar.

He's had only one swig, but Adrian already feels a foamy web of warmth in his head. He seems to float in the bar's dimness.

Adrian hears a voice—but it's muffled by the music.

He takes another pull on the Bud. A haze settles in his brain.

"I said . . . *Adrian?*"

Startled, Adrian peers to his right.

A ruggedly built man in his midthirties stands at the bar. He stares intensely with cold, deep-set gray eyes. The guy's about six two, maybe taller—with sloped, powerful-looking shoulders and a broad, well-muscled chest. He has a bull neck with cordlike veins that look like blood-filled pipes. Even in a flannel jacket, the man's arms are thick, sinewy. His hands are huge, with thick, gnarled fingers.

"*Adrian*? Do I know you?"

Adrian suddenly feels a clenched dread. A knot forms in his stomach. A shudder floats through his chest. He draws back as if by instinct. The man is steep-jawed; he has a Vandyke beard and closely cropped blondish hair cut in a semimilitary style.

"I don't think so . . ."

"Oh, yes . . . I *know* you . . ."

The guy edges closer, looming larger.

Adrian thinks the man's nostrils quiver as though he smells something. Even in the bar's dimness, Adrian registers the strange grayness of the man's eyes, with their pitted-olive black pupils reflecting a purple neon sign. Adrian sees a dark madness there, a smoldering rage, and something cold crawls through him.

"Adrian . . . That's a girl's name. You a faggot?"

Adrian's mouth goes dry. The guy reminds him of a beast—something lethal, soulless. Adrian's fingers tingle; his scalp dampens.

Holy shit. This is unbelievable. It's not from the life I've been living. What's this guy about?

"Look, mister," Adrian says. "I don't know you and I'm—"

"Hey, *you*," Vinnie growls from behind the bar.

The man's eyes shift to Vinnie. The guy has yet to blink.

Voltage charges through the air.

Except for the jukebox, the place goes quiet.

"Vinnie," Adrian says, "there's no need—"

"It's okay, Adrian," says Vinnie as his sumo-sized arm slips beneath the bar. "If you're looking for trouble, you son of a bitch, you've come to the right place." A blue-black baseball bat appears in his hand. "Get the fuck outta here. *Now!*"

Suddenly, the guy's arm lunges out in a mercury-quick movement; his beer bottle slams onto the bar. The bottle bounces, topples, and twirls wildly as foamy beer spurts out its neck. He glares at Vinnie with those cold, unblinking eyes. "I'll be back," he says and then turns to Adrian. "And I'll see you too, faggot."

Adrian's skin feels like it's peeling. His insides go cold, as though an ice floe encircles his heart.

The guy turns, casts another look at Vinnie, and saunters out the door.

Led Zeppelin's chorus fills the room.

Adrian's armpits are soaked. His heart batters his rib cage, and his knees feel weak.

"You know that guy?" Adrian asks, surprised at the steadiness of his voice.

"Nah," Vinnie says, setting the bat behind the bar. "Been hanging around a couple a weeks now. Looks like he's been waitin' for someone."

"Looks like he was waiting for me . . ."

"He's just killin' time—comes in around seven, stays an hour or two, leaves, then wanders in again around eleven, stays another hour. Nurses a bottle of beer, that's all. Doesn't talk to anyone. Strange guy." Vinnie swipes the beer bottle, tosses it into a bin, and wipes down the bar top. "In this business, you meet all types . . ."

Vinnie heads toward the grill area.

Adrian waits for the adrenaline rush to subside. He feels his heart still throbbing in his throat. He swigs his beer, and it shoots right to his brain. His legs are unsteady. He plops down on a stool.

The last stanza of "Stairway to Heaven" resounds through the bar.

The front window shatters. A scorching air blast whooshes through the room as bottles detonate in a percussive blowout. Glass, liquor, and debris scatter as neon explodes and everything flies. Everyone drops to the floor.

Another blast sprays the place.

The lights flicker; one goes out.

Smoke, plaster, and dust float in the air.

"A shotgun!" shouts Vinnie; he leaps over the bar and rushes out the front door.

A dangling ceiling light sizzles.

A babble of voices rises; panic-level fear takes over as patrons stampede toward the back of the place. It's pure mayhem.

"Don't go out the door," someone shouts. "He could be there."

Vinnie bursts back in, looking around. "Anyone hurt?"

"What the hell was that?" someone calls.

"A shotgun," Vinnie says, snapping open his cell phone.

A patron swipes shards of glass from his hair. Another guy curses. Someone whimpers. A few men rush for the front door.

Adrian gets to his feet. "You see who it was?"

"Probably that bastard I kicked out," Vinnie says, dialing 911. "It was a black pickup, a big Ford or Chevy with a steel toolbox behind the cab. He was goin' like a bat outta hell."

"You get his plate?"

"Nah . . . He was goin' too fast."

The place smells like malt and acrid smoke—a trace of whiskey, too. The walls are pocked with pellet holes. Ceiling wires dangle, spit, and sputter.

"It's King's Corner," Vinnie says into his cell. "There's been a drive-by shooting through my front window."

A pause as Vinnie listens.

"No . . . nobody's hurt . . ."

The music builds in a surge of guitars and vocals. The air is hazy, yellowish, and caustic. It smells chemical. Booze drips from shattered bottles.

Vinnie's still on his cell, talking to the police dispatcher.

The music hits a crescendo and then goes serene.

A police siren burps and then whoops. Whirling lights suddenly appear; they carousel everywhere.

The Led Zeppelin vocalist ends the song in a voice that conjures up angels.

Two

Adrian stands on the cafeteria line. It's a hospital lunchtime madhouse. Pure bedlam. The expanse seems to swell like a roiling sea.

A thunderous crash erupts amid the maelstrom. Adrian reflexively whirls and crouches. An electric surge rips through him. *Shotgun!*

Adrian realizes a huge metal tray cart has overturned. The floor is piled with plastic trays and debris. The moment of shock evaporates. People help the cafeteria workers pull the cart upright and slide trays back into the racks.

Last night's shotgun blast tramples through Adrian's thoughts. The air-sucking whoosh, the glass shards, the smoke, the sizzling ceiling wires, the pockmarked walls, all of it. It's life and death—in the OR and at King's Corner.

"Adrian? Do I know you? You a faggot?"

The words bubble through him like a hemorrhage—again and again—and each time, a sickening wave of dread washes through him. He feels his guts contract as he recalls that moment. Adrian tells himself to push the memory away; it's an aberration, not part of his life. His life is here, at Eastport General, where lives can be saved. After all, that's the business he's in.

Amid the oceanic roar of the cafeteria, Adrian slides his tray along the three-barred railing, picks up a container of chicken soup, a slice of carrot cake, and plastic utensils, and then fills a cup with diet soda from the dispenser. No ice.

Adrian spies his surgical team at a table—six people in hospital greens and surgical caps, chomping sandwiches, guzzling mineral water or coffee, talking and laughing. No seat there. The place is a fluorescent-lit sea of white coats and surgical scrubs—doctors, nurses, attendants, technicians. EMS people and visitors in civilian clothes, too.

Adrian looks about for a seat, catches snippets of conversation amid salvos of laughter and aromas of lunchtime fare—chicken soup, meat loaf, pizza, and tuna fish. He and Richie Moscatello see each other and smile. They've known each other since medical school at Cornell, where they did plenty of late-night drinking after exams. That ended when Richie got married and had a kid. Everyone, it seems, has kids.

But not Adrian.

Passing some scrub-suited orthopedic surgeons, Adrian sees a brawny guy with a stethoscope dangling around his neck. The guy's arms bulge in the surgical greens; it reminds Adrian of that madman in King's Corner last night. That face, the neck, those huge hands, the quivering nostrils—and those eyes—unforgettable.

Adrian? That's a girl's name.

You a faggot?

Adrian knows he's still spooked by that steely eyed psycho. The rawness of the encounter has begun fading, but the adrenaline needs time to burn off and dissipate the way a foul odor dissolves with time. But the jangling sensation peaks in an instant—shoots through him—like when the cart overturned. Or earlier this morning when a tire blew out in the hospital garage. Adrian's insides jumped.

I'll be back.

The fucking Terminator—a scene right out of the movie.

And I'll see you, too, faggot.

Adrian scours the cafeteria. Not a single seat in sight. He wonders if it might be better to brown-bag it from now on; it would be easier, much less fuss, but he'd miss the connectedness of the cafeteria, the nearness of life around him.

On the other hand, the camaraderie of the place just heightens his loneliness.

As he passes a group of nurses, Mary Pearson, a tall blonde, winks at him. She's been incredibly flirtatious since Adrian's divorce from Peggy. He and Mary had had a brief, tempestuous fling at Yale, long before he and Peggy had met. Only a few months ago, a message arrived at his hospital e-mail. It said:

Adrian, I'm around. Mary.

He didn't respond; he thought it would be unwise.

Then another one popped up.

We can still be friends, can't we? Mary.

For sure, it's a small universe: Eastport, Yale, and Bridgeport Hospital. Everyone knows everyone—and they know everyone's business, too. It's a gossip mill. But Adrian doesn't want to get into the casual friends-with-privileges thing. Stir up dead embers and you can ignite an unwanted fire—a shit storm of recriminations. And you don't shit where you eat, he thinks. He throws Mary a tight-lipped smile, an unspoken *Yes, we shared a moment of need and convenience back then, but not now.*

He finally spies an empty seat and moves toward it. A woman sits alone at the table. She's drop-dead gorgeous. Adrian feels his knees wobble; he's riveted by her.

"May I join you?" he asks. It's the obligatory self-invitation—not overly friendly, just plain straight-talk—merely asking in a polite and casual way. Walking the social high wire—sending out carefully calibrated cues. Not too hot, not to cool . . . just right. The Goldilocks approach.

She looks up briefly and nods indifferently; he sits down.

Settling into the chair, Adrian realizes he's been on his feet since six thirty. His arches ache and his feet feel leaden. Maybe he's a candidate for orthotic inserts. No wonder most surgeons retire by age sixty. So . . . at forty, he's got twenty more years of cracking chests and mending hearts. Plenty can happen in twenty years, he thinks.

Twenty years . . . I can't think that far ahead . . . and I don't want to think of the past.

Steam rises from his soup in a vaporous cloud. It's too hot to slurp. The bowl, the soup's aroma, and the plastic tray remind him of the dorm food at Cornell; they bring back the verdant rolling hills of the Finger Lakes, rowing on Cayuga Lake and playing center field on the varsity baseball team. It's amazing—Ithaca, New York—merely a whiff away.

He glances across the table—eyeballs the woman. She's staring down at a book; an untouched egg salad sandwich sits on her plate. A container of coffee sits nearby. It's obviously cooled down—there's no vapor. She's wearing green surgical scrubs and a long white coat. Her name tag says, "Megan Haggarty, RN." Beneath it, "Neonatal Intensive Care."

Adrian . . . do I know you . . . ?

That shock-like sensation jolts through Adrian. His legs tighten. Forget last night, he tells himself. It was a few moments of craziness in an otherwise sane world.

He peers at Megan Haggarty. God, she's gorgeous. Her face has the look of unbroken Celtic lineage—beautiful Irish features—unattainable beauty, he thinks. She's in her early thirties, Adrian guesses. She has fiery red hair with an iridescent hint of blond and a coppery undertone. It looks silken soft and shines under the fluorescent lighting. Pulled back, it flows into a hair clip, perfectly framing her oval face. He can almost smell it through the curling soup vapor infiltrating his nostrils.

Is blood rushing to his cheeks? Or is it the steaming-hot soup?

Either way, he feels flushed.

Megan Haggarty's forehead is high; her cheekbones are prominent. Her nose is delicately sculpted, while her jaw is square, firm. Auburn eyebrows accentuate her forehead. Her skin is bone-white and looks creamy, luscious. What would it taste like? he wonders. Staring at her, he knows he's incapable of subtlety.

Her eyes flick up—past him. They're hazel with emerald-green rings around the irises. He's never seen such eyes—so soulful and sad in a way. She's seen hard times, he thinks. It's in those eyes. He could *fall* into them.

She turns a page. Adrian realizes he might as well be a vapor wafting in a wind.

God . . . she's a work of art.

He scans the book upside down, a skill he refined riding on subway trains in Manhattan years ago. *In Cold Blood.* Oh, right—Truman Capote. Four poor souls murdered by two madmen using a shotgun in the Kansas night.

A shotgun. It reminds him of that bastard at King's Corner. "Stairway to Heaven," the guy's piercing, gray eyes, and his quivering nostrils.

I'll be back.

You gotta put that out of your mind. That was then; this is now.

Megan Haggarty's fingers are long and graceful, with perfectly shaped nails—no polish, just natural pink nail beds—with light half-moon crescents above the cuticles. And, the most important feature—the *crucial* one—no ring. Adrian wonders if it's possible she's not married, but he knows lots of nurses wear no jewelry while working in the hospital.

Ring, no ring, married, living together, looking, hooking up, lost and found . . . it's all complicated. Jesus, man . . . what're you, Sherlock Holmes? Looking for clues, bits and pieces . . . trying to dope out this puzzle?

Adrian waits for his soup to cool. He wonders if Megan

Haggarty could possibly make him feel something—anything—because since the divorce from Peggy, he's felt forever soured, emotionally mutilated, as though indifference runs thickly through him, slows his blood, and chills his heart. He knows he's too young to feel this way; there's too much to look forward to, yet life's vividness seems drained, washed out.

It occurs to Adrian that there could be something chemical in one's attraction to another. It could be inborn, something beyond control, hormonal—maybe pheromones, some elemental attractant—that draws a man to a woman and makes someone irresistible. And he suddenly realizes he's nearly leaning across the table, even trying to get a whiff of Megan Haggarty's hair or her milky skin. And he's aware at that moment that approaching women was always emotionally charged with some nascent fear he'd be spurned, or worse, he'd be laughed at.

Megan Haggarty picks up her sandwich and bites into it, eyes still fixed on the page. He recalls first seeing Peggy devour a sandwich. He'd thought back then—nothing original, for sure—the heartier a woman's appetite, the more robust her sexual hunger.

It's kid stuff, pure fantasy.

She sets her sandwich back on the paper plate. A perfect half circle is gone. There's scalloping where her teeth severed the bread. Her throat moves up and then down as she swallows. Adrian notices that she's tall, maybe five ten, though he can't tell for certain. Peggy was tall, too, as have been all the women he's desired.

"Your soup's getting cold," she says, her eyes still riveted on the book.

His throat closes; it feels like a thicket of thorns forms deep inside.

She looks up now, directly at him. Those eyes—emerald-green rings around hazel irises—are simply gorgeous. Be careful, Adrian tells himself. He grins—caught looking—and he sees a smile form on her bow-shaped lips. Her teeth are perfect, and dimples form on her cheeks as she smiles.

And she closes *In Cold Blood.*

He's trumped Capote. Adrian wonders if it's possible a connection is forming. Or will she simply toy with him because now she thinks he was copping glances like a teenager? Maybe she thinks he's a flirt, a third-rate Casanova trying to score.

"Are you new here?" he asks.

"I've been here for two years." Her head tilts.

"Funny, I haven't seen you around."

How lame. What a contrived opener . . . Adrian tells himself.

"Well, Dr. Douglas," she says, a smile filling her voice, "the neonatal ICU's very far from the cardiac surgery center."

So she's read his name tag. Small triumph, he thinks, but he'll take it.

"And I rarely come down to the cafeteria."

"How come?"

"Oh, we're very busy with the newbies. But we get a little time off."

And of all things, he finds himself wondering what she does with her time off. It could be spent with her husband and kids, he thinks. Or, if she's single—which seems unlikely—she could hit the local bars with her girlfriends, go clubbing, drinking, and dancing, or maybe troll the Post Road gin mills, where lonely singles guzzle their nights away, often looking to hook up.

Alone and single? Megan Haggarty? Not a chance.

"I grew up on long shifts, too," he says.

"You must keep very busy fixing God's mistakes."

He laughs, suddenly aware that she's wise to the swaggering bravado of chest-cracking surgeons. "So, you've met cardiac surgeons," he says, grinning self-consciously.

"Oh, yes, but you don't seem to be like the rest of them."

"You mean grandiose?"

She nods and smiles with her eyes.

"Just filled with themselves? Real gunslingers?"

She laughs; her mouth opens. God, those perfect teeth.

"Where were you before Eastport?" he asks.

"At Yale-New Haven."

"*Me* too."

"Our six degrees of separation," she says, canting her head. Her earrings tilt.

"It's a small world."

"When did you come here?" she asks.

"Two years ago. Same time you did."

There's a brief pause. The cafeteria noise hits a crescendo.

"What made you leave the center of the medical universe?" he asks, hoping he doesn't sound too cynical, even bitter about Yale.

"Oh, lots of things . . . ," she says, her voice trailing off.

She won't talk about it; he's certain of that.

She must be very smart, Adrian decides. Yale—it's the core processer of the nursing profession. And neonatal nursing—top-shelf credentials, right up there with OR and ICU work. It's the most technical and demanding nursing work around.

His stomach grumbles; he realizes he's starved.

"It's much better in this little pond than the ocean at Yale," she says.

"Yes," he says, wondering if some upheaval drove her from Yale. Something personal, meaning marital trouble—separation or divorce.

Like what happened to half the people in this cafeteria, a congregation of troubled souls, each with a personal tragedy.

"You live here in Eastport?" he asks.

"Yes. I've rented a condo."

Near the hospital. And she used "I," not "we."

Adrian realizes he's sifting through her every word, each nuance, making inferences. It's fucking Sherlockian.

"And you?" she asks, those hazel eyes questioning him. God, how he could stare at them forever and how he wishes time could slow so this conversation could last longer.

"I have a rental too . . . in Simpson."

"Simpson?"

"Yes."

Adrian's certain she knows Simpson's a bedroom community; so, maybe she thinks he's married, just game-playing. She may feel he's doing the big flirt, that he's ready for a casual fling, a fuck-buddy thing, nothing more.

"The rental market in Eastport's impossible," he adds quickly. "I took a place in Simpson so I didn't have to buy a condo." He purposely used "I," hinting at his single status.

She nods, and he wonders what she's thinking.

The conversation shifts—comfortably for Adrian—to their work. She loves the neonatal ICU and working with newborns. The only shame is when a crack baby is born. The nurses know its mothering will be awful. "It's terrible when a mother doesn't want a child," she says, a tinge of sadness in her voice.

Staring into those eyes, Adrian knows he can't get enough of her.

"But then a fragile little preemie comes along. If we save the baby, it's great, because we know the parents want this child more than anything else."

"So it's more than just a job?"

"Yes, *much* more. And I imagine it's the same feeling for you with surgery."

"Absolutely. It makes my day."

There's a pause in the conversation. The cafeteria hum seems louder in his ears.

Then she says with a smile, "Now your soup's *really* cold."

"And you've taken only one bite of your sandwich."

They laugh. He notices how her lips spread into a smile and

the way her eyes brighten and become lively. The sadness he saw is gone, evaporated. He feels somehow they've shared something as inconsequential as a brief, self-conscious laugh amid the din of this cafeteria, and he feels close to her in a way he doesn't quite understand. It's very strange, and Adrian wonders if she can possibly know he's insanely glad he couldn't find a seat and finally plopped down at this table.

He wonders, too, if Megan Haggarty has *any* idea—even a seminal notion—of the effect she has on him. Can she tell that he's hanging over the table, edging closer to her? He realizes he's engrossed by her. He's looking into her luminous eyes, making intimate and earnest contact, and it feels so terribly comfortable. It occurs to Adrian that if another surgeon could take over his afternoon surgeries, he'd stay right here with Megan Haggarty.

He asks himself if she can even imagine—with the tumult of sound and patina of lights—that years from now he'll try desperately to recapture the memory of the moment he first saw her, surrounded by an ocean of doctors and nurses and aides and hospital workers and porters and cafeteria workers, amid hospital greens and white coats and hairnets and name tags and stethoscopes and the smells and sights and sounds of this stadium-sized cafeteria in Eastport Hospital, and all the while, she was completely oblivious to his existence.

Adrian thinks there's something unadorned, even earthy about Megan Haggarty. He's quite certain she's very different from Peggy, who thought nothing of buying herself a $100,000 Mercedes SL roadster, who shopped tirelessly at Betteridge Jewelers in Greenwich for Van Cleef & Arpels bracelets or Paolo Costagli earrings, or rummaged through the Ralph Lauren Collection at the store, and pushed relentlessly for them to buy a Manhattan pied-à-terre (which he resisted, much to her chagrin) so on weekends they could eat Kobe beef or world-class sushi at Nobu or the latest culinary constructions at Daniel and then take a taxi back to the apartment rather than drive back to Connecticut.

But that was then and this is now, and Adrian wonders if there's a remote possibility this chance encounter with Megan Haggarty could lead to something exciting—a relationship with substance, one that might endure—even though he barely knows her. He questions why he's suddenly thinking this way because until twenty minutes ago, he thought he was limping through his life—steeped in a sour marinade of pessimism—forever brooding, feeling emotionally crippled because of what Peggy did.

Three

Megan thinks Adrian Douglas is quite a physical specimen. He has a great body—wide, powerful-looking shoulders, a narrow waist, athletic-looking from stem to stern. She noticed it as he was ambling toward the table. She'd long ago learned to recognize a man's athleticism from Conrad, her ex—a superb athlete and winner of the Colorado State high school heavyweight wrestling championship. He was also a cross-country skier and a superb mountain climber.

The thought of Conrad sends a galvanic charge through her; and at that moment, Megan wonders if Conrad will always haunt her life. *He's part of your past life, girl, so just live in the present . . . Forget back then.* Without seeming obvious, she focuses on the man sitting across the table.

Adrian Douglas is probably about six one. His hair is light brown and closely cropped. He has cornflower-blue eyes, a strong jaw, and good, manly features. Yes, Adrian Douglas is handsome, but not in a pretty-boy way; he has what she would call rugged good looks. But unlike Conrad, there's a gentleness glimmering through, and Adrian Douglas has kindly looking eyes, so different from Conrad's, which could sear you like a scalpel.

Please, Conrad, go away. Just go and be gone forever.

Adrian . . . It's an unusual handle for a man, but in its own way, quite masculine. *Douglas.* It's likely of English, or maybe

Scottish origin—probably a mixture. It's kind of rare in this part of America—the border between Fairfield and New Haven Counties, Connecticut. Actually, if Megan thinks about it, Adrian Douglas is—what's the old-time expression?—a bona fide hunk; but she senses he doesn't realize how good-looking he is. He exudes a sort of calmness she sees too little of in the hard-bitten, life-and-death world of doctors and nurses. That's especially true with surgeons. And he has a soft voice, not brash sounding like so many of the galloping surgical cowboys she's run into. Probably has a great bedside manner. She nearly laughs to herself. Is this high school back in White Plains? Is there a girlfriend to whom she can give a slight elbow nudge? *Bedside manner* . . . It's been ages since she's had a bed partner.

She peers at Adrian's baby blues. God, his eyes are so different from Conrad's.

But remember how charmed you were by Conrad when you first met him.

So, Megan thinks, *Adrian Douglas lives in Simpson—really, a bedroom community.* When she heard that, she was certain he'd be married, but he's a renter, not a homeowner. Renters can be transient. But he's around forty, not a kid. *So where is he in his life?* Megan wonders.

God, she's been talking her head off about the newbies and her hectic schedule. In the middle of their conversation, she finds herself wondering if Adrian Douglas is simply toying with her because she's just *here*. The hospital's a player's paradise.

He's glanced at her ring finger—twice. He tried to be subtle, but she spotted the furtive looks. There are always messages . . . unsung songs wafting through the air. It's a virtual chorus in this hospital with its singles—divorced and separated doctors and nurses. Megan wonders if he assumes she's married but doesn't wear her ring, or assumes that she's divorced. Does he assume *anything at all*?

Still overthinking it, Megan, like you always do . . . But then, you didn't overthink things when it came to Conrad.

She asks herself why Adrian Douglas should be more than an afterthought to an egg salad sandwich and coffee in a crammed cafeteria in Eastport General.

"How come Simpson?" she asks.

"Well, after my divorce, I wanted to get away from New Haven. Eastport had begun a new heart surgery program. I had to decide about living arrangements, and the housing market in this town is abysmal."

She nods. "So is it Wednesday nights at Applebee's with the kids?" she asks, imagining a dad—guilt-ridden as hell—doting on his spoiled-rotten kids.

"No kids," he replies. The corners of his mouth seem to droop. He blinks.

"I guess I made a silly assumption," she says, shrugging, trying to appear casual but feeling she made a cringe-worthy comment.

"Most people do."

Megan feels exquisitely embarrassed by her supposition. But he's not defensive; in fact, he's smiling, and those eyes of his—indulgent, but not patronizing. And besides, doesn't everyone assume things at some point in life? "Yes, having kids is a big deal and they're complicated," she says.

Now his eyes are wet. Did he lose a child? You never recover from that, ever. And it can lead to mutual blame, resentment, anger . . . divorce.

"How about you?" he asks. "Are you married?"

"I'm divorced, too."

He nods.

What does that mean? God, Megan, you're reading too much into every little thing, each inflection or gesture. Straighten up, girl. Get with it; you're not a kid back in White Plains in the high school cafeteria.

"So . . . we're bobbing along in that sea of uncertainty," she says.

"It's tough out there," he says. He clears his throat and blinks.

Yes, there's a scab there, she thinks, and she's unwittingly picked at it. Now it's raw and exposed.

She nods knowingly.

"You know, it's funny," he says. "I thought medical school was rough . . ."

Megan's certain she knows what he'll say next.

"Then there was the internship and residency, the whole life-and-death thing . . ."

She anticipates his next words.

"And when I got to be a surgeon, I thought the hardest part of my life was over."

She feels her lips spread into a smile.

"But *then* it really got rough."

"And it isn't over yet," she says, giving him a don't-we-know-it look.

They talk on—it's a zigzagging, word-filled blur, a back-and-forth exchange of thoughts and feelings about marriage and divorce—amid a fluorescent-lit sea of people with plastic spoons, knives, forks, plates, and paper cups—all disposable—the air redolent of soup, pizza, tuna fish, and fried chicken, and they're surrounded by a babble of voices, volleys of laughter, chirping beepers, and trilling cell phones. They talk about other things, too: the realty market, the hospital's fund-raising campaign, the demands of the OR and neonatal ICU, comparisons of Eastport to Yale, plenty of conversational fodder for people uncertain of what direction—if any—the encounter will take.

And Megan realizes that not only does she find Adrian Douglas attractive, but feels comfortable with him, and she could actually imagine being with him, doing things together, enjoying each other. She's startlingly aware that it doesn't feel choreographed, like the Waltz of the Singles, that overly practiced art form that's become so old and so very stale at this time in her life—thirty-two years old. She also feels an edge of wariness: after all, how much do you know about someone in a half hour? Or, for that matter, how much can you *really* know in the first few weeks or months?

Don't forget, there was Conrad.

She glances at her watch. "My lunch break's pretty much over," she says.

It's an opening. God, she's on tenterhooks. This is so absolutely silly—even juvenile.

"You haven't eaten a thing," he says.

"Neither have you . . ."

His laugh is robust, uncontrived. Sometimes things can be so simple, so uncomplicated, she thinks.

What happens now? Is there more?

The cafeteria hum peaks. It's a frenzy of movement as people come and go.

"You know, since we didn't really eat lunch, maybe we could get together and have dinner," he says.

"Yes. Eating like *this*, we'll both starve."

There's more laughter.

"That'd be nice." *Nice.* So plain vanilla, she thinks. "Actually, dinner would be fun."

"Can I have your number?"

"Of course," she says, reaching into her lab coat pocket; she sets a pad onto the table and scrawls on it. Then she rips out the page and hands it to him.

He tucks it into his pocket and says, "Are you free this weekend?"

"I can find time . . ."

"Can I call you this evening?"

Her eyebrows rise. "I work until seven."

"How 'bout I call at eight thirty?"

A fluttering rises in her stomach. She nods and picks up her tray. "That would be fine," she says, trying not to sound too casual or overly eager. She gets up and looks into his eyes. "Actually, I'd like that,"

"Talk to you," he says, "tonight . . ."

"At least eat your carrot cake," she says with a grin.

He laughs and picks up his plastic fork.

She wends her way past people chomping, talking, and laughing. Megan feels Adrian Douglas's eyes bore into her. It's like heat searing through her lab coat and greens; it shreds the skin on her back. It's that strange feeling of being watched, of being followed. It reminds her of Conrad, of his rage-filled explosions and his stalking her. As thoughts of Conrad shuttle through Megan's brain, she shudders inwardly.

She suddenly recalls how it felt to look over her shoulder entering a supermarket or a boutique, or going to the hospital. How she wouldn't work the night shift. How she asked a security guard to walk her to her car because the darkness was too eerie. And how she changed her phone number and made sure it was unlisted. How she got an order of protection. How her skin crawled back then. Yes, being watched—that feeling of exposure, a raw sense of nakedness—was creepy.

But maybe with Adrian Douglas, being watched is a good thing.

She feels lightness in her chest. It's been so long since she's flirted with a man, she'd begun thinking she forgot how. But you never forget. *Yeah . . . it's like riding a bicycle.*

Megan asks herself if they'd actually been flirting. They'd spoken about work and marriage and divorce and living arrangements, about nursing, the ICU, and surgery—yes, they'd talked about very *substantial* things.

So, they were substantially flirting.

And . . . she never said a word about Marlee.

But they'd just met, and they knew very little about each other—even after a half hour. It'd be crazy—utterly insane—to talk about Marlee, to dive into the complications of her life.

And yet she felt tempted to tell Adrian Douglas how it all began.

Why on earth would she even *want* to tell him her most deeply held secret? For that matter, why would she tell him a single solitary thing now? That would be crazy.

Four

Megan's apartment is on the ground floor of a two-story, cedar-shingled condominium complex near Eastport's heavily trafficked Post Road. Getting out of the car, Adrian feels his stomach flutter. A first date and he feels the slow burn of anxious anticipation. How juvenile, how incredibly retro it is—to be wondering how the evening will go, if the momentum will slow, if she'll be as attractive tonight as when they met a few days ago. He's amazed at the tingling in his chest and realizes it's the sheer vitality of the unknown. He recalls these feelings as a student at Cornell—dates and mixers—thinking back to when it all seemed new and exciting, all of it muted now in the stream of time.

Megan appears at the door and, God, she's beautiful, even more striking than in the cafeteria. She wears charcoal-gray slacks and a beige sweater. A pearl choker offsets her neck. She looks incredibly different out of her hospital scrubs and white coat—so non–Eastport General, so *I've got a real life and you're about to enter it.* Her hair is swept back in a fiery French braid. Her hazel eyes with those incredible green rings look ethereal. He'd thought of Megan so often these past two days; the reality of her seems chimerical.

Her apartment is a potpourri of contemporary style: the walls are eggshell white; the space is open and airy, with skylights, oak hardwood flooring, and trapezoid windows. The apartment is furnished with a mix from IKEA, Pier 1, and Pottery Barn; the impression is one of casual modernity and slap-dash transience. Adrian suddenly realizes he's squinting as he peers about the place.

"It's strictly utilitarian," Megan says, as though she's read his thoughts. "It's a month-to-month rental until things get settled."

"Settled? What things?"

"Oh, my life," she says with a quick laugh. But Adrian detects discomfort when she says *my life*. "I should really say *our* lives," she adds, pointing to a beige-colored Victorian-style dollhouse with lilac and pink gingerbread trim. "That's Marlee's . . . my daughter . . ."

"How old is she?" he asks, trying to sound casual, as though it changes nothing, but it had been a big problem with Peggy.

"She's five."

"Is she here?" He half expects to see a kid come charging out of a bedroom.

"She's at my sister Erin's for the evening. I couldn't get a sitter," Megan says, slipping into her coat. "And she loves staying with Erin and Bob. It's almost Marlee's second home. My sister's a stay-at-home mom, and Marlee spends the days there when I'm working. She's crazy about her cousins and their little dog." She pauses and then says, "Also, there's something I'm trying to avoid . . ." She looks up at him with those emerald-ringed eyes.

"What's that?" he asks, sensing he knows.

"She can get attached very easily. She really misses out on having a dad."

He thinks suddenly how he and Peggy were childless. But it's a loaded topic, not to be discussed, at least not now.

"Does she see her father?"

"No. He's been in Colorado since Marlee was two."

"You said things need to get settled? What things?"

"Oh, my sister and brother-in-law may move to Hartford. It

depends on his job situation. And I can get a good position at Hartford Hospital, but I'd hate to move again. They're family, and Marlee's cousins are almost brother and sister to her."

Giovanni's is an intimate, candle-lit trattoria on the Post Road in Westport. It has rough-hewn stucco walls, the clichéd checkered tablecloths, and black metal wall sconces. A recording of Pavarotti singing Neapolitan love songs pipes through the sound system. They feast on bruschetta, Caesar salads, shrimp scampi, and a seafood pasta, all washed down with a straw-colored Pinot Grigio. They talk for a while about hospital gossip—it's safe, neutral ground—nothing intimate or overly revealing.

"I see you stay with the low-fat dishes," she says. "Does being a heart surgeon influence what you eat?"

"It probably does. I see decrepit hearts every day," he says with a laugh. "How about you? Does the ICU influence how you feel about kids?"

"It's the other way around. How I feel about kids got me into working with them."

"In the cafeteria, you talked about feeling terrible when a child is unwanted."

"It's a tough topic for me."

He nods, hoping she doesn't think he's too inquisitive.

"I was adopted," she says with a slight tremor in her voice. "It's something that stays with you forever."

"That somebody didn't want you? Gave you away?"

"Exactly." She smiles weakly.

"But somebody else wanted you."

"And that's the lifesaver. There's a special place in heaven for adoptive parents."

"Tell me about them."

"My parents couldn't have kids, so they adopted Erin and me

as newborns—Erin first and then me a few years later. We grew up in White Plains. Dad worked at an ad agency in Manhattan and Mom was a teacher in Yonkers. It was a pretty traditional Irish family."

"Megan and Erin . . . it doesn't get more Irish than that."

She laughs. "Erin's three years older than I am."

"And you two are close?"

"As close as sisters can be."

"Where're your parents now?"

"They died in a car accident when I was nineteen," she whispers.

"I'm sorry."

"Erin and I moved to New Haven, where Erin was working."

"Then what?"

"Erin was at Merrill Lynch; then she met her husband, Bob, an engineer at Sikorsky. I went to nursing school at Yale. When I found pediatric nursing, I knew that was what I wanted. And then . . . the newbies."

"So it's not just a job, is it?"

"It's much more than that to me, Adrian."

A flush creeps into his face when she uses his name.

"How about you? Why cardiac surgery?"

"I guess the easy answer is that my father died when I was six . . . a heart attack."

"My God, how terrible."

"Right in front of me and my mother."

Her hand covers her mouth. "You actually *saw* it happen?"

"Yes. We were in a restaurant and he just keeled over and died."

"How terrible that must have been. A young boy seeing his father die."

He nods. He hadn't expected the conversation to veer in this direction. Not great topics for a first date—abandonment, adoption, and death. His throat thickens and his toes curl.

"That'll make a difference in your life," she says with wet eyes.

"For sure," he replies, watching her hands on the tabletop.

"So . . . we come to our work because of our early lives," she adds. Her voice sounds clogged.

He nods, staring into her eyes. "Is Haggarty your married name?"

"It's my adoptive parents' name."

"Do you know your birth name?"

"No. As far as I'm concerned, I'm pure Haggarty." She smiles. "It's who I am."

"Even when you were married?"

"Even when I was married. It was the name I grew up with and the one I became a nurse with. So I stayed with it." She pauses and then says, "And Marlee's last name is Wilson . . . her father's surname."

"Marlee Wilson. It's a pretty name."

"She's a pretty little girl."

"Well, her mother's very beautiful," Adrian says, aware his pulse is throbbing. And his hand is now resting on the tabletop.

A smile forms on her lips. He thinks she's blushing, though it's difficult to tell in the peach-hued lighting. She looks surprised, even embarrassed. Adrian wonders if Megan Haggarty realizes how ravishingly beautiful she is. He's certain many men have told her that, and he wonders if she carries the burden of beauty. Has she been the target of a lifelong cortege of flattery—mostly genuine, some counterfeit, meant to entice, to seduce—and has it made her skeptical, even untrusting of men? Or is she like some women he's met—beautiful, yet convinced they're ugly, scarred by disappointment, by rejection?

"Torna a Surriento" soars through the restaurant. The wine and music fill him with warmth and contentment.

"This is very different from the cafeteria," he says, knowing the conversation has veered into different territory from hospital gossip.

"Yes, it is. Do you know why?"

"I think I do . . ."

"So do I," she says, leaning toward him. "It's because we want to be here."

"Oh yes," he says, and a moment later, their fingers are intertwined. Her hand is soft, warm, and he feels her fingers pressing his; a hum courses through him. Adrian's heart swells with possibility.

"It's like an adventure, isn't it?"

Yes," he says with a laugh. "I have a confession to make . . ."

"What?" Her grasp is firmer now and her head tilts. A smile stays on her lips.

"I'm glad for that one empty seat in the cafeteria."

"I'm glad, too."

"The second I saw you, I knew I wanted to sit there."

"I was watching you."

"Were you?" he says, genuinely surprised. "I thought you didn't know I existed."

"Oh, I knew," she says with an amused look.

"You didn't give me a glance."

"Oh, I looked. And I was thinking, too . . ."

"Thinking what?"

"I can't tell you that *now*."

"You were very subtle, sitting there with your paperback, never looking at me."

"You can't know what was going through my mind then."

"I didn't think you noticed."

"Life's full of surprises, isn't it?" she says, squeezing his hand.

At her apartment door, she moves close. The scent of her makes his knees weak. "I'd ask you in, but I'm not sure I want to go there . . ."

"Go where . . . ?"

She smiles, touches his arm.

A thrumming courses through his chest.

"You know where," she whispers, her finger brushing his cheek. His skin tingles. "At least not yet . . ."

"We'll just let things go where they will . . ."

"In time, they will," she whispers, drawing closer.

He can smell her hair, her skin, the wine on her breath. The hospital seems forever ago, a lifetime away. Her hand strokes his chin gently; then her palms rest on his cheeks. His face is on fire. His heart flutters as he looks into those amazing eyes and knows again he could fall into them. Her scent is vaguely reminiscent of wisteria, or is it lavender?

When they kiss, her lips are moist, full, and pliant, and the taste of her mouth blends with wine and sambuca.

They draw away and look into each other's eyes. Her hand rests at the back of his neck. "This is the strangest thing," he says.

"What's strange?"

"It feels like . . ." He shakes his head, not knowing what to say.

"Like what?"

"Like we've known each other for a long time."

"Yes. It does."

"And there's something else," he says.

"What's that?"

"I feel like a kid."

"That's a good feeling, isn't it?"

"Like it's all the first time, but I'm too old to feel this way."

"No, you're not," she whispers.

"And . . ." A thousand thoughts cascade through his mind—a frenzy of words and images—but he can't find a thing to say.

"And what?" she says softly, her lips hovering near his.

"How does this happen so quickly? This feeling . . ."

"I don't know. But I feel it, too," she whispers. Then she buries her face against his chest; she looks up and those plush, moist lips press against his neck, kiss him—very gently—and his arms wrap around her, pull her so close, he feels the heat of her body, and a soft moan comes from her throat. Her lips linger on his neck, and his skin feels like it's on fire. He tilts his head downward so their mouths come together.

They kiss again, this time, more deeply.

Five

An autumn moon casts a pale wash on the forest behind the cottage. Adrian savors the taste of Megan still lingering in his mouth. Stepping out of the Audi, he marvels at how rustic the area is. It's quite a change from New Haven, where he lived the first few years of his life in Connecticut. Except for Simpson's town center, the area remained rural, with undulating hills, open fields, and some working vegetable and dairy farms.

Over the two years since he moved in, Adrian's grown fond of this quaint cottage. The stone fireplace, chestnut-beamed rooms, and wood-burning stove provide a cozy ambience, especially on winter nights. The nearest house—the Gibson mansion, for which the cottage was a gatehouse years ago—is three hundred yards away. There's plenty of privacy.

Inside, he's about to plop onto the sofa when he notices a cushion is out of place. He straightens it out and heads into the kitchen for a glass of water. A kitchen cabinet door is open. Adrian stands there, befuddled: he has no recollection of having opened the cabinet that morning. He was in a rush to get to the hospital and had coffee and a doughnut in the doctors' lounge on the sixth floor. He closes the cabinet door, drinks a glass of water, and returns to the living room.

He replays the evening with Megan. It already seems like a dream. How they'd talked about themselves and each other, about mothers and fathers, family closeness, and Megan's sister, Erin, about being adopted, and Megan's words about Marlee.

A child, the little person you've helped create and around whom your life orbits . . . And here he is, forty years old, childless. Adrian's thoughts drift to Peggy. God, what a downer it was. He'd wanted to have a child, but Peggy had jolted him out of that wish. He's certain she'll never have a baby. It's ironic, because she's still at Yale, churning ahead as an A-list gynecologist and fertility expert, of all things. He's sure she's still doing surgery, writing journal articles, attending conferences, and is on a meteoric rise to the top of the surgical food chain. He'd even heard a rumor that she'd been offered a top-shelf position at Harvard but had turned it down.

They'd met at Yale-New Haven Hospital. From the first moment they spied each other, the attraction was high voltage. She ignited something incendiary inside him. It was erotic overdrive. How insatiable their appetites—a lust-driven hunger—were for each other. They were married for two years when the idea of a baby came up—he can't even recall how it did.

"I hadn't really planned on it," she said, "but I'm willing to give it a try."

So they tried, and after eight months, nothing happened.

"It's not *my* fault, Adrian," Peggy said. "And I don't want to start the whole sex-on-a-schedule thing. I could never think of anything more *boring*."

"Isn't that what your patients do?"

"Yes, the ones who want to ruin their sex lives."

"So, what do we do?"

"Maybe you should get tested," she said.

"Why not both of us?"

"I've already gone to the best fertility clinic in the state. Mine, right here at Yale. And there's nothing wrong with me."

Gen-Health Labs was in a nondescript, four-story building on State Street in New Haven, a few short blocks from the hospital. With her connections, Peggy got him an immediate appointment.

First, there was a form. A million questions: his family, ethnic background, health issues, medications, anything affecting seminal fluid, sperm count. There were tests for motility, viability, and an impregnation index. He was a one-man study in reproductive capability.

Then came a physical examination—head to toe. And then prostatic massage, blood tests, urinalysis, and x-ray imaging of his bladder.

Then he made a "deposit."

The results: a fine sperm count—great little soldiers, indomitable infantrymen ready to charge uphill.

Four months later: still no pregnancy.

"Why not give us five or six samples?" said the lab director, Dr. Lefer, a short, frosted-blond woman who wore a starched white lab coat and large, oval-shaped glasses. "We'll store them and then use a concentrated dose when Peggy's ovulating. It's artificial insemination, but with your own sperm."

A megadose—millions of soldiers marching to the front.

Four more samples.

Result: no pregnancy.

Still plenty of deposit left over for another try.

"What will be, will be," Peggy said.

Peggy was losing interest. Lovemaking—by then indolent, rote, and rehearsed—screeched to a standstill.

Peggy got home at nine thirty that night. "A grueling day in the OR," she moaned. "Hysterectomies . . . C-sections. I'm wrecked."

She tossed her purse on the table as she trudged to the bedroom. "I need a shower. Let's order in. Pizza's fine." He could hear weariness and burnout in her voice.

It had been months since they'd done the Manhattan restaurant thing or been to a show—either on Broadway or at Long Wharf in New Haven—and Peggy was working later than ever. And coming home exhausted—*wrecked* and *wasted* were her favorite words. Sexually, she was distant, remote—completely uncaring. The marriage seemed spiritless.

The pizza arrived. Same delivery boy—a tall, greasy-haired kid wearing Reebok basketball sneaks and baggy jeans whose crotch hung between his knees. *Poor fucking kid*, Adrian thought. He can still picture him standing at the doorway with iPod buds in his ears.

No small bills in Adrian's wallet.

He opened Peggy's purse and extracted a twenty. "Here. Keep the change, kid."

Returning Peggy's wallet, his gaze fell on a beige plastic container. A logo was etched on the plastic cover: "FemCap."

He snapped it open. Inside: a thin, thimble-shaped rubber object.

He heard Peggy—out of the shower, tramping around the bedroom, opening and closing dresser draws—and he saw her shadow in the slit of light beneath the door. His hands shook violently as he rummaged through her purse.

A tube of ointment: "GYNOL II." Douche or antifungal preparation? They'd barely had sex in weeks . . . no, in months.

He booted up the laptop and typed "FemCap" on the Google search engine.

It came up: "Cervical Cap (FemCap) condom, diaphragm. Contraception. Female Cervical Cap."

His hands went weak, cold. His scalp dampened.

FemCap. Inserted into the vagina—best done some hours before intercourse—fits snugly over the cervix, provides a barrier to sperm, preventing fertilization.

His heart hammered while his thoughts swirled.

Highly effective; acceptable to both partners—the man won't feel the device if it's properly inserted.

Discreet, comes in a makeup-like container enhancing portability.

Ready to wear, he thought. *How versatile.*

His body hummed and his hands shook. A few typed letters and a couple of clicks: Drugs.com.

Gynol II. Vaginal spermicide: a gel inserted into the vagina before sexual intercourse. It damages and kills sperm in the vagina.

His skin prickled. His heart thrashed in his chest. A sick feeling filled him.

Moments later, Peggy was in the living room, wearing a bathrobe, her hair damp and limp. Adrian smelled terry cloth, Pantene with aloe in still-wet hair, rose-scented body wash—all melding in a sickening wave of nausea. When Peggy saw the FemCap container, she turned ashen.

Adrian pointed to it, feeling his chest would implode.

"How long've you been using this?"

"For a while," she whispered and looked away.

"And the blood tests, the sperm count, I've been jacking off in a *jar* . . . in the lab? *Your* lab."

She swallowed and said nothing. The silence was sustained, ugly.

"This has all been a lie, hasn't it?" His insides felt like they were being yanked apart. Tears burned the back of his throat.

Peggy plopped onto the sofa, her lips a thin, bloodless line. One leg crossed over the other; her foot dangled and jiggled.

"You've been playing me."

She crossed her arms over her chest. The foot kept jiggling. Her eyes couldn't meet his.

"And why's it in your *purse*?"

She blinked wetly; her chin trembled.

"Adrian, I just don't see a child in my life . . ." She still looked away.

"I could've lived with that."

More silence, penetrating. Peggy's eyes darting left and right.

"Peggy . . . ?"

No response.

"The fucking *purse* . . . why?"

"Adrian, can I be completely frank with you?"

No righteous outrage—no explosion, no theatrics, though he trembled with fury.

"I've been thinking about our marriage . . ."

His mouth tasted metallic—something coppery.

"I . . . I . . ." She halted.

"C'mon, Peggy, just spit it out."

"It's not that our marriage is bad . . . It's . . . it's something else . . ."

"What's that?" Something bubbled inside him.

"It was mostly hormones that brought us together," Peggy said, and then she inhaled deeply. "I guess I chose to ignore that marriage might mean having a family . . ."

"So, Peggy—"

"Adrian, our sex life's turned into a baby-making chore."

The edges of the room darkened. The room swayed.

"I . . . I never considered the commitments of marriage. It really comes down to this: I just can't be with only *one* man."

"So you've been having an affair?"

"Yes . . ." Tears snaked down her cheeks. "Adrian, I still love you, but . . . I just can't live the kind of life you want . . . kids . . . a house in the burbs . . ."

He could have launched into a rage-filled rant, a poisonous blitz . . . Words crashed through his brain like an avalanche, tumbled wildly, and littered his thoughts like swirling confetti. *So you lie . . . pretend there's a sperm problem . . . I have to jerk off in a jar . . . and you're using a device? And I'm just a cuckolded sap, and you . . . you mind-fucking bunko artist . . . you played me like a mandolin.*

But he said nothing, just shook his head, his mouth desert dry. A tide of memories swelled through him—of places they'd been, things they'd done, songs they'd shared. They'd traveled the same road—together—but with different destinations.

It was just so over.

Six

"Someone has an admirer," Barbara Conte coos as Megan enters the neonatal unit. She's just returned from the cafeteria, where she'd hoped to see Adrian. But an OR nurse had said, "We have wall-to-wall patients. He'll be tied up all day."

"These came while you were at lunch," Barbara says, pointing to a vase of gladioli. Tall spikes of red and white blossoms rise sequentially from long stems. Sword-shaped foliage protrudes from between the florets.

A wave of astonishment washes over Megan. A lovely gesture, but really reckless of Adrian. The human resources handbook is crystal clear about hospital romances: they're a huge no-no. When it happens, it's discreet, beneath the administrative radar. In the two weeks they've known each other, things have gotten pretty intense, but flowers to the unit? It seems unlike Adrian to do that.

A tag identifies the plant as a Lucky Star gladiola, and there's a small envelope. She opens it. The script looks like a woman's cursive writing.

It says, "To Megan, with love."

But there's no signature—very discreet.

Megan wonders: why today? Then it's clear: it's the first time Adrian hadn't called early in the morning. No doubt, he rushed off to an emergency. So he sent flowers. Probably made a telephone call to a flower shop between surgeries, she thinks, smiling inwardly. The card is from George's Flowers, near the hospital. A quick call and a credit card number was all it took to get them delivered.

During the afternoon break, Megan's cell phone rings. It's when Adrian calls if he's not stuck in some patient's chest cavity. She checks the caller ID and sees it's him. Glad she's alone in the nurses' lounge, she flips the cell open.

"Well, hello," she says in a half whisper. "How's your day going?"

"Hectic . . ."

"I knew that when you didn't call this morning."

"An emergency . . . The heart waits for no one."

They talk for a while—about their schedules, dinner this coming Saturday night, and how he can't wait to meet Marlee—but nothing about the flowers. She knows Adrian is short on artifice; gamesmanship isn't in his playbook. He's a straight shooter, no duplicity.

"I got the flowers," she says.

"Flowers?"

"Didn't you send gladiolas?"

"No . . ." He sounds bemused, but with a hint of astonishment.

A chill slithers down Megan's spine. She suddenly recalls that years ago, after one of his rages, Conrad had stormed out of the house and disappeared for two days. There was no phone call, no note—nothing. Then flowers arrived—not gladioli, but roses—followed by a telephone call. He apologized, begged to come back, and said he'd been a total ass and would never scream at her again. And like a fool, she'd taken him back in.

"Don't tell me I've got competition," Adrian says half-seriously.

"Oh no," she says with a dry throat. "It's just that . . ." And she stops.

"What?"

"Flowers came to the ward . . . and . . ." She falters.

"What, Megan?"

"I assumed it was you." Her voice sounds small in her ears.

"Well, you're a beautiful woman . . . I regret it wasn't."

Megan's hands go cold.

"It was probably some parents whose baby you people saved . . ."

"That's funny. I didn't think of that," she says, but her throat closes. Her skin prickles.

To Megan, with love.

Tingling starts in her fingertips, then around her mouth. "It's weird," she says, as her thoughts streak through a roster of hospital people. Then a vision of Conrad floats before her eyes. The night they met, the quick romance, his almost puerile sweetness—followed months later by his anger, and finally rage and violence . . . especially after Marlee was born. But Conrad's in Colorado.

"What's weird?" Adrian asks.

"There was no signature."

"Oh, Megan, it's some preemie's parents. Didn't we agree the family's thank-you is the best part of the job?"

Blood whooshes in her ears.

Adrian says he's deluged by surgeries and can't talk, but he called for a quick hello.

"I miss you," he says softly.

"Double that, here," Megan whispers as the gladioli flash in her thoughts. A knot forms in her stomach and then tightens.

"I'll call you tonight," he says.

"You know, Adrian, things are happening very fast . . ."

"Yes. It feels like a new beginning."

"I know," she whispers, but something jumps in her chest.

"Tonight, then . . ."

At the nursing station, Megan dials the florist's number.

"Hi, this is Megan Haggarty. I'm at Eastport General and received some gladioli from your shop."

"Oh, yes," says the woman. "Aren't they lovely?"

"They certainly are. Did you pick them out, or did the customer?"

"He asked me to choose something beautiful."

"Was it a telephone order?"

"He came into the shop."

"Can you tell me who he was?"

"I don't know his name."

"Didn't he use a credit card?"

"No. He paid in cash."

Paid in cash . . . rarely done in this plastic world—done usually when you want to hide your identity.

"What'd he look like?"

"What did he look like?" the woman asks; a smile seeps through her voice.

She thinks I'm dying to learn who my secret admirer is.

"I'd say he was nice-looking . . ."

Megan thinks, *Nice-looking* . . . so nondescript—bland—meaning he didn't look like Quasimodo or Godzilla. "Can you tell me more?" This woman is trying to play out some floral fairy tale. "Was he about six three?"

"He was on the tall side."

"Athletic-looking?"

"I don't really know . . ."

Megan switches the phone to her other ear. She recalls Adrian telling her about that insane encounter at King's Corner a couple of weeks ago. *Adrian, what kind of name is that?* How it could have come to blows but the bartender kicked the man out. Then the shotgun blast from a pickup. And now flowers, she thinks, trying to quell a tide of dread rising steadily within her.

"Tell me," Megan says, "was he powerful-looking, midthirties, maybe two hundred twenty or thirty pounds, with a thick neck and short hair?"

"He could've been, but I'm not very good at estimating a man's age and weight."

"Did he have deep-set, bluish-gray eyes? Almost like ice?"

Eyes that could make your blood run cold.

"No, I'd have noticed *that*."

"Was his hair blondish in color?"

"No. Actually, it was dark brown and combed back, kinda slick-looking. And to tell you the truth," she adds, "he had dandruff on his shoulders."

Slicked-back? Dandruff? Never. Not Conrad.

Megan feels her heart slow.

She runs through a mental cache of men at the hospital—guys with whom she'd had casual conversations—in an elevator, in the cafeteria, in the parking garage, or on the ward. Nobody fits the description. She draws a complete blank. She wonders if Conrad's back in Connecticut. Maybe he got someone to go into the shop.

To Megan, with love.

She thanks the florist and snaps her cell phone shut. A film of sweat forms over her upper lip.

There've been a few telephone hang-ups lately, but that happens all the time. Have I noticed anyone following me? Have I seen a black pickup? Is Conrad even alive? It's been three years since I last saw him. God, what's going on?

She closes her eyes and thinks—despite her sense of caution and sound judgment—maybe it's just *one of those things, one of those crazy, inexplicable occurrences that happens to everyone.* She enters the lounge and plops down on the sofa.

Ann Johnson comes in and sits next to her. Ann's a thin,

chain-smoking, twice-divorced nurse who's been Megan's confidant for two years. At thirty-five, Ann's been around plenty of blocks—she's a somewhat world-weary, hard-bitten but empathic friend—and she's seen it all. "You look totally washed out, honey pie," Ann says in her South Florida accent. "What's goin' on?"

Megan tells her.

"You worried it could be Conrad?" Ann asks, popping a Marlboro Light into her mouth and opening a window. Ann usually sneaks a smoke in the lounge.

"I don't know."

"Have you heard from him?" Contrails of smoke pour from Ann's nostrils.

"Ann, it's like he disappeared from the face of the earth."

"Honey, only dead people do that," says Ann, the cigarette wagging between her lips. "Think he's still in Colorado?"

"As far as I know, he is." Megan feels her chin quivering. "I left New Haven two years ago . . . and I thought I was out of sight . . ."

"Megan, dear, you're *never* out of sight. Unless you're in the Witness Protection Program, you're findable."

"I haven't heard from him in . . . forever."

"You still have that restraining order?"

"It expired a long time ago."

"I'd think about getting another one," Ann says; she gets up and begins pacing. "You know, Megan, when I left Donnie—after he beat the crap outta me for the tenth time—I got the hell outta Florida. I hired a no-name mover—the truck had no logo on it—and I had them move my furniture to a warehouse, where it stayed for a few weeks.

"I left for Connecticut by car, in the middle of the night. I didn't tell a soul where I was goin'—left no forwarding address. Canceled all my credit cards and just got the hell outta town. I had the mover send my stuff up separately.

"I began livin' a cash-only existence. Had my name changed,

got licensed under my new name, didn't even open a *charge* account. The first year here, I paid for everythin' with money orders or cash.

"But, sweet pea, it didn't matter . . . Donnie found me. My first mistake was comin' here—'cause your ex knows you're always goin' to your family. Donnie knew I'd move near my brother, knew it like the back of his hand. He started callin' me, makin' threats . . . like he was gonna show me some *tough love*. I got an order of protection."

"Ann, you're scaring the hell out of me."

"Maybe that's not a bad thing, honey, because Donnie showed up here, and it was a good thing my brother was there. Steve beat the crap outta him and called the cops. Donnie did ninety days in lockup and I haven't heard from him since, the sadistic son of a bitch."

Megan tries to control the trembling in her chest.

"Look, Megan, Marlee makes you traceable. And you have the same name as before. You can bet Conrad knows you live near Erin, Bob, and the kids. But it wouldn't matter if you moved to Alaska; he'd find you."

"Ann, I'm sure he's hanging out with some gun-toting crowd, chugging Coors, doing his Rocky Mountain thing."

"You know what, honey . . . you'd best hire a private detective to find out. It'd set your mind at ease."

"I'll think about that, Ann. But if it *is* him, why now . . . ?"

"No idea, sweetie. But you just got flowers, even if it's from a guy who needs some Head & Shoulders. *To Megan, with love*? Unsigned? Gimme a break, hon; it's him."

Megan feels her arms go taut; her fingers cramp.

"Sweet pea, it's nighttime and you're treadin' water in the ocean. And the water moves . . . a sudden surge. Maybe it's a sea swell, but maybe somethin's circling. Even if it's just the water, you know the shark is out there . . ."

Megan sits at the nursing station, swivels her chair, and turns to the computer. She logs in and clicks onto her e-mail in-box.

There's a high-pitched *ding*. She has mail. She's certain it's going to be one of the usual mass notices, an e-mail blast from the administration—double-check all medications before dispensing; use proper disposal techniques for medical waste; make certain you know the location of all fire exits—or a memo about the Accreditation Committee's tour, any of a dozen weekly reminders sent to staff personnel.

She clicks on the envelope icon.

From: "Private."

Subject: FLOWERS

Her heart slams in her chest.

Message: YOU KNOW WHO SENT THEM.

A gnawing sensation forms deep in her belly, as though a rat lives inside her. It crawls around and tears at her guts. Then a glacial chill slithers up her spine even as the nursing station feels superheated, as though the thermostat's set at eighty-five degrees.

Megan's nostrils fill with the cloying fragrance of Lucky Star gladioli. Her heart skips a beat as she reaches for the telephone.

"So, Megan, I have the pleasure of fixing another computer problem for you," says Brian McCoy, the redheaded hospital IT expert who usually makes rounds every week or two. Brian once asked her out on a date, but she'd demurred. Since then, he's been a bit flirtatious, but appropriate.

She tells him about the flowers and the e-mail as a taut feeling eddies through her.

A moment later, he's at the message. "It's not from our internal network," he says. "It doesn't have our domain tag. It could come from anyplace with access to the Web."

"But the flowers were paid for in *cash* . . . at a shop down the street."

"The e-mail's been sent by an anonymous proxy through a series of random nodes, and it's very hard to trace back."

My God . . . all this creepy tech talk is just too much. We live in such a crazy world.

"Anything else unusual going on, Megan?"

"Last night I had two hang-ups at home and a few last week."

"Megan . . ." Brian's voice turns low-pitched. "Have you had any . . . let's say . . . situations lately . . . anyone weird?"

A voltage-filled sensation charges through her.

You know who sent them.

Brian asks if she uses any social media: Facebook, Myspace, Twitter, and a few others.

"Never . . ."

Brian stands. "Well, I'll change your hospital e-mail address."

"So, Brian, what's your take on this?"

"I don't want to worry you, but cyber stalking's a big thing these days."

As he heads toward the elevator, another *ding* comes from the computer. Megan looks up at the in-box.

There's one new message.

Blank, except for the subject line: YOU *DO* KNOW.

A shiver crawls up Megan's spine.

Seven

Entering the apartment, Adrian hears a child's voice. Megan smiles, sets her hand on his arm, and turns to Marlee. The child wears a melon-colored dress with a pink cardigan sweater, red leggings, and pink sneakers. Her rosy face is ringed by reddish-blond curls. Her eyes—every bit as striking as Megan's—are a combination of cornflower blue with glittering green flecks in the irises. She's a beautiful kid who looks up at Adrian with an expectant smile.

"Marlee, this is Dr. Adrian," Megan says.

Marlee's hand goes to her mouth and she looks at Megan and then glances at Adrian. Her lips spread into a smile.

"You can call me Adrian," he says, hearing a smile in his own voice.

She turns to him, takes a tentative step forward, and says, "Are you and my mom going somewhere?"

"Yes we are, honey," Megan says. "We're going out for dinner. And Alice'll take you to Erin's house."

Megan introduces him to Alice, a ponytailed young woman wearing jeans and a UConn sweatshirt.

Marlee cups her mouth and pulls her mother's arm. Megan bends down while Marlee whispers in her ear, still covering her mouth. She glances at Adrian and keeps whispering for quite a while. Megan nods and smiles.

Megan straightens up and says, "We'll be leaving now, honey. Remember, when you get to Aunt Erin's house, don't play rough with Sampson. He's just a puppy."

"But he's so cute," Marlee says, looking at Adrian.

"So're you," Adrian says, grinning. "You're as cute as any puppy."

"I'm not a puppy," Marlee says, laughing. "I'm a *kid*."

"Well, you're a cute kid," he says, realizing he's never felt so drawn to a child.

Giggling, Marlee hides behind Megan and then peeks at Adrian from behind her mother. As he and Megan head for the door, Marlee waves and smiles.

In the car, Adrian says, "She's adorable."

"She'll *charm* you."

"What'd she whisper to you?"

"Wouldn't you like to know," Megan says with a sly smile, fumbling with the seat belt.

"Of course I would."

Laughing, Megan says, "She thinks you're very handsome. And so do I." She leans toward him. Their lips meet in a long and deep kiss.

The Nathan Hale Tavern, with its roaring fireplace, chestnut beams, and colonial wall sconces, has a delightful autumnal ambience—cozy, old-fashioned, and very New England. Their table is near the fireplace, and Megan's hair—lustrous in the firelight—is parted down the middle with a milkmaid braid dangling over her right shoulder. The flickering fire highlights her features—especially her cheekbones—as they dine on hearty American fare accompanied by a California burgundy. Food never tasted so good, Adrian thinks. Nor has he ever been as exquisitely aware of a woman's beauty as he is now in this tavern.

They talk about their friends and their families.

"It's obvious that you and Erin are very close."

"As close as sisters can be."

"It's good to have family," Adrian says, thinking of his widowed mother living alone in Florida. And he wonders how it would have been to have a brother or sister, a blood connection, some enduring tie lasting a lifetime.

As they talk, Megan's hand slides across the table. He reaches for it. The fire's warmth and her hand stir him; she responds with a gentle squeeze. "Actually, part of why Erin and I are so close is we had only each other after Mom and Dad died. We were two adopted kids with no one else." She looks intently into his eyes. "Being adopted always made me wonder . . ."

"About?"

"Who am I? Where did I come from? Why didn't my real parents—want me?"

"Those are very basic questions."

"Because," she shakes her head, "I've always felt that Erin and I were dispensable."

"I never thought of it that way," he says, nearly cringing at the word: *dispensable. Discarded . . . disposable . . . like medical waste.*

"Unwanted . . . given away . . . no returns." She smiles, but her eyes moisten.

"It must've been hard for you."

"Yes. Erin's my only living family member, aside from Marlee."

"What a delightful kid."

"I had very mixed feelings about you meeting her."

"I'm sure, but maybe my meeting Marlee says something . . ."

"What?"

"That you think I'm worthy of it," he hears himself say, and squeamishness slithers through him. "Okay, it's corny, but I mean it."

"It's not corny. It's true." She looks contemplative and then says, "You know, Adrian, you're the first man I've let her meet."

Heat creeps into his face.

"Really. I decided this afternoon that I wanted you to meet Marlee."

"That means a lot to me," he says, knowing something is happening and realizing Megan was saying it through Marlee and now expressing it directly.

"I'm trying to wrap my head around all this because it's . . ." She pauses, smiles. "What can I say? It's complicated."

"I know. It *is* happening fast . . . and it *is* complicated, but I'm comfortable with it," he says, feeling an intense urge to have her in his arms.

The beginnings of a smile form on her lips. "Actually, you know, Marlee's quite taken by you."

"And I am by her," he says, picturing that face—the reddish-blond curls framing it, her impossibly blue eyes, the smile and her whispering as she looked sidelong at him.

"And it's much more than her just wanting some man around. I think it was *you*." One corner of Megan's mouth curls upward.

He watches the flickering flames throw shadow and light onto her face.

"I think she wants *you* as part of her life."

Heat—erotic and longing warmth—spread through him. He brings her hand to his lips, kisses it, and tastes the tang of her skin. "Feeling wanted is very important," he says. "And what about you? Do *you* want me in your life?"

In the firelight, he thinks he sees her nod.

"Because I don't want to be dispensable . . ."

"You're not," she whispers and leans closer to him.

"You know," he says, "wondering *who am I, where did I come from . . . ?*"

"Yes . . . ?" She leans even closer.

"I guess the follow-up is, *Where am I going . . . ?*"

"Sure. We all need direction in our lives."

"Remember that first night I came to your apartment?"

She nods.

"You said it was a month-to-month rental . . . until things get settled in your life."

"Yes?"

"And you said Erin and Bob may move to Hartford . . ."

"Yes . . ."

"I wish you wouldn't go . . . to Hartford, or anywhere else." His throat tightens.

Megan's eyes gleam. She sets her other hand on his.

"I want you to stay here in Eastport."

She tilts her head.

"Because . . . you're not dispensable . . ."

She plants a kiss on the back of his hand.

"Please don't leave," he whispers.

Outside, they embrace and kiss; then, with his arm around her, they walk toward his car.

"Your place . . . or mine?" she asks.

"Wherever you're comfortable." A surge of excitement swells within him, and his insides quiver. But it's more than just desire; it melds with a wish to nurture, to protect and provide for. He wonders if he's ever felt this way before. No, he decides. Not *this* way.

"Then it's my place," she says. "Marlee's with Erin and Bob."

"Did you by chance plan this . . . for Marlee not to be home?"

"Why don't you wonder about that?" she whispers.

They stop walking, turn to each other, and kiss. Their tongues slide over each other's. She tastes of lamb, butter, burgundy, and Megan. When their lips part, they look into each other's eyes. It's a startling moment of intimacy. Adrian takes her hand and sets it on his chest.

"Your heart's beating so fast," she whispers, and she plants a kiss on his lips. They head for the car.

The Audi starts in an instant. A moment later, they turn onto the Post Road. She leans forward and flicks on the radio.

"You like rock?"

"Mostly the older stuff," she says, punching in the buttons.

"How about Pink Floyd and Led Zeppelin?"

"Love it. And I'm crazy about Italian opera."

"I know squat about opera."

"I'll introduce you to it . . . tonight," she says. "It's very romantic."

"Uh-huh."

"And it's tragic, too . . . always tragic."

"What else do you like?" he asks.

"I'm a movie freak."

"What kinds?"

"Oh, drama, sci-fi, almost any kind—even horror films."

"Horror?"

"Oh yes," she says with a laugh. "When we were kids, Erin and I used to watch them and scare ourselves half to death. We'd lie in bed and wait for the Wolfman or Frankenstein . . ."

"And now, do you still like horror?"

"If there's a rerun of *Halloween* or *A Nightmare on Elm Street*, I'll watch it."

Her hand rests on his thigh.

They're cruising at thirty-five, passing a minimall with a Stop & Shop and retail stores. Far ahead, a red light turns green. He steps on the gas and the Audi cruises toward the intersection.

A shadow appears on the left. It creeps up slowly, and a moment later, it overtakes them. Adrian glances to his left—sees it out of the corner of his eye—the shadow looms larger now, dwarfs the sedan. Adrian veers right, sees it's a pickup and it's much too close. *Jesus! What's wrong with that guy?* And then Adrian realizes it's pulling ahead, veering toward them, and it's going to pour into the Audi. It swerves suddenly, violently. There's an explosive slamming—the raw crack of metal on metal as the Audi is hit and the steering wheel jolts in Adrian's hand. His head slams into the side window. There's a momentary starburst of lights as he clutches the steering wheel and fights for control.

He yanks the wheel, pumps the brake pedal, and feels the Audi swerve with a squeal as rubber shrieks on the asphalt. Everything rushes. It happens very fast. There's no control, and the Audi hurtles off the road. He tries to pull left, but it's too late. The Audi pitches and sways—there's screeching, a lurching sensation, and then a blast as the front wheels hit the curb. The car bounces and the seat belt cinches Adrian's shoulder; then there's a downward thrust and the belt grabs his waist. His guts compress. The Audi leaps the curb, tilts upward, and careens onto a grassy area; the harness pulls at him. He's jerked back and then forward. A blasting impact rocks him and something billows about him, blinding and smothering, and he can't breathe. Everything stops. He fights for air and feels his lungs compress, and smoke surrounds him.

The deflating air bag hisses. The car fills with vapor; but it's not smoke—it's powder. Clunking comes from beneath the hood. The smell of engine oil and gasoline fills Adrian's nostrils, and there's a spiderweb of windshield cracks; suddenly, a section falls inward and onto them in a sheet of splintered glass. The car is angled, front wheels in the air, and there's more noise—a strange clanking sound, a pinging—and a wave of fumes. *Don't panic*, he tells himself.

"Megan!" he yells.

He hears a low moan from his right.

"Megan! Megan!"

Hissing comes from behind the fire wall. It's steam and smoke mixed with the smell of gasoline. Heat percolates everywhere.

Megan is slumped in the seat, head down. There's another moan. They're trapped amid crumpled steel and broken glass, half-suspended, fumes wavering around them. The heat intensifies.

He unbuckles his seat belt and lunges for Megan.

There's an explosion of lights—blue, red, and amber—and the wail of a siren, then another. An ambulance, squad cars, police officers, and EMS people swarm everywhere. Glass is smashed and metal creaks and groans. Megan hears shouting, and someone barks commands amid radio static; then comes the tortured squeal of metal shearing, and she sees firemen with crowbars. There's another groaning sound as the Audi's doors are pried open.

Megan's wobbly and her chest aches where the seat belt wrenched her. Blood drains from her head; it's a light-headed, bleached-out feeling, and the night turns white. A cold, prickly sensation rushes up her arms as she's led away from the car. She hears Adrian say something, but it's all so far away. She sits on grass—wet with evening dew—far from the car. The car's crushed front end rests atop the remnants of a low stone wall. Its headlights cast white shafts of light into the air.

Adrian talks with police officers, describing what happened. How calm and unruffled he seems. It must come from doing surgery—life and death, a daily routine for him. But Megan feels hazy, dazed. And above all, so frightened she's shaking.

"No," Adrian says. "I never got the plate."

"Did you see the driver?" asks a cop.

"No, it had darkened windows."

Megan wonders if the cop might think Adrian was DUI and

just lost control of the car. After all, his breath must smell of wine. But there's a young man there—a buzz-cut college kid wearing a Fairfield University sweatshirt and jeans.

"Yes, Officer," the kid says. "I was right behind them and saw the whole thing. A pickup just ran them off the road. No reason."

"What color was it?"

"Dark, but I'm not sure because of the sodium lights," the kid says. "It could've been dark blue or black. Its plates were spattered with mud."

"Any identifying marks?"

"Not that I could see."

"Could you make out the brand? Ford, Toyota . . . anything?"

"It could've been a Ford F-250 or maybe a Toyota Tundra, but I'm not sure."

Cars slow to a crawl on the Post Road as people rubberneck. Cops direct traffic. Headlights pierce the night air; a stream of red taillights snakes off in the direction heading toward Fairfield; horns blare; Megan hears snippets of conversation. She nearly recoils at the smell of gasoline and smoke in the damp night air.

My God! We were run off the road by a madman.

Megan's shaking as she wonders why she didn't take Ann's advice, why she didn't call an investigation agency—some by-the-hour PI who could run a quick check—find out where on earth Conrad is. It might take a few hours, but he could be located quickly. *God, he could be back here in Connecticut.* Was the pickup Conrad's from years back? His was black—and this monster? She just glimpsed it. It's three years now. Who knows if he even has that big Ford.

An EMS guy squats beside her. He looks into her eyes, scribbles something, and asks questions. God, he reeks of cologne—smells like Paco Rabanne or some other crap. Nauseating, cloying, absolutely puke-worthy. It's worse than those gladioli. A sickeningly sweet scent seeps into her nostrils, penetrating her brain. Megan feels she could vomit.

He asks her name, the date, where they are, other questions: time, place, and person—the whole mental status thing. He's trying to see if she suffered a concussion. He shines a penlight into her eyes. The small circle of light is blinding.

"You should come to the emergency room," he says.

"I'm all right," she mutters, though a surge of nausea flows through her.

"Ms. Haggarty, you're a nurse. You know you could have internal injuries."

Oh God, he recognizes me from the hospital.

"I'm fine," she says, looking at his name tag: Rodriguez.

I don't recognize this guy; I never saw him before and yet he knows my name. God, am I getting paranoid?

Another technician rolls a gurney onto the grass.

"I really think you should go to the ER."

"Just give me the form and I'll sign it. You're off the hook."

"Any nausea?"

"No." She swallows, hoping she doesn't hurl on his shoes. That would nail it—she'd be off to the ER.

Lights flash and police radios still crackle. A dispatcher's voice on a handheld radio crepitates and breaks up. A tow truck roars up behind the Audi. It's a huge thing, muscular-looking, if you can say that about a vehicle. A thick chain gets hooked to the undercarriage. The cops wave traffic on, but people still gawk. Adrian's talking with the cops.

The technician hands her the clipboard. With a trembling hand, she signs the form.

The left side of her face burns—feels raw. She touches it and winces.

"It's a slight facial abrasion from the air bag," the paramedic says. "Use some bacitracin on it for a couple of days."

She nods and closes her eyes.

His cologne is overwhelming; nausea swims through her. If she heaves, they'll whisk her off to the hospital. *God, I don't want to go there.* If only he'd move away from her. She needs fresh air.

The paramedic stands. Her queasiness recedes.

"Anyone you want us to call?" he says.

"My sister." She gives him the telephone number.

He dials it, walks a few yards away, and talks into his cell. "She'll be here in a little while," the medic calls back to her.

Megan's thoughts tumble and her inner voice points out the obvious: it must be Conrad. It can't be anyone else, not a chance. There've been the hang-ups, the flowers, the e-mails, and now this. Run off the Post Road and almost killed.

Megan reminds herself to listen to her inner voice, the one that tells her to be very careful after what happened with Conrad. It's the voice that whispers, *Assume nothing when it comes to him . . . absolutely nothing.*

Sitting amid police and ambulance lights, with radio static and the tow truck winch whirring, Megan watches a necklace of red taillights trailing east, passing the burned-rubber streaks on the black asphalt and eyeballing the wrecked Audi. Headlights stream west as exhaust fumes linger in the deep blueness of the heavy night air. V-shaped cones of pinkish light from vapor lamps illuminate the road.

That inner voice hisses in her ear . . . *It's Conrad, a brilliant madman . . . and you're chin deep in a ton of trouble.*

He's back . . . and this time he'll kill you.

Eight

Erin looks pale and her voice is shaky. The Audi—with its twisted hulk and shattered glass—groans as it's hoisted onto a flatbed truck. It's totaled, just a complete loss. A cop waves traffic on. Adrian signs some papers; then he, Megan, and Erin walk to Erin's Subaru Forester.

"This is some way to meet," Erin says as she and Adrian shake hands.

Adrian nods and smiles weakly. A humming sensation throttles through his chest. "There'll be other times," he says, noticing that Erin's nearly as tall as Megan; she also has that Celtic look with reddish-brown hair and cerulean-blue eyes.

"The pickup just ran you off the road?" Erin asks, turning off the Post Road.

"That's right," Megan whispers.

After passing through a series of tree-lined streets, they pull into the driveway of a ranch-style house about a mile from the Post Road.

As they enter the house, Marlee, wearing pajamas, jumps into Megan's arms. Megan lifts her, and the child wraps her legs around Megan. "You okay, Mommy?" Marlee whimpers. Her reddish-blond curls are in disarray; her eyes look bleary.

"Everybody's fine, sweetie." Megan looks pale and depleted. Marlee rests her head on Megan's shoulder and casts a furtive glance at Adrian.

Erin's husband, Bob, a tall, thin guy with a receding hairline, introduces himself and then examines Adrian's head. "You've got quite a goose egg there," he says.

Adrian nods and sits down on a sofa. His head is throbbing and his legs feel weak.

Marlee and her cousins, Robert and Ellie, begin playing with Sampson, a fawn-colored little pug who's getting more excited each minute.

"I'll give you a lift home, Adrian," Bob says.

"No need, Bob. I'll call a taxi."

"It's no sweat. I'll take you." Bob grabs his car keys.

"Thanks. I'll make arrangements for a car first thing tomorrow."

"Are you all right?" Megan asks him at the front door. Her eyes look glassy.

He takes her hands in his and says, "I'll be okay. How're you?"

"I'm taking tomorrow off," she says.

"I don't have that luxury. I'll have to get to the hospital early . . . by taxi."

"This is some way to end an evening, huh?"

"There'll be others," he says, wanting to wrap his arms around her. Instead, he squeezes her hands gently. "You sure you're okay?"

She nods her head, presses her lips together, and then says, "Adrian, why not come to my place for dinner Tuesday night. Just the three of us . . . you, me, and Marlee . . . ?"

"I'd love that," he says, wanting desperately to kiss her, hold her. But it's neither the time nor the place.

"There's something I need to tell you," she says, blinking rapidly as her eyes grow wet.

Their lips meet in a quick kiss. After saying goodbye to everyone, Adrian and Bob head out the door. Walking toward Bob's car, Adrian glances back and sees Megan standing on the front steps. She looks like she's shivering, and Adrian knows whatever she wants to tell him, it won't be a good thing.

Adrian gets out of the leased Altima. It's nine o'clock on a moonless night. The incident on the Post Road two nights earlier—a mere forty-eight hours ago—replays in his head. It's flashed back to him a hundred times since then: the screech of brakes, the slamming impact, the heat and suffocating fumes. And Megan, looking so completely wrecked.

He unlocks the front door and steps into the cottage. The living room is dark. It strikes Adrian that something's wrong. He always leaves a small accent lamp on so he doesn't return to a dark house. It's an early morning ritual—something automatic—one he doesn't even think about. Did he do it this morning? It would've been dark, so he can't imagine he'd forgotten. But then, he's been so preoccupied, it could've slipped his mind.

He snaps on the lamplight and glances at the stone fireplace, chestnut beams, built-in bookshelves, and furnishings. Everything's in place. But there's a hint of an odor—barely discernible. He wonders if he left the kitchen garbage can open. He recalls a few aging items sitting in the refrigerator: a carton of garlicky takeout Chinese and some prepared crap from Stop & Shop.

He opens the refrigerator door, grabs the leftovers, tosses them in a plastic garbage bag, and carries it to the bin outside the rear door. He laughs to himself, realizing how tough it is to find good ethnic food in Connecticut. He was spoiled silly in Manhattan: great exotic cuisine was everywhere—from every nation on earth. And New Haven had plenty of ethnic places, too—especially Indian and Italian restaurants. Every tribe has its cuisine.

He realizes suddenly there was something wrong in the refrigerator, something out of place. He opens the door again.

Yes, it's strange: no milk. He recalls clearly going to the supermarket only yesterday and buying a carton of Skim Plus; he uses it on his Total every morning. But it's not there. Did he throw it out by mistake? Has he been *that* zoned out thinking of Megan—and about what happened two nights ago? Is this an episode of *Fringe*?

Is it the long hours at the hospital, invading patients' chests and fixing God's mistakes? he wonders, knowing he's quoting Megan.

He returns to the outside garbage bin, snaps open the lid, and rummages through the contents. And there it is—an empty carton of Skim Plus with milk sopping through to the bin's bottom. The carton was emptied into the garbage.

Adrian recalls reading about REM Sleep Behavior Disorder. You can have violent dreams and do bizarre things. Some people sleepwalk—trudge into the kitchen in a somnambulistic state and raid the refrigerator. Others punch or kick some dreamed-up attacker, thrash their bed partner—actually beat them. And the dreamer has no memory of the dream when awakened.

But Adrian's never been told he has restless sleep. Not by Peggy, or any other bedmate. He wonders if he's opened the door to some cartoonish universe and slipped down the proverbial rabbit hole.

But he's certain he used milk *this morning*. He plops down onto the living room sofa, re-creates his morning rituals, and tries to understand how milk ended up in the garbage and he didn't turn on the lamp.

Peering across the living room, he sees an empty space on the mantel. The framed photo of Mom and Dad on their honeymoon at Schroon Lake in upstate New York is gone. Startled, he shoots to his feet. Then Adrian sees his guitar. It's upright, leaning against the stone surround of the fireplace.

A jolting sensation pummels him, and his heart feels like it stops.

The guitar strings have been severed. They dangle like limp tresses from the instrument's neck.

Somebody broke in, emptied the milk, took the photo, and cut the guitar strings.

Adrian's body goes taut as a sizzling sensation rips through him.

There was an intruder . . . in the cottage.

His eyes dart to the bookshelves, to his old Leitz microscope from medical school, then to the brass candlesticks on the console, something Mom gave him—all undisturbed. The flat-screen television sits on a credenza; the TV and microscope are what a burglar would take.

But someone was in the house. My place was violated . . . my possessions . . . my space was invaded.

But don't burglars head to the bedroom for jewelry and hidden cash?

And that smell . . . vague, but detectable. Someone or something is upstairs.

Adrian moves to the staircase; he stops and sets his hand on the newel post. He sniffs and thinks there's an odor.

Yes, something smells, and it's rotten . . .

He begins the climb—slowly—moves up the first few steps.

Yes, there's a stench—it's stronger now. Definitely . . . something reeks.

He treads lightly and goes up a few steps, and the wooden planks creak.

As he nears the top of the staircase, the odor grows stronger.

Standing on the landing, he feels his pulse in his wrists.

The bedroom door is shut.

He never closes it—ever.

Frozen, he hears whooshing in his ears. He moves toward the door; the oak floorboards groan.

Adrian hears the night sounds of an old cottage: the water

heater rumbles, a pipe in a wall knocks, and then comes a series of metallic clanks. Outside, crickets chirr, there's the hoot of a night owl, the creaking of the red maple's windblown branches in the autumn air.

At the door, his legs quiver. His tongue feels sandy.

An eddy of air whips against the cottage's cedar shingles.

Ear pressed to the door, Adrian hears the thudding blood rush of his heart. *My God,* he thinks, he can actually feel the hairs on his neck standing.

He turns the doorknob slowly, silently.

He flings the door open and flips the light switch.

It hits him like a bitter cloud.

The bedroom air is putrid and reeks of decay. He tastes it on his tongue—caustic, repellent.

On the bed is the bloodied body of a large bird—a crow.

Its neck is wrung; its head angles grotesquely. The thing is ripped apart, mangled. Dried blood is streaked on the bedcover and pillow—clotted, congealed like currant jelly. Clawed feet poke up. The wings are torn, smeared with bloodied innards. Greenish-black iridescent feathers and quills are scattered everywhere, the tips crusted with blood and rotting flesh.

There's a sudden movement. A feather tilts, sticks up—quivers.

Something white and glistening appears. It rolls; then it's gone.

The smell of the carcass is so penetrating, it burns his throat.

Then he sees them.

Maggots—glistening white, segmented things—writhe wetly through the corpse and bore through its flesh. The dead thing pulses up and down, as though alive; it reminds Adrian of a beating heart. The bird is infested with maggots and rests in the broken rigor of a violent death.

Adrian turns, leaves, and slams the door shut.

He whips out his cell phone.

"Well, it wasn't a burglary," says Sergeant Ford. "I can say that, even though the photo's missing." Ford's a military type—reminds Adrian of a marine drill instructor—has a slate-gray crew cut, is steep-jawed, steely eyed, and wears a tailored uniform to fit his wiry physique. Right out of Central Casting. His partner, Moore, a balding giant, must tip the scale at three hundred pounds—looks like he could wrestle in the WWE.

"You think it might've been kids playing a prank?" Adrian asks.

"Nope," Ford says. "I've been a Simpson cop for fifteen years . . . seen plenty of teen mischief. They leave empty beer bottles and pizza boxes and toss the furniture." Ford rubs his chin and shakes his head. "And they piss all over the place and take a dump . . . They leave a little souvenir for the homeowner." Ford shakes his head. "But that bird? It's a whole other thing, Doc."

"I'll smell it for a long time," Moore says, his salami-sized hand rubbing his bulbous nose. The junior cop reminds Adrian of Shrek.

"Doc, you have any enemies?" Ford asks.

"No." Adrian's hands feel weak.

"Because this guy left you a message . . ."

Adrian nods. A pang of fear stabs his chest.

"What kind of message, Sarge?" Moore asks.

"Maybe this guy blames the doc for screwin' up his life. Could be a warning . . ."

"That goddamned crow," says Moore.

"By the way, that's a raven," corrects Ford. "They're bigger'n crows. Not that it makes a helluva lot of difference. Though, maybe it does. Remember that poem 'The Raven'? What is it the raven says . . . *nevermore*?"

"Nevermore?" Moore asks.

"Maybe I'm just overthinkin' a nutcase," says Ford. "It could just be some road kill he found. Or maybe the guy's an outdoor type, killed it with a shotgun."

A shotgun . . .

Adrian's reminded of King's Corner, the drive-by shooting.

Adrian? Do I know you?

I'll be back . . .

Adrian smells the smoke, hears the sizzling wires, and sees the shattered glass.

"That bird's been dead awhile," Ford says. "It's filled with maggots. He probably carried the thing in a plastic bag."

"Son of a bitch," says Moore.

"You sure nobody's got it in for you, Doc?"

"I don't have a clue," Adrian says, as his thoughts scan colleagues, friends, and casual acquaintances—people past and present.

"Some patient who thinks you ruined his life?"

Adrian shakes his head.

"You have any arguments? Some jerk at a supermarket or a gas station . . . anything?"

He describes the incident on the Post Road.

"Look, Doc . . . maybe there's some connection between the Post Road thing and this. Maybe you oughta talk with Chief Mulvaney over in Eastport. He's got way more resources than we do. We're a small town, only six thousand people."

"Isn't this out of his jurisdiction?"

"Not when you got run off the road. There could be a connection."

"The chief's a friend of mine," Adrian says. "I called him about the Post Road thing."

"What about the photo?" asks Moore.

"Mom and Dad . . . damned if I know," says Ford. "And that milk carton . . . emptied out. It's pretty strange." At the door, he turns to Adrian. “Doc . . . I have a feeling someone’s got it in for you.”

Adrian feels a chill in his heart.

Nine

"A dead bird . . . ?" Megan asks. "I can't believe it." Her voice is trembling. "Do you think it's some angry patient, like the cop said?"

"Megan, I've gone through the hospital log . . . every case over the last year. There're no unexpected bad outcomes. No threatened malpractice suits. There's nothing."

"What about people at work?"

"No problems. It's a great team."

"And the neighbors . . . ?"

"The Gibsons? Elderly people with a home health aide. They can barely walk."

"What about other neighbors?"

"There's no other house for half a mile. And the cop said it wasn't kids."

"What're you doing about the cottage?"

"I called a biohazard removal company. They practically sanitized the place. A new bed's coming tomorrow. And a security company installed a motion detector in the cottage and a photoelectric beam at the driveway entrance. It'll trigger a signal five hundred feet before anyone gets to the front door."

"The driveway's five hundred feet long?"

"It's a gravel-covered roadway."

"Adrian, it's so isolated."

"But it's alarmed now. And Chief Mulvaney said he'd contact Hartford."

"Adrian, we have to talk about something."

He can *feel* the tension in her voice.

"What is it, Megan?"

"It's too important to discuss on the phone. We'll talk about it tomorrow night, when you're here."

Adrian watches Megan tuck Marlee into bed. The child's milky-white skin reminds him of porcelain.

It's really crazy, Adrian thinks, but in a few hours, he'll be driving that sinuous road back to Simpson in the dark, listening to his Pink Floyd CD, *The Dark Side of the Moon,* and thinking of Megan: the redolence of her hair, the taste of her mouth—all a faint ghosting, a memory of desire. And he'll spend the night alone.

Marlee stayed up later than usual to play checkers with Adrian. She's a great kid—smart, too—caught on to the game in a flash and squealed with delight every time she cried "King me!"

With the bedcover up to her chin, she peers at Adrian through partly closed eyelids. She turns to Megan and says, "Mommy, can we go to the aquarium?"

"Of course, honey. That would be fun."

"Can Adrian come too?" she asks in an audible whisper.

"Sure he can."

"We can see the mermaids . . . especially Ariel."

"It's very hard to see the mermaids. You know they can't be with humans."

"And we can see Flounder the fish and Sebastian the crab."

"Yes, we'll see them there."

"You know who Adrian looks like?" Marlee half whispers, glancing at him.

"Who, sweetie?"

"Eric the human prince."

Adrian feels his face flush.

"And Ariel has red hair . . . just like you, Mommy."

Adrian feels lightness in his chest as he and Megan move toward the door.

"Night, Mommy."

"Good night, sweetie."

"Night, Adrian."

"Good night, Marlee."

"I love you both," she murmurs.

The light goes out.

A lump fills Adrian's throat.

"She misses her father," Adrian says in the living room.

"She has no memory of him."

"She misses *having* a father."

Megan nods, sits on the sofa, regards him somberly, and says, "Adrian. I need to tell you what happened with Conrad and me. I think it's connected to the break-in."

A chilled wave sluices through Adrian. Unease invades him, a disquiet he recognizes as a harbinger of trouble, even danger.

"It's hard to talk about," she says. She looks pasty, but a plum-colored flush creeps across her throat.

"Megan, you can tell me anything."

"It's so strange. I always thought it was awful that I didn't know my real parents. Now Marlee asks about her father and all I can say is he's gone." She swallows hard, clasps her hands, and then says, "Adrian, I think he's back."

"Your ex? He's back from Colorado?"

"Yes. And I'm scared to death."

Adrian moves closer to hold her. His throat closes off. "You've never told me about him."

"Things with Conrad changed after we were married. It was gradual, but he changed."

"Changed how?"

"Adrian, the man went crazy."

Ten

"I met Conrad when I was at Yale. I was out one evening with two girlfriends."

Describing it, Megan recalls the Trumbull Roadhouse with its mix of bully-bikers and pretend cowboys. It was like a Western saloon right out of *Unforgiven* or *Shane*, but with a contemporary twist: an electrified band and a twangy country singer who murdered the songs. Actually, it was a bit karaoke, with couples swaying to corny, lovesick ballads blaring across the barnlike expanse. "It was music, energy, and hormones . . . fun for an evening, but not really my style."

When Conrad approached her, the first thing Megan noticed were his ghostly looking eyes. He had a strong jaw, a straight, prominent nose, high cheekbones, and closely cropped blondish hair—almost a buzz cut—which fit with his etched features. He was big, well built, and looked very athletic, which she always liked in a man. He could have stepped right out of a rodeo ring smelling of horses and hemp.

"I've seen four guys talk with you," he said. "And you haven't danced with any of them."

"They didn't ask me."

Megan noticed he wasn't all tanked up, smelling of booze and filled with macho swagger, like the others.

"Well, I'm just asking if you'll dance the next slow one with me."

On the dance floor, he was light on his feet, which was surprising given his size. His shoulders were broad and sloping; she could feel the immense power in his arms.

"You don't sound like you're from Connecticut," she said.

"I'm from Colorado . . . a town called Red Rock."

He'd been living in New Haven in a rental apartment, working for a construction company. The housing boom was in high gear. He was making good money and living a freewheeling life.

"There was something endearing about him," Megan says. "He was sort of a callow, country boy. There was something unpretentious and honest about him, which I've always liked. We danced a few slow numbers, and I realized I was not only attracted to him, but I felt almost motherly toward him."

"They were right," Conrad said when the music ended. "Those guys who came on to you."

"Right about what?"

"You *are* beautiful."

Blood rushed to her cheeks.

"In fact, you're the most beautiful woman I've ever seen."

She knew then, he lacked the capacity for caprice.

"By the third date, we talked about our families," Megan says. "That was when we made a very deep connection. Because it turned out that Conrad was adopted, too. He never knew his birth parents."

"My mother told me when I was seven," Conrad said. "My so-called father didn't care. He never wanted me. I had lots of trouble with him."

"What kind of trouble?"

"He beat me every day. And he left when I was ten."

"Well, what about your mother?"

"She died after I graduated from high school. It was cancer," he said. "After that, I was on my own."

"**S**o," Megan says. "We shared not only being adopted, but we were both orphaned early. When I think about it now, I know *pity* played a part in my feelings for Conrad. But he was very affectionate, and smart, too. I must tell you, Adrian, he was one of the most brilliant people I've ever met.

"He was a carpenter, but he learned to read architectural blueprints. He learned plumbing and electrical work—all on the job. He could memorize things in a flash, and was a whiz with a computer. Actually, he could do anything technical. His boss paid him to do all kinds of jobs—off the books—so he didn't have to bring in licensed tradesmen. If Conrad had come from a different background, who knows what he'd have become?

"When we got married, I kept my name, Haggarty, which really bothered him. That's when things started to go downhill. Erin saw it too."

"Saw what?"

"Conrad's jealousy. At first it was little things, like thinking other men were looking at me. If we were in a restaurant, he thought guys were staring at me. It got to the point where no man could look in my direction. He even threatened a few.

"Then he began showing up at the hospital, checking on me. He accused me of flirting. He once thought I looked at some guy in a shopping mall and the guy glanced back; Conrad punched him out. He was arrested and sentenced to thirty days of community service.

"Then he began talking about having a baby. I thought maybe it was his way of proving that unlike his real father, he could *keep* a child, especially a son. You know, sort of rewrite history through his own child. Lots of people try to do that. And naively, I thought it might cement things.

"So I stopped taking the pill. But there was no pregnancy.

Conrad thought my work was wearing me out and I wasn't getting pregnant. He wanted me to quit, do private duty nursing . . . something less pressured. But he really wanted to keep me away from the hospital and doctors . . . actually, he was jealous of any man.

"I saw my gynecologist, and we went through the whole routine when couples're trying to have a baby."

"Oh, I know it well," Adrian says.

"Yes, you know the nightmare. The ovulation test strips, the thermometer, sex on a schedule . . ."

"Uh-huh."

"After a year, Conrad was just freaked out. He wanted me to get checked. I resented his assumption that *I* had a problem, but there was no harm in my seeing a fertility specialist.

"So I went for the tests—a blood workup, ultrasound, everything. I had no biological family, so there wasn't a clue about whether there might be a problem. It turned out, I was completely normal."

"And then . . . ?"

"The specialist said that about forty percent of fertility problems are caused by a sperm defect. That it could be Conrad. We'd need a semen analysis. But I knew that would never happen with Conrad."

"So what happened?"

"I never brought it up. We kept trying, but nothing happened. And then, many months later, my period was late. I bought an Early Pregnancy Test kit. And I was pregnant." Megan shifts her weight on the sofa. Adrian notices her chin quivering.

"Conrad wanted a son . . . desperately. He began doting on me, like I was a ripening fruit. He insisted that I retire. He wouldn't consider child care."

Megan's thoughts race back to the arguments.

But, Conrad, I can leave the baby with Erin.

Erin's not his mother.

Erin would love to watch the baby.

You belong at home . . . with the baby and me. I don't want you hanging around with those goddamned doctors. All they wanna do is get into your pants anyway.

Conrad, this jealousy . . . it's crazy.

Crazy? I'm crazy in love with you.

"And I'd wonder if he was crazy in love, or just plain *crazy*," Megan says. "He wanted a son more than anything. And when Marlee was born, I knew he was disappointed. And of all things, he was insanely jealous of her, too.

"After maternity leave, I went back to work. Marlee stayed with Erin and her baby, Robert. That's when Conrad really got crazy. First, there were his rages. They came out of the blue, and I was afraid for Marlee and myself.

"He thought I had a *boyfriend* at the hospital. He began staying out at night, going to bars, getting all tanked up. He'd stumble home by midnight—drunk. Erin kept saying, 'You need to get out of this marriage. You're married to a madman.'"

Megan's thoughts lurch back to her last fateful evening.

He came home early—at nine o'clock—barged in the door and staggered around the apartment, reeking of alcohol. Marlee was asleep.

"Is there anything to eat in this fuckin' place?" he snarled, and then slammed the refrigerator door so hard, the appliance rocked.

"How can you ask me that?" she shot back. "You're never home. We're not living like a married couple."

"Why don't you *tell* me how we're living, huh? When you work every day and spend the rest of your life at your goddamned sister's?"

"Conrad, we're there because you're never home. You're out drinking and—"

"Well, I'm home *tonight*. And the fuckin' refrigerator's *empty*."

He stomped into the living room and the walls seemed to shake. "And this work of yours—nursing newborns—is getting in the way."

"Getting in the way of *what*? I'm home by five fifteen, but you're not here."

"Goddammit! I want you *home*." His face was blotted with rage.

"I *am* home. But you're out. You drink too much and you're angry all the time. And you don't care about Marlee—"

"And just what the fuck *do* you do at that hospital?"

He kicked over a chair; a huge purple vein on his sweat-soaked forehead pulsed. "You keep those little bastards alive." He shouted, moving closer, looming over her. "Tell me this . . . tell me this *one* goddamned thing." His bloodshot eyes looked crazed. His neck veins bulged like thick ropes.

"Tell you *what*, Conrad?"

"Who're you fuckin' at the hospital?"

He clutched her arm and clamped down on it tightly.

She tried pulling away, but his grip was viselike. She felt her arm going numb.

"Conrad, you're hurting me."

"I want the *truth*."

His eyes were wild-looking, bloodshot, and saw nothing. His face was crimson. Gobs of saliva formed on his lips. He shook her so violently, she thought her neck would snap.

"Please, Conrad . . ."

"Who're you fuckin'?"

"Conrad. *Stop* it." The room swayed, then began spinning.

"You'd better tell me, you slut," he shouted, pulling her closer. Her arms were pinned to her sides, losing feeling.

"You're *crazy*. You're—"

His palm cracked across her cheek. She toppled; but he held

her up. He shook her again; her body shuddered like a bobble-head doll.

He flung her onto the sofa.

"Tell me, you *whore*." His fist hovered. One hand clutched her neck, squeezing.

Choking, desperate, her eyes watered. Dimness, breath going, crushing pressure on her chest, the room spinning, she was fading.

She twisted, turned away from him, and gasped.

He got up and raged through the apartment.

She lay on the sofa, shaking, with her eyes closed.

Suddenly, she heard frantic squealing. She leapt to her feet and stumbled toward Marlee's cries.

What she saw nearly made her heart stop.

Conrad held Marlee in his left arm. His face was bloated with rage; Marlee screamed.

"Tell me whose baby this is. Whose kid is this?"

Marlee shrieked, reaching for Megan.

Still holding her, Conrad rushed into the kitchen. Dishes crashed to the floor.

Megan tottered after him. Her legs shook and felt weak. Trembling coursed through her body.

A carving knife was poised at Marlee's neck. "Who's this bastard's father?"

Megan's body jangled. "Conrad, she's yours . . . she's *our* child." She sputtered a stream of words in a weak voice and whispered, "Conrad, please don't hurt her."

"Tell me or I'll slit this little bastard's throat."

"Please . . . Conrad . . . please . . . let her go . . ."

A dark current of fear ran through Megan. "Please, Conrad . . . give Marlee to me. I'll tell you whatever you want." Her voice rasped, frantic, pleading. Shaking, she inched closer on legs of water. "Conrad, please, just give her to me."

She stepped closer, her breath ragged. Her hands shook violently.

His eyes were ruthlessly bloodshot, crazed. "Tell me *now*. Whose kid is this? Who's the father?"

"Conrad! What are you talking—"

"Because it isn't mine."

"She's *yours*, Conrad. She's our *baby*," Megan cried, certain he was out of his mind. She inched closer, her body shuddering.

The knife rose.

"Fuckin' whore—tell me, whose is she?"

Megan's heart jumped. Her stomach dropped. She felt sick.

Another inch closer, then another, then she stopped, arms out, begging with her eyes, tears snaking down her cheeks. Her skin felt raw, like it was shredding.

Oh, just a little closer . . . a few inches . . . if I can get close enough . . .

Suddenly, the telephone rang.

"Who's that?" he roared. "Is it your *boyfriend*?"

"No, Conrad. It's Erin."

"Oh yeah? We'll see," he said, snatching the telephone.

Megan lunged at him; he fell backward.

She seized Marlee and bolted away. She grabbed her car keys, threw open the apartment door, dashed down the hallway, stumbled, and kept going, rushing wildly.

Conrad stormed into the foyer, crashed drunkenly into furniture, fell down, got up, and then came after her.

Doors opened; neighbors' heads popped out; the hallway flew by. Megan scrambled down three flights with Marlee shrieking in her arms.

Conrad thundered down the stairwell. She heard him closing in—the second floor, then the first. She could hear his rage-filled, drunken grunting. Then he tumbled over, bounced heavily on the stairway, headfirst, rolled, roared, and cursed; then came more thumping and shouting as he got to his feet, fell again, got up, and came after her.

At the car, Megan fumbled with the keys, hands trembling, knees quaking, and then—after groping and foraging—she was behind the wheel; the ignition whirred, as the engine coughed and finally turned over. She threw the car into reverse and backed away from him as he bounded toward her.

Her breath left her as he came closer. She was frantic, in a frenzy of fear.

Limping, Conrad bounded closer.

She turned the wheel, and the car swerved.

The headlight beams shone on him and swung away. His hand slammed the rear fender—a deep and jarring thump. She gunned the gas pedal and burned rubber; the car fishtailed and then sped away. She held the wheel with one hand and clutched Marlee with the other.

On the main avenue, she glanced into the rearview mirror. Was his pickup behind them? Not yet. No traffic. Thoughts scuttled in a frantic mind rush; the streets flashed by, lamplights, headlights, signs, crosswalks, all in a nighttime blur.

Another glance in the mirror: nothing. Nobody was behind her. She passed a red light, the tires shrieked and then hammered on the road as she sped down Chapel Street.

The engine howled as she gunned the gas pedal and stomped it to the floor. She held Marlee. No time for the baby seat—just time to get away, to Erin's place or the police. But what would they do? Arrest him—a holding cell, maybe till tomorrow. Then what?

She'd go to a safe place, to people she loved and who loved her because they were family, the only thing that could ever matter in this crazy world. It was all she had; it was everything.

Yes, family. Not Conrad's madness.

"So I lived with Erin and Bob," Megan says. "And I got a restraining order. Conrad wasn't allowed near us. Then I filed for divorce."

Looking pale, her voice watery and weak, Megan shudders on the sofa. Adrian feels a twinge of sadness—raw, penetrating sorrow—reaches for her hand and caresses it.

"Then flowers began to arrive . . . along with notes."

"Flowers?" Adrian says.

"Yes."

"Like the gladioli that came to the hospital?"

"Yes." Megan swallows and then takes a deep breath. "The flowers I thought you sent that day."

"What happened then?"

"Erin wanted me to call the police, but I ignored Conrad, didn't want to fan the flames. He began sending notes saying he loved me and wanted me back. He never even mentioned Marlee, and I was amazed at the irony of it. For Conrad and me, learning who our real parents were was the burning issue of our childhoods. It was our personal dragon. And now my husband was accusing me of having a bastard child. It was crazy. As Erin put it . . . *His own flesh and blood and he thinks it's someone else's. How crazy is that?*

"There were telephone hang-ups. But they tapered off after a while. I guess he just gave up. Then I heard he left for Colorado. Bob hired an investigator, and we learned that Conrad relocated out West."

Megan's eyes are red-rimmed, puffy-looking.

"For a while, I had the strangest feeling he was following me, even though he was gone. Whenever I saw a black pickup, my heart would stop."

"A black pickup?"

"Yes, like the one that ran us off the road, Adrian."

"I'm getting the picture," Adrian whispers as the edges of the room darken.

"I had this uncanny sense he was around—lurking—because I realized he'd always know where to find me. You can't just disappear into thin air. With a man like Conrad, you can never feel safe . . . ever."

"You mentioned his eyes."

"Yes."

"Blue-gray . . . they seemed ghostly . . ." he says.

"Yes."

"That guy at King's Corner . . . those were the kind of eyes he had."

"Oh, my God." Megan gasps and blanches.

"And, Megan, that night we got run off the Post Road . . ."

"I know. I think it was Conrad."

A coppery taste forms on Adrian's tongue.

"He's back. I'm sure he is," she whispers.

Adrian shivers; his chest feels like it's filled with ice.

"I thought I'd left it all behind. Bob and Erin had just had Ellie, and their place in New Haven was too small, so they moved here. I rented this place to be near them and got the job at Eastport General."

Megan looks drained, pallid. "Now there've been telephone calls, the flowers, those e-mails, and the break-in at your place."

That coppery taste on Adrian's tongue turns to acid—hot, bilious.

"Didn't you say that Chief Mulvaney had the forensic people in Hartford examine that bird and they found that it was filled with buckshot?" Megan says.

"Yes, twenty-gauge shot."

"That's the kind of shotgun Conrad had. The New Haven police confiscated it when I got the restraining order."

"Is it still in effect?"

"No. It expired."

"Well, my love, I know someone who can find out if Conrad Wilson's here."

"What if he *is*?"

"Let's take it one step at a time."

"And, Adrian, there's something else I need to tell you about Conrad and me. It's important, and . . ." She falls silent, stares down, and covers her mouth. And she says, "My God, I'm so scared."

"What is it, Megan?"

"I just can't . . ." Her voice trails off. Her shoulders shudder and her hands go to her mouth. "I feel so terrible . . . and if I tell you this, I worry you'll think less of me. I worry you'll never want to see me again." Tears drip from the corners of her eyes.

"Oh, Megan, how could you even think that? There's nothing that could make me feel that way . . . nothing."

"There's something else I need to tell you about Conrad and me."

"What is it?"

"Well," she whispers, "in his own crazy way, Conrad's right. But it isn't . . . it isn't anything he could ever know, because it's a secret. The truth is," she says as tears roll from her eyes. "The truth is, Marlee's . . . Marlee's *not* his. But, Adrian, it's not what you think."

Eleven

"How's my favorite heart surgeon?" asks Patrick Mulvaney, the Eastport chief of police.

Adrian always finds himself smiling when he and Pat talk. He loves the big guy's laugh, a genuine marker of pleasure in a man who'd been near death and now laps up every possible delight life offers.

"I'm fine, Pat. How're you doing?"

"Can't complain, thanks to you and your chest-crackin' buddies. Ticker's goin' like a damned Swiss clock, and I haven't had a chest pain since the bypass. I'm back to playin' golf now, walking the full eighteen. And I keep it light on the Nineteenth hole. No more corned beef and cabbage, either, and only one measly beer a day. Can ya believe it . . . an Irishman drinkin' only one shitty beer a day? That's the downside; the upside's I get to live my life, thanks to you."

Adrian reminds himself that Pat always focuses on the absurdity of life—even when trouble rears its ugly head. And trouble—big or small—is Patty's business.

"How's Marge?" Adrian asks.

"She wants your ass over here for dinner real soon; *that's* how she is."

"It's a date, Patty. Just let me know when."

"I know I've said this before Adrian, but I wish I had a

daughter for you."

Adrian smiles, knowing Pat Mulvaney's quite the father figure. It's always been part of the mix in his feelings about Pat. After all, the infamous left anterior descending coronary artery—known in the heart trade as *the widow maker*—left Adrian fatherless. Whenever he's inside a patient's chest, a thought of Dad flashes in his mind; and now he thinks of Patty, too. It's a momentary thing, but it's always there. And that artery, along with others, was as clogged as an old rusty pipe when Adrian opened Pat up.

"You seein' anyone special these days?"

"You'll be happy to hear, Pat, I'm seeing a beautiful Irish girl."

"An Irish girl? Really?"

"Megan. Megan Haggarty . . ."

"A *lovely* name. You'll bring her for dinner. Marge and I insist."

"Sure thing, Pat."

"Sorry I don't have any more on that pickup, Adrian. It's a dead end. And that bird . . . I had the thing examined by the forensic unit in Hartford. There's nothin' more . . . just the buckshot."

"That's not what I'm calling about," Adrian says as dread slithers through him and chills his flesh. He feels goose bumps on his forearms, and the back of his neck tingles.

Adrian . . . what kind of name is that? I'll be back . . .

"Pat, I need help on something." Adrian hears a nervous treble in his voice.

"Name it, Adrian."

"Well, there's a good chance there's a guy stalking Megan."

"Your girl's getting stalked?"

"Yes. In fact, Pat, I may've run into him. Remember that drive-by shooting at King's Corner?"

"Sure do."

"The guy who did it may be Megan's ex." Adrian's tongue goes to his lips and tries to find moisture, but they're Sahara-dry.

"You have time, Pat?"

"For you, Adrian? Of course I have time."

Sitting at his desk, Mulvaney dials Adrian's cell. It's eight in the evening, a day after they talked on the telephone. Adrian picks up after the second ring.

"Adrian, guess who we found."

"Conrad Wilson?"

"Yup, he's here at the station. I'd like you to come down and ID him . . . see if he's the guy from King's Corner."

"How'd you get him?"

"We picked him up early this evening. He was in New Haven."

"So he *is* back. How'd you do it?"

"Easy. We ran Wilson's name through Colorado DMV. His pickup's registered there. We got an address, contacted Denver PD. They learned he broke his lease and left no forwarding address, so they talked to a neighbor. The guy said Wilson went back East, somewhere in New England. So we assumed it was New Haven. In this business, you learn people are creatures of habit. We spoke to your girl, Megan, and she told us that Wilson used to hang out at a Tex-Mex place, the Mesa Bar & Grill in New Haven.

"So we contacted the New Haven PD, and they were on the lookout for a black Ford F-250 with Colorado plates. Bingo. The thing was parked there, right at the corner of State and Beech Street. Can you get down here real soon?"

"That's the guy," Adrian says, peering through the one-way mirror. Looking at the man in the interrogation room, Adrian feels a cold tingling run down his spine. And something drops in his belly; it feels heavy, like a dead weight.

"No doubt about it?"

"Patty, I'll never forget that face or those eyes. The Vandyke's gone, but that's him."

"So he was at the bar that night, and he owns a black pickup. Doesn't prove he shot the place up," Mulvaney says. "But it says somethin' about him."

"It shows he's been hanging around, stalking Megan."

"Yeah, and maybe you, too. We'll find out what we can. The ID helps, Adrian. I'll let you know what develops."

Back in his office, Mulvaney thinks about the call he made to his old friend Lieutenant Joe Morris, district manager of the State Street Patrol District in New Haven. As a courtesy, he told Joe his men picked Wilson up for questioning.

"Looks like a stalking situation, Joe. The guy may've also done a drive-by at a bar in Eastport and possibly a B and E."

"Pat, do whatever you gotta do," Morris said.

Leaning back in his high-backed leather chair, Mulvaney thinks about his job. He's thankful he's Eastport's police chief. It's a lovely town, for the most part: stately homes and high-end condos in Fairfield County—one of the wealthiest in the nation—filled with law-abiding citizens, especially compared to New Haven. Even with Yale, a good part of New Haven's still a shithole. And it was just his luck to be recruited by the Eastport Town Board after thirty-five hard-core years on the New Haven force.

In Eastport, you got mostly upper-middle class types—commuters into the Big Apple—and some leftovers from the old days of the blueblood WASP elite. Yup, there's plenty of old money still lingering in Eastport, especially in the Green Hills section. And there's no serious crime, just the everyday bullshit of the burbs: traffic enforcement, neighbors' petty squabbles over dogs or noise, and underage drinking, teen pranks, DUIs, minor crap like that.

Yup, Mulvaney thinks, it's good to be chief. Actually, he's lucky to be alive, thanks to Adrian Douglas. He'd just begun his stint as chief when the chest pains began—felt like the Jolly Green Giant sitting on his chest—crushing pain right in the center and goin' straight up his back and down both arms. He was rushed to Eastport General.

Adrian got in there and fixed his pipes—real fast, skin to skin in less than three hours. Since then it's been a social thing—no more doctor-patient bullshit. Adrian's a regular guy, and he's modest, too. Not some grandstanding braggart like so many of these guys with sheepskins. Mulvaney realizes Adrian's got all the bases covered. A top-notch surgeon and a former baseball player too—center field at Cornell. He was scouted big-time by the pros—was offered a trip down to Vero Beach to try out for the Dodgers. But he nixed it for med school.

Because of Adrian, Mulvaney'll work another five years, till he's sixty-five. Then he and Marge'll head down to the Carolinas, where retired cops fade away on the golf course. It's what Marge has wanted for a while now, and it's time to give her a break, get her away from these Connecticut winters, which make her arthritis flare up.

Mulvaney's reverie is broken when Lieutenant Ed Harwood pokes his head into the office.

"It's been nearly two hours and we're getting nowhere, Chief. Soon he'll be all lawyered up."

Peering through the one-way mirror, Mulvaney knows Wilson's a rough customer, not like most of the punks he's dealt with over the years. He looks like a rugged guy, one you'd never wanna run into in a dark alleyway. Mulvaney turns to Harwood and says, "We won't get much outta him, Ed."

Harwood's a twenty-year veteran and knows the nuts and

bolts of police work. "He fits the profile of a stalker," Harwood says. "Was married to the vic, was abusive, she left him, and he's stalked her before."

"Any priors?" Mulvaney asks.

"Not here. We contacted Colorado. Just some minor barroom crap, nothing serious. There's no real rap sheet." Harwood grunts. "He's just tumbleweed and trailer trash; that's how I see this guy."

"Too bad the prints on the beer bottle at Kings Corner were smudged."

"Yup," says Harwood.

"Anything from NCIC?"

"Nope, not a thing."

"This stinks out loud," says Mulvaney. "It's the kinda thing you hear on the six o'clock news. He stalks the ex, kills her, kills the kid, and then shoots himself in the head." Pressure builds behind Mulvaney's eyeballs. He feels another headache comin' on—a real brain squeezer. Maybe he'll take that antimigraine shit, Imitrex.

Mulvaney enters the interrogation room, a cinder-block cubicle with semigloss painted beige walls. The place is cramped, brightly lit by a recessed fluorescent light above the oak veneer table. A faint odor of cheap cologne—the crap Detective Bill Casey uses—lingers in the air. Casey's his best interrogator; he took courses with the FBI down at Quantico. The guy could sweat a block of granite. He spent an hour and a half with Wilson and got shit-on-a-stick outta the guy.

Up close, Wilson's even bigger-looking than before. And those eyes: like some strange fish peering up at you from the depths—a shark. Mulvaney feels a hole in the pit of his stomach. Wilson's wearing a light-blue work shirt and faded Wrangler jeans along with tan hiking boots—typical workman's outfit. The guy's thighs bulge with massed muscle and look like they're ready to burst outta the jeans.

"What do we have here, the chief of police?" Wilson says, eyeing the row of silver stars on Mulvaney's starched blue collar.

Sitting opposite Wilson, Mulvaney tastes acid in his throat. "Pat Mulvaney, police chief," he says, meeting Wilson's eyes. Mulvaney makes sure to hold Wilson's stare—eyeball-to-eyeball, no flinching.

Wilson sits casually, his hands—with fingers clasped—rest on the table's laminated top. Jesus, those mitts are huge meat pies, thinks Mulvaney. They're thick-fingered, rough, calloused—a working man's hands.

"Mr. Wilson . . . you were livin' in Colorado?"

Wilson nods.

"Whendya come back to Connecticut?"

"A few weeks ago."

"Why was that?"

Wilson shrugs his massive shoulders. Fuckin' guy's built like an NFL linebacker, thinks Mulvaney. It's rare to see a guy with such dense muscle bulk.

"Get fired?"

"Laid off . . ."

"These are bad times, huh?"

Wilson nods. He seems to be merely tolerating Mulvaney's presence.

"You been workin' since you got back to New Haven?"

He shakes his head.

"Why not?"

"Like you said . . . bad times."

"Mr. Wilson, you own a Ford pickup, don't you?"

You go from the known to the unknown. Take it step by step; ask yes-and-no questions to pin him into a corner; get some tidbits that might begin opening the door a crack.

Wilson nods again, a slow, ponderous motion of his head.

"Mr. Wilson, you ever been in King's Corner here in Eastport?"

Wilson shrugs.

"Someone shot the place up . . . used a shotgun."

Wilson's stare reminds Mulvaney of the prefight stare downs when he was heavyweight champ in the interdepartmental boxing matches in New Haven—a thousand years ago. Beat the shit outta plenty of cops and firemen.

"You own a shotgun?"

Wilson shakes his head.

"*Ever* own one?"

Wilson nods.

"Where is it?"

"With the New Haven police, last I knew."

"Why?"

"They took it."

"Why?"

"Part of a restraining order . . ."

"Who got the order?"

"My ex."

"Why'd that happen?"

"She claimed I got physical with her."

Mulvaney wonders where to take this little chitchat. Wilson stonewalled Bill Casey, so Mulvaney's certain he's going to have to settle for this Q and A going nowhere. Maybe it's time to use some of what he's learned from Adrian.

"Got any kids, Mr. Wilson?"

"Nope, not one."

"Most men I know have kids."

"The ex has one, but it's not mine. Kid's a bastard."

"How do ya know?"

"I know."

"Speakin' of your ex, you telephone her?"

"Nope."

"Send her flowers?"

"Why would I send flowers to a whore?"

"A whore? Why do ya say that?"

"Just is."

"So, you're not workin'. I guess you have plenty of time on your hands."

No response.

"Lots of time to spend here in Eastport?"

He says nothing.

"In your black pickup . . . Colorado plates 254WKB."

The guy still says nothin'. No blinking, no movement.

"A Ford F-250 with an overhead light rack and a silver toolbox in the back of the cab?"

Wilson's eyes remind Mulvaney of a blizzard of pure nothingness. Those pupils—deep black holes in the middle of that icy paleness—fuckin' creepy.

"Ever been to the flower shop near Eastport General?"

Wilson shakes his head.

Wilson's sitting in this hard-backed interrogation chair—purposely designed to give you ass-ache—with those huge, lunchbox-sized mitts clasped, looking like they could rip the New Haven County Yellow Pages in half.

"No flowers?"

"Flowers are for faggots."

"I send flowers to my wife every Valentine's Day. That make me a faggot?"

"Only you can know, Chief."

"You a homosexual, Mr. Wilson?"

Mulvaney looks for a tell—a flicker in the eye, a twitch, a few blinks—anything to show he's touched a raw nerve, penetrated the guy's armor, put a needle up his ass. But the guy sits there, calm, unruffled; he's impenetrable.

Mulvaney leans in, palms on the table, his face inches away

from Wilson's.

"I asked if you're a homosexual, Mr. Wilson." *Jesus. This guy's coldness could cause freezer burn.* "In my experience, a guy who calls other guys a faggot has homosexual tendencies," Mulvaney says. "Ya know what I'm sayin'?"

"Maybe you got lots of experience with faggots, Chief . . ."

"I wonder if I'm lookin' at one now."

"Am I under arrest?"

"No."

"Then I'm outta here," Wilson says, rising from his chair.

"You're outta here when I *say* you're outta here." Mulvaney feels his heart kick into a gallop.

Wilson sits down. Stays cool, unshaken.

A twinge of apprehension crawls through Mulvaney. It's Wilson's stare, the brooding silence, the guy's fearlessness—even lifelessness. And right now, of all the goddamned things, the fuckin' guy's nostrils are widening. Even quivering, just slightly; Mulvaney *sees* it. It's barely detectible, but Mulvaney can see the nostril edges flaring outward. Maybe the guy's getting' annoyed, or maybe, just maybe, the son of a bitch smells somethin'. Mulvaney recalls reading that people give off fear odor; it comes from somewhere deep inside. Actually, all animals give it off. And Mulvaney realizes he's thinking about fear odor because he's certain Wilson's sniffing *him*.

Yes, Mulvaney's sure the bastard's getting a whiff of his damp pits. It's not a Niagara of sweat, but it's there. So Mulvaney finds himself inhaling—discreetly—trying to sniff his own sweat, but there's not a hint of that primal juice. Yet Wilson's sniffing him like a goddamned dog. *Jeez, is this guy some kind of animal?*

"Lemme tell you something, Mr. Wilson."

The man stares. The fluorescent light buzzing above them reminds Mulvaney of a horsefly on a hot summer day, or maybe a goddamned hornet.

"We have our eye on you."

The light keeps humming.

"You'd better be careful about who you follow or harass."

"Are you accusing me of something?"

"I'm telling you to be careful."

"I'm always careful. It's my nature."

"Well, we're onto your *nature*." Mulvaney waits a beat, then says, "And I'll tell you somethin' else . . ."

Wilson waits, silent and stone still.

"We know it was *you* who shot up King's Corner. We know you've been hanging around Eastport General . . . and we know you've been following Megan Haggarty. And ya know what? You show up in Eastport, we'll be on you like shit on a pig."

Wilson stands. It's a sudden movement, quick, catlike.

Mulvaney feels his pulse bound as he pushes back from the table.

Wilson walks casually toward the door.

Mulvaney rises and nods to the men on the other side of the one-way mirror.

Mulvaney wonders if sweat stains show beneath his underarms. He feels a droplet slide down his back. He's wearing a wife beater today, nothing to absorb the sweat. So he decides he'll keep his arms hanging at his sides till he's back in his office. Then he'll turn on that table fan—the little one stowed in the file cabinet—and lean back in his chair with his hands clasped behind his head.

The door opens. Two detectives and a uniformed cop stand there.

Wilson says, "Will one of your detectives give me a lift back to New Haven?"

Mulvaney heads back to his office, suddenly aware his clothes feel sodden and heavy, and he smells something. He wonders if it's his pits, or if it's the stench of a madman lingering in his nostrils.

Twelve

"I don't like it, Adrian," Mulvaney says on the telephone. "We had our best guys go at him and we got *nada*."

"Any idea why he's back?"

"Not really, but I think Megan should renew the order of protection."

"Anything else you can do, Patty?"

"I'm afraid not. He hasn't done anything we can prove. But I've talked with a few higher-ups in New Haven. They'll keep an eye on him, but that won't do much."

"At least we know he's here."

"Adrian, I'm sure he's got his eye on *both* of you. Getting' run off the road was no coincidence. And that break-in . . . it wasn't some harmless prank. He was definitely sending you a message. Just be careful. And call us if anything unusual happens. *Anything*. Got it?"

"Sure, Patty. And thanks for everything." Adrian's voice sounds foreign to him.

When they hang up, Adrian goes to the refrigerator, pops open a bottle of Bud, and returns to the living room. He settles onto the sofa. Sipping the beer, he thinks about Mulvaney's words, and a feeling of dread penetrates him like an icicle. It seems so strange to Adrian that three years after they separated and then divorced, a man would travel across the country to stalk his ex-wife, send e-mails and flowers, run her off the road and break into the home of the man she's now seeing. Adrian is certain from what Megan's told him that Wilson has no one meaningful in his life. He's a lone wolf, an introvert, and has no essential core to his existence, no family—no center of being. He's alone in the world, and he's on some sick mission.

I'll be back . . .

The words thread coldly through Adrian and penetrate his bones. He feels a slight inner shudder. He takes another slug of beer. The carbonation bites his tongue, feels good going down, and seems to bypass his stomach and shoot directly to his head—permeates to his brain. He feels a bit fuzzy. It's been a long day—complicated surgeries, the trip to the Eastport police station, seeing Conrad Wilson, and then driving back to the cottage.

Adrian's thoughts meander to Megan, Marlee, Erin, and Bob, to their kids, and the little dog, Sampson. It's family . . . warm and loving, caring for one another. That was part of what was so obvious when he was over there—the care and concern they have for one another. Adrian suddenly realizes there are now people in his life with whom he's made connections. He feels it—deeply—and in a very short period of time. It occurs to him that he really needs a foundation—an emotional nucleus—in his life, that it's been missing for so long.

God almighty, here I am, forty years old and my only blood tie—my one living and direct genetic link—is Mom.

Adrian realizes suddenly he forgot to telephone her today. That's a rarity; in fact, he can't remember a day over the last few years when he hasn't called Mom. Adrian usually calls her every evening—the OR schedule permitting—even if they can talk for only a minute or two before the early-bird dinner specials are served at the myriad restaurants catering to the swarms of seniors living on Florida's Gold Coast.

His mom lives in a white stucco, two-story garden apartment

condo on Southeast 10th Street, one block from hibiscus-lined South Ocean Boulevard in Pompano Beach. The place crawls with newly constructed high-rises, condos, co-ops, and the occasional bungalow built forty years ago. The boulevard's only a short block from the beach and the sparkling blue-green Atlantic waters. Mom moved to Florida to live with the snowbirds after inheriting the place from her spinster sister, who died five years earlier.

Adrian dials. Mom picks up on the first ring. She was probably waiting for him to call.

"Hi, Mom."

"Adrian, dear, how are you?"

"Fine, Mom. How's everything?"

She mentions a movie she saw with her friends and how they enjoyed it and then talks about her weekly bridge game, some renovation issues with the condo board (she's the treasurer), and the ever-present Florida topic—the strange weather patterns and hurricane alerts. After a brief pause, she says, "So, Adrian, how's your woman friend, Megan?"

"She's fine, Mom," he says, knowing exactly where she'll take this conversation.

"What's happening with you two?"

"We're getting serious."

"Getting serious . . . so quickly?"

"You know, Mom, we're not kids; we know what we want."

"She sounds lovely, Adrian. But do you really want to get involved in that kind of thing?"

"What kind of *thing*, Mom?" He tries not to let his irritation percolate through. Adrian could kick himself in the ass for letting her steer the conversation in this direction.

"You know . . . another man's child . . ."

"The father's not around," Adrian says, as a prickly current ripples through him. He feels his thighs tighten, and that hollow feeling forms in his stomach. "The father hasn't been in Marlee's life since she was two. She wouldn't recognize him if he walked in the door." Adrian knows he sounds defensive.

"Adrian, a child's father is *always* around. It's *his* flesh and blood, not yours."

A shiver begins at the back of his neck; something frigid slithers down his spine.

"I have a great relationship with Marlee."

"But, Adrian dear, she's another man's daughter."

There's a pause; Adrian knows Mom's getting emotional.

"Listen, Adrian, you're not a father, so it may be hard for you to understand, but a child forms a permanent link between a man and a woman—and also between the child and her father. It's the natural order of things, and no matter how you feel about this little girl, there's a connection between the child and her father—it's a biological thing—and you can never be part of it."

"I'm not so sure, Mom."

"And, Adrian, you know this woman for only a few weeks."

"How about you and Dad way back when? It was three months, right?"

"Yes, but times were different then, dear, and we weren't young, either," Mom says with a quaking voice.

Adrian is about to protest that he and Megan aren't young or inexperienced in life's affairs, and he regrets even more deeply allowing himself to be sucked into this dialogue. It's discouragingly the same—each time—and he seems powerless to alter it. He knows he should've diverted the subject to something less charged.

Mom's breathing sounds choked, and he thinks she's sobbing, though she's doing her best to stifle it. A twinge of sadness stabs at him. He hears her Swiss chalet cuckoo clock strike the hour—the clock that telescopes time because he's heard it as far back as he can remember, the clock on the kitchen wall of their brick-faced attached house in Queens, where he lived until he left for college at Ithaca. Now it's a Florida cuckoo.

How time can telescope on itself. Things from years ago can come back in a split second . . . and can have incredible emotional pulling power.

Silence on the line until the clock finishes its last cuckoo.

"I still miss him . . . so much," Mom says in a strangled whisper.

"I do too, Mom," he says, as a mammoth lump fills his throat. The conversation's gone south; it's in the tar pits of his memory, of times long gone, but it's part of the matrix of their lives. Adrian knows that talking with Mom can bring on a bone-deep ache as ugly images of that night assault him.

He was nearly six years old. They were at a Chinese restaurant—he recalls the festive ambience, the aroma of garlic and ginger, the egg rolls and steaming wonton soup with sliced shallots and pork-filled wontons steeping in the broth—when midway through the meal, Dad clutched his chest. His face turned chalk white and then sagged, as though life suddenly washed out of it. Dad keeled over, the table tilted, and dishes clattered. Adrian recalls the horror of seeing Dad inert on the floor, hearing Mom scream, seeing the tumult of patrons, then the ambulance, the ride to the hospital, the medics working on Dad—the oxygen mask and the frantic pumping on his chest—and then they stopped. He recalls his father's open shirt, the limp body, his slackened face, the clouded, blank look in his still-open eyes, and his own terrified disbelief that Dad was gone.

It's still difficult for him to feel comfortable in a Chinese restaurant—especially a Cantonese place. The decor alone makes his stomach lurch—fantail goldfish in a tank, the butterfly and flower wall fans, chopsticks and cylindrical paper lanterns—it's too evocative of that night and brings it all back in an instant. He's never eaten wonton soup again. Even the sight of it in a bowl would sicken him.

Adrian recalls the funeral: it was a dreary day with his aunts and uncles crying at the chapel. He remembers his mother hunched over the coffin, her shoulders shaking in disbelief and despair. They wouldn't let him look in the casket.

"No . . . No . . . the boy shouldn't see this," Uncle Al said.

"Not even a last look?" asked Aunt Bea.

"No, he's too young."

At the cemetery—a mammoth expanse of granite tombstones near the Long Island Expressway with the Manhattan skyline looming beneath a sickly steel-wool-gray sky and stacks of gray-black, even greenish clouds—his relatives shielded him from seeing the coffin lowered. Dad sank slowly into the grave, never to be seen again or be part of his life.

Quoth the raven, "Nevermore."

The men shoveled dirt, and Adrian remembers the smell of freshly turned earth, the sound of soil thumping heavily onto the coffin lid, the grave filling quickly, Mom pressing him close, and her grief-stricken shuddering while her tears dripped onto him. God, the horror of it all was overwhelming, and Adrian recalls the feelings—the shattering upheaval in a boy's life.

He felt so lost, so empty and bereft—as though life cheated him of his father—he was upended in the world. Adrian knows he felt cheated of what they could have shared; it was stolen from him. His dad would have been so proud of him at Cornell—his grades, the varsity baseball team, the honor society.

Adrian knows that losing a father so early does something to a boy. Megan could be right: maybe now—doing heart surgery—he *is* trying to fix God's mistakes.

And Megan: working with newborns—*newbies* as she calls them—wanted and unwanted, is she trying to redo her own past?

But in this life there are no do-overs. What's done is done and can't be made whole again.

He recalls saying to Megan a few evenings ago, "I think injury brings us to our work," and she'd nodded.

"They're deep wounds, and they lead us to what we've become," she said.

He knew then that Megan has a certain emotional savvy—an affliction-induced wisdom. And now, on the telephone with Mom, he's reminded of what Megan said that same evening: "Life is so fragile. Everything we are and all we know can be gone in a moment."

When Mom talks this way, it all comes back to him—the hollowness of loss, feeling dispossessed—feeling wanting and deprived.

"Oh, Adrian, just be sure you know what you're getting into."

"I will, Mom. I will," Adrian says, feeling sadness so deep, he fears his heart will burst.

Thirteen

Megan throws her Ford Fiesta into park, kills the engine, and steps out of the car. The parking lot in front of the Stop & Shop is clogged with cars and SUVs this sunny autumn afternoon, and she angles between them toward the store.

Then she sees it; her heart feels like it'll burst through her chest.

A black, muscular-looking pickup sits two rows over from where she's parked. Darkened windows; she can't see inside the thing. A huge silver toolbox sits behind the cab and a row of amber-colored lights sits atop the cab. She wonders if it has Colorado plates. But she can't tell from this angle. The engine is running—gray-white exhaust fumes billow from dual tailpipes. The air shimmers where the vapors pour out the back of the thing. The parking lot is brilliantly bright; chrome and glass glare in the low afternoon sun in a whitish sky. Megan suddenly feels light-headed; her knees begin buckling and she nearly trips. She angles herself to get a rear view of the truck.

It has Connecticut plates. It's not him. Or is it possible that by now he's registered the truck in Connecticut? She recalls her conversation with Chief Mulvaney. He said there was no DMV record of Conrad Wilson registering a vehicle in Connecticut. But that was a few days ago. She walks toward the store entrance, exquisitely aware of that eerie feeling of eyes boring into her. The skin at the back of her neck prickles, and she suddenly feels like prey.

Ann Johnson was right, Megan thinks as she grabs a shopping cart and moves past the automatic doors. She could be bobbing in the ocean, adrift in the inky darkness of a watery night with no stars or moon above. She's treading water and her feet dangle . . . just like in *Jaws*.

A cold swell rises beneath her.

Girl, you've got to stop thinking about movies. It never helps.

Entering the store, she passes the floral section; a faintly sweet scent fills her nostrils—it reminds her of the gladioli. Queasiness seeps through her and drops to her legs, turning them to jelly. It's the same feeling she gets when she's looking down from a great height. A sickly sensation invades her belly. She's had these feelings before. She knows what it is: pure nerves, that queasy, on-edge, heart-fluttering sensation—the skin-crawling edginess of anxiety.

She glances at her shopping list. It's her usual routine. She'll wind her way through aisles she long ago memorized and grab pretty much the same items as always, and she'll end up at the dairy section. But she's aware she's in a rush and can't wait to get out of the store.

She heads for the fruit and vegetable section first, picks out some lettuces for a salad—packaged cores of prewashed romaine and one of baby lettuces—and selects a cucumber and a clump of radishes. She doesn't even bag them in plastic—just tosses them into the cart.

Megan glances up, feeling tense, jumpy. She scans the other shoppers—mostly women, a few preschoolers, and some retired older men filling idle time by shopping for their wives.

She makes her way to the center of the store. Marlee's running low on Apple Jacks, the only breakfast cereal she'll eat. Megan tosses two boxes of cereal into the cart and moves to the next aisle.

She passes a sky-high facade of shelves stacked with Pringles, Utz chips, Fritos, Doritos, and Tostitos, wheels the cart past an endless assortment of sugary soft drinks in bottles and cans, and then heads for the pasta aisle, tosses two boxes of Barilla penne into the cart, and grabs a bottle of Colavita olive oil.

Suddenly, the hairs on the back of her neck bristle. She feels, rather than sees, a shadow behind her, and a cold, sickening feeling pervades her. Her insides shudder. She whirls around.

A woman with a shopping cart peers at the shelves. Behind her, a perplexed-looking man with a furrowed brow holds a box of linguine, staring at it with that befuddled-husband-who-never-really-shops look. Megan turns and peers in the other direction. There's no one there. An internal humming begins in her chest, and she knows she's pumped herself into fight-or-flight mode; she's shooting adrenaline into every part of her being.

She rolls her cart to the next aisle. She's certain someone was behind her only a moment ago. Or was it her imagination, her overprimed, hyperattuned expectation, knowing Conrad's back in Connecticut? God, she feels brittle, as though if she fell to the floor, she'd shatter into a thousand pieces.

Megan feels this strange tingling sensation around her lips and at her fingertips—a low-level electric buzz. She knows she's hyperventilating, sucking air in and out, and if it continues, she'll be light-headed and fall into a faint. And now her chest heaves like an air bellows. A bristly rush spreads through her. She slows her breathing, willfully controls her intake of air, and closes her eyes for a few moments. Calmer now, she decides to pick up the other items and head home.

About to head toward the dairy section, Megan sees a shadow out of the corner of her eye. Her stomach drops. She abandons her cart and slips over to the next aisle.

Suddenly, there's a crashing sound. Voltage shoots through

her body; she spins around. A woman stands over a pile of display cans her shopping cart has knocked to the floor. Megan's knees wobble and her body feels weak, as though she'll keel over. Her lips feel numb, and without another thought, she heads for the supermarket's exit. For a moment, she thinks of going back for her cart, but her heart pumps violently and she's on the verge of collapse. *The hell with the cart*, she thinks without another second of hesitation and rushes out the doors to the parking lot.

Breathless, she threads her way between Beemers, Escalades, and Suburbans ranging in color from Tuscan bronze to vanilla latte. The black pickup is still sitting there; it rumbles ominously in place amid a bluish cloud of fumes. Megan feels the blood drain from her head as she fumbles with her car keys; she nearly drops them and knows she can't get out of this place fast enough.

I just want to get out of here. I want to get home.

She hits the remote, unlocks the Fiesta's doors, gets behind the wheel, and locks the car doors. She clutches the steering wheel and, suddenly, her fingers cramp. She turns the key, starts the engine, and pulls out of the parking spot.

At the exit leading onto the Post Road, she looks left and right, realizing she's near the spot where she and Adrian were nearly killed by the maniac in a huge black pickup, just like the one in the parking lot. Traffic is heavy—vehicles pour down the Post Road in a honking rush; she'll never make it out in time to cross over for a left turn. She'll have to wait until the light down the road turns red before pulling out. She feels so edgy, so completely amped, she's tempted to hit the gas pedal and lunge into traffic heading west in the lane closest to her. She can then make a series of right turns and get back onto the Post Road heading in the right direction.

She waits for a break in the traffic as her heartbeat rampages through her. Cars flow in an unending stream of horns and exhaust fumes. Drivers cruise bumper to bumper in the early-autumn brilliance. She squints in the near-blinding glare of light bouncing off this shimmering vehicular procession. Her eyes dart in each direction of the fast-food-franchise-filled Post Road—a commercial artery of on-the-run eateries: Taco Bell, Wendy's, Boston Market, and scores more.

Glancing into the rearview mirror, Megan sees it: the black pickup is right behind her. A jolt of galvanic tension ramps through her body. The thing is massive, with a sky-high cab, chromed grill, and growling engine. She can't see into the darkened front windows. Her heart sends a heated rush of blood into her face. Then she's aware of a tight feeling, like a clenched fist inside her chest.

The light changes.

She turns onto the Post Road, heads east, and stays in the left lane. She glances into the mirror and sees the pickup lunge onto the Post Road. It's behind her, following closely. Her heart tumbles and her hands curl tightly around the wheel. She realizes she's driving erratically—one eye on the road, the other in the mirror. She may even have run a red light, but she isn't sure. The pickup's still behind her in the shimmering glare. She reaches into her purse for the cell phone and pulls it out.

Dial 911? And say what to the police? There's a pickup following me on the Post Road? It's ridiculous.

There's a sudden horn blast. She's veering into a car on the westbound side. Jolted, Megan yanks the steering wheel to her right and straightens out. Shaking, she drives on and tells herself not to look into the mirror, but glances up and sees the pickup turn suddenly off the Post Road. Her breath flutters in relief; her fists loosen on the steering wheel.

Megan heads home, feeling damp and weak.

Fourteen

It's sunday, a late-afternoon October dinner at Erin and Bob's house. Adrian realizes that this get-together reminds him of those Sunday-afternoon dinners at Dad's sister's house in Hempstead, Long Island. Though he was only four or five at the time, he has hazy memories of Dad driving from their modest attached house in Ozone Park, Queens, taking the Cross Island Parkway to the Southern State Parkway and then heading east to the Hempstead exit.

A boisterous throng of aunts, uncles, and cousins gathered around a large table at Uncle Al and Aunt Bea's ranch house, a short distance from the Southern State. Adrian recalls the festive Thanksgiving dinner only a few months before Dad died. Everyone watched Dad carve the turkey. Adrian sometimes jokes that his surgery career was inspired by watching his father slice the bird that day. He recalls the laughter. Most of all, Adrian remembers the *feelings* of that November afternoon. He was part of a family.

He feels it today—a sense of connectedness with Megan, Erin, Bob, Marlee, and Marlee's younger cousins, Robert and Ellie. Marlee and her cousins are playing with Sampson in the living room. The little pug yaps furiously.

Puccini arias play on the sound system. That's Megan's doing, Adrian thinks, as the melody soars through the house. An intense feeling of well-being seeps through him as he sips a robust Barolo wine. Erin sets a roast beef–bedecked platter onto the table.

"Let's have the good surgeon carve the roast," Bob says.

"What's your fee for this surgery?" jokes Erin, handing him the carving knife.

"I think Bob should do it," Adrian says.

"No way, Doc. I defer to you."

"Come on, Adrian," urges Erin. "Just *do* it."

"Yes, Adrian, we'd like to see your surgical technique," Megan says. "Your fee for services comes later." She grabs his hand and squeezes.

Dinner is over. The kids play again with Sampson in the living room.

"We have an announcement," Bob says, and he clinks a spoon against his wineglass.

"Yes, we do," Erin rejoins. Her cheeks look flushed.

"We won't be moving to Hartford," says Bob. "I'm staying with Sikorsky."

"Bob won't tell you because he's too modest," Erin says, her eyes shining. She stands behind her husband and sets her hands on his shoulders. "He got a huge promotion—with appropriate compensation, of course—and we're staying put."

"That's *great*," Megan says and claps her hands together. "I'm so happy for you." She grabs Adrian's hand, moves it to her lap.

"Congratulations, Bob," Adrian adds.

"So then we're all staying here in Eastport," Erin says.

"That's another reason I'm glad," Adrian says, caressing the nape of Megan's neck. She leans closer to him. His arm goes around the back of her chair; he rubs her shoulder.

Erin nods, casts a Cheshire-cat smile at Megan, and glances at Bob. He barely smothers a knowing smile. "Here's to you two,"

Bob toasts, raising his glass.

"Here's to the future," Erin says, grabbing her wineglass. They clink glasses. Adrian looks into Megan's eyes; she purses her lips in a mock kiss.

Sampson scuttles around the living room, the kids crawling after him. An aria from *La Bohème* drifts through the house. There's laughter, congratulations, and some jokes. Bob pours more wine, the kids giggle and yell, Sampson yaps, and Adrian realizes that this is what he wants: family.

"Any new developments?" Erin asks.

It's been unspoken, but Adrian knows they all worry about it.

Megan shakes her head; her lips look thin, bloodless.

"He's keeping a low profile," Bob says. "That's Conrad—a *very* smart guy."

"Yes, he is," Megan says. "You know, he once took a car engine apart and reassembled it just for fun."

"Yeah," Bob says. "I once explained force vectors to him and soon he was talking like an engineer."

The kids turn on the TV; it mixes with another rousing Puccini aria: a soprano, a tenor, and SpongeBob.

"Why can't they arrest him?" Erin asks.

"Because he hasn't *done* anything," says Megan, her voice brittle.

"Oh, he's doing plenty," Bob says. "Just nothing the police can act on."

"I'll tell you what he's *really* doing. He's making my life hell. I cringe every time I open my e-mail."

"Has he sent any more?" asks Erin.

"He doesn't have to. Even on my home computer, I hate opening my e-mails. And when the telephone rings, I jump out of my skin."

Adrian clasps her hand. It feels cold and damp.

"I pass the flower shop near the hospital and my stomach does flip-flops. Every time I see a pickup, my heart pounds. I'm just . . .

I don't know. I'm on the lookout everywhere—the Trumbull mall, the supermarket, leaving the hospital, especially that indoor garage. I can't tell you how many times I thought I saw him in a parking lot, at the CVS or Staples, the library—everywhere. I just know he's around, following me. I don't feel safe in the apartment anymore. It's the first floor, glass doors to the patio, lots of windows and skylights . . . Anyone can break in."

"Your friend Ann at the hospital, she must have some advice," says Erin.

"I don't even want to tell you what she says."

"Oh, c'mon, Megan."

Megan closes her eyes, shakes her head. "She says I should get a gun."

"You're *kidding*," Erin says.

Adrian feels his insides cringing.

"You renewed the restraining order," says Erin. "Can't the police do anything?"

"He has to make *contact* before he violates the order," Adrian says. "They can't arrest him for what he *might* do."

"Who says?"

"Chief Mulvaney said the police are powerless."

Erin shakes her head. "It's like waiting for the hammer to fall."

"There's nothing I can do. I'm stuck."

"You just have to be careful, Megan," says Erin. "And make sure you always have your cell phone with you."

"God, this is scary. I'm so creeped out."

Fifteen

"The baby otters are so cute," Marlee says as they leave the Norwalk Maritime Aquarium. "But I didn't see Ariel anywhere." She looks up at Megan. "Mom, I think your hair's more beautiful than Ariel's."

"I agree," Adrian says.

"Is she more beautiful than Ariel?" Marlee asks, wide-eyed.

"Definitely. She's far more beautiful."

"Is she the most beautiful woman in the whole world?"

"Yes, she is."

"Stop it, you two," Megan says, smothering a self-conscious smile.

"And when you grow up, you'll be beautiful, too," Adrian says.

"Will I be as beautiful as my mom?" Marlee asks with a giggle.

"Yes, you'll be just as beautiful."

Marlee looks up at Adrian, grabbing his right hand and Megan's left. "Give me a ride," she says with a smile.

Still walking, they swing her between them as they cross the parking area. It's a warm, breezy Saturday for late October, six days since the dinner at Erin and Bob's house. The air smells of brine and kelp from Long Island Sound. A ship's horn croons in the distance.

Megan stops suddenly. "Look at *that*," she says.

A huge black pickup truck is parked nearby. A Ford F-250

with a gleaming steel toolbox behind the cab.

Adrian's heart throbs in his neck; then something tunnels through his chest.

"That's *it*," Megan says in a trembling voice.

"Mommy, what do I do with this gum?" asks Marlee.

"In a second, honey," Megan says, staring at the truck.

Viselike pressure builds in Adrian's head.

Megan opens her purse and grabs her cell phone. It falls to the blacktop. She picks it up and snaps it open. "I'm calling the police," she rasps, but the phone again clatters to the asphalt.

"Adrian, do you have any paper?" She picks up her cell and snaps it shut. "I'll take down the plate."

He grabs a crumpled envelope from his shirt pocket and opens it. It's the invoice for the leased Altima. He stuffs the bill back in his pocket and is about to give Megan the envelope. "Wait, Megan," Adrian says. "Use the cell phone and take a picture of it."

Suddenly, a tall, thin man wearing a Red Sox jacket and baseball cap ambles toward the truck. He casually opens the driver's side door and climbs inside.

Megan closes her eyes and exhales. Adrian sees how pale she looks.

"Mom, this gum has no taste," Marlee says.

"Well, let's get rid of it," Megan replies. "We're going for lunch anyway, sweetie."

"Pizza?"

"Yes, at Rizzuto's in Westport."

Marlee pulls the pink wad from her mouth.

"Not on the ground, please. Someone will step on it," says Megan.

"Here you go, little one." Adrian holds the envelope out. "Put it here."

Marlee deposits the gum in the envelope. Adrian folds it and slips it into his pocket.

The pickup rumbles and pulls away. The tailpipes churn a cloud of fumes. A grayish haze lingers in the air.

Standing in the parking lot, with Megan and Marlee at his side, Adrian recalls seeing Conrad Wilson in the interrogation room. He remembers the encounter at King's Corner—those lifeless eyes.

Oh, yes, I know you.

I'll be back . . . and I'll see you, too, faggot.

He looks at Megan: her face is chalky white. It's bloodless.

Sixteen

It's eight o'clock in the evening, seven hours since Adrian and Megan had pizza with Marlee. They're at a black-tie cocktail party thrown by some megabucks donors to the hospital. Though Adrian hates these gatherings, he's glad they're there; it's a distraction from Conrad Wilson and the dread of his nearness.

The Bainbridges—Old Guard denizens of Southport, scions of a long line of industrialists—have donated an avalanche of money to the hospital, enough to warrant an entire pavilion bearing their name. They host an annual party for the hospital honchos and its wealthy patrons; Adrian is always invited by the surgery department's chairman. As a concession to the politics of hospital life, he attends, though he always makes an early exit. At least one hundred people are crowded into the towering Normandy-style manor overlooking the waters of the Long Island Sound.

The manse is furnished with Louis XV gilded settees, patinated chairs, and ornate sofas with chestnut trimmings. Adrian guesses the furnishings alone cost more than he earns in five years at Eastport General. Multitiered crystal chandeliers hang from gilt-coffered ceilings. Large, mullioned French doors open from the expansive living room into a massive library lined floor to ceiling with books and furnished with gilded walnut easy chairs and an inlaid mahogany Louis Philippe desk. Passing through the dining room, Megan exclaims, "This table could seat forty people."

"Only the right *kind* of people," Adrian adds with a laugh.

"You mean we're not the right kind of people?"

"We're definitely not."

Megan sighs and nods. She grasps his hand.

Sipping from a flute of champagne, Adrian notices Renoir and Manet oil paintings on the walls. "It's a bit ostentatious, don't you think?" Megan says.

"This is robber baron money. It's been around for a hundred years."

A platoon of bow-tied waiters weaves through the crowd, offering exotic dips, French cheeses, and wild mushroom profiteroles. A string quartet plays Vivaldi and Handel while the crowd talks of politics and the economy.

Adrian presses Megan's hand; she squeezes back, seeming relaxed; she's definitely calmed down since seeing that black pickup earlier today. Megan looks like she's trying to be casual as she observes the fauna—eyeballs the Versace, Fendi, and Prada evening gowns—and she's joking *soto voce* about the jewelry-draped women. "This place is a walking advertisement for Tiffany," she says.

"Not Zales?" he says, and they laugh. It strikes Adrian that he and Megan are the only couple holding hands. Everyone else, it seems, is busy talking politics—hospital and national politics—trying to make impressions on one another.

Adrian decides to refill his champagne flute and threads his way to the bar. He's snared into an exchange with a bloated blue-blood type—a dewlapped board member whose neck wattle overhangs his bow tie. The guy's half-lit; he slurps champagne like a drunken monkey and talks nonstop with a mouth full of food. His breath reeks of Camembert. Adrian tries not to inhale too deeply.

Adrian manages to extricate himself graciously, grabs another flute of champagne from a passing waiter, sips, and feels the astringent burn at the back of his throat; it warms his gullet and heats his chest. It permeates his brain's circuits, a soothing infusion of social confidence. The taut wire in his head loosens. The string quartet now plays Bach, but Adrian wishes he could hear some Led Zeppelin or Aerosmith. *I'm just a working stiff, wandering among this crowd of country-club, old-money conservatives.* Wondering why he dragged Megan to this pompous gathering, he gazes past guests nibbling on sushi, Beluga caviar, and melon wrapped in paper-thin prosciutto and sipping Veuve Clicquot.

His eyes fix on Megan.

She's wearing a black strapless cocktail dress with a pearl choker around her throat. Her neck looks amazing: long, elegant, creamy white, with a slight concavity at its bottom; shadows form in the hollows behind her collarbones. Her hair is in a fiery updo, and the red-orange color has a brilliant sheen. He regards the sensuous slope of Megan's shoulders, her toned arms, and the curve of her hips and graceful flanks. A charge thrums through him as every nerve ending in his body fires. The supple curve of Megan's bare back is exquisite—a thing of incredible beauty. He studies the porcelain whiteness of her complexion, the lush fullness of her lips, and the plump underbelly of her chin.

He notices men casting furtive glances in her direction—old and young alike—there's nodding and whispering—*Eat your hearts out, you jealous bastards*—and Adrian finds it difficult to believe this amazingly gorgeous and intelligent woman is actually part of *his* life and will spend the night with *him* and no one else. Suddenly, amid the crowd, music, and mumbling, through the pomposity of it all, Megan turns and looks directly at him.

There, amid the mellifluous strains of a Bach sonata, Adrian sees the look in Megan's glistening eyes; it's a combination of tender longing and connectedness, a deeply felt sharing. It hits him with startling intensity: they've been together only a month, but even now Adrian wonders what life was like before Megan. Was it real before her? Was there even a life before her? Because he feels as if they've always been together, that inexplicably, their lives have intertwined for years.

Megan's eyes lock on to his, and then, in a barely discernible gesture, she purses those luscious lips. Suddenly feeling weak-kneed, Adrian finds himself moving—as though dragged by a powerful undertow—and Megan, seeming to know exactly what he wants, drifts toward him.

They clasp hands and slip through the crowd.

"Let's get out of here," she whispers. Her breath feels hot in his ear and sends a delicious tremor through him. He nods and murmurs something back as they head for an enormous set of French doors facing the Long Island Sound.

On the veranda, the blathering crowd, baroque music, and hobnobbing are muted; they're just a backdrop to the washing sound of the sea. A pale-yellow three-quarter moon casts a golden swath on the rippling, black water. Wavelets buffet the shoreline rhythmically, gently. The night air sends a shoreward breeze redolent of brine with a vague hint of iodine. Adrian sucks in the salty air and whispers, "It feels so natural . . . so good."

"I don't need anyone else right now. Just you," Megan whispers.

In the autumn coolness, they pull close to each other, kissing gently. Carrying their shoes, they walk onto the beach. The sand is cool and soft as their feet sink in. They stand where the water laps onto the wet, slick sand. With his arm around Megan's shoulder, hers around his waist, they watch the incoming surf and the blinking lights of a distant freighter.

"I love being with you," Megan murmurs, leaning her head on his shoulder.

"What's going on in there seems so unimportant."

"Yes, it does," she says and raises her lips to his. He kisses her deeply and hungrily, and her mouth opens.

"You taste delicious," he whispers.

"I want more than just a taste of you," she murmurs.

They kiss again, urgently.

"Let's get out of here," she says.

They walk to the parking lot, brush sand from their feet, put on their shoes, and get into the car. He turns the ignition key and starts the car; they drive along the shoreline road. Her hand rests on his thigh. His erection threatens to erupt through his pants. He finds a secluded cove near Compo Beach, stops the car, and kills the engine. Bulrushes and water reeds rise from the shallows, all lit by the pale light of the moon.

They kiss again. "It's like we're eighteen-year-olds," Megan says.

"It's like we ducked out of the prom."

"In a *car*," she says with a soft laugh.

They embrace, parked amid sand and willows bending in a gentle night breeze.

She presses herself to him; he can feel her heat.

"I wish we'd met years ago," he says.

"You probably wouldn't have cared for me back then."

"You're very wrong there . . ."

"Am I?"

"Yes. Forget back then. It's now that counts."

"Oh, Adrian."

"I think about you all the time," he whispers, inhaling the tang of her skin.

"Same here."

"I'm so glad you and Marlee are in my life. Before this, I was just drifting. And now . . . it feels so different. I have the two of you."

"Marlee's crazy about you. I don't want this to end. Ever," she whispers, looking into his eyes.

"I can't begin to tell you how I feel," he whispers.

"Words won't do it, Adrian, but I'll say it . . . I love you."

"And I love you. My God, I've fallen so in love with you."

"Let's make love," she whispers.

"Here?"

"Yes, like teenagers. We've snuck away from the prom, so let's do it," she whispers, slipping her hand beneath his shirt. His skin tingles; he trembles in anticipation. He takes her in his arms and she moans as they kiss again.

"I feel so close to you," he whispers.

"I know, Adrian. I know. And I want it to be like this . . . always."

His arms circle her waist, hers go around his neck, and she sits on his lap, pressing herself close, her breasts full and lush against him. Her mouth is hot and sweet, and they kiss deeply. She tastes faintly of champagne and vanilla. She slides her hands beneath his shirt, and a shudder of pleasure goes through him. Still kissing, they pull gently at each other's clothes; they whisper, and moments later, she moans as he sinks into her. Still kissing, they move slowly, and Adrian is lost in the pleasure of it, and he knows there's nowhere else on earth he would rather be.

Part II

Seventeen

Megan hurries from the neonatal ICU to the elevator. She's on her way to the temporary locker room downstairs, since the third-floor facility is being renovated. Her thoughts drift back to Compo Beach three nights ago, and a hot flush envelops her. It was the most exciting lovemaking of her life.

But right now there's no time for fantasy. It's six o'clock and she's running late. Her shift ended and the day nurses are gone. She'd been held up by an emergency—a newborn in fetal distress. But that's been resolved. Another little life saved.

She and Adrian will be taking Marlee and her cousins to the Carvel stand in Westport to celebrate Marlee's birthday, which is tomorrow. Megan's always been aware that birthdays—her own or anyone's—remind her of the circumstances of her birth. They're a big unknown, and it's always haunted her. Doesn't every orphan wonder about her origins, the beginnings of her life, her so-called real parents and where they might be?

Who am I and where do I come from? Those are the burning issues of my life.

Looking back, she knows those questions were painful for Mom and Dad Haggarty. They must have felt marginalized—even rejected—when, as a kid, she asked again and again about her *real* parents.

"It's only natural you'd ask, dear," Mom would say. "All we

know is we wanted a child for so long and then Erin came along. We loved her so much and we wanted another . . . and then . . . there you were. Just three days old and already so beautiful. You were a gift from heaven. We were the most fortunate people in the world to get you two."

Yes, given away at birth, but taken in by the most loving people on earth.

When Mom and Dad died, it had seemed like the end of the world. Megan was still a teenager; Erin was twenty-one.

"We began life as orphans," she said to Erin.

"And we're alone again."

"No, we're not. We have each other."

"Let's face it, Megan, we were dumped at birth."

After crying and holding each other, Erin said, "Let's sell the house and get an apartment. We'll live together."

We were dumped at birth. It can haunt you for a lifetime . . . unless you're lucky enough to meet someone who makes you feel wanted as much as the people who took you in and nurtured you, someone like Adrian.

These thoughts are both warming and haunting, but right now she's in a rush. She reaches her temporary locker, spins the wheel on her combination lock, opens the door, hangs up her lab coat, and retrieves her purse. She flips open her cell phone and hits the speed dial for Erin.

"Hi, Erin. I'm running late, but I should be at your place in ten minutes."

"No hurry, sweetie. Adrian called; he said he'll be a little late, too. The kids're excited; they can't wait."

"Sure . . . he'll get them all worked up. And Sampson, too," she says, thinking it's like a cyclone when Adrian, the kids, and the dog get together.

"I swear, Megan, if you don't marry this man, you should see a shrink."

They laugh. Megan has a quick flash of the other night at Compo Beach.

"You know, Megan, it's only been a month, but I think it's clear . . ."

"What's clear?" she asks, hearing a smile in Erin's voice.

"I can tell by how Adrian looks at you—and at Marlee, too—he cares so much for you both. And Bob and I think he's great. Robert and Ellie do, too."

"That's so important to me, Erin."

A few more hurried words; then Megan snaps the cell phone shut. She's about to pocket it when a draft rushes over her—as though a door is open.

An open door from where?

Megan scans left and right.

The basement is creepy: six rows of lockers, recessed fluorescent lights that buzz constantly, cinder-block walls painted in a high-gloss off-white, a gray cement floor; a ribbon of multicolored, rubber-coated wires snake along one wall; aluminum ductwork and PCV pipes crisscross the ceiling. It's the newer section of the hospital. Modern, sanitized.

And Megan suddenly realizes she's completely alone.

Her skin feels like it's rippling, moving in corrugating wavelets. She feels the hairs on her arms stand on end. Yes, her skin feels cold and it's definitely gooseflesh. She's always hated this feeling unless it came over her while watching a movie. And lately she feels like she's living in a John Carpenter movie . . . *Halloween* . . . or is it *Nightmare on Elm Street*?

I've got to stop thinking about movies. It's too creepy. And why do I think of horror films? It always makes me feel weird.

Megan shivers. It's the same feeling she had as a kid when she and Erin imagined monsters beneath their beds. Could they get under the covers before a huge arm reached up from beneath the bed, clutched an ankle, and pulled them under? They'd lie there, shuddering, frozen, waiting in anticipation of being grabbed by this huge, hairy arm, the horror of it.

But it's not then; it's now, and she's leaving the hospital. She has everything—book, purse, coat—and she realizes suddenly that her thoughts are rushing as though she's pumped with adrenaline. She shuts the locker door, slips the lock through the loop, fastens it, and gives the combination wheel a quick turn.

She stops, frozen in place. Megan has that strange feeling again. It's a *sense* more than an actual perception. A strange awareness of some sort—that eyes are boring into her. It's so powerful, it has texture.

God, nerves can make you hear or see things that aren't there. You can even *feel* them. It's amazing how fear feeds on itself and can eat you up. Imagination, fantasy—they can be a burden, a true curse.

Then she sees him.

A man stands at the end of the row of lockers.

He's wearing a black leather car coat, black gloves, and a black ski mask. Narrow slit for the mouth, openings for the eyes. He's huge, the size of Conrad.

In his gloved hand, a knife gleams.

A riptide of terror streaks through Megan. Her heart jumps in her chest.

Hands shaking, she flips open her cell phone. God, her hands are uncontrollable. Her fingers go weak; she can't dial, and her thoughts streak in a jumbled rush.

He's coming toward her.

Fear surges through Megan, pulses through every muscle, and jangles every nerve in her body. A shriek erupts from her throat, but it's stifled, and she emits a guttural gasp. She turns, somehow; her legs move and she bolts away.

Yes, run. Just run.

She lurches, stumbles, nearly falls, but keeps going. Her purse tumbles to the floor; she clutches the cell phone.

She looks frantically to her left, then right. Where can she go? There's only one place to run: there's a door at the far end of the locker room. Where does it lead? It doesn't matter. Just run as fast as possible and get there.

Steel cabinets flash by, one row, then another. Her breath whines in her ears.

She's at the door; it has a push bar, and she slams it down. The door flies open. She's in a narrow hallway, dimly lit. There's another door at the end—maybe ten feet away. Where is she going? It must be the old East Wing. Shut and sealed, it'll be torn down soon. If the next door's locked, she's a goner.

Oh, God, please let it open.

On legs of rubber, she reaches the door and slams the handle down; it opens. She's in another short corridor. Gray plaster walls and a bare lightbulb—dimly lit—hangs from the ceiling. There's another door, twenty feet away. She races toward it. Oh, God, please be open!

She's there. Down goes the push-bar handle. It opens. She plunges into a dark, musty room. What is this place? Must be a storage room—piled with old mattresses, crates, and gurneys. She's in the hospital's old East Wing. She's certain that's where she is. It's an eighty-year-old, four-story building—the original hospital from the 1930s. A mausoleum, it's been closed since last year. It's ready for demolition. You can't get in from the outside.

She rushes into the darkness, crouching behind a carton as her pulse thumps through her. She covers her mouth and waits, aware of her chest heaving. Her heart pounds as she peers from behind the carton at the doorway.

He stands there, backlit by dull light, knife in hand. His silhouette reminds Megan of a bear on its hind legs. Megan's sure his body looks like Conrad's.

She has the cell phone, but it's useless. He'll hear it beeping if she presses the keys. She slips it into her pocket.

Can't call . . . just wait . . . for what? She's trapped in this storage room unless there's another door out. And then where?

Her heart pounds violently and thuds deeply in her chest. Can he hear it? If it's Conrad, his hearing is incredible.

His head rotates left, right. He's waiting for his eyes to adjust to the darkness. And he's listening, perched like a predator.

He moves into the room.

Raw fear burrows through Megan; her body quakes. She feels like she's turning to jelly.

He reaches out and feels for the light switch.

Oh, God . . . once the light goes on, I'm a goner.

The switch snaps up and down. There's nothing. It's broken. She waits in darkness.

She's safe, for the moment.

But fear throttles through her—blood rushes through her arteries, thrums to every part of her, throbs in her head, and she even feels her eyes pulse.

He moves into the room and closes the door. He's swallowed in blackness.

Megan strains to hear him. She takes shallow breaths—ready, tense. She tingles—from scalp to toes—as though a current simmers through her body.

He's closer. She can hear his breath—a ragged intake of air.

Squatting, shivering now, she moves slowly to her left, away from him. *Slowly now . . . don't make a sound.* Maybe there's another door out of here, she thinks. She's behind a pile of mattresses—the ammoniacal stink of urine fills her nostrils. She shifts to a slow crawl on damp, rough concrete. She feels her way slowly, careful not to brush against anything. She moves on hands and knees, an inch at a time, silently.

Oh, please . . . let there be another door. And if there is one . . . let it be unlocked.

She's at a wall, drowned in darkness; she inches her way along cinder block, feeling its cold, coarse texture. It's damp, or is that the sweat of her palms? *Careful now, slow . . . a few inches at a time.*

Then she sees it. A yellowish sliver—a pale light, maybe ten feet away—slants from beneath a side door. Maybe it's a way out.

There's whooshing in her ears as blood pulses through her brain; she feels like she's on fire and dribbles sweat.

She hears a rustling, chafing of clothing on skin, the squeaking soles of his boots. It's him, coming closer in the darkness.

She reaches the door. Cold metal—feels reassuring; her palm presses its surface. Her fingers crawl slowly up the metal, find the knob—smooth, cold—and she rises from her knees very slowly, inch by inch. Her leg muscles burn, strain, and tremble with tension; her breath sounds like a wind tunnel in her ears. *What if my knees creak or crack? Oh, please . . . don't make a sound.* Crouched, she clutches the doorknob. Her thighs quiver and feel incendiary, as she reaches her full height, in blackness, barely breathing, listening for him; then she leans on the door. Her heart slams rampantly in her chest—so strongly, her entire body pulses.

At just the right moment; she'll make her move. That is . . . if the door opens.

It's so dark and she's so very scared and he's so close now. She thinks she hears him—maybe ten feet away. This is it . . . her last chance . . . the doorknob. She begins turning it slowly.

Oh, God, please don't squeak. Don't make a sound . . . and please, please . . . don't be locked.

The doorknob turns silently, a quarter rotation and then more. Half a turn, more, and now it's fully turned. She holds the knob in position, closes her eyes, and waits. Some pressure should do it. That is, if the door's not locked.

She'll do it in the burst of a heartbeat and maybe catch him off guard.

The door flies open.

She's in a corridor. She whirls and slams the door shut.

She's rushing down a hallway now, taking deep gulps of air with breath whining in her ears. The corridor spins as she races. Her legs wobble, but she keeps going. She could be shrieking, but she's not sure. She dashes along the corridor. Gray walls, peeling paint, dim lightbulbs in steel ceiling cages, a porter's sink, electric meters, pipes, wires, and cinder blocks stream by her, and she feels breathless, dizzy—suddenly sluggish, stumbling—ready to collapse. At the end of the corridor, a door looms—gray, metal, huge, heavy-looking.

She's almost there; in a second, maybe two, he'll be in the corridor.

She's at the door.

There's a metal crossbar. She pushes down. It clanks. She shoves the door outward. It scrapes against the concrete floor. It's stuck—won't move outward.

She wrenches down on the handle, throws her weight onto it, and then leans her shoulder against the metal and pushes.

It scrapes on the floor and moves—an inch.

The crossbar shakes in her fists. Up and down. She rattles the bar savagely, then once more. She throws her back against the door and pushes so her thighs strain; every muscle quivers, and her legs feel like they'll explode from tension, and then she slams her back into the door, but it's stuck.

The storage room door bashes against the far wall. He's there. He's coming fast—closing the gap.

She glances to her left. There's a freight elevator. She slaps at a button.

The door slides open.

She's inside now, punching at buttons, frantically, any button, doesn't matter.

"Close" . . . "One" . . . "Two" . . . "Four" . . .

The doors slide together suddenly, and she's shut inside.

There's violent thumping on the outer door. So loud it penetrates the cubicle and thrums through her bones. She's closed off—in a freight elevator with gray metal walls and a steel floor with studs. The door has a round Plexiglas window reinforced with wire mesh. Overhead: a low-wattage lightbulb in an iron-gray sleeve. It casts a sickly, yellow glow through the compartment.

Her breath whistles through her nostrils; her heart feels like it will burst. Megan's thoughts hemorrhage in a frenzy of fear and confusion. What now? Where can she go? What options does she have? What does she do? She's light-headed, weak, and can barely stand, and she shudders as the pounding on the door grows louder, shakes the elevator, drums through her ears, and penetrates her brain. With each thump, she shrinks farther back against the rear wall as fear blitzes through her like a freight train. A steel door separates her from a madman, and she's trapped in this cubicle—inside the elevator shaft of an abandoned building. She closes her eyes, tries to catch her breath, and does her best to quell the shaking of her body.

But as long as she stays in this compartment, so long as bricks and steel surround her, so long as she stays in this suffocating compartment, she's safe. But she's trapped.

In this box.

Eighteen

A slamming so powerful she *feels* its force—it has sledgehammer intensity. He's bashing the elevator door, blasting at it with his fists. His power is incredible. It must be Conrad.

Suddenly, there's a whirring, then creaking. The elevator lurches upward. Megan's stomach drops as she feels the upward thrust in her thighs.

Cables squeal as the elevator rises. She feels light-headed, faint, as though she'll drop to the floor.

Destination: first floor or second. She doesn't know; she's slapped every button.

Tears flood her eyes with near-blinding wetness.

Two . . .

Three . . .

She glances about the elevator. It's maybe eight feet deep, six or seven feet wide, gray, and has cast-iron walls with rust blotches, a dull, metal-studded floor, and that murky overhead yellow light—a freight elevator.

Her arms feel spaghetti limp, weak. A sick sensation billows up from her stomach, eddies through her chest and then to her head. Her entire body trembles.

There's a bounce.

Rapid jiggling, cables groan. The elevator stops and shudders. The indicator says it's the fourth floor.

The doors part silently, quickly.

She peers out at the hallway's cinder-block walls. Everything is gray, dull, and dimly lit by a few bare lightbulbs. It's deserted and damp; the air is still.

Megan wonders if she should scramble down the stairway to the third floor, dash from there through a series of fire doors—if they're even open—and back into the main building. But the doors could be locked. Then she'd be dead meat. There's her cell phone. *Yes*. She reaches into her pocket and flips the cell open. No signal in this old building. But maybe if she moves, she'll get one. Megan holds the phone up, watching the screen as she moves left, then right.

No signal. It's the building—thick walls—brick, reinforced concrete. It's old-time construction with cinder blocks, mortar, and rebar steel. She's deep in the building's innards, far removed from any open space.

Inertia envelops her—a static, paralytic feeling. If she moves, will she fall? If she does, can she get to her feet?

My God, I'm frozen. I've got to get out of here.

Calm yourself. Think this through. Use your head.

At the stairwell door, she pushes at the crossbar; the door creaks open.

She steps onto the landing.

Then she hears him.

He's bounding up the stairs. The thumping of heavy boots courses up from the bottom, thumping and echoing. Louder now, rising so fast, it's unbelievable. Only Conrad has such power and stamina. Guttural snorting rises through the stairwell.

She spins and looks to the other end of the hallway.

There's a door—leading to what? It could be locked; then she's trapped.

She jumps back in the elevator and pushes the "Close" button.

The stairwell door slams open, banging against the wall.

The elevator doors slide shut.

She presses another button.

The cab begins its descent.

Don't panic. Stay calm.

Megan knows he'll watch the indicator to see where the elevator stops. And he'll come for her. She presses "Three."

The elevator bounces to a halt. It jiggles up and down. Megan's teeth rattle with the bouncing. *Oh, my God . . . don't let this elevator get stuck.*

The elevator levels off with the landing.

She's at the third floor. The doors slide open.

She hears tramping boots rushing down the stairwell.

She presses the "Close" button. Then she presses "Basement."

The doors shut. The elevator slips downward and then shudders.

There's a jolt, a yanking sensation. Megan nearly falls to the floor.

The elevator bounces up and down and then stops.

She hears creaking cables, a shearing sound, and then squealing.

Megan looks up at the indicator. No light.

The elevator is motionless.

The doors slide open.

It's a red brick wall.

Something electric charges through her as her knees go weak and her body stiffens. *Oh, my God! Is this really happening? I'm trapped like a small animal?*

She's between the third- and fourth-floor landings, closed off from the world.

Nobody knows she's here except this madman.

Megan's thoughts swirl in frenzied circles. The cell phone is useless. No one can hear a scream; she's trapped, isolated. This elevator's ancient. She's stuck between floors. No camera or video. Even if there were, who would view the monitor? The building's deserted.

Then she sees it right there—a box with a handle. It's in the wall. *Why didn't I see it before?* "Telephone" it says. A landline. No transmission problem. It's hard-wired—a solid connection.

She grabs the small latch, turns it, and pulls. The door flips open.

There it is: a massed tangle of wires coiled like a nest of colored snakes—red, yellow, and black—stuffed inside.

No telephone. It's gone.

Megan feels she's withering. She's out of options—stuck in an elevator shaft with a maniac outside. She reaches into her pocket and snaps open the cell. Still no signal.

Just keep calm. You have time . . . It's all you have right now.

Her eyes dart about the compartment—walls, floor, doors, the ceiling.

There's a recessed fan in the ceiling, but it's not stirring. It's coated with dust and years of grime. Hasn't been used in God knows how long. There's a suffocating stillness to the air.

Stay calm; keep it together. He can't wait forever.

It's stifling in here, but time is on her side. Megan tells herself not to lose her cool. If only her cell phone worked here; if only . . . *if* . . . the biggest little word in the English language.

She can't control the panic surge flooding her like a river gone wild. She feels her pores open; a trickle of sweat slides down her back. Her skin feels like it's cringing.

Think . . . think . . . of what?

Let's face it, girl, you're out of options.

But if she just waits and time passes, Erin will get worried. She'll call the hospital, maybe the police, and then they'll look for her . . . maybe . . . if she can just wait him out.

There's a creaking sound above her.

She peers up.

She sees it: a service hatch—a small ceiling door. There's no handle inside the elevator. It's a rescue hatch that opens from on top of the compartment—from the outside. No doubt for firemen and rescue workers; but there isn't a soul to save her.

It occurs to Megan that he's pried open the outer door on the fourth floor. Conrad could be sliding down the cable—just rappelling down the thing. He was a canyoneer in Colorado, cable-dropped hundreds of feet down cliff walls—like the mountain climber he is—and soon he'll drop down onto the elevator roof. She'll hear the thump of those huge boots, then the scraping sound as he pries open the hatch. He'll drop down into the compartment. And then what happens?

If this was a movie, he'd stomp around on the elevator roof and then lift the door, drop down, and materialize right in front of her. And then he'd be on her with those massive hands, those powerful arms, and he'd crack her neck, snuffing out her life. But in the movie . . . something else would happen—something dramatic, life-saving, something implausible, *impossible.*

C'mon, girl, get real! You're not in a theater; you're in this horrible little box, hanging in a shaft, and there's a madman out there . . . and he wants you. He wants you to die.

Her body trembles, it feels like it's melting.

God, what can I do?

She sees it: the alarm button, a red knob. Why hadn't she seen it before? Panic, that's why. Her arm shoots out and presses the button.

Clanging reverberates through the shaftway, up and down its length, shrill, echoing, penetrating her brain. She keeps pressing though her arm feels like lead.

After what seems a very long time, she pulls her thumb away and listens. There's silence.

Her thumb shoots back to the alarm button and presses. The ringing resumes. Shrill, strident, the bell sound shrieks through her bones.

He can't stay forever—not while this clamor pours through the shaftway.

Don't look at the bricks, she tells herself. It's too frightening. Just watch the floor and keep pressing the alarm. Someone's bound to hear it. Is there a chance in this deserted building that a single soul could be within earshot of the bell?

Megan knows she's desperate for *something* to happen, for *someone* to come. If she just keeps ringing, she tells herself, yes . . . yes . . . keep pressing. Keep up the noise; don't stop. The sound blares through the shaft. He'll have to leave. Eventually, someone will hear the bell and call for help.

She's losing track of time: seconds, minutes . . . how many?

Her eardrums are throbbing. Tremors go through her, but the bell's her only hope. Its harsh shrill piping goes on and on, clanging mercilessly.

She releases the button.

Her ears ring—a high-pitched, tinny sound—and she feels her heart flutter like the whirring wings of a caged bird. Her body is damp, and an inner trembling ripples through her—wavelets of fear and terror. The compartment's more oppressive now and she feels she'll smother in its closeness.

Megan lets herself stare at the wall. In any other circumstance, she'd feel panic gazing at this impenetrable facade—brick and cement in layered patterns. But right now, the wall is sanctuary. Safety. She could stay here for hours, for days, forever—just to keep him away.

Now she listens to the thundering of her heart. Feels like it'll burst through her breastbone.

Then, strangely, calm comes over her, a sense of inner peace, tranquility. In those moments, Megan thinks of Marlee and Adrian and then Erin and Bob and their kids, Robert and Ellie. That's the trick. Let her thoughts drift to the life-affirming people who love her. Detach from the here and now. Disconnect from *him*.

There's the past—not the present.

There were the days with Mom and Dad—only memories now, but filled with sweetness and love. There were Sunday brunches after church; and she was high scorer on the girls' high school basketball team. And there were the days—so many years ago—when Mom and Dad took them to Rye Playland, where she and Erin went on the Dragon Coaster, skated in the Ice Casino, and ate piping-hot pizza, pulling on cheesy strings of mozzarella. Those days seem so long ago, so lost.

Oh, those memories. Megan thinks of them as so sweet and so painful. Painful? Why? Because they're *gone*. And suddenly it seems to Megan that everything before this moment—before this *very* second in this horrid elevator—all the seconds and minutes and hours and days and years, all the thoughts and feelings and all the things she did with all the people she knew in her life, are gone . . . are just a series of memories. And yes, her entire life before this very moment is only a memory.

Suddenly, the door closes. The elevator lurches upward.

As quickly as it starts, the elevator stops.

She peers through the door's wire-mesh Plexiglas window.

The cab is hanging just below the fourth-floor landing. Through the window, she sees the hallway ceiling and part of the corridor wall.

She sees him: he's *there*. He's only inches away—the black ski mask over his head, the rounded skull. The eyes are red, wet, gleaming.

A sound erupts from deep inside her; it's as inhuman as the thing outside the window. She tumbles back to a corner of the compartment.

But she can't let the doors open, so she rushes back to the panel and hits the "Close" button.

A thump shakes the compartment.

Then another—more powerful. He's bashing again at the

outer door.

There's a creaking sound.

The elevator rises a few inches.

It stops—closer to the landing.

This is it. He's going to get me.

She presses harder on the "Close" button, pressing the heel of her palm on it. How stupid, useless—how feeble she feels.

There's another thump—deep, penetrating.

The light in the elevator flickers. It dims, brightens, and flickers again.

Please, please . . . not in the dark. I can't take the darkness.

The compartment rises—slightly. A few more inches will do it. The elevator will line up with the landing. And the door will open.

She's quaking nonstop and feels her guts squirm in her belly.

She presses "Stop" even as she holds the "Close" button.

Her insides crawl; she's shredding from within.

Thump! Thump! Thump!

The light flickers again.

She slaps frantically at the panel buttons—first one, then another, then another.

"Basement . . ."

"One . . ."

"Four . . ."

"Stop . . ."

"Alarm . . ."

Ringing rises through the shaft.

Just keep pressing and don't stop. Don't give up. Do whatever you can.

Thump! Thump! Thump!

Then it happens: the elevator slides down, moving slowly, steadily, glides past "Three," then past "Two," and bypasses "One," still going down.

And then . . . "Basement."

The elevator stops.

Is he rushing down the stairwell?

She presses "Open." The doors slide apart.

I have to get out of here. Move . . . move . . . now.

She's in the corridor, where she'd begun. Same cinder-block walls and pipes, same sink, meters, the open door to that musty storage room. Should she bolt back there, race through it and then beyond those doors and back into the locker area? She could trip over the debris in the darkened room. And what then? Would he burst into the room?

To her right, the stairwell door is open. He'd pushed it out before he stomped up the stairs. She peers into the stairwell: cinder-block walls, cement stairs, and a glossy red handrail. It's a double flight of stairs to the next landing.

Rush . . . run . . . make it to the first floor.

She pushes off on one foot. Then the stairwell fades; she's fainting.

She clutches the railing, yanks herself upright, and begins the climb.

Her chest feels like it'll explode, and how endless these stairs are. She stumbles and sprawls on her hands and knees. Pain—searing, shocklike—shoots from the heel of her palm to her elbow, and her knee slams into the step. Her skin is raw, scraped, burning.

She rises and scrambles up the stairway. Her mouth opens, and her breath comes in short grunts. There's a flame deep in her chest, and Megan feels pressure, as though her lungs will collapse within her rib cage.

Now she hears it: a thumping of feet—a furious scrambling, coming closer, thundering—racing down the stairs. He's coming. She hears his footfalls—pounding, raucous, clamoring and echoing, louder now—closer and right above her.

Her feet find a rhythm, and she moves so slowly. There's a door on the first floor, and she lunges ahead on cement legs—lurches and grasps desperately at the handrail—and there's that fusillade of noise caroming down the stairwell.

She's at the door; she thrusts down on the bar and bursts forward.

She's in a corridor and there's another door. She plunges ahead, stumbles again, nearly falls, shambles sideways, regains her balance, slams against the door, pushes the bar handle down, flings the door open, and then lunges and sprawls onto a linoleum floor. Megan thinks she sees doctors and nurses and a security guard, but the corridor tilts, her head hits the floor, and a white starburst detonates in her eyes. There are voices as arms lift her, the blood drains from her head, and the security guard's radio crackles as she thinks of Marlee and Adrian and Erin and floats in pale ether.

Nineteen

"The hospital's in lockdown," says Pat Mulvaney, leaning forward with his hands clasped on the table. "Everything's closed off . . . the ambulatory care center, ambulance bays, all of it."

It's seven thirty in the evening. Adrian, Megan, Mulvaney, and Harwood are in the third-floor doctors' lounge. A siren whoops outside. Megan shudders; Adrian wraps his arm around her shoulders.

"How're ya feelin', Megan?" Mulvaney asks.

"Just a few scrapes and bruises. I'll be okay," she whispers.

But Adrian feels her body trembling. And she sounds drained, wasted. He rubs her back and whispers, "It'll be okay."

"Megan, can you talk now?" Mulvaney asks. Harwood stands nearby with a digital recorder.

"I don't know," she stammers. "I'm feeling calmer now. That sedative's kicking in."

"Can you tell us anything else?" Mulvaney asks.

"I couldn't . . . not really . . . He was very fast . . . and . . . and strong . . . and . . ." Her voice warbles; her hands shake.

"You think it was your ex?" Mulvaney asks.

She nods and swallows hard. "Yes."

"We're combin' each floor, goin' in every room," Mulvaney says. "Everyone's being interviewed. The only ones we're not talkin' to are patients in *comas*."

"He's gone," Harwood says.

"Can't know," Mulvaney says.

"You're pretty sure it's Conrad Wilson, aren't you?" Adrian says.

"Believe me, Adrian," Mulvaney says. "It's almost always the husband or the ex. And I'll tell ya somethin' else. He's probably lookin' for you, too. That night at King's Corner wasn't a coincidence."

"But Megan and I hadn't even *met* yet."

"Still, Adrian, he was lookin' for someone . . . and he picked *you*."

"You mean the break-in at my place, don't you?"

"By *then* he knew you were in the picture. It's that old jealousy thing. 'If I can't have you, then no one can,'" Mulvaney says. He turns to Megan. "We're gonna make arrangements for you, Megan."

"Huh?" she says, and peers vacantly at Mulvaney.

"We're takin' you to a hotel. The tab's on the governor. It's not the Ritz-Carlton, but you'll be comfortable. I can't tell you where right now—protocol, ya know?"

"But I can't leave Marlee."

"You'll both go."

"What about Erin and her kids? They could be in danger."

Adrian realizes it's extraordinary; after what she's been through, Megan worries about her sister and the kids.

"She'll be here soon . . . with the kids," Mulvaney says. "You'll *all* go. And her husband, he and the dog are stayin' at a friend's place in Avon."

"I'm going with them," Adrian says.

"Not a good idea," Mulvaney says.

"Someone can cover me. I'll—"

"Adrian, you're *both* targets. We're gonna separate you. You'll stay at a hotel in Fairfield, on the Eastport border—near the hospital—until this is over."

"He's probably left Connecticut," Adrian says, feeling both hope and dread.

"New York's only forty minutes away. And Rhode Island's an hour from here on I-95. But my old cop's gut tells me he's around."

Harwood's cell phone trills. He snaps it open, listens, thanks the caller, and then closes the phone.

"That's New Haven PD," Harwood says. "They got a warrant and went to Wilson's place. Empty coffee containers, pizza boxes, and half-eaten cartons of Chinese are everywhere. But he's not there."

"So you'll be looking for that pickup?" Adrian asks.

"My guess is he garaged it somewhere," Mulvaney says. "Or maybe he sold it for cash to some illegal."

Mulvaney pauses and then says, "Adrian, you need anything from your place?"

"Just some clothes, a few things . . ."

Mulvaney glances at his watch. "It's safe to go there now. I spoke with Chief Toscano in Simpson. Just in case Wilson decides to pay you another visit, Simpson PD's got your place staked out. The cruiser's probably been there for a half hour by now, so it's safe. But don't stay long."

Adrian nods.

"Look, I gotta be up-front with you," Mulvaney says. "Wilson may come back. Megan, we've got your place under surveillance—twenty-four-seven—with state police and my men. Adrian, Lieutenant Harwood's made arrangements at a hotel for you in Fairfield. You'll use a different name . . . Tom Cunningham."

"I don't see why I can't go with Megan."

"Please, Adrian, you're in *my* operating room now."

Mulvaney rises to his full height. Then he says, "Adrian, talk with Lieutenant Harwood, then go home, pick up a few things, and head over to the hotel. Remember . . . the name's Tom

Cunningham."

Mulvaney peers at the throng outside the hospital. There are klieg lights and a clot of reporters. What a goddamned zoo, he thinks. A battalion of microphones bobs in his face. One aggressive reporter nearly pokes him in the nose with his digital recorder.

Jesus, buddy. Watch it, will ya? I only got one nose, Mulvaney thinks, scowling at the guy. He makes his way down the hospital's steps, thinking he should have used a side door.

News 12 Connecticut has a truck sitting there. Local reporters and TV crews jostle for position.

"Chief! Can you give us any details?"

"I'm afraid not, Harold," Mulvaney says to Harold Fallon, a reporter for the *Connecticut Post*. He and Fallon go back two decades to Mulvaney's days in the New Haven PD. "We're sortin' through everything."

Mulvaney tries to quicken his pace, but the pack is too thick. He stops on the mezzanine between the upper and lower stairway.

"Any idea who it was, Chief?" calls a reporter. The guy's face is thin, mottled—some goddamned skin condition—and under the lights he looks reptilian.

"Is there a boyfriend involved?" asks a guy from the *New Haven Register*.

"No comment."

The horde cascades down the steps with him, mikes, cameras, recorders held high.

"Does it look like a random thing, or was it a stalker?" shouts a reporter for the *Eastport Bulletin*, the town weekly. The paper's biggest stories usually center on the new school budget or rising property taxes. Not tonight.

"People . . . people . . . it's an ongoin' investigation."

Mulvaney plows through the mob, but they follow him like a swarm of pilot fish on a shark's ass. A forensic team's just arrived from Hartford; it's combing through the place. If something's found—a hair, fiber, anything—they'll tag it and bag it.

Everyone's here—TV crews, the daily rags, the local weeklies. Mulvaney gets to the sidewalk and keeps walking. One guy with a camcorder crouches down to get a close-up of Mulvaney—a goddamned nostril shot. Mulvaney keeps trudging as two beefy cops commandeer Camcorder Guy and shove him back.

This stinks out loud, Mulvaney thinks, quickening his stride.

I gotta get away from this pack of shitweasals.

A contingent of state police brass is coming to an eight o'clock meeting at the town hall. So is Eastport's first selectman, Kevin Russell, and members of the town council. Mulvaney's gotta hustle now, gotta talk with Inspector Bruce Howard, state police deputy chief of the Central District's Major Crime Unit.

This shit storm's coming down the pike—like an eighteen-wheeler on I-95.

Twenty

Dinner is taken in the hotel dining room, a drab expanse of off-white, Formica-topped tables. Soggy, warmed-over preparations sit in tarnished tureens on a long, cloth-covered buffet table. Cloying music is piped in—tinny Muzak stuff that reminds Megan of the saccharine music she hears at the Danbury mall. She glances at a clot of hotel conventioneers picking over the buffet offerings.

"We'd be better off at the Olive Garden," Erin mutters.

Trembling ripples through Megan's chest, and a hum courses through her insides. The food smells like cheap meat and reused cooking oil. It makes her feel nauseous. Even the *thought* of food makes Megan's stomach churn. She's not certain she'll be able to swallow an Ambien before bedtime. Yet another drug . . . She'll be a junkie before this is over.

God, when will this shaky feeling end? I don't want to take another Xanax . . . I feel zonked already. But this shaking just won't quit. Will I end up like Nurse Jackie on Showtime—drug addicted and sneaking meds out of the dispensary?

"I can't believe this place," Erin mutters, pushing Robert's plate closer to him. "It's totally bargain basement."

Erin's right. The hotel—a nondescript six-story, prefab structure—is situated between the Connecticut Convention Center in Hartford and the choking exhaust fumes of I-91. It's cookie-cutter generic, with zero personality. It's typical of the world we now live in—homogeneous. You could be in Hartford or Baltimore or Cleveland, for all it matters; they all look the same. But who cares? It's only temporary, till this nightmare ends.

"This place should be called Hotel Purgatory," Erin says. "You just kill time here, waiting to go somewhere else."

Why do I feel this is my fault?

"Don't worry, honey," Erin says. "Adrian can handle himself."

Marlee pokes her fork onto Robert's plate and snares a chicken wing.

"Marlee, let Robert eat in peace," Megan rasps. She feels brittle, ready to crack apart. No, not ready to crack. There's already a deep, raw fissure in her being. She's been shredded, chopped, and churned in this food processer called life.

"I want chicken wings, too," Marlee whines.

"Then ask and we'll go to the buffet table."

"It's been going on nonstop," Erin says.

Megan mouths the word *Jealous*. Then she crosses her arms in front of her and squeezes, holding herself together so she won't collapse in front of the kids.

Megan sits in her room at the edge of the bed. A muted orange glow comes from the bedside lamp. She gazes at the room's grayish walls. Yes, Erin's right: the place is a dump—Burger King cheap.

During dinner, Erin kept muttering about Conrad. "I hope they find him soon because we can't stay very long in this hole," she said. "And the kids have school . . ."

Erin's antipathy toward Conrad had always been out there, especially as he'd become more unhinged years earlier.

"He's a caveman," Erin would say. "Okay . . . so he's smart, even with that callow country-cowboy act. Actually, I think he's a bipolar maniac."

Megan recalls the time Erin—jokingly, of course—called him *Connie*. You'd think she'd castrated him—purposely. Sometimes Erin can be really cutting. It's just her personality. But Conrad reacted as if she'd called him *faggot*, his favorite word. His face turned plum-purple and he looked like he'd implode.

Megan wonders why she fell for him so quickly back then. Yes, Erin nailed it—part of her sister's social intelligence. It was that callow, *aw shucks* cow-puncher way of his. At first he wasn't particularly jealous. And there were no rage-filled, paranoid rants until later.

But now she understands what attracted her to Conrad. It was the seduction of shared circumstances. They'd both been adopted, and she fell into that vortex of commonality. God, how pathetic it all was; how completely naive it was of her to think that their both being orphans made for some deep and abiding connection.

How stupid could you have been, girl?

The telephone rings in a nerve-jangling burst of noise, and Megan nearly jumps. She picks up the receiver.

"How're you feeling, sweetie?" Erin asks.

"I'm okay," she says, trying to stifle the motor in her chest. "I'm glad Marlee's staying with you and the kids tonight."

"For them, this is an outing. It could be Rye Playland."

A high-pitched yowling derails the conversation.

"You two have *got* to stop this," Erin calls, her hand over the receiver.

"What's going on?" Megan asks.

"Oh, Robert wants to watch *SpongeBob* and Marlee wants something else." Erin's voice fades as she yells, "You'll take turns!" Then, speaking into the telephone, she says, "Marlee's bullying Robert . . ."

"Well, she's in this shitty hotel—and she knows I'm all screwed up. She picks up on everything. You know how kids are."

"Megan, maybe Marlee's got Conrad's . . ." Erin's voice trails off.

"*Say* it, Erin," she whispers. "She's got Conrad's *temperament*, right? She's got his lousy genes?"

"I'm sorry, Megan. It's . . . just stupid . . ."

Megan's eyes well up with tears and feel swollen. "No, *I'm* sorry, Erin. I shouldn't take this out on you."

"Forget it, sweetie. I was being a jerk."

"I'm so glad you're here," Megan murmurs, as that internal motor shifts to low gear.

"Oh, Megan, this must be terrible for you . . ."

"I just can't believe this is happening . . . to you, Bob, the kids . . . and Adrian."

"It'll be over soon, sweetie."

"I feel like a nerve dipped in the ocean, like I have no skin."

"Honey, you just need some time to get past this."

Megan nods; she tries desperately to convince herself Erin's right. Yes, she needs time—the great healer. Tincture of time will do it. Isn't that what the doctors always say?

But her head pulses and her chest feels clogged. God, she can still smell that storage room, the cement and moldy cardboard mixed with dust and rat droppings. It's embedded in her nostrils. And she can't rid her thoughts of him . . . the mask and the knife.

A *ding* comes from the hallway elevator. Megan's insides lurch. Her pulse stampedes. There are voices—a man and a woman, then laughter.

"What's wrong?" Erin asks.

"I just heard the elevator." Her chin quivers.

"Megan, we're *safe* here. Don't let your imagination run away with you. And remember, sweetie, there're cops in the lobby."

"And Marlee's okay?"

"She's fine."

Megan's shoulders hunch with tension; she's so tight, her muscles ache. She hears the ice machine rattle in the alcove off the hallway.

*Clunk . . . clunk . . . clunk . . .*Cubes drop heavily into a plastic bucket. The sound shoots through her like a machine gun.

Music floats down the hallway from an open door.

A woman says, "Oh, don't be stupid . . ."

A door slams. The music dies.

Another door opens. She hears voices, laughter. It must be a party. There's more music. Sounds like rap—ugly, brutal. Violent words in forced rhymes. It gets louder, peaks, and then fades. Turns to a bass thumping and penetrates the room's walls.

Paper-thin walls, cheap fiberboard, joint compound, and spackle, Home Depot construction . . . what a prefab world it all is.

Erin says, "Can you believe it? The kids love this place—no school, a flat-screen TV in the bedroom . . ."

Megan nods, wanting desperately to believe something good will come of this.

"Just try to get some sleep," Erin says. "Did you take that other pill . . . ?"

"I will . . . but you know me, I'm not a pill person."

"Tonight you need a pill or two. Just take it."

When they hang up, Megan lies back on the bed and stares at the ceiling. She tries to connect the dots of her life—reviews the seemingly random yet linear chain of events all leading up to this moment where she's in this hotel room on this awful night and she fears for her life. And she's afraid for Marlee and Adrian, too. Despite the sequential connections of her life's events, it strikes Megan that none of it makes sense. It's all so crazy.

The phone warbles. She nearly jumps, grabs the receiver, and puts it to her ear. But before she can say a word, a harsh buzzing comes from the earpiece.

Is it a hang-up?

Conrad?

How can he know she's here? It's impossible. She's so wired, she thinks she needs another Xanax. Maybe even two . . . just to take the edge off. There are three more inside that little capped bottle the ER doctor gave her. Maybe she'll just let the medication snow her; she'll drift into a mindless fog. She's taken maybe three pills in her whole life, but now Megan understands why some people become addicts, complete junkies.

She trudges into the bathroom, opens the plastic bottle, dumps a Xanax tablet in her palm, peers at its whiteness, shakes her head, and then thrusts it in her mouth. A cup of sink water washes it down.

Back in the bedroom, the telephone jangles; it seizes her.

Her hand hovers.

Pick it up . . . The known is better than the unknown . . .

There's another ring.

"Hello . . ."

"Megan, it's Adrian."

"*Adrian*," she gasps. "Where *are* you?"

"At the hospital. I'll be leaving soon. More important . . . how're you?"

"I'm okay," she hears a small voice say. "Did you just try to call me?"

"I don't know. The police patched me in to you. Why?"

"The phone rang and nobody was there."

"My call must've been dropped. But you sound so nervous . . .Maybe you need another Xanax."

"I just took one."

"You'll take the Ambien tonight, right?"

"Yes . . ."

She can hear—even feel—the worry in his voice.

"Adrian, I'm worried about *you* . . . about what Mulvaney said. He could come for you."

"He doesn't know where I am."

Biting on her lip, Megan feels the flesh between her teeth. A sliver of skin peels back. She licks her lip and it burns. There's a fissure where she bit; it's as raw as she feels inside.

"Adrian, why don't you just stay at the hotel . . . ? Don't go to the hospital tomorrow."

"Megan, my love, Eastport's crawling with cops. Besides, they'll find him."

"Find him? No way. He grew up in the Rockies, Adrian. He could live in the wilds if he wanted to."

"Megan, this is *Connecticut*, not the Wild West."

"Adrian?"

"Yes, darling?" he whispers.

"Do you realize how much you mean to me?"

"Nothing'll happen. Listen—"

"And to Marlee." Her eyes are so wet, the room blurs. Her voice bubbles in her ears, and tears collect at the back of her throat. "Marlee's become so attached to you in only . . . what is it, a month . . . ? A little more . . . ?"

"Megan, I—"

"*No*, Adrian, I want to say this," she blurts, nearly gurgling through her tears. "Other men"—she quivers—"other men've been interested, but I didn't want Marlee to get attached, to be disappointed. I didn't let them in. But, Adrian, I let you in. I let you into our lives."

"I know, Megan. I know. I love you and I love Marlee," he whispers. "I love you both *so* much." She thinks she hears him choking. "Okay, Megan," he says. "Just tell me where you are and I'll leave now. I'll come and stay with you."

"No, Adrian. I'm being selfish," she says, closing her eyes. "Erin's here."

"Megan, you and Marlee are all that count. I'll talk to the chairman. He'll get another surgeon—"

"No, Adrian. We'll be fine. But I love you, and I can't stop worrying."

"Megan, when I saw the way you looked tonight, I couldn't bear the thought of losing you. It made my heart ache."

"Oh, Adrian."

"Megan, my love, we'll be together . . . the three of us," he says, his voice cracking.

"Adrian, you and Marlee are my whole world now. I just want us all to be safe."

Megan senses he's about to offer some anemic reassurance—but he doesn't, thankfully. As a doctor, Adrian knows better than to mouth empty promises. *You don't use balm on an open wound*, she thinks, recalling when she worked in oncology. Morphine dulls pain. It's palliation—an attempt to relieve suffering—but the cancer marches on, metastasizing everywhere.

And that's what Conrad is: cancer.

In the bathroom, Megan slides the vinyl shower curtain aside, turns on the bath spigots, and adjusts the valve so water pours into the tub. She knows she needs sleep, desperately.

No, girl . . . If you think you're going to sleep well tonight, you're in another world; you're in some dreamlike fantasy of a place. You have to stay real. You've been through a trauma, as the psychologists would say.

It's so strange, she thinks, because she never in her life dreaded sleep. In fact, years before, when Conrad was getting crazier, sleep was a welcome sanctuary.

But tonight Megan *knows* he'll come back to her in her sleep. He'll haunt her. *God, it's like Freddy Krueger.* She'll shoot awake in a clammy cocoon of sheets.

At the bathroom sink, she picks up the other translucent orange vial and reads the label.

Ambien. For the short-term treatment of insomnia.

She unfolds the insert and reads about the side effects: dizziness, drowsiness, a "drugged" feeling, weakness, a bunch of others. It occurs to Megan that it might be a good idea to take one now, to give it time to do its thing—dope her up before she crawls into bed. But she's already half-bombed from the Xanax. It's going to be some combination.

Knock yourself out, girl. Just go for it. Get some sleep. That's what you need.

She pops the container lid, drops a tablet into her palm, and slips it onto her tongue. She pours water into the glass and lifts it to her lips. Swallows. The Ambien drops down.

Go ahead, work your magic, Mr. Ambien. Are you the one with the butterfly hovering over the bed? No, that's Lunesta.

Bath water pounds heavily into the tub and turns hot. The bathroom steams up; fog covers the mirror. The air is heated, dense, wet. She turns the directional lever up so water spurts from the showerhead. She strips off her clothes, steps into the tub, and slides the shower curtain shut. Water sloshes over her. She lathers up. The hotel soap smells like tangerine—bringing on a hint of nausea. Reminds her of the paramedic's cologne that night they were run off the Post Road. Her legs quiver like gelatin, but the water feels soothing and forms a hot liquid wrap.

Megan looks down and sees soapy water circling the bathtub drain. Her heart jumps. She should have known this would happen: she thinks way too often about movies.

She's reminded of the shower scene in *Psycho*. Anthony Perkins and Janet Leigh: the shower curtain is ripped aside; Megan recalls Norman Bates in an old woman's dowdy garb and then black-and-white quick shots, a close-up of the showerhead, water streaming out in arcs, the knife slicing through the air, screeching violins, the blade plunging into Janet Leigh's body, the soft *thushing* sound of the steel puncturing flesh, blood circling the drain, washing away, and suddenly—in less than the second it takes to recall it—Megan's knees buckle, and she's ready to collapse in the tub with the water running, lying with open, dead eyes, just like Janet Leigh. She realizes she's left the bathroom door open.

She slides the shower curtain aside, reaches through the steamy air, closes the door, and with a shaking hand, turns the latch and locks it.

My God, I'm going berserk. I'll drive myself as crazy as Conrad.

Megan thinks it's difficult to believe her life's funneled down to being in this tub with its yellow, floral nonslip bathtub appliqués, showering in this cookie-cutter hotel, right off a major, clogged highway, and she realizes that no matter how long she lives, she'll always see herself as a *survivor. Yes, from now on, each day is a gift,* she thinks, *life granted by nothing more than luck.* Everything good—whether it's time spent with Marlee or Adrian, helping a fragile preemie struggle for life, watching the ecstatic parents of a newbie or anything else, for that matter—is little more than a bequest.

Lying in bed, Megan is thankful the bass beat from down the hall has stopped. With a thermal-pane window, the room is sealed off from the distant roar of I-91.

She hears footfalls in the hallway. Then that ice machine churns again; the elevator bell dings; the doors slide open.

My God, it's so loud.

I'm going out of my mind.

More footsteps, then sibilant whispering, a woman's voice; then there's a high-pitched giggle in the hallway. It grows distant, recedes down the corridor, and fades like the drift of a radio station at night, a ribbon of sound lost in darkness.

She lies there, stone still, trying to ease her tense muscles, the covers pulled to her chin, waiting for sleep, amnesty.

The telephone sends out a shrill tone. She bolts up, fumbles for it, picks it up, and puts it to her ear. She hears only a buzzing dial tone. She slips out of bed, turns on the lamp, and dials reception. "Did anyone call my room?" she asks.

"No, Ms. Haggarty," says the operator.

"Are the police there?"

"Yes, two officers are in the lobby. One's near the elevators."

"Thanks," she says, and slips the phone onto the receiver. She switches the lamp off and slides beneath the covers.

The sodium vapor lamps three floors below cast pastel illumination onto the hotel; shadows of sycamore branches form a dancing tracery on the room's ceiling. Eerie, but better than darkness, Megan thinks. She hates the blackness of night and has always feared how it makes her feel there are no boundaries, just dark emptiness. Like the universe—an endless void. But those shadows are so creepy. Why didn't she pull the drapes closed?

But no one can see into the room. She's on the third floor. There's a huge parking lot across the street, and it's surrounded by a high chain-link fence. Beyond that, darkened warehouses, low-lying buildings, and in the distance, cars are snaking along in a pall of fumes on I-91, their headlights piercing the night air. In the other direction, a ribbon of red taillights stretches to a black horizon.

She decides to close the drapes. Pitch blackness is better than those ghostly shadows on the ceiling. Slipping out of bed, Megan turns on the bedside lamp. Feeling weak, she plods unsteadily to the window—a double-paned glass expanse. About to pull the drapery rod, she peers down at the parking lot. The sodium vapor lamps cast pink, pyramidal-shaped spotlights, and amid the bleached-looking tints of a hundred parked cars, she sees him. A large man, he wears a hoodie and jeans, stands stone stock-still. She can't make out his face. Is he looking up at her? Megan's heart falters and then flutters in her chest. She feels every nerve ending in her body fire. As her heartbeat drubs heavily, she squints, trying to focus on him, but everything's blurred and then seems to tilt. Megan blinks a few times and then closes her eyes, rubs her face, opens her eyes, and looks again.

Yes, he looks up, right at her. She realizes she's backlit by the bedside lamp, so she backs away from the window. She stands there for a few moments, trembling. Then she moves slowly back to the window, angles herself to the right side, and peers down to the parking lot.

He's gone.

She looks left and then right, cranes her neck, presses her cheek against the cold window glass, and peers down the street, both ways. She sees no one. How can that be? She's certain she saw him. Was it her imagination? Can she even trust her senses now? Between the double dose of Xanax and then the Ambien and her fear, the anticipation of terrible things, and after what happened tonight—was it tonight or forever ago?—she can't trust her senses. Everything's disjointed, so out of place, and here she is, uprooted and alone in this dreary hotel room. Maybe she *is* going crazy.

She slides the drapes closed and turns off the lamp.

Back in bed, Megan's thoughts swim back to high school, to Mom and Dad and Erin back in those days, and it occurs to her that the Ambien, now mixed with Xanax, is doing its thing. She's floating languidly through space, and there's a brief flash of Adrian as she recalls their first meeting that day in the cafeteria—*Your soup's getting cold*—and everything tumbles in some pleasantly cascading stream.

It's so drifty-dreamy, and there's no linear thread; everything's a delicious hodgepodge of stuff. Even as it's happening Megan knows she's hovering in a silken web of sleep—some netherland. It's almost like being drugged. Yes, she's getting deliriously bombed by the Ambien and Xanax and fear-driven fatigue, and she's thinking about another movie—not something scary for a change. She won't do that to herself again. Instead, she recalls *Hope Floats*. That line: *Childhood is what you spend the rest of your life trying to overcome . . .*

But right now, Megan's no longer certain where she is, and nothing is quite real. She's just floating in darkness . . . somewhere . . .

It must be much later—she can't tell after that *Psycho* shower; everything's so hazy, so completely lost in time, and she thinks she's been dreaming. Megan's eyes open even though she may still be sleeping—she really isn't sure. Her eyes sift through the darkened room to the drapes, then the ceiling, then slowly to the door.

A man stands there.

Fear ramps through her like a squall. It's a body-numbing fright mixed with a shivery feeling, like icicles beneath her skin.

He stands there, unmoving. She blinks, thinking for a half second that her eyes are deceiving her.

But he's *there.*

Megan doesn't move—not a single fiber in her body—because it's an all-encompassing paralytic fear, a terror so primal, she feels like a trapped animal. Like when she was on the elevator, but worse. There's no barrier. Megan lies there with her mind racing, her thoughts plummeting and churning like a heaving ocean. But through it all, Megan wonders if she could slither out of bed, slip to the floor, and crawl to the bathroom.

She could grab her cell phone, make it to the bathroom, slam the door, lock it. But she'd never be quick enough. Conrad's lightning fast, and he'll be on her in a second. And even if she *does* make it, he'll shatter the flimsy door with one malletlike punch. So she lies there, frozen, in a state of terror-stricken inertia.

Play possum. He wants to torture you with fear. So if you stay asleep, you're safe . . . for a while.

He's toying with her—and she realizes that while she was sleeping, he'd slipped stealthily into her room. In the dark, Megan can make out the thick slope of his shoulders, his powerful arms and chest, and there's that horrible ski mask with its rounded contour. She can see his eyes through the holes, those dull, penetrating, bluish-gray eyes.

Through the current of her fear, Megan hears a mousy voice. It says, *Isn't this just a dream, Megan? Isn't it some stupid mix of fear and fatigue and Xanax and Ambien working in the dark?*

Then another voice, this one stronger, more confident. It's Megan's from when she was captain of the girls' basketball team. It says, *Don't be a jerk, Megan. He's here, and he's going to kill you . . . so you'd better get with the program, girl.*

But the mousy voice whispers, *It's your imagination, Megan. Remember when you were kids in the darkened bedroom, how you and Erin thought the clothing on the chair looked like Lon Chaney as the Wolf Man, or one of those ghouls after you watched* Night of the Living Dead *on television?*

Megan knows it's the voice of capitulation, and she can't let that happen. So, in an adrenaline-fueled moment, with her blood surging, she rolls out of bed and leaps toward him. She's amazed at the power in her legs and arms. In a blind fury, crazed by fear and rage, knowing her life's on the line, and Marlee's, too, she pummels him furiously, but feels nothing. She crumples against the wall, breathless and spent, and flips on the light. Gasping and trembling, with her knees buckling, she realizes she's alone and there's no one else in the room—it was a fear-fueled dream.

Swooning, with her back against the door, she slides down, reaches the floor, her knees at her chest, and sobs, waiting for the night to end.

Twenty-one

Adrian pulls the Altima up to the cottage. No Simpson police officer on stakeout. Not yet, even though it's been hours since the attack. It's a typical miscommunication. Happens all the time in the hospital. Why not with the cops? Mistakes are a part of life. But it doesn't matter; Adrian will be in and out in three minutes—just grab a few things and then head for the Fairfield Holiday Inn.

He gets out of the car and stares up at the autumn night sky. A bone-colored full moon gives the cottage roof and woods an eerie luminescence. An unending carpet of stars is visible on this clear, warmish October night. A few strands of clumped clouds drift by, heading east, their fluffed edges backlit by the moon's radiance. A breeze swishes through the swaying tree branches and rustles the desiccated leaves. The windswept redolence of a fireplace is in the air. Someone at the Gibson mansion is burning oak mixed with ash. It melds with the scent of pine needles, dried leaves, and lichen.

Thinking of Megan fills Adrian with an aching sadness. He feels her absence like an open wound. And when she said, *Adrian, with you it's different. I let you in. I let you into our lives,* he felt a sob deep in his chest. The image of her after the attack brings a surge of melancholy that makes him want to cry for every sadness he's ever known. Like losing Dad and then seeing Mom's shriveled life. Like the patients he couldn't save and their loved ones lost in grief. Adrian knows when this outbreak of madness is over, he and Megan will change everything. It's time to make a commitment—to Megan and Marlee.

In the cottage, Adrian deactivates the alarm. He's struck by a sense of estrangement. It occurs to him that he's lived here for two years, but never really grew attached to the cottage. Yes, it's been a pleasant, homey place—but it's always seemed temporary, transitional in his journey from life with Peggy to whatever would await him. Here he is, forty years old, and it's all transient, lacking permanence. He's still foraging for meaning beyond the operating room, still searching . . . for what? Happiness? Contentment? The pleasure of settling into a life of stability? Maybe now—in the middle of his life—he's closing in on what he's always wanted. Adrian is certain Megan has changed everything for him.

He's made a mental checklist of things he'll need: his laptop and a few other things, just basics. Anything else, he'll buy in Eastport. And when Megan and Marlee are back, they'll all go on with their lives—together. When he looks about the cottage, it occurs to Adrian that it makes no sense for him to have come back here. There's very little he needs. Maybe it's his way of saying goodbye to the life he's been leading. Yes, he decides; it's a final farewell.

He pulls a small duffel bag from a closet and goes upstairs to the bedroom. He grabs underwear and socks. In the bathroom, it's a toothbrush, razors, dental floss—slipped into a plastic bag and then into the duffel. He skims through some hanging shirts, trousers, a belt, and his New Balance running shoes and stuffs them into the bag.

There's nothing else he needs. It's only for a few days, and there's always Walmart or CVS. It occurs to Adrian right then that material things are trifles, utterly replaceable. It's easy to figure out the things that count—the people who have meaning in your life.

He glances at the living room, thinking this is the end of the line for life in Simpson. The horror of what happened to Megan forces things into focus. That's what facing death can do to you. Adrian realizes his patients deal with it every day—clogged arteries and failing hearts put them at the edge of that dark precipice. They know how fragile—how precarious—life can be.

Then he hears it.

The warning buzzer rasps. The photoelectric beam's been broken.

The police car's arrived. Some poor son of a bitch'll spend a lonely eight-hour shift in a patrol car outside the house, sucking down Dunkin' Donuts coffee and killing time.

He hears tires crunching on the gravel pathway.

Adrian drops the bag and moves to the front window.

A monster-sized Hummer appears. Adrian's insides jump.

The thing swerves amid a cloud of gravel dust, stops suddenly and sways in place, facing the cottage. The headlights are brilliant, blinding. Dust particles swirl in the light shafts, clearing slowly in the night breeze. Suddenly spotlights detonate on top of the Hummer. Blinding illumination floods the cottage. The living room seems superheated in strobelike incandescence.

Adrian reaches for his cell phone.

Beep, beep, beep . . . Nine-one-one.

With the cell to his ear, Adrian looks through the window.

A man stands beside the truck, his silhouette hulking, ominous. It's him. Wilson. No doubt about it. Adrian can make out his face; he sees the brutish, bulked-up build. It's the same guy from King's Corner and the interrogation room. He's unmistakable.

"Simpson Emergency Service . . ."

"Officer, this is Adrian Douglas at 38 Turtleback on the Gibson estate in Simpson. I'm in the gatekeeper's cottage. Conrad Wilson's *here*."

"Hold on," says the officer.

Adrian squints through the glare; white halos dance before him in a nimbus of dust and vapor—blurred and hazy. His heart slams in his chest, sending a rush of blood to his brain, where his thoughts whirl in a frenzied tumbling.

"You're sure it's him? It's the guy who attacked the nurse at Eastport General?"

"It's him," Adrian says and feels his breath coming in short bursts.

"We're on the way," says the officer.

"Make it quick," Adrian says, his heartbeat throttling through him. With his hands going weak, Adrian backs away from the window, the phone still at his ear.

The officer says something, but it's garbled. Adrian hears mangled voices, excitement, and there's static on the line. The connection's breaking up.

A flame flickers in Wilson's hand.

Holy shit . . . He's gonna burn me down.

"We're dispatching officers," the cop says.

The flame sputters. A cloth ribbon ignites. An orange tongue licks its way up the strip.

"He's gonna firebomb my house!" Adrian yells, snaps the cell shut, and pockets it.

Then he sees it: a shotgun in the man's other hand. Wilson strides toward the cottage, rears back, and the lapping flame arches through the night air.

Adrian bolts to the back of the cottage. At the rear door, he rushes into the night as he hears glass shatter; then a muffled *whoosh* comes from behind him and sounds like a blast furnace. An intense heat wave hits his back, and he smells gasoline and smoke.

He's out the door, running into the moonlit night.

Out back, he sees a police cruiser parked at an angle. He

rushes to it and peers inside. The front seat's empty, and where the on-board computer screen would be is a hole; tendrils of ripped wires dangle in disarray. On the rear bench seat, a cop lies facedown. He's hog-tied—feet bound with wire, handcuffed, gagged. With fear-filled eyes, the cop peers up at him. Adrian yanks at the door handle; it's locked. He runs to the other side and tugs. It's locked.

"Help's coming," Adrian yells, then turns and dashes toward the timber line.

He glances back. A red-orange glow fills the cottage. Flames lick up the walls as an instant later, a firestorm engulfs the cottage. It's an inferno.

Adrian stops, gazes at the blaze, and then sees Wilson circle the flaming cottage, his silhouette shimmering in orange heat waves. Wilson advances with the weapon—it looks like a stubby shotgun.

A flashlight beam pierces the night.

Adrian whirls and sprints toward the woods.

The light shimmers on the tree trunks, swiveling right, then left—searching him out.

Adrian crashes through underbrush, deeper into the forest, his thighs pumping as he churns his way through dried leaves and a fungal smell, with branches snapping, whipping at his face, his legs pistoning over pine needles, stones, jagged rocks, roots, and damp soil.

A hasty glance back: Wilson's coming. A light beam flickers through the tall timbers and shimmers on gray tree trunks, white pines, and a twisted tangle of honeysuckle tendrils and climbing vines.

Keep going. Don't stop.

The clear starlit night sky and moon illuminate the woods.

Adrian rushes, turns one way and then another, and keeps going as his legs churn through brush and bramble. He's run a few hundred yards, trampling through the woods. The burning cottage is no longer visible but for an orange halo in the night sky.

The light blinks behind him, casting flickering shadows slanting through the trees. The forest is filled with rocky outcroppings, bushes, and a meshwork of tortuous vines, broken tree limbs, and vegetation. The smell of pine resin fills Adrian's nostrils. His face burns where branches lashed him. He scrambles over a hillock and then half tumbles down a leaf-strewn swale into the woodland.

Just keep moving; don't stop. This bastard's come to kill you. He didn't want the cop. He wants you.

The blinking flashlight is far behind, but coming.

Adrian comes to a steep, leaf-covered gully. It dips to Comstock Brook far below. Adrian's been here before; he hiked in this area a few times last summer. He drops to his haunches, then onto his butt and skims down the embankment. Soil, dried leaves, and pebbles sift up into his pants. He descends amid cracking twigs and rustling leaves. The sound of rushing water caroms up from below.

At the bottom, the brook roils in white fury. Moonlight shimmers off rushing water, giving off a blue luminosity. Eddies swirl and boil with agitation. The air feels cold and damp. There's no real room to run, so he sloshes through the shallows. The embankments form a sheer drop on each side. White birch trees overhang the water in an arching canopy. He lurches through the ankle-deep water, then onto solid ground, running at the brook's edge.

He comes to a waterfall, maybe ten feet high. The brook rushes and tumbles to a turbulent pool below. White foam gives off moonlit phosphorescence.

He slides down a leaf-strewn path beside the falls, following the water.

Keep going. He can't be far behind.

The brook narrows and the water rushes faster. He leaps to the other side, where the bank is less dense with underbrush. He trots along a pebble-strewn path, using the thudding water rush as a guide. At one point, the brook slows to a gurgle; water slaps against the rocks.

The light flickers through the thicket. It's far behind now, but still coming.

Why am I following the water? He just moves along the brook and keeps coming after me. Didn't Megan say he's a hiker and cross-country skier . . . a goddamned mountain man? I'm making it too easy for him.

Adrian knows the trail. He'll head for open ground and trek over Ambler Hills toward Bald Hill. It's near Route 33, a country road with traffic where, if he's lucky, he can stop a car and get some help.

The brook widens. Massive moss-covered boulders jut from the water. The banks grow steeper. The current pounds its way over rocks and broken tree boughs. White water swirls in truculent eddies, sloshing back and forth.

The terrain is rocky now, covered with moss—wet and slippery. He could fall, sprain or break an ankle, twist a knee; then it's over. He'll lie there helplessly as Wilson advances. He edges along the water, weaving among the rocks. Adrian has no idea how far he's gone. Now everything looks different, foreign. And he's lost all sense of time—distance, too.

Just keep going . . . Don't stop.

Adrian knows, too, that a hiking trail meanders high above the brook. He looks up through the pale cast of moonlight. It's maybe twenty feet to the top. Looking at the steep wall, he finds a spot that looks scalable. He claws and kicks his way up the embankment. Soil crumbles in his grasp. He slips back.

He clutches a projecting rock and pulls himself upward. He kicks hard, alligator-style, and hauls his way up. Stones loosen and tumble down in a clattering mass. Loam, moss, and pebbles rain down on him—into his hair, eyes, and mouth. He spits, sputters, and shakes his head, grappling his way up the wall. His arms quiver; a burning ache penetrates his biceps and sears its way through his shoulders and back as he inches his way up toward the crest. Finally, his hand slaps over the top; his fingers curl around an exposed root.

Hoisting himself to the brim, he drags himself over, rolls onto his back, and lies there, staring up at the star-strewn sky. His body quakes; he's muscle-weak—depleted, feels wasted. His arms quiver, his chest heaves, and a burn comes from deep in his lungs. It's air hunger. He needs oxygen; he needs fuel to burn. He gulps frantically.

Jesus, I can't keep going like this.

He lies there spent, drained. He stares at the sky. There are billions of stars—a cloudy ocean of them—and they'll exist forever, no matter what happens on this night.

Still on his back, Adrian waits. It occurs to him that the shotgun and flashlight will make it hard for Wilson to scale the embankment. He won't have free hands for the climb, assuming he realizes Adrian scaled the wall.

Don't kid yourself. He'll know. Rocks and dirt are scattered everywhere. It's a trail as clear as daylight.

A light shimmers through the woods below.

An icy shiver crawls through Adrian. He's got to get up and keep moving. He stumbles to his feet and crashes through the woods. He's moving in a shuffle, an erratic shambling on unsteady legs, but he's moving.

Just keep going. Move your ass . . . and live.

The trail is a dreamscape of gray timber—ash trees, huge oaks, and scrub pines—bathed in a pale light. The path twists through saplings and brush and leads steadily uphill. Tree trunks loom over him, crouching eerily beside the path.

He's in a thicket now; it's nearly impenetrable. Twigs snap; stones crunch. He trips over a rock, sprawls forward, and scuffs his palms. Burns like hell. Burrs cling to his hair and prick his scalp—needle-sharp, penetrating. He rips out a clump; a patch of hair comes with it. Pain sears through his flesh. His hands are flayed, bloodied.

He crawls and shimmies ahead desperately on hands and knees. Thorns and bristles puncture him. A barberry bush rakes his face. He's amid dense undergrowth with needle-sharp projections. He lies still, panting, and then closes his eyes.

Twigs snap nearby. Another sound is followed by a shrill chirring. Adrian's heart jumps as he leaps to his feet, whirls, and sees two eyes glowing at ground level. It's a raccoon. The beast crashes through the brush and scuttles into the darkness.

On leaden legs, Adrian tramps through shadows in a gray glow. He forges ahead, through a thick tangle of sinewy vines where the trail comes to an abrupt end. He's out of the woods.

Adrian steps into the open and looks ahead to a vast series of fields and hills. He'll be in open country and easy to see in the moonlight.

He'll be a clear target—and the bastard has a shotgun.

Twenty-two

It's the first slope of Ambler Hills, bathed in murky moonlight—an enormous undulating expanse of hills where dairy farms once dotted the land. Now it lies unused; it's fallow pastureland—been this way for years. The fields are crisscrossed by man-made stone walls a few feet high. Over time, the hillsides have been overgrown with thistle, brambles, and thick field grasses. There are no trees or swales; Adrian knows he'll be a clear target on open range.

But he knows he has no choice if he's ever going to reach civilization. *Gotta take the chance; gotta go this route.* He guesses he's been running for ten minutes, maybe more, but he can't really tell. He breaks into a slow trot, jogging uphill through yellow, knee-high field grass. He churns his way upward, thrashing through the weeds and clogged growth of vegetation.

Adrian's cheeks burn. He swipes at them. In the moonlight, he sees a dark bloodstain on his hand. Thorns, bristles, and branches did it, lashed and cut him. This night's insane, but if he's going to live, he's gotta keep going.

Fighting gravity, he churns uphill. He's underestimated the incline's steepness and the toll it would take on him.

Keep going . . . Just keep moving. There's no time to think or worry . . . Just run.

His pace slows, but he slogs forward. His legs get heavier,

more leaden.

Staggering and gasping, Adrian closes in on a stone wall. It's a low outcropping, and he drops onto the stones, rolls over them, and tumbles to the other side, feeling spent. It's been years since he played baseball, ran laps around the field, did crunches, or lifted weights. His body's gone to hell.

He's gagging, legs quivering, muscles burning, vision fading. A spasm begins in his right leg, an incipient cramp that'll cripple him. If it happens, it'll all be over.

Wait . . . wait . . . muscle fatigue passes . . . You need time.

Lying there, looking up at the night sky, Adrian feels the violent drubbing of his heart and a crushing sensation in his chest. For a moment, he thinks he might be having a heart attack—just like Dad did all those years ago. That night in the Chinese restaurant flashes before his eyes.

But Adrian waits, knowing his heart rate will slow; he's certain his breathing will get less ragged with time. *Time . . . need more time, maybe a minute or two.* Slowly—forever, it seems—the burn in his legs subsides; the cramping sensation eases too, and his breathing's less coarse, not as labored. Oxygen will get to his muscles—burn off the lactic acid—and fresh blood will pump its way to his heart, lungs, and brain. He'll think clearly and devise a plan.

What fucking plan? Just run for your life. Keep going. That's all you can do.

Adrian struggles to his knees; he leans on the wall and peers at the woodland below. It's a black shadowline in the night, a distant mass at the edge of the downward slope. He sees only a dark heap of forest—a dense backdrop. He knows he's come a long way since the brook—through forest and tangled brush, up this endless incline. Every step's been uphill.

The embankment at the brook was treacherous. He wonders again if Wilson can scale it carrying both the shotgun and flashlight. Should he wait longer to see if he follows? It could be a mistake, but it might be worth the chance.

A breeze whispers across the field and washes over him, tussling his hair and cooling his damp scalp. The draft is redolent of willow, weeds, and wet earth. He inhales goldenrod, moss, and desiccated clover. He smells the night, wishing he could vanish into its dark mystery. A billowed cloud scuttles by, obscures the moon, and throws the field into a clutch of darkness. It passes; pale light returns.

In the distance, a siren wails. It reminds Adrian of a coyote's howl. The cops are nearing the cottage, a smoldering heap by now, he's certain. And he's here, on this hill, waiting to see if Wilson comes for him. The thought occurs to Adrian that maybe he'll survive this night, that he might outlast Conrad Wilson.

He squints toward the tree line, across the pallid wash of moonlight. He has some protection: semidarkness, a stone wall, and night shadows—all on a moonlit incline in the Connecticut foothills.

A light flickers through the woods.

It's Wilson. He's coming.

Adrian's skin crawls. A sick feeling rises from the pit of his stomach, and he feels like retching. His heart begins thumping, and its rampant beating pulses in his throat.

He's coming . . . How can he track me at night? This guy's some kind of animal.

The light advances and glimmers like some ghostly radiance.

A perilous realization seizes Adrian: there's something strange about this man; he's primitive, animal-like. He just keeps coming. A chill seeps through Adrian's blood and spreads to his flesh, invading him. He feels like prey.

The light stops, scans the field, and moves up the slope, right to the wall. It fixes on him, shining in his eyes. Adrian squints and fractures the beam into a white starburst.

Adrian suddenly realizes that in his uphill trek, he left a wake of trampled vegetation—an obvious path leading right to the wall.

The light begins moving up the slope and bobs up and down in cadence with Wilson's stride. He's advancing steadily toward him. No pause; Wilson just keeps coming.

Adrian pivots and dashes in a rushing crouch. The afterimage of the light speckles his retina. That slow burn begins in his lungs and spreads through his chest like a hot blade piercing his heart. He churns up the slope on legs going dead. Every cell in his body screams for oxygen, but he can't stop. He shimmies over another low wall and tumbles heavily to the ground. Jesus, it's so tempting to give up, to just lie here and gulp air, let it nourish him, and give him strength.

But he gets to his feet and trudges uphill.

In the distance, a siren pops and then keens through the night. It sounds closer than before.

The cops are coming. I dialed 911. Isn't it true that when you dial 911 on a cell phone, the connection gets locked and the phone turns into a GPS? Yes, the cops know where I am.

Adrian's thighs burn; they begin trembling. His pace slows to a shambling walk. He staggers sideways, then slips over another wall and glances back.

A cloud scuds across the sky and obliterates the moon. The hills darken in a somber shroud. A wind kicks up; the swishing of the grasses grows louder. It's black but for the light below—coming uphill. Wilson's advancing.

Adrian stands, then bends over, sets his hands on his knees, and sucks air desperately.

Gotta wait for the moon to come back . . .

The light keeps coming. He'll soon be in shotgun range.

Adrian's breath comes in wheezing, guttural bursts.

The cloud courses across the sky and obliterates the moonlight.

With each passing second, the light, bobbing up and down,

comes closer.

Suddenly, Adrian's right hamstring muscle cramps; a wrenching pain sears through the back of his thigh and the spasm drops him to one knee. The pain is blinding. *This could be it*, he thinks. He stretches the leg, rubs his thigh, massages the muscle, and feels the cramp ease.

The cloud streams away and bathes the field in watery light. Adrian gets up, limps uphill, then moves faster, trotting over the next hill. He comes to another wall, slips over it, and realizes he's on a rocky promontory.

He's on Bald Hill, a rock-strewn hillock where the early settlers buried their kin. How strange this is, how otherworldly: he's being chased by a madman to the entrance to Bald Hill Cemetery.

It's me and Wilson among the dead.

Twenty-three

Adrian stumbles past half-toppled tombstones in the old section of the cemetery.

Staggering along a stone wall, he coughs, begins retching, and feels he'll vomit, so he stops, leans on the wall, hangs his head, and feels ready to collapse. Time passes—a few seconds, maybe more—and the nausea fades. He grabs a hand-sized oval-shaped stone from atop the wall, then scrambles behind a grave marker, crouches, and waits with his breath rattling in his chest.

A few moments later, the light appears at the cemetery entrance.

Another siren wails—sounds closer. But Adrian can't tell where it is. It could take some time for the cops to get here.

Wilson's flashlight's at the edge of the cemetery; it scans left, then right. Adrian huddles behind the stone as the light moves over it and goes back and forth. Wilson moves forward—slowly—and stops and shines the flashlight down one aisle of tombstones and then another. He moves cautiously to the next row.

He knows I'm here. He'll comb through the place methodically—one row after another. I'm dead meat.

A tickle begins at the back of Adrian's throat; he fights it, knowing it's an incipient cough. He presses his tongue to the roof of his mouth, holds his breath, then swallows though there's no saliva. The tickle nags from deep behind his uvula. He licks his lips for moisture, but they're dry.

The tickle intensifies. He swallows—again and again—trying to stifle the cough. His eyes feel like they're swelling in their sockets. Adrian's chest heaves less violently; the flame in his legs subsides. The throat tickle ebbs, bit by bit, very slowly.

In a few minutes, the flashlight will come to Adrian's row. He knows he must move to better cover. It's risky; a snapping twig or crunching pebble could give him away. Then he's a dead man. But he'll be exposed if he stays behind this tombstone. He has no choice.

Still hunched, he looks behind him and sees a ten-foot-high tapered obelisk. Crouching, Adrian moves away from the light until he reaches the monolith, then ducks behind it. It's about four feet wide at the base and will give cover, so long as Adrian keeps to the far side of Wilson. Adrian realizes suddenly that his cell phone might go off; it would be the police calling. Then it's over. He reaches into his pocket, grabs the cell and, from behind the obelisk, hurls it into the night. It clatters against a distant headstone. The light beam flashes toward it, hovers, and then resumes its search.

Adrian angles himself at the obelisk's far side as Wilson moves closer.

The light beam scans row after row, coming closer.

Adrian moves laterally as the shaft illuminates each row of gravestones.

The light comes closer.

Adrian holds his breath.

Wilson treads between tombstones, shifting the beam left, then right, then straight ahead. He'll come to the obelisk, and then he'll be inches away from Adrian.

Adrian's body goes taut and then quivers in anticipation. He clutches the rock.

The light shaft shines on the ground, forming a white oval.

A sudden wind kicks up and gusts through the graves in an

eerie whine. Adrian can no longer hear Wilson. But he can see the light beam on the ground.

Adrian's pulse thunders in his ears. His face feels hot, flushed. He's coiled in readiness, quivering.

The beam hovers on the ground. Its shape changes from a circle to an oval. The cone of light elongates and moves closer.

Wilson is beside the obelisk.

The shotgun barrel appears, waist high. It stops, hangs in midair, and slants downward.

Adrian waits, pressed to the monument's granite, inches from the gun's muzzle. His entire body shudders.

Wilson must be straining to hear him. But the wind gusts in shrill eddies through the graveyard. Adrian is poised, ready, rock in hand.

The shotgun barrel hovers so close he can touch it. It hangs there, a lethal-looking blue-black tube.

With a burst, Adrian's legs uncoil; he swings, and the stone slams into Wilson's head. There's a deafening blast as an orange tongue of flame leaps from the gun.

Adrian grabs the barrel. The percussion shock shakes him as he yanks the muzzle upward. Blood pours from Wilson's scalp, over his ear, forming a wide runnel. Adrian realizes the rock only grazed Wilson's head. It's a scalp wound.

Adrian's right hand locks on the barrel; his left clutches the stock. He yanks the shotgun and pulls with all the force he can muster. Wilson has the trigger housing and clasps the barrel; he pulls. The weapon is between them, angled to the side.

Adrian pushes, then pulls, trying to twist the gun away. Wilson swerves and yanks with such power that Adrian's feet leave the ground. He's launched into the air, hurled aside like a hand puppet. He lands on his feet, still clutching the shotgun. He knows he can't let go. But his grip feels slippery—from blood, sweat, and the rawness of his hands—and he knows he can't hold on for long. But he holds, pushes, pulls, and turns, and both men grunt as the struggle goes on.

Suddenly, Wilson propels Adrian backward. He's rammed against the obelisk. A cracking shock shoots through Adrian's back and head as he slams against the stone. A starburst of white lights explodes in his eyes, but he holds on. Wilson forces the barrel upward to Adrian's throat; Adrian's skull is pressed to the granite while the steel tube presses his windpipe. Adrian sees the feral look in Wilson's eyes and the spittle on his lips. He smells Wilson's sour breath, sees a stream of blood on his face, hears his guttural grunts, and feels his power.

Adrian gurgles and chokes. He can't get air, so he twists his head to the side, keeping his windpipe open. He tries to shove the gun back and let in precious air, but the barrel is wedged deeply into his neck, squeezing the carotid artery and cutting off the blood supply. Adrian feels dizzy. The night starts going hazy and white, and he knows he's fading.

Adrian's vision dims. He's weakening, going down. His eyes bulge in their sockets. His head swims. He feels a frantic surge, knowing he can't last much longer. As if by instinct, Adrian snaps his right knee up—into Wilson's groin. Wilson grunts as breath bursts from his lungs.

Adrian pushes and drives Wilson back. They grapple for control—pulling, pushing, twisting—left, then right, up and down. Adrian is thrust sideways—all two hundred pounds of him—like an empty sack.

A half step back—Adrian jerks, pushes, and twists the gun. His arms cramp; a spasm clutches his shoulders. He realizes he's no match for Wilson. The muzzle moves toward him—nears Adrian's ear. He tugs the barrel. In a desperate move, he tries to flip Wilson over his hip, but Wilson yanks back. They stumble to the right, and Adrian's grip weakens. Wilson will soon have the shotgun.

Suddenly, Wilson's feet fly up—damp moss on stone. He arches through the air, and his head slams into a gravestone; Adrian hears a sickening thud. Wilson bounces and lies still, inert, his head angled to the side.

Weapon in hand, Adrian—with a swift plunge—slams the gun butt into Wilson's face. The impact sends a thump through Adrian's arms. He hears bones shatter—a sharp, snapping crack, almost like cellophane crumpling—and blood sprays everywhere. Adrian raises the weapon, ready to smash again. He feels a primal surge of power and realizes a beast within him has roared to life.

Wilson lies in a limp heap. Adrian wonders if Wilson's faking, playing possum.

He whirls the weapon; the muzzle snaps into position at Wilson's head. He pumps another round into the chamber.

Goodbye, motherfucker.

A rush of rage ramps through Adrian. He knows he can pull the trigger and blow out Wilson's brainpan.

You're one squeeze away from over. Yes... Goodbye, motherfucker.

Adrian's hands shake—a violent and sick trembling. His finger slides onto the trigger and begins the squeeze; the mechanism engages, ready to release the hammer, hit the load, and spew a burst of pellets.

But he doesn't do it. Instead, his foot slams into Wilson's groin.

No response.

Adrian tastes it and smells it—the urge to kill—to batter Wilson, smash him into pulp. He's in another world. The graveyard's pale light, the weight and heat of the shotgun, its oiled smell, the scent of earth and sweat and blood, and the singed stench of spent buckshot in the wind—it's woven a sick spell, taken Adrian from himself.

A shell sits in the gun's chamber, waiting to take a life—the life that would have taken Megan's and his. This man would've killed him—wasted him with no remorse. He deserves neither mercy nor pity. Adrian knows he can snuff him out, ending his existence, and in that moment, he feels an overpowering wish to bring death to this man.

The sirens are closer. There's still time. Adrian can kill this maniac—blow him away—and no one would ever know the difference. Not a soul on earth would know it was in cold blood.

And you're not a physician, not here, not now. This is no operating theater. You're standing in dirt and mud and rocks, you've come through woods and hills where you've been hunted like prey, and you've survived. You should terminate this son of a bitch. For Marlee's sake, for Marlee's, and for yourself; too, you should end it, here and now.

Adrian yanks the pump mechanism. It slides back, clacks loudly, and a shell ejects and hits the ground. Don't murder him . . . The man's crazy, he thinks. But then an overpowering urge—an insane surge of rage seizes Adrian—and he pushes the pump action forward. There's a snapping sound. Another cartridge slaps heavily into the chamber. The weapon is locked and loaded—ready to fire.

Nobody gets out of this life alive, motherfucker.

The barrel's at Wilson's head. The trigger yields gently. It takes so little pressure—an ounce, maybe two—and he presses harder so the trigger nears the point of no return.

Adrian jerks the shotgun skyward. A hot flash roars from the muzzle. He feels the blowback from the gun's breech as it blasts into his shoulder.

He racks the gun again and pumps another shot into the night.

He pumps again—a shucking sound—and shoots, then pumps and shoots again and again, emptying the chamber.

Eight shells, one after another, all blown out. Yellow plastic casings litter the earth. The air smells of propellant powder—a mix of charcoal and sulfur. The sooty odor stings Adrian's nostrils. His ears ring and his arms feel dead. His eyes fill with water.

Wilson will never know how close to death he came. He'll know only the bleakness of prison—the cinder-block walls and razor wire—caged like the beast he is, behind bars with the scum of the earth, extruded from society with tattooed shit-flingers and bellowing psychos in some gang-infested, filth-ridden hellhole.

Adrian pats him down. No weapon. No cell phone. No wallet, nothing. Just Conrad Wilson, lying in a lake of his own blood with his tongue protruding.

Adrian's blood hums. He feels incendiary, yes, like he's on fire and could explode. Adrian tells himself his job is to mend, not destroy. Not to shoot, stab, smash, or pound. He's spent years studying biology, chemistry, anatomy, physiology. Countless hours in hospital wards and operating rooms, forestalling death, preserving life. Adrian realizes he's viewed it with a certain reverence; it's been his life's work. He's a healer. It's been his way in the world.

Fixing God's mistakes.

But nothing stays the same. Everything changes if you give it enough time.

The moon's luminescence gives Wilson's shattered face a ghoulish look, with his blood-drenched hair and crushed cheekbone, blood leaking onto the granite slab.

Adrian wonders how this man could have been someone with whom Megan shared her life.

The puddle of blood spreads, glistening like an oil slick in the moonlight. Scalp wounds can be nasty. The bastard will bleed out, go empty, and die. It serves the fucker right. And you'll go on with your life and try to forget this night and what you did.

Or you could rip off your shirt, stanch the bleeding until the medics get here . . . You're a physician . . . a healer . . . You know what to do.

Pressing his ear to Wilson's chest, he hears the man's heartbeat rushing in a thready symphony, like a hummingbird's fluttering wings—a sure sign he'll lapse into shock. In maybe a minute or two, he'll bleed out and be gone.

Does he really want this bastard to die?

Yes, he does.

Shame shudders through him. He's appalled by his own fury.

Adrian waits for numbness, hoping for some kind of disconnect from the rage, from the wanton wish for this man's death, from his own remorse, from fear and guilt and the absolute horror of it all. He's appalled at himself. It's stomach-churning revulsion, and it sickens him to his core. Jesus, how he wants to not care, to not give a shit, but that's not him. It's an impossibly callous level of indifference. So Adrian tears off his shirt and presses it to Wilson's scalp. Blood blossoms into the cotton and seeps through the fabric, soaking Adrian's fingers. He presses harder; the bunched shirt squishes in his hand.

The wind kicks up and whistles in a shrieking eddy between the granite stones. Adrian's feet are soaked, numb. His palms burn; he's torn and bleeding. His arms and legs feel weak, jelly-like—dead. There's a high-pitched ringing in his ears—he's shotgun deaf—and everything sounds muffled, clogged, distant.

Sirens wail, then burp; then there's a dying whine. Adrian hears car engines. The cops are here. Doors slam. Shouts carry on the wind, which now gusts through the headstones with lusty howls. Lights whirl in a multicolored frenzy; some pulse and flicker while others shoot blinding beams into the night. Adrian hears voices, radio static, crepitating commands, police jargon, men running.

On his knees between the graves, in milky moonlight, Adrian presses his blood-soaked shirt to the slippery wetness of Wilson's wound, trying to keep a life from leaking away—trying to stop the dying of this man so mired in hatred, rage, and violence.

The wind gathers more forcefully, and a shrieking eddy of air lashes between the gravestones. Flashlights approach, gravel crunches beneath jump boots, voices grow louder and frantic, and Adrian hears a police dog's throaty barking, followed by growling; the dog must smell blood.

Crouched beside the man who tried to kill Megan and then him, Adrian shivers, surrounded by tumult, and inhales the organic smell of earth and blood and torn flesh. He waits in this graveyard above the dust of the dead—weak, drenched, bruised, and bleeding—and amid a swirl of lights and clamor of voices, he cannot believe he somehow managed to survive this night.

Twenty-four

Dr. John Grayson nods at the cop sitting in the chair outside Conrad Wilson's hospital room. The cop nods back. It's the same Eastport officer who was here yesterday, and he's been told that Grayson is evaluating Wilson's mental state.

Wilson occupies a single room. He lies in bed, wearing short-sleeved, blue hospital pajamas. His left wrist is cuffed to the bed-rail. Entering the room, Grayson notices the television is on and muted. Wilson's bed is in the half-raised position, and he stares off into space.

As a former NCAA basketball player at Duke, Grayson's encountered some pretty big guys, and while Wilson's by no means the tallest, he's possibly the most formidable-looking man Grayson's ever seen. He looks like what he once was, a champion wrestler—a bulldozer of a man. He has plenty of bulk, but he's sinewy and athletic-looking, too. His thick forearms ripple with bands of tendon and muscle, as though heavy-duty cables reside within them. And his face—tough-looking, sullen—reminds Grayson of the mixed martial arts fighters he's seen on Spike TV.

Huge purple swellings bulge beneath Wilson's eyes. His right cheek was reconstructed by the plastic surgeons and it's swollen and discolored. The hair over his right ear has been shaved where the scalp was sutured and bandaged. Grayson thinks the guy looks like a gargoyle.

"How're you feeling?" Grayson asks.

"Could be better," Wilson says with a grimace. His nostrils quiver slightly, as though he's sniffing something. Wilson pulls at the handcuff and rattles the bedrail. His forearm muscles writhe beneath snakelike cords of veins.

Grayson pulls up a chair, sits down, and crosses one long leg over the other.

Wilson shifts his bulk. "Hey, Doc, you're not gonna ask me where we are or what the date is, are you? Or if I can spell 'world' forward and backward?"

"I won't insult your intelligence."

Wilson exhales. "I don't have time for dumb questions."

"Just one more question," Grayson says. "How much is one hundred forty-four divided by twelve, plus the number of days in the month of April, divided by two, minus the number on a clock when the long hand is at three forty-five?"

"Twelve," Wilson says quickly. He peers out the window, obviously bored.

Grayson can barely believe the mind-blowing speed of Wilson's calculation. He's megasmart; his intelligence level is off the charts. He decides he'll have Jim Morgan give him a battery of neuropsychological tests and then an MMPI.

"You're right," Grayson says, nodding.

"Piece of cake . . . and boring, too."

"Let's get back to three nights ago," Grayson says. "You stashed the pickup in Tommy Parker's garage. Then took his Hummer and drove to Dr. Douglas's house, right? What then?"

"There was that cop in his cruiser out front. I snuck up on him, dragged him outta the car, and punched his lights out, roped him like a rodeo calf, and drove the thing to the back. Then I waited for Douglas down the road. You know the rest of the story. And I woke up here. And now you guys're testing me every hour . . . neurologists, X-rays, an MRI, and now you . . . a tall shrink who needs a shave," Wilson says, glancing at Grayson's three-day stubble.

"Hey, look at that bitch," Conrad blurts, his eyes fixed on the TV. A redheaded reporter is speaking on CNN. "She reminds me of that whore Megan Haggarty."

"Why do you say Megan's a whore?"

"It's obvious. She hooked up with this Douglas bastard at Yale six years ago."

"Six years ago? What makes you say that?"

"I checked the cafeteria out at New Haven and at Eastport General, too. I could smell sex in the air."

"But they met only a little more than a *month* ago."

"Bullshit. We break up. She gets a restraining order. I go to Colorado. Then she and Douglas leave Yale—together. And they *both* come here . . . to Eastport General. That's no coincidence. It was planned. And the restraining order was part of the deal. I couldn't get within five hundred feet of the cheating bastards."

Grayson's thoughts whirl. Wilson's opening up, showing some emotion. Not acting like an android or automaton, the way Pat Mulvaney described he'd been at the police interrogation. Though Grayson isn't sure, he finds himself thinking that maybe someone can reach Conrad Wilson, bring out some humanity.

"Conrad, tell me about your father."

"I don't have one . . ."

"I mean your adoptive father."

"The bastard beat the shit outta me. He'd take off his belt and strap me across the ass till I couldn't sit for days."

"And your mother . . . ?"

"You mean the woman who adopted me?"

"Right."

"She let that bastard abuse me. She bought a cushion so I could sit after he beat my ass."

"How did you feel about your father?"

"He wasn't my father."

"But how did you feel about him?"

"How the fuck ya think I felt?"

"And your mother?"

"She never stopped that bastard."

"You think it's why you're so angry now?"

Wilson stares out the window.

"Don't you want to understand your anger . . . your rage?"

"There's nothin' to understand. Except my ex-wife was doin' another guy and it's gone on for years . . . like I was a worthless nobody."

"Like the way you felt as a kid . . . worthless? You didn't know your real parents?"

"Go *fuck* yourself, Doc."

"But how can you be so sure about Megan and Adrian Douglas?"

"I just am; that's all."

"It would be good to have proof, wouldn't it?"

"What're you tryin' to imply, Doc, that I'm paranoid?"

"I didn't say that. I'm—"

"That's *exactly* what you're sayin'. You shrinks gotta label everyone. If a guy can't get it up, it's erectile dysfunction. So you prescribe Viagra 'cause you're hooked into the pharmaceutical industry."

Grayson smiles and says nothing.

"I know your game, Doc, because I read. I'm smarter than you think."

"I know that, Conrad. But the past can explain some things."

"Ah . . . that's all crap that can't be redone."

"You think it scarred you? Never knowing your real parents and being abused?"

"It killed part of me. But it doesn't matter."

"Why not?"

"All that matters is what's ahead of you. And you know what's ahead for me? Some Legal Aid lawyer was in here. Guy named Kovac. He talked about coppin' an insanity plea."

"Kovac's a damned good lawyer. You're lucky, Conrad."

"So what do I have, a shrink and the public defender? What a team."

"Maybe . . . we'll have you seen by a few psychiatrists."

"Like I don't know which end is up?"

"Well, this whole thing about Megan Haggarty . . . and Adrian Douglas."

"Is that *crazy*? That I still think about what that whore did? That's crazy?"

"Well, I . . ."

"In a way, *love* is crazy. It's fuckin' mad, isn't it? It means that someone . . . Ah, fuck it!" Wilson turns away and stares out the window once again.

Grayson's eyes follow his. The air is dazzling on this sunlit autumn morning, so radiantly clear, Grayson thinks he sees across the Sound to Long Island's North Shore, to Stony Point, where he was a high school point guard before going to Duke on a basketball scholarship.

"And just *who* defines crazy, huh?" Conrad says. "The psychiatrists? The lawyers? The crooked judges? The corporate crooks and the union big shots? White-collar robbers pickpocketing the public? All a bunch of money maggots? Who're *you* to decide I'm nuts?

"And Megan Haggarty—the bitch kept her maiden name. I'm surprised she didn't name the *kid* Haggarty, too . . . or *Douglas*. After all, I didn't match up to the fancy doctors at the hospital." Wilson pauses and seems to be thinking. "So now I dream about snappin' her neck, and in the dream I hear the bones crack. The whore."

Grayson realizes that for the first time, Conrad Wilson's eyes seem alive.

"And when I think about Douglas, I just wanna kill 'em both for what they did."

"She's a big part of your life, Conrad."

"It's all so goddamned crazy," Conrad says, gazing out the window.

Grayson notices Conrad Wilson's huge right hand curl into a white-knuckled fist, and sitting there, he has a strange feeling about Conrad Wilson—an eerie sense that this man is like no other patient he's ever seen in his entire career.

Part III

Twenty-five

Adrian enters Bridgeport Superior Court with Jack Farley, the ADA assigned to the case. Farley wears a blue-black suit with barely visible pinstripes, a white shirt, and a navy-colored cloth tie. He looks like a mortician. They've already met to discuss Adrian's testimony.

Farley shows the court officers his attorney's pass as Adrian goes through the metal detector. "It's the defendant's right to a speedy trial," Farley says at the elevator bank. "But this is a competency hearing to see if Wilson's fit to stand trial. The whole thing is moving at lightning speed because of Walter Kovac, Wilson's attorney. He's a very aggressive guy. In fact, he's leaving the public defender's office and joining a criminal defense firm. This is a trophy case for him because Wilson's pleading an insanity defense."

"So that's why there's a competency hearing?"

"Yes. If he's claiming insanity, the judge has to be satisfied Wilson understands things and can cooperate with his lawyer."

"Insanity defense . . . like he's just nuts, so he can get away with what he did?"

Farley laughs and says, "People have misconceptions about the insanity defense. It's used very rarely and hardly ever succeeds. It gets attention because the big-name cases are in the public eye—John Hinckley, the Unabomber, Ted Bundy, John Wayne

Gacy. And believe me, Kovac wants publicity."

Adrian thinks, *Maybe Wilson is nuts . . . Megan certainly believes so.*

"I'm glad you could come," Farley says. "I know you're busy, but I want you to see Kovac in action." Farley smiles, showing pink gums with squarish teeth. They remind Adrian of a row of Chiclets.

The walls, benches, desks—everything in the courtroom—is blond oak. The windowless room is lit by recessed fluorescent lighting.

A woman and two men sit in the gallery's first row. Farley tells Adrian they're the psychiatrists who evaluated Conrad Wilson for the competency hearing. Farley and Conrad's attorney, Walter Kovac, shake hands; each stands behind a lectern facing the bench.

When he sees Conrad Wilson sitting at the defense table, Adrian's heart begins pounding. The hulking man is manacled and wears an orange jumpsuit nearly bursting from the pressure of his muscular frame. It's hard to believe Adrian is sitting a few rows behind the man who tracked him so relentlessly that night. It all floods back to him at that moment.

Judge Henry Burke enters from chambers. He's a portly man with a drooping double chin and dewlaps; the horseshoe-shaped hair on his scalp has been shaved bald. He wears wire-rim glasses that reflect the overhead lights, and his black robes flow freely over his generous belly.

Burke sits at the bench and glances at the court reporter. "Gentlemen, we're on the record," he says.

Kovac's in his late thirties; he has a salt-and-pepper crew cut and a squarish face. His eyes seem distorted behind the thick lenses; they remind Adrian of goldfish in a round bowl. Kovac wears a brown suit that looks like it came off the rack at Kohl's.

"As you know," Burke says, "there was a hearing in accordance with Connecticut General Statute 54-47, which allows for a court determination of probable cause. The hearing determined there was sufficient evidence to warrant a trial. Are we all in agreement?"

"Yes, Your Honor," Farley and Kovac pipe up.

"I understand the defendant has made an NGRI plea. Is that correct?"

"Yes, Your Honor," says Kovac.

"And since he's pleading not guilty by reason of insanity, we're holding a competency hearing to decide if the defendant understands what a trial is and if he can cooperate with his attorney."

The court reporter's fingers glide over her machine.

"Mr. Kovac, I assume you've informed your client about an NGRI defense?"

"Yes, Your Honor, I have."

"Now," Burke says, shuffling papers. "I understand the defendant has been examined by two forensic psychiatrists and a neuropsychologist, correct?"

"Yes, Your Honor," Kovac says.

"Are they present in court today?"

"Yes, Your Honor," Kovac says.

"I read their certified reports," says the judge. "If I were to question the doctors at length, would they testify in accordance with their reports?"

"I think the doctors can speak for themselves, Your Honor," says Kovac.

"Dr. Grayson," asks the judge, looking at a tall man seated in the first row, "if you were to testify, would it be in substantial accordance with your very detailed report?"

"It would, Your Honor," Grayson says. He appears to Adrian to be about forty years old, at least six four, and well built. An athletic-looking guy, for sure. He has short brown hair and sports a three- or four-day growth of facial stubble.

"And Dr. DuPont?"

A willowy, chestnut-haired woman stands. She's in her midthirties, with large, almond-shaped eyes and a gamin face. Her hair is stylishly short; her lipstick is crimson and her upper lip forms a perfect Cupid's bow. She wears a smart-looking charcoal-gray suit that accentuates her trim yet curvaceous figure.

"The same question is put to you."

"I would testify in accordance with my report, Your Honor," says DuPont.

"And the psychologist, Dr. Morgan?"

A pudgy, rumpled-looking guy wearing a tweed sport jacket and black slacks says, "I would testify in accordance with my report, Your Honor."

The judge nods. "Okay, then, the reports will be entered into evidence as sworn testimony. Do both attorneys agree that we can dispense with the doctors' live testimony?"

"Yes, Your Honor," respond Farley and Kovac together.

"Good," says the judge. "We'll save time." Burke adjusts his glasses and looks at the attorneys. "It's clear . . . the mental health professionals agree unanimously that the defendant is competent to stand trial." Burke looks over at Kovac. "As you surely know, gentlemen, the Constitution guarantees the right of the defendant not to be put on trial unless he has sufficient mental ability to consult with his lawyer and understands the proceedings against him."

"Yes, Your Honor," both attorneys say.

"So, Counselor," Burke says, peering at Kovac, "is it your position that despite his presumed mental illness and the insanity plea, your client can understand the proceedings and can assist in his own defense?"

"It is, Your Honor. It's also our contention that when he

committed these acts, Conrad Wilson was suffering from a severe mental disorder—"

"Mr. Kovac," Judge Burke cuts in, "you're getting ahead of yourself. We're here to determine the defendant's *competency to stand trial*, nothing more. I'm concerned about his state of mind *now* . . . as we proceed to trial."

Adrian is glad Megan chose not to attend the hearing. He imagines her shuddering at the sight of Conrad, and he's certain the lawyerly arguments about Conrad's state of mind—either when he attacked them or right now—would throw her into a state of high-voltage panic.

Judge Burke peers at the defense table. "Will the defendant please rise?"

Conrad stands with his manacled hands in front of him. His biceps and forearms bulge from the short sleeves of the jumpsuit. Two beefy court officers stand nearby; they peer warily at him.

Thoughts of the night on Bald Hill flood Adrian.

"Mr. Wilson," Burke says, "who's the man standing closest to you?"

"Mr. Kovac, my lawyer."

"What's his job here in court?"

"To defend me."

"What does that mean?"

"He'll question witnesses and he'll protect my rights."

"And, Mr. Wilson, what's the difference between the truth and a falsehood?"

"The truth tells the reality of things, not something made up. A falsehood is a distortion of the truth or a fabrication such as the—"

"And, sir," Burke interrupts, "Do you believe Mr. Kovac will do his best to defend you against these charges?"

"Yes."

"And do you understand the consequences of this trial that

you're pressing to have very quickly?"

"Yes."

"And what are they?"

"I've already admitted what I did. If I'm found guilty, I'll go to prison. If I'm found not guilty because the jury thinks I'm crazy, I'll be sent to a mental institution."

"And you're willing to take the legal advice of your counsel, Mr. Kovac?"

"Yes."

"Is there anything else you want to say at this time?"

"Just that Megan Haggarty lied to me . . . She—"

"You can assert that at trial, Mr. Wilson. Thank you. You may be seated."

The judge says, "I want the record to reflect that both sides agree on the issue of competency. Is that correct?"

"Yes, Your Honor," say the attorneys.

"Then it's settled. I find based on the evidence provided that Mr. Wilson is capable of participating in his defense. I find further that he understands the nature and consequences of a criminal trial and of pleading NGRI.

"I hereby order—on the record—in accordance with the defendant's request under the Constitution's due process clause that we proceed to trial within sixty days as requested by the defendant. It so happens that my calendar is open and I'll be the sitting judge. Meanwhile, the defendant is remanded to the Bridgeport Correctional Center's psychiatric unit to await trial."

Twenty-six

"I understand there's another issue," says the judge, rubbing his lower chin.

"Yes, Your Honor," Kovac says. "The state is trying to *force* my client to take an antipsychotic drug called Risperdal. It's my client's right to refuse the medication."

"Your Honor," Farley says, "the people want to ensure that the defendant *remains* competent during the trial. It would be a terrible waste of time if, during the trial, Mr. Wilson became so disturbed that his competency is lost. We want to avoid a mistrial if he has to be institutionalized for competency to be restored."

"Restoration of competency?" Burke says. "That's not an issue, Mr. Farley."

"Your Honor," Kovac calls, "Mr. Farley's being disingenuous. Forcing Mr. Wilson to take the drug violates his civil rights. In fact, I have an expert here who will testify about Risperdal."

"Who's the expert?"

"Dr. Nicole DuPont, Your Honor."

"I'll hear the doctor's testimony, but let's keep it brief. I don't want to turn this into a minitrial."

"Yes, Your Honor." Kovac turns and says, "The defense calls Dr. Nicole DuPont."

Nicole DuPont walks quickly across the well to the witness chair. She strikes Adrian as an attractive and self-possessed woman.

After she's sworn in, Kovac asks, "Dr. DuPont, will you tell the court about your professional training and education?"

She turns to Burke and says, "I attended college and law school at Yale. I then went to medical school at Harvard and did my psychiatric residency at Massachusetts General."

"So, Dr. DuPont, you're a physician, a psychiatrist, *and* an attorney?" Kovac says.

"Yes, I am."

"And your current work is where?"

"I work at Whitehall Forensic Institute with a team of mental health professionals."

"I'm familiar with Whitehall," says the judge. "A highly respected institution for the criminally insane. And your credentials, Dr. DuPont . . . most impressive."

"Thank you, Your Honor." A hint of a smile forms on DuPont's bow-shaped lips.

"So, Doctor, you're a *forensic* psychiatrist?" Kovac asks.

"Yes."

The judge's lips curl into a smile. He nods and closes his eyes.

Adrian has the impression that Nicole DuPont is seducing the judge—intellectually. And there's nothing wanting when it comes to her looks, either.

"Doctor," says Kovac, "will you please tell the court about Risperdal?"

"Risperdal belongs to the class of antipsychotic drugs that are benzisoxasole derivatives. Among other things, it suppresses serotonin receptors in the brain."

"Doctor," Burke says, "can you please put that in plain English?" He smiles self-deprecatingly. *He's playing—acting the down-home country judge,* thinks Adrian—*the judicial equivalent of your favorite uncle.*

"Yes, Your Honor." DuPont's lips curl into a fleeting smile. "By altering the brain's chemistry, Risperdal can stop hallucinations and delusions. It tamps down psychotic thinking and perceptions."

Burke nods and leans back in his leather chair. Adrian is certain the judge enjoys watching and listening to DuPont.

"So it would wipe out the defendant's delusional thinking?" Kovac asks.

"Probably."

"Now, Dr. DuPont, what, if any, dangers does Risperdal pose?"

"First, there's neuroleptic malignant syndrome. It includes high fever, muscle rigidity, altered mental status, irregular pulse, and blood pressure changes that can cause death. Then there are abnormal muscle movements, which may be irreversible."

"Are there any other dangerous side effects of these drugs?"

She launches into a toxicologic tsunami of reactions: blood disorders, diabetes, and thinking abnormalities along with difficulties such as somnolence, fatigue, and rashes.

Judge Burke's face turns pallid. "Doctor," he says, "is there a less-intrusive way of obtaining the same antipsychotic effect?"

"No, Your Honor."

Burke peers at Farley and removes his glasses.

"Your Honor?" says DuPont in a honeyed voice that reminds Adrian of syrup.

She has her act down . . . cold. She's a real pro . . .

"Yes, Doctor?"

"May I remind the court of a Supreme Court case in 1992, *Riggins v. Nevada*?"

"Objection, Your Honor," calls Farley, red-faced. "Dr. DuPont is testifying as a physician and psychiatrist . . . not as a legal expert."

"Your Honor," Kovac counters, "Dr. DuPont is also an *attorney*. She's worked for the ACLU and won the Edgerton Civil Liberties Award. She's eminently qualified to testify about legal issues."

"So," Burke says, "you're offering the doctor as an omnibus witness?"

"Yes, Your Honor."

"I see no reason to preclude the doctor's opinion." Burke turns to DuPont and says, "Doctor, I'm vaguely familiar with the case, but will you refresh the court's recollection?"

Nicole flashes a demure smile. "David Riggins stabbed a man to death in Nevada, was arrested, and then complained of hearing voices," she says. "A psychiatrist prescribed Mellaril, another antipsychotic. Riggins was found competent to stand trial. He planned to present an insanity defense and asked that the Mellaril be stopped so the jury could see his mental state *first-hand* rather than get a false impression induced by the medication. He claimed that for the jury to see him in other than his mental state at the time of the crime would deny him due process. His request was refused."

Burke nods and leans closer to Nicole DuPont.

"The Supreme Court decided that the forced administration of antipsychotic medication violated the defendant's rights guaranteed under the Sixth and Fourteenth Amendments."

"The opinion was . . . ?" Burke asks.

"The court held that a defendant has a valid right, protected under the due process clause, to refuse these drugs. In order to *force* the drug on the defendant, the state must prove the medication is necessary for the defendant's safety and that of others."

Burke turns to Farley. "Is the defendant dangerous to anyone?"

"*Look* at this man, Your Honor," says Farley. "He could take down five men."

"How he *looks* is not at issue. I asked if he's *dangerous*."

"He's dangerous to Dr. Douglas and to Megan Haggarty, Your Honor."

"But the defendant's incarcerated. They're safe now. Isn't that correct?"

"Yes, Your Honor."

"Has he threatened suicide?"

"No, Your Honor."

"Has he threatened anyone else?"

"Not that I know of, Your Honor."

"Your Honor," Nicole says from the witness box. "If I may?"

"Yes, Doctor." Burke faces her. His glasses glimmer in the lighting. A hint of a smile forms on his lips. He's enchanted by Nicole DuPont.

"Mr. Wilson has a *monomania* about Ms. Haggarty and Dr. Douglas. His psychosis is limited to *them* and them *alone*. He's not a threat to anyone else."

"Thank you, Dr. DuPont," Judge Burke says with a quick smile. "You've been very helpful. You may step down."

Nicole walks back to the gallery carrying a small purse clutched to her side. She sits next to Grayson.

Burke says, "My recollection of the Riggins case is refreshed. Any proposed treatment must be to ensure his safety or that of others. Mr. Wilson remains incarcerated, so Ms. Haggarty and Dr. Douglas are safe."

Adrian feels his chest tighten.

"The defendant has the right to refuse medication so the jury may evaluate his state of mind as it was when he committed the acts for which he's being tried. We will *not* deny the defendant due process. The defendant's motion is granted."

Burke looks down at some papers and says, "Now, as for the trial, how long do you estimate it will take?"

"I have only three witnesses," says Farley.

"I also have three witnesses," Kovac says. "Two of the experts whose reports you've read and the defendant himself."

The judge flips open his calendar book. "I estimate a three-day trial, not including jury selection, to begin on Monday, December 12," says Burke. "Jury selection will begin on the fifth. No delays, no excuses, gentlemen."

The gavel slaps down.

Twenty-seven

Sitting in the witness chair, Megan's innards tremble. She suddenly feels light-headed, and the courtroom sways. She keeps her eyes focused on the gallery and avoids looking at the defense table.

Farley's voice sounds distant. There are questions about the marriage and Conrad's fits of jealous rage. Megan thinks she's controlling the shaking, but her voice warbles and sounds clogged, small and insubstantial in her ears. Conrad is an immense blur to her right, about thirty feet away at the defense table. She's intensely aware of his eyes scouring her.

Farley asks her about the breakup and Conrad moving to Colorado. Then there's a series of questions about the night at Eastport Hospital.

Megan's stomach churns, and her pores open as sweat trickles down her back. She feels a wave of coldness, yet the sweat seems to boil on her skin. Describing the locker room, her voice falters.

Farley prods her gently. "So then you saw him there . . ."

Megan shudders as it all flashes back: the gurneys and mattresses, the dank smell of the place; then she sees—actually visualizes—the elevator and that brick wall; she hears the shrieking bell, and her thoughts tumble. Suddenly, the courtroom walls move in. The room lurches and begins spinning; she clutches the arms of the witness chair.

"Your Honor," calls Kovac, "there's no need for this. Mr. Wilson has admitted what he did, and the jury knows every detail of it from Mr. Farley's opening statement. This is really a victim impact statement and doesn't address the issue at trial, namely my client's *mental state* at the time."

"We'll have a sidebar," Judge Burke says, summoning the lawyers with a wave of his hand.

Megan looks down at her hands. They look like they belong to someone else. Her skin feels like it's shredding, about to fray and drop to the floor. Muffled words come from the bench.

. . . Your Honor . . . the jury needs to know what happened.

. . . But, Your Honor, Conrad Wilson's state of mind at the time is all that's relevant.

Megan's thoughts swim, and she wishes she could look at Adrian somewhere in the gallery, but Farley warned them not to make eye contact. The lawyers continue with their sidebar argument; their voices are rasped mumblings, barely audible.

Finally, Judge Burke leans toward her. "Ms. Haggarty, you may step down. Thank you very much," he says with a weak smile.

On melting legs, Megan rises, moves down the steps, and walks along the center aisle toward the courtroom doors.

"I love you," Adrian whispers as she passes him.

She mumbles something but feels like she's in a dream.

The judge turns to the jury—eight women and four men along with three alternates. "I'm sustaining Mr. Kovac's objection," Burke says. "You heard a description of the defendant's attacks during Mr. Farley's opening statement." He turns to the prosecutor and adds, "Mr. Farley, call your next witness."

"The people call Dr. Adrian Douglas," Farley says.

"Same objection, Your Honor," Kovac calls.

"I'm going to sustain the objection."

"Your Honor," Farley says, "I'll be asking this witness about a *different* encounter with the defendant, one that happened *before* the events that are the subject of this trial."

"Dr. Douglas," Farley begins, "did there come a time when you met the defendant—purely by happenstance—at a bar known as King's Corner?"

"Yes," Adrian says, feeling Conrad's eyes boring into him. A chill crawls through his chest and seizes his heart. The very mention of King's Corner brings a flash of the bar, the smell of malt, spilled booze, and sizzling wires.

"When was that?"

"One night this past September . . . about three months ago."

"What, if any, relationship did you have with the defendant, or for that matter, with Ms. Haggarty at that time?"

"I'd never met either of them."

"Now, Dr. Douglas, will you please tell the jury what happened that night . . . before you'd even met Ms. Haggarty?"

"Objection, Your Honor. This is irrelevant."

"Your Honor," Farley says, "I'm trying to establish that Mr. Kovac's theory of a *monomania* about Dr. Douglas and Ms. Haggarty isn't true; Mr. Wilson's violent tendencies are completely independent of the victims."

"I'll allow it."

"Please, Doctor, tell the jury about that encounter."

With his heart drubbing, Adrian describes the confrontation at King's Corner. Adrian's voice sounds distant in his ears. Even as he recounts the incident, he re-envisions shattered glass and smells shot propellant. And suddenly, the night on Bald Hill floods his thoughts—the struggle, the blood, and the shotgun blasts. A shiver travels down his spine, and the back of his neck tingles.

"Objection, Your Honor," Kovac calls. "There's no proof Mr. Wilson shot up the bar."

"Sustained."

"Certainly, Your Honor," Farley says, "but only to establish the date of the incident, I would like to introduce the police report into evidence."

Farley gives the police report to the court clerk.

"Dr. Douglas, did you provoke the defendant in any way?"

"No, I did not."

"How would you characterize his aggression?"

"It came out of the blue."

Farley asks a few more questions and then says, "So, Dr. Douglas, the defendant threatened you *before* you'd even met Ms. Haggarty?"

"Yes."

"Thank you, Doctor. I have no more questions."

"Mr. Kovac, cross-examination," says the judge.

At the lectern, Kovac says, "Doctor, you said you met Ms. Haggarty *after* the incident at the bar?"

"Yes."

"And you'd never even seen Ms. Haggarty before then?"

"That's right."

"You're sure about that?"

"I'm absolutely positive."

"Well, Conrad Wilson believes that you and Ms. Haggarty met *six years ago*. Is that true?"

"No. It's not."

"He also believes that you and Ms. Haggarty were having an affair . . . and it's continued over the years. Is that true?"

"No. It's not."

"So, Doctor, Conrad Wilson's belief about an affair six years ago is mistaken?"

"Yes, it is."

"It's a false belief?"

"Yes, it is."

"If I tell you that he clings to this notion, that he believes with all his heart you and Ms. Haggarty have been lovers for six years, would his belief be a *sick* one?"

"Objection, Your Honor. The doctor isn't a psychiatrist," Farley calls.

"Sustained."

"Is Conrad's belief supported by any facts?"

"No. It's absurd," Adrian says, his voice shaking.

"Thank you, Dr. Douglas. I have no further questions."

Twenty-eight

Adrian stands in the hallway during recess. He dials Megan's number and it goes straight to her voice mail. "It's me, my love," he says. "I know how hard that was for you. I wish I could be with you now. My testimony was very short. Farley's sure the trial will be over in a day or two. I'm canceling my OR schedule till it's over. I love you and we'll talk later."

"I'm John Grayson," says a tall man, extending his hand. "One of the psychiatrists who evaluated Conrad Wilson." Grayson has that unshaven who-gives-a-shit Hugh Laurie look from TV's *House*. Actually, he has a cleft in his chin so deep it would be hard to reach those dark bristles with a razor. He has clipped, brown hair and strong, regular features, and he wears a light-gray suit with a blue tie. He towers over everyone. "You look familiar," Grayson says, narrowing his powder-blue eyes.

"So do you. Where'd you train?"

"At Yale."

"We were probably doing residencies at the same time. I'm a surgeon."

"You look like an athlete. You play a sport in college?"

"Baseball at Cornell. How 'bout you?"

"Basketball at Duke. A lifetime ago."

They laugh. Adrian feels a bond forming with this psychiatrist who will obviously testify about Conrad's craziness. He knows they can't talk about the case.

"The world makes for strange acquaintances," Grayson says.

Dr. William Sheffield takes the stand. He's in his late fifties, has grayish hair, and wears a tweed suit. As he rattles off his credentials—college at Amherst, medical school at Tufts—it's obvious to Adrian that Sheffield's been in court before. He sounds rehearsed, even canned as he describes his psychiatric residency at Yale and membership in the American Academy of Forensic Psychiatry.

Farley asks that Sheffield be qualified as an expert witness.

"He is so qualified," says Burke. "As such, he may render a psychiatric opinion."

"Can you describe your examination of the defendant?" asks Farley.

Sheffield details his interview with Conrad at the Bridgeport Correctional Center. He finally says, "Mr. Wilson was quite hostile. He clearly resented the evaluation and, frankly, I thought I might be attacked."

"Doctor, was there a reason for his hostility?"

"Well, he knew I was the prosecution's examiner, and he tried to malinger."

"Malinger? What's that?" Farley asks, glancing at the jurors.

Adrian is certain the jurors resent Farley's self-serving line of questioning. He's too obvious, too agenda-driven.

"Malingering is feigning or exaggerating a physical or mental illness for gain."

The jurors are taking notes. It strikes Adrian as surreal: jurors writing on court-issued pads as he peers at the man who tried to kill him and Megan. And Sheffield's a shrink who says Conrad Wilson's trying to game the system. And two others—Grayson and DuPont—will tell the jurors the opposite. Is there any such thing as truth? Is it all a legal chess game? Is it possible that Conrad Wilson is competent to stand trial but totally insane when it comes to him and Megan? It sounds absurd.

"You said 'exaggerating illness for *gain*'?" Farley asks. "Meaning what, Doctor?"

"There are many reasons for malingering or faking. Usually, we see it when someone wants to gain something, such as getting money in a lawsuit or to avoid prison, as in this case."

"So, Dr. Sheffield, what's your psychiatric impression of Conrad Wilson?"

"That he's an angry man, but he wasn't insane at the time of the attacks."

"Why was he *not* insane when he attacked Ms. Haggarty and Dr. Douglas?"

"He had full cognizance—meaning he was completely aware—of the wrongfulness of his actions. He planned them meticulously. He was *not* acting on an uncontrollable impulse. He methodically followed—actually stalked—the victims, was *lying in wait* and tried to kill them, whether by stabbing, firebombing, or with a shotgun."

Adrian shudders as he recalls the nightmarish chase through the woods to Bald Hill. He glances at the jurors; they look mesmerized.

"And all this means what, Dr. Sheffield?"

"That he was definitely able to act in accordance with the law; after all, he waited until an opportune time to attack."

"And his claim that his ex-wife began an affair with Dr. Douglas years ago?"

"It's a ploy by which he hopes to avoid prison. He's just a jealous ex-husband who tried to murder his ex-wife and her current boyfriend."

"Thank you, Doctor. I have no more questions."

"Dr. Sheffield," Kovac says, "can you explain to the jury what defines a successful insanity defense?"

"Yes. It must be shown that the accused suffers from a mental disease or defect such as brain damage and is unable to distinguish right from wrong, or cannot control his conduct in accordance with the law."

"You mentioned *brain damage*. Are there other mental disorders that qualify for an insanity defense?"

"Yes. There's schizophrenia, bipolar disorder, dementia, mental retardation, or any combination of those disorders, among others."

"Among others? How about paranoid delusional disorder?"

"Yes . . . that *could* qualify."

A few jurors lean forward in their seats. Adrian glances at them; they look questioningly at Sheffield. Two jurors narrow their eyes. Adrian feels his legs tightening; he can tell Kovac's going for Sheffield's jugular.

"Doctor, if a person holds a paranoid belief, is it possible that he couldn't act in accordance with the law because his belief is so powerful that he acts on it? Like a man who believes the CIA is after him so he moves from one location to another? Changes his telephone number? Tries to change his identity?"

"I don't think that's the case here. Usually, a paranoid person is suspicious of *everyone*. It's hardly ever limited to one or two people."

"But let's just say, Doctor, that this person is convinced his wife is having an affair. Even though there's no evidence of it, he insists his belief is *true* and it's limited to this *one* situation. In other words, it's a well-contained false belief. Is it possible that he could be unable to act lawfully because of this belief?"

"I suppose so. It would have to be a very strong and sick belief."

"Like a sick belief that his wife cheated on him and still does?"

"I don't believe that's the case here."

"So you don't believe that Conrad Wilson has such a sickness?"

"No, in my view he's faking."

"Based on what?"

"My opinion is based on my training, education, and on my experience in forensic psychiatry."

"But do you know with absolute certainty that my client is faking?"

"The only absolute certainty in this life, sir, is death."

Two jury members smile; the others appear poker-faced, even somber. Adrian wonders if Kovac can penetrate Sheffield's armor.

"I see," Kovac says. He moves toward Sheffield. "But, Doctor, didn't you just acknowledge that an individual with a sick belief might not be able to control his conduct?"

"Yes, *possibly* . . . if he was truly psychotic as you *hypothesized*. But I don't believe it applies to *this* defendant."

The jurors' eyes are locked on Kovac. "Doctor, how many times have you testified in court over the last fifteen years?"

"Maybe three or four times a year."

"If I tell you that court records indicate you've appeared fifty-four times in the last fifteen years, would that be right?"

"Probably. I haven't counted." Sheffield's forehead furrows. He leans back in the witness chair. His forehead shines. Adrian thinks some jurors regard Sheffield skeptically.

"Have you ever testified on behalf of a defendant?"

"Yes, I have."

"How many times?"

"I can't really recall."

"Records say that over the years you've testified *twice* for defendants. Is that accurate?"

"I think so. I'm not sure."

Adrian feels his stomach lurch; Kovac is making headway with Sheffield.

"So you've worked pretty much exclusively for the district

attorney?"

"*Predominantly*, sir."

Kovac pauses, peers at the jury, and then says, "Doctor, how much were you paid for your evaluation of Conrad Wilson?"

"Three thousand dollars."

Kovac waits and lets it sink in with the jury. One panelist's eyes widen. She shakes her head.

Adrian feels his throat close.

"And how much are you being paid for testifying today for the prosecution?"

"Eight thousand dollars."

Murmuring rises from the jury box and gallery.

"I have no further questions," Kovac says, and he turns away.

Adrian feels a sinking sensation in his chest.

Twenty-nine

"The defense calls Dr. John Grayson," says Kovac. As Grayson is sworn in, Adrian realizes that physically, the guy is very impressive. Grayson has the muscular, toned look of the college athlete he was. Adrian notices the women jurors stare at Grayson. He definitely has that *House* look—minus the arrogance.

Kovac asks about Grayson's professional background.

"I went to college at Duke and medical school at Yale," Grayson tells the jurors. He's a board-certified psychiatrist, recognized by the American Board of Psychiatry and Neurology with specialty training in forensic psychiatry. He's a member of the American Academy of Psychiatry and the Law.

"Doctor, will you tell the jury what forensic psychiatry is?"

"It involves psychiatric training applied to the interface between law and psychiatry."

"And, Doctor, what work do you now do?"

"I'm medical director of Whitehall Forensic Institute, a state psychiatric hospital under the auspices of the Connecticut Department of Corrections. We treat people who've been found not guilty by reason of insanity."

"And, Doctor, are you being paid for your appearance in court today?"

"No. I'm a state salaried employee. This is part of my work."

"Were you paid for your three meetings with Conrad Wilson

and the preparation of your narrative report?"

"Only my regular salary."

Kovac waits, letting Grayson's statement marinate with the jury.

"Doctor, can you describe your psychiatric evaluation of Conrad Wilson?"

Grayson details the interviews with Conrad and explains Conrad Wilson's thoughts, feelings, and considerable intellect. He covers the ground thoroughly. "Mr. Wilson feels angry at the world," he concludes. "Especially since he lost his job. That threw him over the edge, but his hatred for and beliefs about his ex-wife are psychotic."

It occurs to Adrian that Grayson projects a sincerity that Sheffield lacked. He's a no-bullshit kinda guy—a straight shooter who's connecting with the jury.

"Doctor, what diagnosis, if any, did you make of Conrad Wilson?"

"Conrad Wilson has paranoid delusional disorder."

"Is that some pie-in-the-sky diagnosis?"

"No. It's a well-recognized psychotic disorder."

"And by 'psychotic,' what do you mean?"

"Mr. Wilson can't distinguish reality from fantasy, at least in one specific area of his life."

"Does paranoid delusional disorder qualify as a mental disease or, to use the legal terminology, a *defect*?"

"Yes, it does."

"So in that regard, you and Dr. Sheffield are in agreement?"

"Yes."

"Dr. Grayson, what exactly is paranoid delusional disorder?"

"It's a disorder in which the person believes things that aren't real are true. He has a delusion about something."

"And what is a *delusion*?"

"A delusion is a false belief. It's an *insane* belief. And it's fixed,"

Grayson says. "Meaning, it's a belief the person clings to, *no matter what.*"

"Such as?"

"Such as Conrad Wilson's belief that Ms. Haggarty and Dr. Douglas began an affair six years ago. It's a delusion of jealousy. But there's another layer to Conrad Wilson's delusion."

"What's that, Doctor?"

"He believes that Adrian Douglas is the *father* of his daughter, Marlee Wilson."

A collective gasp comes from the jury. Adrian's heartbeat pummels his chest, and a violent shock lances through him.

"Conrad Wilson believes that Marlee Wilson is *Adrian Douglas's* daughter?"

"Yes."

"What makes that a delusion?"

"It's completely false," Grayson says. "Dr. Douglas and Megan Haggarty met only *a few months ago*. I know it's hard to prove a negative, but I got collateral information by talking to other people."

"Who else did you talk with?"

"Megan Haggarty's sister, Erin, confirmed that Megan and Adrian Douglas met only *three months ago*. Megan's brother-in-law, Bob, confirmed it, too. So did two nurses at Eastport Hospital who've known Megan Haggarty for the last two years."

"You interviewed *four* other people besides Conrad?" Kovac asks.

"Yes. You need to know the reality before you conclude something's false."

"And, Dr. Grayson, at my request, did these four people sign affidavits—sworn statements—saying that Dr. Douglas and Ms. Haggarty met only recently?"

"Yes."

"Your Honor, I ask that these affidavits be admitted into

evidence for the jury to read if they so choose."

"Granted."

Adrian's heart pumps like a Porsche unwinding down a racetrack. *Wilson thinks I'm Marlee's father? How the hell did he come to that conclusion?*

"Tell us more about this part of the delusion," Kovac says. "Tell us about Conrad's belief that Dr. Douglas is *Marlee's father*."

"Conrad's delusion is multigenerational," Grayson says. "He believes that Marlee is evil, since, in his delusional belief, she's *Adrian Douglas's* child, conceived six years ago—before Dr. Douglas and Ms. Haggarty even *met*. For Mr. Wilson, they're all linked—biologically—and he believes they must all die. That's the essence of his delusion."

"You say these beliefs are the essence of his delusion?"

"Yes. And he acted on that delusional belief when he attacked Ms. Haggarty and Dr. Douglas. In other words, he acted on an *insane belief*."

"Did he recognize right from wrong?"

"Yes. But *he couldn't obey the law* because of his *insane beliefs*."

"In other words, Dr. Grayson, he couldn't conform his behavior to the requirements of the law because of his mental disorder?"

"That's correct."

"Doctor, we know that over the years Conrad's worked, paid rent, had friends, and *seemed* completely normal. How do you explain that?"

"Conrad's psychosis—his insanity—is limited to *this* specific area of his life—to his relationship with his ex-wife, to Dr. Douglas and Marlee Wilson. Otherwise, he's normal."

A kinetic throbbing beats its way through Adrian, reaches his neck, and pulses into his head.

"And, Dr. Grayson, is your testimony given with a reasonable degree of medical certainty by virtue of your training, education, and experience as a forensic psychiatrist?"

"Yes."

"Thank you, Doctor. I have no further questions."

"Dr. Grayson," Farley says, "you said the defendant is angry and bitter, correct?"

"I said that . . . and much more."

"Especially since he lost his job, yes?"

"Yes, that kicked him over the edge."

"So, Doctor," says Farley, "the defendant lost his job and felt enraged?"

"Yes."

"So he can go out and murder two people?"

"That's not what I said."

"He lost his job and he's angry. *Yes*?"

"Yes."

"He loathes his ex-wife and her boyfriend. *Yes*?"

"Yes . . ."

"So we just let him get away with attempted murder?"

"That's a simplification of what I said."

"Well, let's look at what you've said, Doctor. You've told this jury that this man knows right from wrong. You've said that he's extraordinarily intelligent, maybe the smartest man you've ever evaluated. He has many skills—carpentry, plumbing, masonry, auto mechanics, architectural drafting, even electrical work—and after losing his job, he feels enraged, put upon by the world. So, he comes back to Connecticut and stalks his ex-wife, then tries to stab her to death. He locates her boyfriend, firebombs his house, tracks him through the woods, and tries to blow him away with a shotgun.

"And we should just say he's upset, bitter, he's *delusional* about all this . . . or at least he claims it? So, Dr. Grayson, this man's just sick and shouldn't go to prison?"

"No. That's a caricature of what I said."

Adrian sees two jurors smile. The others look stone-faced. Adrian now thinks Farley's betting on the wrong horse; he's pushing all the wrong buttons.

"But aren't you saying, Doctor, we should just call this man *disturbed* or *troubled* or maybe even *delusional*, that we shouldn't hold him *criminally accountable* for what he did, even though he was abusive and threatening to Dr. Douglas—a complete stranger who hadn't even met Megan Haggarty—that night in the bar?"

"No, that's not what I'm saying."

"But didn't he threaten Dr. Douglas *before* he even met Megan Haggarty?"

"Yes."

"So his violence isn't just limited to his *ex-wife and her lover*, is it?"

"He didn't try to kill Dr. Douglas that night at the bar."

"That shotgun blast *could* have been directed at Dr. Douglas, right?"

"Objection, Your Honor," calls Kovac. "There's no evidence my client fired anything at anyone."

"Sustained."

"And he attacked a police officer, didn't he?" Farley asks, raising his voice. "He beat him brutally, tied and gagged him, and locked him in a car, yes?"

"Yes. To get to Dr. Douglas, he did."

"Was that part of his delusion?"

"It was in the *service* of his delusion."

Farley pauses and rests an elbow on the lectern. "Doctor," he says, squinting, "do you have *proof* that Conrad Wilson is delusional?"

"Proof?"

"Yes, Doctor. We rely on *proof* in court. Can you prove your assertion?"

"If you listen to this man, if you have him tested by a psychologist and you evaluate him psychiatrically, that's your proof."

"So you're saying we should take *Conrad Wilson's* word that he believes these things, and that makes him delusional. It renders him mad. It makes him *insane*. *That's* the proof you're offering?"

"No, I'm using my training, education, and experience and conferring with other mental health professionals and interviewing other people to arrive at my conclusion."

"I have no more questions for this witness, Your Honor," Farley says, returning to the prosecution table.

Thirty

The male jurors' eyes track Nicole DuPont as she strides to the witness stand. Adrian watches them carefully.

Jesus, the men on the panel are already transfixed by her.

Her chestnut hair frames her pixyish face. As she's sworn in, her eyes appear even larger than they did at the competency hearing. She wears a figure-revealing taupe skirt, stiletto heels, a light-blue blouse fitted snugly over her breasts, and a tan jacket. Adrian detects in her an aura of not-so-subdued sensuality beneath a crust of academic austerity.

Kovac elicits DuPont's impressive credentials. Her testimony is virtually a carbon copy of Grayson's as she describes her three examinations of Conrad and details his considerable intellect, skills, and his delusion about Adrian, Megan, and Marlee.

She too concludes that Conrad is psychotic and within the context of his distorted beliefs was unable to act according to the dictates of the law.

"In other words," she says, "his delusional thinking forced him to break the law."

Adrian feels his insides shivering. He knows the case for an insanity acquittal is growing—exponentially, it seems. And Sheffield—who Kovac made out to be a paid hack—wasn't the most impressive witness in the world. Yes, he was smooth, but the bullshit needle jumped when Kovac went gunning for him on cross. And Adrian decides—despite rooting for Farley—that if he ever got into legal trouble, he'd definitely want Kovac on his side.

"Doctor," says Kovac, "did you learn anything else about Conrad?"

"Yes, I did," Nicole says.

Adrian realizes Nicole projects plenty of smarts and hits a scale-tipping ten on the confidence meter. The jurors—men and women—are riveted by her.

"What else did you learn about Conrad?"

"He was abandoned as an infant and then adopted. His adoptive father abused him."

"Abused him? How?"

"Objection, Your Honor," calls Farley. "This is irrelevant."

"Your Honor," says Kovac. "Conrad Wilson's mental health is at issue, and it's only fair that the jury evaluate him in the context of his background. After all, Your Honor, we're all products of our early environments."

Nicole DuPont gazes up at the judge. Adrian detects—through her body language—that she's imploring the judge to rule Kovac's way.

"I'll allow it," Burke says.

Adrian is convinced Kovac's dancing circles around Farley. He glances at Conrad, who sits impassively as his mental life is being dissected beneath the legal microscope—splayed open in a public forum.

"Doctor," Kovac resumes, "how was Conrad abused by his adoptive father?"

Nicole makes sequential eye contact with each juror. She's connecting with them like a laser beam, Adrian thinks. He's worried that Farley's case is going down the tubes.

"Conrad's adoptive father was a deacon in the church, but he led something of a double life," Nicole says. "He would lead Conrad down to the basement and abuse him. He would *rape* him. And while doing it, he would chant passages from the Bible. It was a perverted religious ritual: rape and prayer. It began when Conrad was five or six and lasted for five years."

The jurors' eyes dart back and forth. One man shifts in his seat. The female panelists look aghast. One woman's face blanches to an alabaster white.

"One thing, Dr. DuPont . . . Are you betraying Conrad's confidentiality by telling the jury about this violation?"

"No. Conrad's put his mental state at issue. So he's forgone any confidentiality."

"I see," Kovac says. "So Conrad was raped by his adoptive father?"

"Yes. He was raped repeatedly. And beaten and threatened every day of his early life."

"How often did these rapes occur?"

"So often that his adoptive mother bought a special cushion for Conrad to sit on."

"Did she know about this sexual abuse?"

"She seems to not've *let* herself know. She used denial and in a real sense betrayed Conrad."

Adrian sees three women on the jury nodding.

"And what effect did this have on Conrad?"

"He grew up with a devalued self-image. He hated and feared his adoptive father and felt betrayed by his adoptive mother. His adoptive father deserted them when Conrad was in elementary school, and his mother died of lung cancer when Conrad finished high school. He now believes fervidly that *any* woman will betray him. And he's obsessed with *manliness*, with proving that he's a virile, capable man . . . that he's not effeminate.

"So," DuPont says, "he became a wrestler, which involved close contact with other men, often one on top of the other. He symbolically repeated these early sexual experiences, but in an adaptive way."

"Objection. Speculative!" Farley calls.

"I'll allow it," Burke says.

Dr. DuPont continues, "Those early experiences—the threats, the beatings, the rapes, the prayers, his mother's silence—set the stage for the onset of Conrad's delusional disorder."

"Tell me, Dr. DuPont, how come this never came up with the other doctors?"

"I think he felt very comfortable with me. He opened up to me. It was as though we began psychotherapy right away. In a strange way, Conrad became that pathetic little boy all over again."

Grayson knows Nicole's dug deeply into Conrad's inner turmoil. It's her way, especially with male patients. She's able to dip into their roiling cauldrons of sickness. And they open up to her, more so than with anyone else. It's a gift, and she uses it effectively to get to the core of these men—NGRI acquittees at Whitehall, deluded men with mangled minds. She unearths psychological detritus—rapes, incest, cringe-worthy fetishes of every kind—the most deeply held secrets in these men's emotional caches.

Jim Morgan, the psychologist sitting next to Grayson, whispers, "She really dug down, got into this case."

"That's Nicole," Grayson whispers. "Always looking for the how and why."

"She thinks she's still with the ACLU," Morgan whispers.

"She feels for the patients. It's part of who she is."

"Yeah, every session's gotta be a therapeutic milestone," Morgan mutters. "I've told her a hundred times, these sessions with defendants and NGRI acquittees aren't Rent-a-Friend psychotherapy."

"Dr. DuPont . . ." Farley begins his cross-examination. "What percentage of children are sexually abused?"

"For girls," DuPont says, "it's about fifteen to twenty-five percent. For young boys, it's between five and fifteen percent."

"Okay, so it's reasonable to assume about ten percent of boys are abused?"

"I suppose so. Sexual abuse is quite prevalent in our society . . . far more than people think."

"I'm sure it is, Doctor. Now, assuming that ten percent of boys—maybe more—are sexually abused, do we have ten percent of the adult male population—maybe fifteen million men—attempting to murder their ex-wives and their boyfriends?"

"No. Of course not," Nicole says, closing her eyes. Grayson is certain Nicole is indulging Farley, tolerating this self-serving line of questioning. She's too cagey a witness to get snared into a pissing match with a cross-examining attorney.

"Do millions of men attempt murder because they were sexually abused as children?"

"No. But they're damaged people."

"Damaged? So damaged that they lie in wait and try to *kill* other people?"

"No. They're damaged and they develop distorted and stunted emotional lives."

"Damaged in a way that they *stalk a woman for weeks*, ambush her with a knife, firebomb her boyfriend's house, assault a police officer—all preplanned—and try to slaughter the boyfriend?"

"No, of course not."

"And, Doctor, who told you that Conrad Wilson was sexually abused as a child?"

"He did."

"And you took him at his word?"

"Yes. When a man divulges that kind of thing, it's a core issue in his life."

"Would you consider his *word* to be scientific evidence?"

"No, it's not *scientific*." Her eyes look like they're laughing.

Yes, Nicole is suffocating the urge to verbally decimate the prosecutor, thinks Grayson. *She's restraining herself. She's a damned good psychiatrist and a fabulous witness, even though she sometimes advocates too strongly for a defendant.*

"Is it objective medical evidence?"

"It's the patient's history. All patients give history."

"But isn't medicine supposed to be based on science?"

"Mr. Farley, let me assure you that the practice of medicine—every specialty from surgery to psychiatry—is as much *art* as it is science."

"And Conrad Wilson's *history*, as you called it, is what *he* told you, isn't it?"

"Yes."

"So, speaking of *art*, could he have been *artfully* lying?"

"That's possible."

"Do patients ever lie to doctors?"

"On occasion they do."

"Has a patient ever lied to you?"

"Yes."

"And, Doctor, in a legal proceeding such as this one, is there an incentive for the defendant to lie—especially to a psychiatrist evaluating him for *trial* purposes?"

"There can be."

"Thank you, Doctor. I have no more questions," Farley says, sitting down.

"Mr. Kovac, any redirect?" asks Judge Burke.

"Yes, Your Honor," says Kovac, going to the lectern.

"Dr. DuPont, is Conrad Wilson lying when he talks about an affair between his ex-wife and Dr. Douglas and about Marlee being their daughter?"

"No. He's telling the truth."

"*Truth*? How on earth is that *true*?"

"He's telling *his* truth. It's *his* sick, psychotic, inner truth. It's a *delusion*. He believes it to be completely true, even though it's ridiculous. And he acted on this jealous delusion and sought revenge."

Thirty-one

To Adrian, Conrad looks like a hulking bear sitting in the witness chair. Conrad stares straight ahead with that menacing look Adrian recalls from King's Corner. Those eyes smolder as though something dark and unknowable lurks within him. Adrian shudders as Conrad's eyes scan the gallery and finally fix on him. He feels malevolence pouring from Conrad like hot lava.

Conrad is cleanly shaved, and his hair is no longer shorn in a military buzz cut. Obviously, Kovac has advised him to change his look to something softer and less threatening. Conrad's sloping shoulders, massive arms, and chest bulge through a gray sports jacket. His blue work shirt, open at the collar, reveals his thick, corded neck.

Conrad doesn't wear handcuffs during the trial. It could prejudice the jury to see a defendant manacled. Adrian notices five court officers lining the oak-paneled wall near the witness stand.

As if that doesn't send a clear message to the jury.

The jurors glance furtively at Conrad and then avert their eyes. On the gauge of menace and intimidation, Conrad throws the needle way past the meter's maximum number, Adrian thinks. That metallic taste forms on Adrian's tongue as images of the cemetery wash over him.

"Now, Conrad," Kovac says, "You don't deny attacking Megan Haggarty and Adrian Douglas, do you?"

"I did what I did," Conrad says in a monotone.

"So you tried to kill these people?"

"Yes."

"Why in your mind did they have to die?"

"They're *evil*." Conrad virtually quivers in the witness chair. "They betrayed me." A purple vein on his forehead bulges and seems to twitch. Redness creeps into his face, and the pipelike veins on his neck bulge. A court officer edges closer. Judge Burke leans back in his high, padded chair.

"Conrad, how were you betrayed?"

"They were lovers for years."

"But, Conrad, how do you *know* that?"

"I know. I visited the hospital at Yale where they worked."

"But that was years ago. They didn't even *know* each other then."

"Yes, they did."

"How do you know that?"

"I know what I know." His jaw juts with certainty.

A juror in the front row shakes her head. Another furrows his brow and tilts his head. To Adrian, it seems the jurors instinctively lean away from Conrad, as does the judge.

"Can you prove they had an affair?"

"Yes, I can."

"What proof do you have?"

"She bore *his* child . . . not mine."

"But Marlee Wilson's *your* daughter, isn't she?"

"No. She's *Adrian Douglas's*."

"How do you know that, Conrad?"

"I can *smell* it on her," he hisses. His face turns venom-red.

A gasp comes from the jury. Frenetic whispering rises in the gallery. Adrian feels a spasm begin in his foot. His ears feel hot and begin ringing.

Grayson leans forward, watching Conrad intently.

"You can *smell* it?" Kovac asks with arched eyebrows.

"Yes. I smell it coming from the little bastard's pores, and it's on her breath. Even her innards reek of him. She's *his*, not mine."

Adrian's pulse throbs in his throat. Heat flares in his chest as though his heart is bathed in acid. It occurs to him that Conrad is completely insane about Megan, Marlee, and himself.

"How can you *smell* it on her?" Kovac asks, moving closer to the jury box.

"Her stench fills my nostrils."

One juror's mouth hangs agape. Another blinks repeatedly and then squints at Conrad; disbelief is etched on his face.

"So you're convinced that Adrian Douglas is Marlee's father, even though other people've said that Megan first met Dr. Douglas only three months ago?"

"They've kept it a secret."

"Conrad," Kovac says, moving closer, "are you familiar with DNA testing?"

"Yes."

"That it can be used when there's a question of paternity?"

"Yes."

"What if we swabbed Marlee's inner cheek and yours and had the samples tested for DNA? Would that prove she's *your* daughter . . . ?"

"No."

"Why not?"

"The lab can't be trusted. There could be a conspiracy."

"What if I told you—just hypothetically, Conrad—that we could get a sample of *Dr. Douglas's* cheek cells, so his DNA could be tested against Marlee's? And they wouldn't match. Would *that* change your mind?"

"It wouldn't prove a thing. Whose samples would they use?" Conrad's jaw muscles contract as though he's clenching his teeth. The guards edge closer.

"So, Conrad, you're convinced . . . the fix is in?"

"It's been a secret for six years."

Judge Burke stares at Conrad. The jurors are wide-eyed; a woman in the second row covers her mouth.

"So, Conrad, why did you try to kill them?"

"There's so much evil and betrayal in the world. They must be destroyed."

"Can't you forgive them, Conrad?"

"Forgiveness is for the weak. Those who're strong and righteous must eliminate the evildoers. They murdered my soul. It's soul murder."

A sucking sound comes from the gallery. Judge Burke glances at Farley as if to tell the prosecutor this man is insane. The jurors stare, wide-eyed and open-mouthed.

The courtroom is so silent, Adrian hears the overhead fluorescent lights buzz like a swarm of insects.

Farley begins his cross-examination. "Mr. Wilson, this conspiracy you talk about, how did it start?"

Conrad stares coldly at Farley. He says nothing.

"Can you answer the question, sir?"

"I already have."

"I don't believe you have, Mr. Wilson. Again, how did this start?"

Conrad shakes his head and says, "If you don't believe me, I can't convince you. What you think is irrelevant."

"What about the jury? Are they irrelevant?"

"Yes. Only the truth matters."

"Don't you want the jury to understand *your* version of the truth?"

"They don't matter."

"They don't *matter*? Even though the rest of your life is in their hands?"

"My life ended long ago. My soul is dead."

"Let me ask you something, Mr. Wilson. You say this conspiracy involves your ex-wife and Dr. Douglas, correct?"

"Yes."

"Yet when you saw Dr. Douglas at the bar, you didn't know who he was. It was a random encounter in a bar one night. Am I right?"

"Correct."

"But you were aggressive with him—a man who did nothing to you, correct?"

"I confronted him."

"But he was a stranger. In fact, he hadn't even met your ex-wife yet."

"So he claims," Conrad says, as his eyes bore into Farley.

"But you didn't know his name or who he was, right?"

"Yes."

"Yet you *confronted* him. Why?"

Conrad's hands hang over the ledge and curl again into huge hammerlike fists.

"Mr. Wilson, why did you confront Dr. Douglas?"

Adrian's heart throbs; blood thunders in his ears; it feels like his skull will explode.

"Why were you aggressive with Dr. Douglas that night?"

Conrad's eyes gleam. "Because I knew he was the kid's father."

"How on earth could you know that?"

Conrad's face darkens and he says, "I could smell it on him. He stank. It was the stench of that bastard kid."

Thirty-two

In his closing argument, Farley scoffs at the notion that Conrad Wilson couldn't obey the law because he was insane. He emphasizes how Conrad's acts were meticulously planned. "He knew what he was doing was wrong and he was stealthy," Farley cries. "And he's using *insanity* as an excuse!"

He reviews the evidence and then says, "The defendant's excuse is his childhood and the loss of his job. My God, every convict in prison has a reason, an *excuse.* In this society, we're held *responsible* for our actions. We can't blame our parents or our circumstances, our job, our luck, or our genes. We *are* responsible for what we do.

"The people ask that you hold *Conrad Wilson responsible* for what he did. The people ask that you find Conrad Wilson guilty for the attempted murders of Megan Haggarty and Adrian Douglas."

Kovac begins his closing argument. "Now, ladies and gentlemen, you heard the doctors. And most of all, you heard Conrad testify. It's clear that he was acting under the influence of a delusion—an *insane* belief. He even thinks he can *smell* his own daughter on another man he bumps into at a bar. And this was a man whom his ex-wife didn't meet until a few months ago. And he tries to kill them both.

"If this twisted conviction isn't insane, then what on earth *is*? Ladies and gentlemen, you *must* conclude that Conrad suffers from paranoid delusional disorder, which caused him to act outside the requirements of the law. Ladies and gentlemen, I ask that you find Conrad Wilson *not guilty by reason of insanity*."

After a short recess, Judge Burke addresses the jury. "Ladies and gentlemen, I'm going to instruct you about the law. In this case, the defendant has admitted to his actions, so that's not at issue.

"What *is* at issue is the defendant's *state of mind* when he acted. The defendant claims he was insane at the time. The burden of proof rests with the *defendant*, not the state. He must prove his claim by *a preponderance of the evidence*. This means that based on the evidence, you may conclude that the defendant's claim is *more likely true than not true*. Or it may not be. That is the decision before you."

The jurors appear to be listening intently.

"The defendant claims that because of a *mental disorder*, he acted the way he did. *That* is the issue you must decide. It doesn't matter that he can work as a carpenter or a mason or that he may seem normal to the casual observer. What matters only is his state of mind as it relates *specifically to the crimes he's charged with*.

"Now, your verdict must be unanimous. Your only decision is this one: did the defendant suffer from a mental disorder at the time of his crimes and, *because* of that disorder, was he unable to act lawfully?"

The jurors' heads nod in unison.

"In other words, you may find the defendant either guilty, in which case he will be sentenced to a penal facility. Or, you may find him not guilty by reason of insanity."

Burke pauses and looks along both rows of jurors.

"Now, I'm required by Connecticut statute to tell you the following: a finding of *not guilty by reason of insanity* does *not* mean the defendant is a free man.

"If you find him not guilty by reason of insanity, he'll be confined to a state mental institution for *long-term treatment*. The acquittee—as he is known at that point—will remain confined *involuntarily*. He will remain committed until such time as he is no longer mentally ill, which may take years, or may never occur. So a finding of not guilty by reason of insanity does *not* mean the defendant leaves court a free man.

"I hope I've explained this clearly and concisely to you and wish you Godspeed in your deliberations."

The jury returns after three hours.

The courtroom settles down as coughing and throat clearing come to an end. Adrian watches as the jury files into the two rows of the jury box. He realizes he can't read them; each juror maintains a sphinxlike face, inscrutable, not a hint of their determination. His insides hum and nearly vibrate, and his legs tense. He glances at Grayson, who sits next to DuPont. They both stare straight ahead at the judge.

"Ladies and gentlemen, have you reached a verdict?" Burke asks.

The jury foreman, a balding man of about fifty, stands and says, "Yes, we have, Your Honor."

"Is the verdict unanimous?"

"Yes, it is, Your Honor."

"Will the defendant please rise," Burke says.

Conrad and Kovac stand behind the defense table.

Burke says, "What say you in the matter of the State of Connecticut versus Conrad Wilson?"

The hissing in Adrian's ears sounds like steam rushing from an open valve.

"We the jury find the defendant, Conrad Wilson, not guilty by reason of insanity."

Gasps come from the gallery and then murmurs and whispers followed by a choral drone. Grayson, DuPont, and Morgan stand. Grayson glances back and looks around the courtroom. His eyes rest on Adrian and he nods in what seems to Adrian a sympathetic way. A cadre of court officers converges on Conrad. He's handcuffed and stares straight ahead; he neither looks at nor speaks to Kovac.

A poisonous tide swirls through Adrian as a chill invades his flesh. The jury's decided that Conrad Wilson is a madman. Adrian is again thankful Megan isn't in the courtroom.

"So it has been decided," Burke says. "I remand the acquitted to the Whitehall Forensic Institute in Ansonia for involuntary treatment on an indefinite basis, subject to further review and hearings."

The gavel slams down.

Thirty-three

Adrian and Megan sit on the living room sofa. Marlee is asleep in her bedroom. Megan's head feels heavy on Adrian's shoulder. He realizes she's drifted off to sleep.

It's been nearly three weeks since the trial. Last night was the fourth in a row Megan slept without the elevator dream waking her in a cold sweat. And she hasn't taken an Ambien in more than a week. She's been back at work for nearly a month, and it's going well. The old building's completely sealed off, and plans for its demolition are on an ultrafast track.

It's clear to Adrian that once Conrad was sent to Whitehall, the horror of what happened receded to some distant backwater of his own mind. And with today's explosive new development—an absolute life changer—a new and exciting world has suddenly blossomed.

The TV is playing softly. Jay Leno is warming the audience up with a monologue. Adrian presses the remote's "Mute" button. His thoughts return to the evening in Megan's apartment many weeks ago when she described the night Conrad nearly killed Marlee. Looking pleadingly at him, Megan had said, "Adrian, there's something else I need to tell you about Conrad and me."

She described the visits to Dr. Green, her gynecologist, and then the referral to a fertility expert. "So . . . my husband wanted a baby. And frankly, Adrian, *I* wanted one, too. But there was no pregnancy, and I knew Conrad would never go for a semen analysis. The fertility doctor said there was only one option available."

"Which was?"

Megan's lips quivered and her eyes grew moist.

"It would have to be artificial insemination."

"Using *another* man's sperm?"

"Yes. But I could never tell Conrad."

"It would be a *secret*?"

"Oh, Adrian. I know . . . it's a *terrible* secret," she said, with quivering lips. "But I was desperate. I thought having a baby was the only way to save the marriage."

"But—"

"I was just *so* desperate to save the marriage. The fertility doctor convinced me it was a good idea. Conrad would have a child, and things would get better between us."

"Okay, I can understand that."

Adrian realized Megan's mind-bending bind—it was an insoluble problem.

"Also," she said, "I could pick the donor's eye color, height, and ethnic type, so the baby would resemble Conrad. And all donors are college graduates. I wanted that because Conrad's so smart."

"So to this day, Conrad doesn't know Marlee's not his?"

"Adrian, only *you* know," Megan said with a brittle laugh. "Not even Erin knows the truth."

"It was an impossible situation."

"I was trying to do the right thing. Can you *understand*?"

"Yes, my love. I do."

"And it's all so strange," Megan said. "Conrad claims Marlee's not his, and even though he's crazy, he's *right*. He's absolutely right."

"And you've shared this with me," he said, pulling her closer.

"Only you, Adrian. It's my deepest secret."

"It was a secret of good intentions," he whispered.

"I wanted to preserve Conrad's self-respect and hold the marriage together. So I've been living a lie."

Megan stirs and suddenly startles awake. She looks into Adrian's eyes and plants a kiss on his neck.

Adrian nuzzles her, inhales the fragrance of her hair. "You and Marlee are so much a part of my life. I want us to be together, always."

She looks up at him. "What's wrong? You look so sad."

"I'm so happy, I could cry," he says, nearly trembling. He feels a strange lightness in his chest, the one he sometimes feels when Megan and Marlee laugh at some inane joke he's made or when they're in the car singing the lyrics to a song on the radio. He picks up the remote and turns off the television.

Is there an easy way to tell her about today's development?

"How much do you know about DNA paternity testing?" he asks.

"I know it's used in child support cases, but why?"

"Because—"

"Do you think Conrad'll have Marlee *tested*?" She jumps up as though she's been scalded. "Oh, my *God*," she blurts. "And now he has this lawyer, Kovac . . ."

He clutches her hands. They're cold and clammy.

"I can see it in the *Connecticut Post*," she says. "A man claims his wife had another man's baby and she tried to pawn it off as his, so now he's in an insane asylum, but he's demanding DNA testing." A knuckle goes to her lips. "This could be *terrible*—"

"Megan, *listen*. Have you ever heard of DNA testing with PCR?"

"No."

"PCR stands for polymerase chain reaction. Any sample can be used. Blood, saliva, a piece of skin; anything with cells can give a profile."

"So if Kovac demands a DNA profile, he'll prove Marlee's *not Conrad's*. And if he supervises the test, there won't be any doubt—"

"Megan, half of Marlee's DNA matches *yours*, and the other half—"

"Of course, but, Adrian, what's this about?"

"Megan, do you remember when you told me about the AI?"

"Yes," she says as her chin trembles.

"And I told you the lab concentrated my sperm so Peggy could get pregnant."

"Yes."

"Well, they cryofroze my semen."

"Yes?"

"What I didn't mention was that a few months later, the lab called. They wanted to know if we'd be using the sperm."

"So?"

"They wanted it for their sperm bank inventory."

"And?"

"I said it was fine. And they sent me a nondisclosure contract."

"So, where does this lead?"

"It leads to *Gen-Health Labs*."

"The lab in *New Haven*?"

"Yes. Where you told me *you* went. *I* was a donor there."

"Oh, darling," Megan says. "The odds of *you* being my donor are ridiculous."

"Listen my love, after you mentioned Gen-Health, I went online and ordered a paternity testing kit. I wanted to—"

"Adrian, it's *absurd*."

"It came in the mail. It has swab sticks, vials, and a prepaid mailing box. You take a tissue sample from the child and from the presumed father—"

"You're suggesting we test *Marlee*? And we test *you*?" Megan folds her arms across her chest and says, "Adrian, the odds are so remote."

"Listen, Megan. After you mentioned Gen-Health, I made an appointment with their geneticist."

"A geneticist, why?"

"Her name's Dr. Lefer." He pauses, recalling the conversation. "I told her I'd been a donor there. She had my file and the non-disclosure contract. She said if my sperm *was* used, she couldn't tell me a *thing* about the recipient. It would violate privacy laws."

"What were you looking for?"

"Their records confirmed that my sperm *was* used. Lefer said the lab matches donors based on characteristics the woman specifies."

"Like I did. So?"

"She said their donor population comes from New Haven and Fairfield Counties, an area of about one point seven million people."

"Oh, Adrian, the odds are insane." She swallows deeply.

"Listen, Megan," Adrian says, barely able to contain himself. "Half the population is women, so it's about eight hundred thousand men. But really, it's far fewer, since they only take men between nineteen and thirty-five and only college graduates."

"Oh, Adrian, that's still thousands of men."

"Then she asked me an interesting question."

"What?"

"She asked if I personally know *any* sperm donor. I realized that I don't. Very few men are willing to go through the screening process, even if the lab pays them to donate. So the actual donor population's very small. And they don't take men with personal or family histories of mental illness, diabetes, or MS, lots of skin conditions, and other things. So it boils down to a small group of *actual* donors."

"Yes?"

"They called me because they couldn't fill a request. A client—whom she couldn't name—asked for a donor between *six feet and six two*, with *blue eyes* and of either *English or Scottish* descent."

Megan's eyes dart from left to right.

"Lefer said 'We had no donor who fit that profile.'"

Megan looks chalky white.

"Only *my* semen fit the bill, and they used it for that client."

He feels her hands shaking.

"She couldn't say more without violating the nondisclosure agreement."

"Oh, Adrian, I don't want Marlee to go through DNA testing."

"Well, my love, after seeing Lefer, I ordered the testing kit . . . and . . ."

"Oh, Adrian, don't be silly."

"Megan, do you remember that day when we went to the Maritime Aquarium?"

"Yes."

"In the parking lot, we saw that pickup. Marlee was chewing gum and you told her not to throw it on the ground. Remember?"

"Not really."

"Marlee put the gum into an envelope. I realized that chewed bubble gum has gobs of saliva and cheek cells with plenty of DNA. When I got home, I dropped the gum into a vial from the collection kit. Then I swabbed my inner cheek and put it in another vial. And I sent the kit off to the lab."

"You did genetic testing on Marlee and never *told* me?" Megan's eyes narrow.

"I'm sorry, Megan, but I just *had* to know. I love you so much . . . and Marlee, too. I *had* to find out." Heat crawls into his face. He feels his pores open.

"You did this without *telling* me?"

The question hits him with stunning impact. "Megan, I—"

"You did DNA testing on Marlee—on *my* child—and never

told me?"

"Yes. But you have to—"

"Oh, Adrian, how *could* you?"

"Please forgive me, Megan. But you told me about the AI and you said you were *desperate* to save the marriage and not hurt Conrad . . ."

"Yes." Her lips quiver and her eyelids flutter.

"That's how *I* felt . . . *desperate*. I had to learn the truth. I *had* to find out, and I didn't want to complicate your life even more, so I did it secretly."

Tears pool in her eyes. Adrian wonders if she'll slap him, walk out of the room, or sink to the sofa, but she stands there, mouth agape, wide-eyed.

"Yes, I did it," he says with his voice quivering. "And I'm sorry I violated your privacy . . . and Marlee's, too. This is *my* deepest secret. Megan, please forgive me."

She stands there—staring at him in bewilderment. And Adrian gazes at those gorgeous green-ringed hazel eyes, now so wide, as her mouth hangs open with her lovely, fair face and her coppery-red hair pinned behind her like it was the day they met. With her hands shaking, she nods her head frantically, as though she understands how tortured he'd felt when she'd mentioned Gen-Health Labs. She seems to realize—he hopes, oh yes, how he fervently hopes—that she understands the urgency of his need to know more about the woman he loves and this delightful little girl Marlee. It's all so intense, Adrian feels he could collapse from the anticipation of hoping Megan can appreciate his desperate wish—no, his absolute *need*—to know more about the two of them, Megan and Marlee, who are now so intertwined in his life. He can't imagine living without them. His entire body feels damp. His heart pounds like a sledgehammer in his chest, and every nerve ending on his skin fires away in bursts of nervous energy. He looks into her eyes and hears Megan whisper, "Adrian, what—what were the results?"

"They came back today."

Megan blinks again and again, and she looks frozen in anticipation.

"Megan, my love . . ."

She nods at him frantically as her lips and chin tremble. He wants to hold her in his arms, nuzzle and kiss her tenderly, and he can barely believe what he's about to say, but it's the deepest and most abiding truth in his world.

"She's ours—yours and mine, Megan," he says, nearly choking. "I'm Marlee's father."

Her hand goes to her mouth and a gasp erupts from somewhere deep in her throat. Her eyes widen in stunned disbelief, and she's speechless. She plops onto the sofa, and he drops down beside her, wrapping his arms around her. Her shoulders shake, and she seems to convulse as he feels a coarse shuddering go through her. He can't tell if she's crying or laughing, or simply quaking from the shock of it all. And then she leans against his chest and buries her face against him, and he presses her close and feels the beating of her heart, knowing she and Marlee are the most precious beings in his world.

Megan draws back, her hands in his; she looks into his eyes and whispers, "This is unbelievable. It's unreal. It's . . . it's just . . . Adrian, of all the people in the world, they used *your* sperm?" Her intake of breath is ragged and her look of incredulity is mixed with that of deep revelation blended with shocklike astonishment. She gasps again. She seems unable to process what she's heard and incapable of uttering a word. Megan shakes her head and stammers, "Here we are . . . all these years later . . . and we met in the cafeteria . . . just a few months ago and . . . and all these years I didn't know it, but Marlee . . . she's yours, too? I . . . I don't even . . . I can't get my *head* around it all," she says in a tear-filled voice.

"I've been in complete shock," he whispers, feeling light-headed.

The clock on the mantle ticks so loudly, it seems to reverberate in his ears along with a low-level hissing sound. A minute passes, maybe two, perhaps three. Adrian can't really tell because his head spins and his heart flutters and a sizzling sensation sears through him as Megan tries to process this fate-filled and incredible denouement in their lives. And Adrian can tell she's trying to absorb—to digest and process—the sheer craziness of it all, the statistical improbability of it. Then, looking bewildered, even staggered, Megan nods, blinks, and gazes at him with those incredible eyes, and while they'll need more time to truly understand this, Adrian can tell that Megan realizes how everything in their now shared little world has changed—completely, permanently.

Their bedeviled little universe—after years of Megan's misgivings about Conrad and Adrian's regrets about Peggy and not having a child—has all funneled down to this single unalterable fact: Marlee's paternity is no longer a mystery. Her identity and Adrian's role in her life—and in Megan's, too—has been forever changed.

After a long and shared silence, as they hold hands and gaze into each other's eyes, Megan whispers, "Who'd have ever dreamed that . . . How can this *really* be true . . . that when I went to Dr. Margaret, I'd—"

"Dr. who?"

"Dr. Margaret . . . she put me onto AI."

"I can't *believe* this," he says. He stands up as voltage shoots through him, and his pulse throbs. "That's what *Peggy's* patients called her . . . *Dr. Margaret*. She didn't like being called Dr. Yanes. Way too formal for her."

"Dr. Margaret's last name *was* Yanes. She was your *wife*?"

He nods as the room swirls and his knees wobble.

"Adrian, this is so strange. It's so . . . so unbelievable. Your ex-wife, the woman who didn't want *your* baby helped *me* get pregnant."

"Yes and with *my* child."

"With *our* child . . ."

"Thank you, Peggy Yanes," he whispers, almost reeling at yet another revelation. "Thank you for this wonderful gift," he murmurs as his blood hums.

"It's so *crazy*," Megan whispers. "Conrad's absolutely *right*. Marlee's not his. She's *yours*. He's insanely right! Marlee's *your* child. She's yours . . . and mine. She's ours. I can hardly believe it." Her hands go to her cheeks. Adrian hears the intake of her breath.

"I've been thinking about it all day," Adrian says as a sob threatens to burst from his chest. His words bubble in his ears. "It's the greatest thing that's ever happened in my life." He shakes his head; his entire body tingles, and he says, "It's hard to believe . . . Peggy brought us together this way."

Tears drip down Megan's face, and he pulls her so close, he feels her heart beating against him. He kisses her cheeks, then her lips, and she sobs with joy and wonder and excitement; and it all seems a gorgeous mystery to Adrian as he tastes the tang of Megan's skin, the saltiness of her tears, the sweet wetness of her mouth, and he's overcome by the astonishing, incredible madness of it all.

Thirty-four

"So this is the place," Megan says, getting out of the car. "It's Whitehall Forensic Institute . . . long-term housing for the criminally insane."

"Looks like a college campus, not a mental institution."

"It reminds me of Harvard," Adrian says, gazing at the Federal-style brick buildings with shuttered symmetrical windows, low-pitched roofs, and balustrades. Stately sycamores and gnarled maple trees line the walkways crisscrossing a parklike setting. The air is crisp and cold; it's mid-January. The afternoon sky is a deep indigo. A cooing blizzard of pigeons flutters upward; feathers spiral and swirl through the air.

"You know, I'm still trying to get my head around this," Megan says as they walk arm in arm toward the main building.

"You mean what we are to each other and to Marlee?"

"Yes, that I'll be marrying Marlee's father. It's just insane. Actually, it's insanely wonderful."

"It brings things full circle."

Megan stops at the stairs. "I sometimes wonder if this is all a dream."

He wraps his arms around her waist and pulls her toward him.

"For all these years, the donor was a phantom. I'd wonder who he was, what kind of person he was. Had I been fair to Marlee with my decision to have a mystery man as her father? And now that mystery man is right here."

She plants a kiss on his lips. The taste of her arouses him.

"And I always felt cheated, even angry," Adrian says. "I blamed Peggy for my not having a family. And now I learn that with *you*, I have a smart, beautiful little girl. Thanks to *Peggy*. Life is so crazy, isn't it?"

"Yes, it's crazy and wonderful."

"You know," he says, "sometimes at breakfast when I pretend to steal Marlee's Apple Jacks and she shoots that little smile at me . . . ?"

"Yes?"

"I realize it's my mom's smile."

Adrian also knows that Marlee's laugh is a distant ghosting of Mom—and Dad, too—a glimmering trace of genetic indelibility. Yes, he sees in Marlee slight insinuations of Megan and himself and his parents. Marlee's a mirror of lineage, of kinship.

Suddenly, Megan's brow furrows. "I just wonder," she says.

"About what?"

"If it was known that Marlee *is* yours, would Conrad have a legal basis to go to court because he was right?"

"Yes, he's right, but for all the wrong reasons."

"But could there be legal complications? I mean, if Kovac—"

"Megan, Conrad tried to kill us both. He's a madman. That's all that counts right now."

"And the rest is our little secret," she says.

Standing amid the twittering of sparrows and cooing of pigeons, he says, "It'll be our secret. And when she's old enough, we'll tell Marlee."

"We sure had her in an unusual way, didn't we?"

He pulls her close again and inhales the fragrance of her hair.

"I have an idea," she says, moving back and smiling.

"Yes?"

"Let's have another baby. But in a more traditional way."

"Let's get to work on that when we get home."

Dr. John Grayson greets them. He wears dark slacks, a blue shirt, no tie, and a white lab coat. He sports that three-day stubble.

"Thanks for agreeing to see us, John," Adrian says.

"It's my pleasure, Adrian. And it's good to meet you, Megan."

"You have quite an elaborate security system," she says.

"We've never had an escapee at Whitehall. It's a hospital facility within the Department of Correction." Grayson sits behind his desk and gestures toward two leather chairs facing him.

Grayson's office is book-lined and cozy. The shelves brim with medical and legal volumes. A skull of what Adrian guesses is a Neanderthal man sits on a black pedestal in a corner. A chart with drawings depicting the evolution of a fish crawling out of the sea to become an anthropoid hangs on one wall.

"We need to know what to expect since Conrad was found not guilty," Adrian says.

"I understand," Grayson begins. "Let me explain a few things, especially for you, Megan, since you weren't in court when Judge Burke gave his instructions to the jury. As the judge said, an NGRI verdict isn't the same as being found not guilty in a regular criminal trial. The jury decided Conrad acted out of an *insane belief* and that's why he's here and not in prison."

"But what if he gets better?" asks Adrian. "And gets out? *Then* what happens?"

"We don't want to live under a cloud," Megan adds.

Grayson says, "I understand completely. But contrary to popular belief, a defendant found NGRI isn't just treated and released. In 1983, a forensic case was tried before the Supreme Court—*Jones v. United States*. The court ruled that the sentence a defendant would have received if he'd been convicted has *no bearing* on how long he can be committed after an insanity acquittal.

The crime could have had a fifteen-year sentence, but he can be hospitalized for *thirty years*, or a lifetime, if necessary."

"Really?" Adrian says.

"Yes. Our NGRI acquittees are under maximum security. Patients in Whitehall come under the purview of the PSRB—the Psychiatric Security Review Board."

"Which means?" Megan asks.

"It means that twice a year, the patient's status is reviewed by a committee. I'm in charge of the PSRB. All staff members who've had contact with the inmate participate. We evaluate everything, from the patient's relationships with inmates and nurses to his treating psychologist and psychiatrists—everyone. The board votes on whether or not the commitment continues or is modified in some way."

"Please don't take this personally, John," Adrian says, "I just don't trust hospital committees. People with different agendas butt heads."

Grayson laughs knowingly. "I know, Adrian. But these patients are very sick, and there's little chance they'll be restored to any semblance of mental health."

"So how long are they kept here?" asks Megan.

"Good question. The average commitment in Whitehall is twenty-five years. Whitehall's no walk in the park. Of course, we're usually dealing with very sick paranoid schizophrenics and, basically, they're lifers."

"That's encouraging," Adrian says, glancing at Megan.

"Conrad's not schizophrenic or retarded, to say the least, but he's paranoid—very disturbed."

"So he'll be here for a long time?" asks Megan.

"Probably. Megan, if you'd been in court, you'd have seen how sick he is. He convinced a jury of that. And his delusion about you two makes him dangerous."

"To *us*," Megan says.

"Yes. I don't see Conrad leaving Whitehall for a very long time, if at all. I have to say that Wilson's an intriguing patient." Grayson gets up, moves to the pedestal, and sets his basketballer's hand over the Neanderthal skull. "You know, I've always been interested in anthropology and evolutionary biology . . . the blending of science and animal instinct. And in that context, Conrad Wilson's absolutely fascinating."

"How so?" asks Megan. She looks milky white.

"First of all, he's brilliant. We've given him all the standard tests: the WAIS, the Stanford-Binet, the Reynolds Intellectual Assessment Scales, and the Woodcock-Johnson Test of Cognitive Abilities. Conrad tests off the charts. Our neuropsychologist, Dr. Morgan, says Mensa would take him in a heartbeat. He masters any subject in no time and can apply what he's learned in practical ways."

"Conrad was always very smart," Megan says.

"He's interesting in other ways, too," Grayson says, sitting again. "I'm sure you've noticed that he's quite a physical specimen."

"Oh, yeah," Adrian says. "If he hadn't slipped and hit his head, he'd have killed me. And he tracked me at night, over very rough terrain."

"Well, his abilities aren't limited to strength, speed, and agility . . . though they're extraordinary. He has some other unique physical characteristics," Grayson says. "At Eastport General, they did CT scans and MRIs of his brain. It was fascinating. The studies showed a very large olfactory bulb, the part of the brain's neural system responsible for smell. In animals with a strong sense of smell, the olfactory bulb is relatively large. We humans have a smaller olfactory center in proportion to the rest of the brain.

"Conrad has an extraordinary sense of smell. Our neurologist tested him using the common test materials: banana, cinnamon, chocolate, onion, and a few others. They come as scratch-and-sniff test strips. You put the strips beneath the nostrils, but

Conrad can smell them from across the room.

"And our audiologist used an audiometer, brain stem evoked potentials, and quantitative EEG brain mapping to test him. He has incredible hearing."

"So what're you saying?" Adrian asks.

"I'm saying that Conrad's a perfect storm of extraordinary physical and mental abilities. From an evolutionary standpoint, he has many atavistic animal traits mixed with the highest human mental attainments.

"You see," Grayson continues, moving to the Darwinian drawing of man's rise from the ape. "In human evolution, from lower creatures to Homo sapiens, we lost certain abilities. Our sharp eyesight, the ability to smell and to hear at great distances, our capacity to run fast and leap high—they were watered down over millions of years as our brains became more highly developed. But Conrad retains these physical traits, which are integrated with the higher mental capacities of humans. Conrad almost straddles the evolutionary scale. He's a Darwinian exception of some kind."

Megan's face is drawn; Adrian sees fear etched on her features.

"Something dawns on me," Adrian says. "That night he tracked me, he kept coming. I wonder if he could hear me, maybe even smell me."

"I suspect it was his hearing."

"You know . . . when I was hiding in the cemetery, a sudden wind blew in; maybe that's why I surprised him. He couldn't hear me."

"I find this all very scary," Megan says. Adrian squeezes her hand. It feels cold yet sweaty.

Grayson adds, "Another thing: he's been reading like crazy, all kinds of things—medicine, law, psychiatry, you name it. He's gone through half our library."

Megan glances at Adrian. He knows she's worried about

Conrad contacting Kovac.

"And he's becoming religious. I don't mean in an apocalyptic way like some of our schizophrenics who hear God talking to them. He's been seeing a pastor from Bridgeport, a guy who works with inmates, Pastor Wilhelm. It seems like a sincere interest, but with someone as manipulative as Wilson, we take nothing about him at face value. He's a complex man, but a very delusional one. And his sickness is deeply entrenched."

"You mean he won't stop being paranoid . . . deluded?" Megan asks.

"Exactly," Grayson says with a nod. "I will say, though, that Conrad's delusion is unique. Most of our inmates are globally deluded about lots of things—the government, the CIA, the Mossad—in that sense, Dr. Sheffield was pretty much on target at the trial. But Conrad's delusion orbits around you two and your daughter. As Dr. DuPont—who, by the way, is his primary therapist—said at the trial, Conrad has a *monomania* for you two."

"So," Adrian says, "*we're* at the center of his delusional universe, aren't we?"

"Exactly. He's created this crazy cosmos." Grayson looks contemplative and adds, "There's one thing that's a bit odd about his delusion, though."

"What is it?" asks Megan.

"Well, in my experience, every delusion forms around some *slight* kernel of truth. The deluded patient recruits some small grain of truth and builds an elaborate delusional system around it. I can't find Conrad's kernel of truth. And Conrad's distortion starts with his daughter, Marlee."

"Yes?" Megan says, visibly trembling.

"He's convinced she's *your* child—the two of you."

"Well, as you said, a delusion is a *false* belief," Megan says in a quivering voice.

"Of course it's false," Grayson says. "Yet it keeps coming back to that amazing sense of smell of his. Adrian, do you remember when he said he could *smell* that Marlee's not his? And he could smell her on *you* that night at the bar?"

Adrian's pulse thuds in his throat. He nods his head and feels like choking.

"That statement probably tipped the scales for an NGRI verdict. But there's an interesting element to all this."

"What's that?" Adrian asks, as something gnaws in his guts.

"It's Conrad's sense of smell. Olfaction develops in the forebrain. It's an early mammalian development. I'm sure you know that dogs sniff each other as a way of greeting. Smell is used for sexuality and survival in most species—but not really in humans.

"In animals, it's particularly important with offspring. You've probably seen nature films on Animal Planet, where a calf gets lost but its mother finds it. They know their own offspring by its *smell*. We've lost that primitive capacity." Grayson pauses and shakes his head. "But Conrad insists his sense of smell tells him Marlee's yours," Grayson says, looking at Adrian.

Adrian feels his guts squirm. "He *smells* that I'm Marlee's father?"

"That's part of his madness," says Grayson.

Adrian's thoughts eddy. *Conrad's right. But he's still crazy . . . with a great sense of smell.*

"Dr. Grayson," Megan says in a trembling voice, "did I somehow kick Conrad over the edge?"

"No, he was always jealous and insecure. Maybe when the baby was born, it became the core element of his delusion. As Dr. DuPont testified, deep down Conrad doesn't feel he's manly enough to have fathered a child. So in his mind, you *must* have had an affair."

"Conrad never told me about his adoptive father," Megan says.

"Well, his early life set the stage. And part of what kicked him over the edge was the trouble conceiving the baby. I've tried convincing him to have DNA testing to prove that she's his daughter."

Adrian's stomach lurches as a pang of tension shoots through him.

"But he refuses. Conrad can't entertain the *possibility* of the truth contradicting what he *believes* it to be. He selectively ignores anything that might disprove his belief."

Adrian casts a quick glance at Megan.

"You see, a delusional person recruits whatever he can to support the delusion. For Conrad, the DNA testing would all be a massive conspiracy."

"So, the delusion *itself* prevents Conrad from reaching the truth?" Megan says.

"Yes. The delusion perpetuates itself. That's why Conrad'll be here for a very long time."

Relief percolates through Adrian. DNA testing is on the back burner—at least for the foreseeable future.

They fall silent. Afternoon sun filters through the window.

"Is there anything else you want to ask me?" Grayson says.

Adrian looks at Megan.

She shakes her head.

"Let me assure you, the delusion is a permanent fixture in Conrad's mental landscape. Some of our insanity acquittees seem to make some changes, but it's a sham to get out of Whitehall."

"Is it possible he'll get out?" Megan asks.

"Megan, a delusion is a delusion is a delusion."

"But if it improves, if he gives it up?" Adrian asks.

"Conrad will have to convince the PSRB. And while I always push very hard for mental health, I don't think we can *drive people sane*."

"Well put," Adrian says with a laugh. He feels his muscles uncoiling.

"I'm very aware of what lurks in the dark corners of Conrad's mind . . . the animal within. But science will outwit instinct. And I have science on my side."

Late-afternoon sunlight casts slats of golden light onto the Neanderthal skull. Dust particles swirl in the luminescence.

"Conrad will have to get past me and the PSRB."

Adrian and Megan get up. It's getting late and they'll be stopping at a cozy French bistro in Fairfield, where Adrian's made reservations.

Grayson moves from behind the desk and walks them to the office door. He shakes their hands and smiles reassuringly. "I hope you're both a little more at ease," he says, opening the door. "You can both go on with your lives. And Marlee can, too."

Part IV

Thirty-five

Grayson glances around the conference table. The entire PSRB is present—doctors, nurses, aides—everyone who's had significant contact with Conrad Wilson. Pads, pens, laptops, coffee mugs, and cell phones are scattered about. Nicole DuPont, sitting at the other end of the table, peers at him in that intense way of hers; Grayson feels his pulse quicken. He senses an air of dissension and feels an impending adversarial discussion is about to occur. His skin prickles.

"Okay, let's talk about Conrad Wilson," Grayson says. "He's asking for a weekend pass with Pastor Wilhelm and his wife. They're willing to assume weekend guardianship."

"Conrad's been here for eighteen months," says Nicole DuPont, making eye contact with each panel member; she then fixes her gaze on Grayson. He thinks he detects the beginnings of a smirk on her face. "As his primary therapist, I meet with him twice a week, and it's hard to believe he's an inmate. He's made remarkable progress."

"But, Nicole," says Grayson, feeling his armpits dampen, "we've never had *any* inmate eligible for a pass before three years."

"Yes," says Dr. Scott Williams, a psychiatrist with a reddish beard. "This is unprecedented."

"Eighteen months?" says Albert Channing, an older psychiatrist with a shock of white hair. "Most of these guys are lifers who're in cold storage."

"But we've never had anyone like Conrad," Nicole says, her eyes widening. "He's not schizophrenic or retarded or brain damaged. He's not bipolar or psychotic in any global way. He had a very well-defined delusion—one limited to three people—and that's dissipated completely."

"Have you challenged him about it?" Grayson asks. His pulse kicks up a notch.

"Yes, I have," Nicole says with an emphatic nod. "His delusion has been eradicated. When I ask about Marlee being Adrian Douglas's child, he laughs. I feel ridiculous for even asking about it."

"You think he's telling the truth?" Grayson hopes he doesn't convey the incredulity seeping through him like an oil slick.

"What constitutes truth?" Nicole asks, her eyes widening again mirthfully. "I don't know if there's any absolute *truth* in the world."

"We're not looking for absolutes," Grayson says, keeping his tone neutral. He knows Nicole's über-opinionated and quite proprietary about her patients; she dislikes being challenged about them. *Watch yourself. Don't get into a pissing match*, he tells himself. "But, Nicole, we've seen inmates make sudden conversions to sanity. Is Wilson just parroting what he thinks you want to hear? Is he trying to manipulate us?"

"I see no evidence of that, John. And believe me, I've probed repeatedly. But I think we should hear from Jim, who's tested Conrad extensively."

"I agree with Nicole," says James Morgan, the neuropsychologist. "Wilson's a completely different man from the one I evaluated before the trial. There's no evidence of psychosis, and we see no marker suggesting deception."

"I'm skeptical," says Scott Williams. "A deeply ingrained delusion doesn't evaporate into thin air."

"I appreciate that, Scott," Nicole says as her lips form a brittle smile. "But Jim's testing confirms it—there's no psychosis. The medication, the therapy—individual and group—and Conrad's meetings with Reverend Wilhelm have been vital. The pastor's become something of a father figure to him . . . a good father."

"That doesn't impress me," says Williams. "There's plenty of religious fervor on the ward, all of it psychotic."

Nicole shakes her head. "But more than that, Scott," she says, "Conrad's focused on his *future*. He wants to go back to Colorado to start a lay ministry, thanks to the pastor. He doesn't want to stay here, so I see no risk to Dr. Douglas, Ms. Haggarty, or the child. And they were the sole objects of his delusion. I truly believe his sanity's been restored."

"I agree," says Morgan. The psychologist's sallow look—a sixty-watt tan—reminds Grayson of patients in terminal toxicity, in liver failure. "I've given Wilson the MMPI-2, and Wilson places in the normative population."

"Normative?" Grayson asks. "What's *normal*, anyway?"

There's laughter around the table. Nicole frowns and shoots him an aggrieved look.

"The MMPI is the most revealing test ever devised," Morgan says. "And Wilson shows no signs of paranoia."

"C'mon, Jim," says Channing. "The MMPI's been around since the thirties. It's older than *I* am, for Christ's sake. And it can be faked."

"Oh, really?" Morgan asks, his face reddening. "If you'd kept up with developments, Albert, you'd know the test was revised to near perfection. Plenty of new questions were added, and new validity scales are now included."

"Still, a savvy test taker can fake it," Channing says.

"The test *can't* be faked now," says Morgan. "There are five hundred and sixty-seven questions along with different scales. Scale Four measures for psychopathic deviation, and Scale Six tests for paranoia. It's *very* accurate. There's no way a delusional individual can keep his paranoia from showing. It's like asking a starving lion not to tear into raw meat."

"Still, Jim, it's self-reporting," Channing says. "You can't control the results."

"You're trying to undermine the test results, Albert," Nicole replies, staring icily at Channing. "Do you have a bias against Conrad?"

"No, but—"

"Let me set you straight, Albert," Morgan interjects. Grayson feels the table shaking; Morgan is being confronted about the sacredness of the MMPI, and it's driving him up a wall.

"There are time-tested validity scales. The L Scale detects attempts at faking and lying. It can determine if the test taker contradicts himself at any point during the test."

"A brilliant guy like Wilson can fake it," Grayson says.

"Rest assured, John—and you too, Albert—*nobody* can remember a response from three hundred questions earlier; it's *impossible*. The questions pick up even the most subtle contradictions. And the VRIN scale—the Variable Response Inconsistency Scale—cross-checks the L Scale. It fine-tunes the detection of any inconsistencies."

"C'mon, Jim, don't you recall Wilson's memory?" Grayson asks.

"Of course I remember his abilities, John," says Morgan.

"Wilson's memory is almost savantlike," Grayson says. "You yourself marveled at how he memorized thirty random words in sixty seconds. I'll bet Wilson remembers every question with that photographic memory. And with all the reading he's done, he knows plenty about the MMPI."

"That wouldn't help, John. The test is exquisitely sensitive to manipulation."

"I wish I had your confidence in it, Jim."

"John, you *are* being adversarial," Nicole says.

"No, he's not, Nicole," says Channing. "He's just being circumspect."

"What does Pastor Wilhelm say?" asks Nicole.

"I'm a bit leery of the pastor," says Williams. "He sees the good in everyone."

"I think he's a very thoughtful man," Nicole says, her eyes boring into Williams. "Do you question the pastor's judgment?"

"I'm just not sure he's objective anymore. Remember, Nicole, as a man of the cloth, the pastor's focused on redemption . . . the triumph of good over evil."

"So you *are* questioning his judgment," Nicole says with a nascent smirk.

"Maybe . . . when it comes to his assessment of Wilson," Williams adds.

"Just what's so threatening about Conrad's request?" Nicole asks. "And, John, I don't think you've explained your reservations about him."

Her stare penetrates Grayson, conveying an invitation and a challenge. He tries not to let it irritate him, so he changes position, pivots, sits sideways, and crosses his legs. But he feels tension grip him. His toes curl as his eyes lock on to Nicole's gaze. He feels his jaw muscles twitch, and a vague stirring starts in his groin. He suddenly recalls what happened three years earlier.

My God . . . the incident.

Nicole had just begun at Whitehall after a brilliant stint with the ACLU. She had potential for forensic work: she was smart, articulate, an experienced attorney, *and* a psychiatrist. She came alone to Grayson's office to insist that some petty ward regulation be rescinded, and they argued vehemently—he can't even recall the issue. Grayson refused to change the rule and Nicole got progressively annoyed.

When the meeting ended, they got up and walked to the door. As Nicole passed close to him, nettled and bristling with righteous indignation, he inhaled the exquisite scent of her hair and skin. It might have been soap or body lotion—he couldn't be certain. It was so sweet, so clean-smelling, and at the same time, so alluring that a swell of desire rose in him. It was so powerful, he felt his blood rush and he grew light-headed as his groin tingled. In a moment of sheer insanity, the intensity of her sensuality and of his own need nearly overcame him. He almost reached for her—wanted desperately to touch her—and he imagined the wetness of her mouth, the aroma and feel of her skin. At that fleeting instant at his office door, he was appalled by his own venality, by his willingness—without plan or intent—to quickly accede to this appetite and be driven by a raw draft of desire.

Despite the tide of lust coursing through him, he held himself in check, and suddenly Nicole turned to him. Her look—a knowing one—told him she knew exactly what he'd felt in that moment of erotic overdrive. Had he imagined her stifling a knowing snigger of superiority?

Grayson thinks of it as the *incident*—and it dangles in his memory like a pointed dagger. He feels it could have been a ruinous moral lapse, jeopardizing his marriage, career, and reputation. Grayson's certain that single moment three years ago curdled his relationship with Nicole. When she's around—especially at board meetings—he feels the strain of her challenge. That's what it was that day, a contest of wills. He feels embers of smoldering tension, intellectual and sexual. In Nicole's presence, he feels a nervous charge—as though there's electricity in the air. He's terribly aware of her manner of walking, the swaying of her hips, the tilt of her head, the nape of her neck, and above all, her smell. She emits an essence he finds intoxicating. Whenever she passes near him, he inhales deeply, and a blood wash of desire fills him.

Breaking away from Nicole's stare, Grayson says, "What do the nurses and aides say about Wilson?"

"I wish every inmate was as cooperative," replies Peter

Woodruff, an aide.

"I second that motion," says Don Compton, another aide. "Wilson helps out on the ward and uses the treadmill and the weight training room. I'd have to say he spends most of his time in the library. And another thing, about six months ago, I taught him how to play chess. He picked it up in no time flat. As some of you know, I've won the Fairfield County Chess Association's tournament for the last four years. And within a few weeks of learning the game, Conrad was beating me every time. He spends his time poring over chess books and manuals. It's not only his memory that's so fantastic, but he has the ability to see ahead on the board—to anticipate his opponent's moves. It's amazing."

"Well, we know he's up there in the genius category when it comes to intelligence, especially with numbers and mechanics," says Scott Williams.

"How's he been about compliance with medication?" asks Grayson.

"No problem," says Lynda Becker, head nurse. "He takes his Risperdal every morning. The pill goes right down the hatch. And when I ask him, he fetches some of the more disturbed patients . . . escorts them to the nursing station for morning meds. I'd say the Risperdal's worked. He's done very well."

The discussion goes on and ranges from Conrad Wilson's activities, his sleep pattern, exercising, his reading, the assessment of Pastor Wilhelm, staff interactions, his relations with other inmates, his test scores—everything.

"I wonder . . . if we refuse his request, will he petition for a pass?" Grayson says.

"Oh, I'm *sure* he will," Nicole says.

"What makes you so certain?"

"He and I discussed it. I advised him of his rights."

"You're not his *attorney*, Nicole." A twinge of annoyance nips at Grayson. The voltage in his chest increases. "What'd you tell him?"

"That if we don't give him a pass, Kovac can petition for a judicial hearing."

"Sounds like you're giving him legal advice, Nicole."

"He should know his rights, John."

"Patients have petitioned over the years—without attorneys," says Williams.

Grayson adds, "We all know Kovac will invoke the Mental Hygiene Statutes, Section 17a-584, and I'm afraid he'll succeed."

"Why're you *afraid* he'll succeed, John?" Nicole says with a bitter smirk.

"C'mon, Nicole, you know delusions never disappear. I'm sure he'd still go after Adrian Douglas and Megan Haggarty, who, by the way, are married now with a child of their own. Wilson's just masking his craziness."

"I'm sorry, John, but I don't share your therapeutic nihilism," Nicole replies.

"Nihilism? It's *realism*, Nicole. I'm sure Wilson harbors the same delusion he always has. He's just toned it down for us."

"Don't you have faith in the medication, John?"

"Faith doesn't have a place in this discussion."

"Right. That's the pastor's area of expertise," Williams says with a laugh.

Grayson regards Nicole's chilled smile and cold stare. It makes Grayson suspect—no, he's absolutely certain—she's dismissing him completely. She's merely waiting to hit back with a lawyerly riposte.

"Excuse, me," Nicole blurts, her tone steely, "but I think faith *does* belong here, John. Conrad's been a model patient—inmate, if you prefer that horrid term. In *my* opinion, Conrad *is* ready for a strictly supervised weekend pass."

Nicole waits a beat and glances around the table; her eyes again rest on Grayson. "As for *faith*," she says with an icy look, "I *must* have faith in the system . . . that it's equitable, because above all, we have to guarantee patients' rights under the law. And we owe it to Conrad Wilson to be fair."

"Look, Nicole," Grayson says, a bolt of irritation sizzling through him, "I'm all for fairness and for whatever you deem *equitable*, but this man is psychotic. And as a direct result of his psychosis, he tried to *kill* two people. The jury, in its collective wisdom, decided he acted out of a delusion and that he's dangerous to three people. And probably to anyone who gets in his way. To paraphrase the statute . . . he's a *desperate and dangerous individual*."

"Oh, John, you're not going to quote the law, are you?" Nicole asks with narrowed eyes.

"So, the court decided," Grayson says, ignoring her, "that Wilson should be extruded from society—not in prison, but at Whitehall. And it's as much our job to protect the innocent as it is to guarantee Wilson's rights. So please, Nicole, let's not talk about being fair—or *equitable*, a word you lawyers just love. This may sound corny, but there's a greater societal good at stake here . . . not just Conrad Wilson's fate."

"Don't you *dare* lecture me, John," Nicole shoots back, her face now crimson. "We still have an obligation to this man, whether *you* like it or not. And our goal is to be *therapeutic*; it's restoration of sanity, in case you've forgotten, and—"

"*Restoration of sanity?*" Grayson interrupts, slapping his hand on the table. He's nearly shouting now and hates the way he sounds. Yet he keeps going. "That's a *legal* concept, not a *medical* one. Now *you're* quoting the law. We're not in *court*, Nicole. You're not at the *ACLU* anymore. And we don't need a legal brief. There's no such thing as *restoration of sanity*. Not in the *real* world. All we get is a temporary reprieve from this man's madness, assuming he's not faking his improvement."

Grayson's voice drops an octave. "And let's face it, Nicole, the reprieve is *partial*, and it's contingent on our pumping antipsychotic medication into him. The moment his Risperdal's stopped, he's as mad as ever. So don't preach to us about *restoring sanity*. We're not some religious order. We're not here for restoration, redemption, revelation, or salvation. Let's keep it *real*."

"For your information, John, you could say that about *any* committed patient . . . in a civil institution or at Whitehall," retorts Nicole. She looks like she's seething. "When the medication stops, the patient regresses and the psychosis returns. So, we just lock 'em up and toss the key?"

"I think the man's still delusional," Grayson says.

"You may *think* that," replies Nicole, "but there's *no* evidence of it. I challenge anyone to point out one instance of psychosis Conrad Wilson's demonstrated in the last six months. *One* instance," she says, her gaze roaming around the table. "And I would remind you that the MMPI doesn't lie. And Conrad Wilson passed the test with flying colors. And I have news for you, John," she says, fixing her eyes once again on Grayson, "unless Conrad can be shown to be psychotic, we can't hold him anymore."

"He's still dangerous," Grayson says.

"Well, John, now I *will* quote the law, since you brought up dangerousness. Need I remind you of the now-famous case of *Foucha v. Louisiana*?"

"Oh, shit. Here we go. Nicole's going into her lawyer mode. She's—"

"In 1992," Nicole interrupts, "the Supreme Court ruled that *potential* dangerousness alone is *not* a justification to retain an insanity acquittee if there's no longer evidence of *mental illness*. An NGRI acquittee cannot be confined as a mental patient without some *medical* justification for doing so."

"Oh, c'mon, Nicole—"

"And the court ruled that even if the individual *is* potentially dangerous, the NGRI acquittee who's regained his sanity cannot be indefinitely confined on the sole justification that he *might* be dangerous. He must be both *ill* and *dangerous* for an involuntary commitment to continue."

"Nicole, you're such a fucking bleeding heart—"

"That's *enough*, John," shouts Nicole, shooting to her feet. Her eyes flash furiously. She radiates anger like a halogen light. "I won't tolerate a personal affront. This isn't your private fiefdom. I'm *outta* here." She pivots, heads for the door.

"*Wait* a minute, Nicole," Scott Williams says, standing.

Nicole stops, turns, and faces the group. Her features are floridly red.

"Let's just calm down," Williams says. "Everyone, please. You're *both* right. We've gotta preserve Wilson's rights, but we have to consider the *societal* good—in this case, the intended victims of his crimes."

"He didn't get convicted of any crime," Nicole snaps.

"He may not've been convicted, but he tried to murder two people," Williams says. "So let's forget *conviction*, Nicole. That's the *legal* system. We're mental health professionals, and this isn't a courtroom; it's a medical board meeting. And we have to make a *medical* decision—one that can have very serious consequences for *other* people, not just for Wilson. Our decisions can have life and *death* consequences. In that respect, John's one hundred percent correct. What we decide could affect *real* people in the *real* world.

"So let's do this rationally," Williams says. "Let's not get into petty squabbles. This meeting isn't about *us*. It's about Conrad Wilson—his rights, his progress, and the danger he could present to other people. It's about our obligations—to him and to those people who could be harmed if he's released. So please, Nicole, sit down and let's go about our business."

Silence blankets the gathering.

Blood throttles through Grayson; he feels his face flush.

Nicole edges back toward the conference table.

"I'm sorry if I offended you, Nicole," says Grayson, aware his voice is quivering. "Please accept my apology." Grayson feels like he's sitting in a nest of scorpions. Stingers poised.

"Apology accepted," Nicole murmurs and then sits down. She clasps her hands on the table and gives Grayson a steely look.

"Obviously, there's sentiment to allow Wilson a weekend pass," Channing says.

"A show of hands?" Grayson says, sensing he may be the only serious holdout.

All hands go up, though Grayson observes Albert Channing's and Scott Williams's hands rise tentatively.

"It looks like I'm in the minority," Grayson says.

"Frankly, John, I'm sure Wilson'll file a petition and the judge will grant him the pass," says Channing.

"That's how the system works," Nicole adds.

"It's too liberal," says Channing. "And, Nicole, it's not your job to be the inmate's advocate."

"Albert, I believe in civil rights," she says. "They're the cornerstone of—"

"The system's partial toward inmates," Channing cuts in.

"That's because of abuses in the past," Nicole rebuts.

"Okay, people, let's get back to this case," Grayson says, peering around the table. "Albert's right. A judge will probably grant Wilson a weekend pass, if not now, in a few months. He has a spotless record. And Nicole's right, too. Patients' rights are a big deal. So it's inevitable that Wilson's gonna get the pass, and we have to protect *everyone's* rights."

"Okay, so what do we do?" asks Channing.

Grayson says, "I'll go along with a pass, but with very strict conditions."

"Like what?" Nicole asks as her eyes narrow.

"First, Pastor Wilhelm and his wife dole out Wilson's medication. I think you can speak with the pastor, Lynda," Grayson says, turning to Nurse Becker. "They have to know exactly what to look for if Wilson misses a dose."

"We can arrange that," she says.

"Second, Wilson'll spend the weekend at the pastor's house, but we use an electronic monitoring system."

"That's *absurd*," Nicole says.

"What's absurd about it?" Williams asks.

"It's coercive. It's just so . . . it's antithetical to everything I ever thought about medicine and psychiatry."

"First of all, Nicole," Grayson says, "you yourself said he's ready for a pass under *strict supervision*. And this isn't pure psychiatry. *You* know that more than anyone else."

"We're dealing with a prison population, Nicole," says Williams. "It makes sense." He turns to Grayson. "We've never done this before, John. How does it work?"

"Wilson wears an ankle bracelet during the weekend."

"A Martha Stewart arrangement?" Morgan says with a laugh.

"That's right," Grayson says. "The bracelet communicates with a receiving device in the pastor's home. The device has a limited range. Any tampering with the bracelet or receiving device sends a signal. The device reports when the bracelet moves out of range. It connects to the monitoring station through a telephone line or a 3G network to a cell phone."

"A monitoring station?" asks Williams.

"Yes, to a private security company. And I'd be willing to have it programmed to send an alert to my cell phone if Wilson moves out of range," Grayson says. "Or if he tampers with the bracelet."

"Sounds good," Morgan says.

"Will the pastor consent to this?" asks Channing.

"He'll have to if there's gonna be a weekend pass," Grayson says.

"What if the pastor and Wilson want to go somewhere?" asks Nicole.

"Not for the first few visits. Wilson's limited to the house and church."

"I agree," says Williams. "Let's go slowly and see how things develop."

"One other thing," Grayson says. "The pastor lets us install a GPS tracking system in his car. And the wife's car, too."

"You really want to do *that*?"

"Absolutely, Nicole," says Grayson. "The latest models have a six-month battery life since they're motion-activated. When the car stops, it switches off. It's attached to the inside of a bumper, or a wheel well, and transmits to a GPS Web site."

"Sounds reasonable," Williams says.

"There's one other provision."

Everyone eyes Grayson. Nicole sighs, shaking her head.

"The pastor can't tell Wilson about the GPS system," Grayson says.

There are nods all around. Nicole sighs again, this time more heavily. Grayson tries ignoring her, but it's difficult.

So he says, "If we agree on these precautions, we can grant Conrad Wilson's request for a weekend visit with the pastor and his wife."

Thirty-six

Pastor Wilhelm maneuvers his 2001 Chevy Impala up the fume-filled ramp to level two of the Danbury mall parking garage. Conrad sits to his right. The pastor feels a deep sense of satisfaction as he remembers first meeting Conrad at Whitehall more than a year ago.

It was early afternoon and the dayroom was deserted except for Conrad, who was slumped on a couch, lost in thought. His muscular frame bulged beneath a blue shirt and faded jeans. The man was an incredible physical specimen. But most of all, the pastor remembers those eyes, how devoid of spirit they were, how dormant—even dead—as though life had drained from him. The pastor's heart went out to him.

"I'm Pastor Wilhelm," he said, and when they shook hands, Wilhelm was struck by the sinew of Conrad's forearm. He realized this man could mangle his hand in a moment, and yet, despite Conrad's physicality, subjugation permeated his very being. The man was defeated, imprisoned in a spiritual vacuum. Wilhelm had known many such men from his days as a youth in the Bridgeport slums. And later as a Lutheran minister visiting the prisons, working with inmates to revive and nourish their souls.

"Conrad, you're the first prisoner who ever asked for me," Wilhelm said, sitting beside him. "What made you do that, son?"

Conrad's face seemed to sag on itself. "Pastor, I just feel . . . dead," he said softly, even plaintively. Indeed, he seemed steeped in the agony of Hell's Grim Tyrant. With wet eyes, Conrad said, "I want to feel alive again."

"Conrad, how can I help you?"

"Maybe we could talk and . . ."

"And what, Conrad?"

"And maybe you can suggest Bible readings for me."

"Readings? Such as . . . ?"

"I'm not sure . . . passages about forgiveness."

"The Book of Daniel says, 'The Lord our God is merciful and forgiving, even though we have rebelled against him.'"

Conrad's eyes beseeched the pastor—desperately.

"Do you want to be forgiven, son?" Wilhelm asked.

"Yes, but I also need to learn to forgive those who've trespassed against me."

Yes, as he heads for level three of the garage, Daniel Wilhelm recalls feeling something truly divine occurred that day. As he and Conrad talked, a feeling of lightness came over the pastor. He felt the Holy Spirit fill his soul with Truth. Looking back, he realizes it was a powerful aura—one he'd never before experienced, even at his own ordination. It intensified when Conrad said, "Pastor, though I'm here for my sanity to be restored, above all, I need restoration of my soul."

Sitting in the sun-drenched dayroom, Wilhelm felt he was truly doing God's work. Because he'd never heard a congregant—or anyone for that matter—ask for such a thing: restoration of the soul. Conrad's withered soul and his unusual request distilled for Daniel Wilhelm everything meaningful in the church: the Holy Communion worship, the fellowship meetings, the choral hymns, the word of God, and the sacraments. And right then, the mystery of God—of truly knowing and feeling a divine presence—came to him. This was the work he'd been born to do.

So they began meeting. Conrad told him his life's story—every unfortunate detail. Daniel Wilhelm listened carefully and was deeply touched. At each meeting, he gave Conrad pastoral counseling and suggested Bible passages to read. Conrad studied them—sedulously—and they discussed their layered meanings.

Daniel Wilhelm was astonished: Conrad not only recalled each biblical passage, but applied them to his everyday experiences—turned the beauty and poetry of the Bible into a living, breathing thing with relevance and deep meaning. For the first time in his life, Daniel Wilhelm could *feel* the abiding truth of words written thousands of years earlier.

Some months later, Conrad said, "Maybe I could form a Bible study group here on the ward."

"That would be wonderful, Conrad."

Conrad soon formed a group with three other inmates.

"I can feel you growing as a person, Conrad," Wilhelm said a while later. He found himself anticipating each meeting with Conrad and knew he was witnessing the redemption of Conrad's God-given soul.

"I'm thankful for your guidance," Conrad said. "With you and the Bible to guide me, I feel an inner calm, maybe even peace."

"There's far more goodness residing in you than you realize, Conrad. I know that in time you can live a life free of anger at the wrongs done to you."

"If I ever get out of here, Pastor, I'd like to start a lay ministry."

"That would be wonderful. Dr. DuPont says you're making excellent progress. And I *do* think God will lead you out," he said, with deep feeling. "Conrad, over these months, I've come to view you as I would a son."

"I think everything happens for a reason, Pastor; you're helping me see that."

Now, on Conrad's fifth weekend pass, the pastor pulls into a parking space. "This is our first trip away from the house or church," the pastor says.

"We could've gone to the Trumbull mall. It's much closer."

"That's all right, Conrad. Those hiking boots look pretty worn out. How much do you run on the treadmill?"

"An hour every day."

"Well, it's time for a new pair."

They get out of the car. Conrad wears cargo pants and a blue work shirt. The pastor wears a light-gray suit and a gray clergy shirt with a white tab collar. They tramp down the oil-stained ramp to the garage exit. "Afterward, we can go to Ruby Tuesday," the pastor says, realizing his stomach is growling. "I told the monitoring company we'd be here until two, so we have plenty of time."

Eastern Mountain Sports brims with a dizzying display of camping, hiking, kayaking, and mountain-climbing equipment.

Conrad tries on a pair of Salomon GTX hikers. "I don't know," he says. "They cost a hundred and forty-five dollars."

"They'll last a lifetime."

"But the expense, Pastor . . ."

"Don't worry. It's been donated by the congregation." Wilhelm peers at Conrad's left foot. "Does the boot leave enough room for the ankle bracelet?"

"Yeah."

"That thing makes me feel like I'm part of the corrections system," Wilhelm says, shaking his head.

"Ah, forget it, Pastor. You and Martha have given me a new life."

"We believe in you," Wilhelm says, breaking into a smile. "We're sure you'll be out of Whitehall before long."

"I'm grateful for your faith in me, Pastor."

"Those boots look like a perfect fit. How do they feel?"

"They're fine."

"You know that Dr. Grayson will want to examine them before you go back to the ward, and your backpack, too."

"Dr. Grayson always goes through my backpack. If I bought a box of trail mix, he'd sift through every nut and raisin."

The pastor chortles. "I don't think Dr. Grayson appreciates the progress you've made. I know Dr. DuPont does."

"She's a tough taskmaster."

"True, but she's your strongest ally. Without her, you wouldn't have these passes. She spoke with your attorney about petitioning the court if the review board didn't grant your request for the passes."

"I have a good feeling about Dr. DuPont."

"I'm glad for her efforts. Because, Conrad, you've enriched our lives. Martha and I look forward to every weekend with you."

"I do too," Conrad says, his eyes glistening.

Wilhelm peers around the store. "Does all this hiking equipment make you nostalgic for Colorado?"

Conrad nods. "It makes me think of the Rockies. I'd give anything to go back there."

"Well, just keep up the good work. You'll get back."

"That's my plan, Pastor. To go back and start that lay ministry."

"I'm sure that'll happen. But when you leave us, Martha and I will miss you," Wilhelm says, as a lump forms in his throat.

At Ruby Tuesday, Conrad orders a veggie burger with french fries and a vanilla milk shake. Wilhelm orders a hamburger and a coke.

"You know, Conrad, this almost feels like a normal outing."

"Yes. Makes me feel"—Conrad searches for words—"like there's someone who cares." He swallows hard and blinks a few times. His eyes moisten. "You know, Pastor, for the first time in my life I feel like I have a family . . . like I have a father," he says, looking into Wilhelm's eyes. "I feel like I have a *good* father."

The pastor's throat thickens. "You're like a son to us . . . the son we lost the day he was born years ago. I even had this thought . . . that if you were willing, we could adopt you. I know it's absurd, but that's how Martha and I feel about you."

Tears brim at Conrad's lower lids. "I never had a father. And now . . ." Conrad's voice breaks. "I can only thank you for everything."

Wilhelm leans across the table and sets his hand on Conrad's thick arm. "I have a thought. Since you're thinking of starting a lay ministry, why not lead the congregation during part of tomorrow's service?"

"You think I can?"

"The way you've been reciting scripture, I'm sure of it."

"When I think about what brought me to Whitehall, I realize it's important to forgive," Conrad says.

"Forgiveness is one of the pillars of our faith, Conrad. If I quote from Ephesians, chapter 4, the verse says: 'Get rid of all bitterness, passion, and anger. No more shouting or insults, no more hateful feelings of any sort. Instead, be kind and tenderhearted to one another, and forgive one another, as God has forgiven you through Christ.'"

"And it says in Mark 11:25–26," Conrad says, "'And when you shall stand to pray, forgive, if you have aught against any man: that your Father also, who is in heaven, may forgive you your sins.'"

"Conrad, forgiveness can lead to redemption. I wasn't always the way I am now. When I was a young man, I ran with a bad crowd. Many of my friends' parents abused or abandoned them. So my friends were filled with anger, even hatred, and turned to crime; some went to prison. The same fate awaited me if I didn't change my ways. I felt cheated, as though I was robbed of life's good things. Anger burned like a flame inside me and took its toll. Visiting my friends in prison, I realized there was a way out of this life's misery. It meant turning to God. And that's how I found my calling. Those prison visits changed my life.

"So believe me, Conrad, there *is* such a thing as redemption. It means giving yourself over to a higher power."

Conrad nods and clasps his hands together.

"Conrad, I think you could recite a brief homily on forgiveness at tomorrow's service."

"I'll work on it tonight."

"Martha and I are blessed that you came into our lives."

Conrad whispers, "You've brought my soul back from the dead. You've given me hope. Thank you, Pastor. Thank you for everything."

Thirty-seven

Conrad wakes up suddenly. He thinks he was dreaming about Colorado—the vast mountains, sweeping moraines, endless vistas of Colorado spruce and white pines, the sweet resinous scent of the air and the rushing streams. Sitting at the bedside, he raises his arms, cracks his knuckles, and then pops the bones in his neck.

It's the last Saturday in July, his sixth weekend with the Wilhelms. The bedside table clock reads seven thirty. It's almost the middle of the day for Conrad. At Whitehall, he's up at five, does his two hundred crunches, followed by a hundred push-ups, and then reads a book he's borrowed from the hospital library.

Conrad thinks about his time at Whitehall. It hasn't been bad. He sees Nicole DuPont twice each week—Tuesdays and Thursdays—and the psychologist, Jim Morgan, once a week. Even though Jim looks like a pencil-necked geek, he's really a good guy and has worked hard with Conrad—not as effectively as Nicole DuPont—but Jim's got a good heart and really tries to help. Conrad sees Grayson every other week, which is always tough. The guy's a straight shooter and takes shit from no one—doesn't move the needle a micron on the bullshit gauge.

Then there's group therapy: a gabfest of nonstop insanity from the inmates. The food at Whitehall is institutional—doesn't compare to Martha Wilhelm's—but it's wholesome and plentiful.

Conrad uses the treadmill and pumps serious iron; he's added plenty of rock-hard muscle. He now weighs two hundred fifty-five pounds.

Conrad can read as much as he wants: law, medicine, chess, anything. He knows it's his right as an insanity acquittee. His rights are enumerated in Part III of the Connecticut Statutes relating to the Department of Mental Health.

And he's thoroughly familiar with the US Supreme Court's recognition of the special status of criminal acquittees as set forth in *Jones v. United States*, 463 U.S. 354, 370, 103 S. Ct. 3043, 77 L. Ed. 2nd 694 (1983). The US Constitution permits the government to confine him to a mental institution until he's achieved "restoration of sanity."

Lord Jesus, restoration of sanity could take years and years. He *had* to get better.

So how'd he do it?

First, he kept his cool, suffered through the amiable chitchat with inmates, even with the craziest of the loony bin bunch. It wasn't easy, but he suffered through it.

Second, he never missed an appointment with Jim Morgan, with Grayson, or with Nicole DuPont, his primary therapist and lifeline.

When he first got on the ward, he was on CO—constant observation. An aide escorted him everywhere. Even in the crapper. They were worried he might hang himself in the shower stall. Bedsheets can be dangerous.

But the staff learned to trust him. Which was important because their input was crucial about his eligibility for a weekend pass and eventually, for discharge.

He'd researched plenty on Don Compton's laptop, especially the case of John Hinckley, the guy who tried to impress Jodie Foster by shooting Ronald Reagan. Hinckley was found NGRI. He had a monomania, just like what the shrinks said Conrad had.

Hinckley was confined to St. Elizabeth's Hospital but eventually got temporary release time.

Yes, it was crucial that Conrad got better. So he began searching his soul and realized that Marlee *is* his very own. Of *course* she is. To believe otherwise would be absolutely crazy—delusional. And as he said to Dr. DuPont, it was ridiculous to think Megan was carrying on with Douglas all those years ago; Conrad would have known *something*. After all, the hospital gossip mill at Yale-New Haven was ubiquitous.

Conrad read all about delusions. Patients rarely renounce them; and if they do, it's a slow, painful process. It's rarely a revelation. Rather, it's a soul-searching evolution. Pastor Wilhelm would call it a spiritual enlightenment. You must labor long and hard to attain such spirituality.

Still, sitting at the bedside, Conrad thinks about the Mental Hygiene Law.

Part II of the General Provisions of the Connecticut Statutes governs state hospitals and the Department of Corrections. Section 17a-521 is very clear: "The Director of the Whitehall Forensic Division, under provisions he deems advisable, may permit a patient—under the provisions of Section 17a-584—to temporarily leave the institution, in the charge of his guardian, relatives, or friends."

Conrad knew he needed a place to go—one the PSRB would find acceptable.

So he contacted Pastor Daniel Wilhelm, a sixty-year-old Lutheran minister he'd heard about through the hospital grapevine. The pastor worked with former inmates, parolees, and psycho-acquittees.

He and the good pastor read the Bible regularly—from Genesis to Apocalypse—and now Conrad's virtually memorized the scriptures. Has it all down cold.

He's on his sixth weekend pass, not locked up in Bedlam—that state-sanctioned snake pit where the psychos—in their soul-sapping sicknesses—shuffle through the hallways, drool like ghouls with glazed eyes and spastic gaits, grunt garbled word salad, and shout shit-twisted obscenities. Twice each day they line up at the nursing station amid the funk of unwashed bodies, where they wait like cattle for their medications.

Since his sanity's been restored, he spends weekends with the Wilhelms, away from Whitehall with its mind-dead zombies, locked doors, the electronic monitoring system, exposed commodes, the straitjackets and isolation room—the sheer madness of it all.

Conrad stands, bends forward, and touches his toes. He holds the position, letting the muscles in his lower back and hamstrings uncoil from their sleep-induced tightness. Then he reaches for the ceiling, stretches, and hears his spine put out a series of cracks.

No time for his morning crunches or push-ups. He has too much to do. He pads over to the window and looks out over the lacy green canopy of sycamores and Norway maples. The sky is quite light at this hour, and finches flutter from bushes to trees. Conrad can hear the house wrens' bubbling calls. And a dove coos in the early morning light. Through the slightly opened window he catches the scent of cedar and Scotch pine in the neighbor's backyard. He can smell the earth, too, an organic mix of soil, loam, and mulch. It's going to be a clear July day with very little humidity. Last night the radio said the temperature would be seasonable, in the mideighties—just perfect for an outing.

He puts on his sweat socks, making sure the left one slides beneath the ankle bracelet; he steps into his jeans, dons a T-shirt, his new hiking boots, and a lightweight work shirt, grabs his day pack, and slips out of the bedroom. He treads lightly on the hallway's polished oak floor, knowing the pastor's a light sleeper.

He moves stealthily to the Wilhelms' bedroom door and stops. He hears the pastor and Martha breathing—deep, regular intakes and exhalations of air. It's the rhythm of sound sleep. Conrad hears the rustle of sheets as the pastor rolls onto his side. There's a snort, then a series of deep breaths.

Conrad slips down the stairway, silent as a hand passing through a spider's web. He's thankful the stairway's carpeted because every floorboard in this old colonial farmhouse creaks and groans. The worn wood of the banister slides smoothly beneath his hand as he descends, and he thinks the stairs should be replaced. He could renovate the entire place by himself in three months.

Crossing the living room, Conrad steps lightly on the hand-hooked rug and slips into the pine-paneled den. Holding his breath, he listens and hears soft breathing from the upstairs bedroom. He closes the den door—very gently, not even a tick of the metal latch—switches on the Tiffany desk lamp, peers beneath the computer table, and lowers the speaker volume to "Mute." He boots it up.

Conrad thinks of the trail he's followed, thanks to Don Compton's laptop. A few months after the trial, Douglas and Haggarty got married and moved to Trumbull—set up house in a small ranch-style place. But they soon moved back to Eastport, probably to be closer to the hospital. Conrad followed their little migratory trail on Don Compton's laptop, and though he doesn't have their exact address in Eastport, it's only a few clicks away.

He opens the Web browser and clicks on the address bar. He types in eastportct.gov and hits "Enter" on the keyboard. The town of Eastport's Web page appears on the screen.

Eastport's Web page displays the town's fancy emblem. Plenty of information about the town's history, population, demographics, more than you'd ever want to know.

On the right side of the screen, a heading appears: Online Services.

Beneath that, a list appears. It includes Board & Committee Meetings Minutes, Pay Taxes Online, Search for Online Forms, and Others.

He clicks on "Others."

A new link appears: Offices.

He clicks on it.

A drop-down menu appears.

He clicks on one entry: Town Clerk's Office.

A link appears: Public Records.

Beneath it: Mortgages, Liens, Property transfers. It's all public information. There are very few secrets in the digital age. Yes, the information highway's a treasure trove where almost anything or anyone can be found. Conrad hopes he's doped it all out.

A click on "Public Records" brings up two boxes:

Upper box: Last Name

Lower box: First Name

He types "Douglas" in the upper box. He types "Adrian" in the lower box. He hits "Search."

It comes right up: Adrian and Megan Haggarty Douglas.

The address: 14 Maplewood Lane, Eastport, Connecticut.

Mortgage: Chase Bank.

He disregards the other information. Not relevant.

They moved right back to Eastport, thinking Conrad would be locked away for years. Not that it matters: it's all public—at any town hall. You're only a few clicks away from anyone, anywhere in the world. Unless you're in the Witness Protection Program, you can't disappear. Besides, no one could've anticipated the progress he's made, thanks to Nicole DuPont and Daniel Wilhelm. *It's been restoration of sanity and salvation of soul.*

In the address bar at the top of the screen, he types in "Google Maps" and then hits "Enter." A map of the United States comes up. The cursor blinks on the left side of a rectangle at the top of the page. Conrad types "14 Maplewood Lane, Eastport, CT" in the box.

He hits "Search Maps." A schematic map appears. The picture automatically zeroes in on southwestern Connecticut. A balloon-shaped icon pops up and pinpoints 14 Maplewood Lane in Eastport. Conrad zooms in for a closer look.

Oh, yes . . . that's gotta be it.

On the left side of the page, there's a street level photograph of the house—a midsized center hall colonial—not one of these absurd McMansions that've cropped up like weeds, but an older structure, built maybe fifty, sixty years ago. It sits on a tree-lined cul-de-sac. The picture's a frontal view of the house taken on a bright summer day.

Conrad slides the mouse so the pointer rests on the photograph; he moves the mouse so the picture rotates in each direction—providing views from different angles—left side, right side, front view. He rolls the scroll wheel for a close-up.

It's pretty much what he'd expect in any of the tonier towns in Fairfield County, where people drive high-end Audis, BMWs, Porsches, Volvos, or Mercedes coupes and live in million-dollar-plus homes. The Douglas house shares the cul-de-sac with three others, all variations on colonial architecture.

Fourteen Maplewood Lane is a two-story, white clapboard house with a cedar-shingled roof, a centrally placed front door, multipaned windows, black louvered shutters, and stately pilasters. Pink and lavender azalea bushes are out front; lush rhododendrons, yews, and boxwoods flourish along the sides, and three apple trees form a small grove out front. A detached two-car garage with a covered portico leads into the house—no doubt, right into the mudroom, if it's like the scores of houses Conrad's worked on as a freelancer in the construction trade.

It makes for easy access, either through the mudroom door or the typically flimsy rear door. Conrad can tell the rear is shielded from the neighbors by a dense wall of lush Colorado spruce, like the evergreens he'd see back home. Privacy guaranteed.

He hits "Map" for a schematic of the streets surrounding Maplewood Lane. Moving the cursor to the Altitude Bar, he hits the minus sign and gets a view from five hundred feet in elevation. Each street is labeled.

Another click on the minus symbol: the map view soars to one thousand feet in elevation. It's an eagle's-eye view.

The map shows the sinuous course of the Merritt Parkway and all access streets running from the Merritt leading right to Maplewood Lane. Driving at moderate speed, the house is maybe ten minutes from the Merritt.

Conrad studies the map and quickly memorizes every street on the grid. In his mind, he delineates the precise route he'll take.

He shuts the computer down.

Conrad opens the den door, stands stock-still, tilts his head, and listens. There's not a sound except for the upstairs bathroom sink faucet dripping. A slow drip, which started last weekend. In the basement, the water heater kicks in, rumbling heavily. It's straining. The intake valve needs an adjustment to let in more air. Morning light streams into the living room through the east-facing double-hung windows. Dust motes rise in the golden glow.

Conrad treads softly into the kitchen, opens the louvered pantry door, and reaches up to the top shelf, where the pastor keeps a two-tiered toolbox. He sets it on the Formica kitchen counter, unlatches it, and takes out a Phillips-head screwdriver, a folding knife, a long-handled paring-blade chisel, and a roll of black electrical tape. He sets them all on the kitchen counter.

He goes to the hall closet and removes a wire hanger.

Back in the kitchen, he sifts through the toolbox and slips out a wire cutter. Using the tool, he snaps through the hanger near its curvature, makes another cut, and sets the wire cutter back in the toolbox. He straightens the wire and pulls it to a length of two feet. Using pliers, he fashions a curve at one end of the wire and then returns the pliers to the toolbox. He wraps the hanger's curved end with electrical tape—four complete revolutions—so it'll grip well and won't slip. He sets the wire on the counter.

Then it happens.

A sound—a sudden snort, a gulp of air comes from upstairs. Conrad can tell the pastor's awake. That sound precedes his getting out of bed each morning.

Conrad hears the bedsprings squeak. The pastor's moving, rolling onto his side, about to get out of bed. Then there's a rustling of fabric—bedcovers folding back. The pastor sits at the edge of the bed, bare feet on the floor.

There's a yawn and then groaning floorboards beneath the bedroom carpet.

Judging from the sound, Conrad knows it's the pastor's weight—maybe one hundred eighty pounds—on the floor beside the bed. He's standing.

The floorboards creak as the pastor crosses the room. No doubt, he's at the rocking chair where his bathrobe lies.

There's another sound—clothing rustling—the pastor moving about the bedroom. The bedroom door opens.

Then there's movement in the upstairs hallway and the floorboards squealing.

The door to Conrad's room opens with a barely audible click.

A voice—the pastor's—in a husky whisper says, "Conrad?"

Conrad hears feet padding to the upstairs bathroom, a soft knock on the door, another whisper. The pastor's wondering where Conrad can be. He can imagine the pastor's thoughts.

Footsteps approach the stairs and then descend slowly. Despite the deep pile of the stairway's avocado-green carpeting, Conrad hears the pastor's footfalls moving down the stairs; actually, it's a stealthy descent—sneaky. Hearing the pastor come down the staircase reminds him of the staircase leading to the basement, where Conrad was pushed down the stairs as a boy to the cellar with its dampness and cold floor, where his adoptive father pulled Conrad's pants down and forced him onto his hands and knees. The belt would loosen, then the zipper would go down . . . then the trousers . . . and then mumbled prayers as the bastard undid his own pants.

The pastor descends the stairs—such a pathetic attempt at stealth. Why sneak up on him? Goes to show that you never know who trusts you. Trust is difficult to come by. Take Grayson, for instance. Of all the people at Whitehall, Grayson most lacks basic trust. And basic trust is the foundation of personality development, according to Erik Erikson, the famous psychologist.

Conrad picks up the screwdriver, folds his arms across his chest, hides the tool beneath his forearm, and leans with his back against the kitchen counter.

Conrad hears the pastor's morning shuffle as he crosses the living room.

Pastor Wilhelm enters the kitchen wearing blue-and-white-striped pajamas, a blue terry-cloth bathrobe, and brown leather slippers. His white hair is mussed; a tuft in front stands straight up like an unruly cowlick. He looks sleepy, with puffy eyes and pillowcase creases on his face. He blinks a few times and peers questioningly at Conrad. His eyes shift to the toolbox and the tape and then to the chisel and hanger wire on the kitchen counter.

"Conrad," he says groggily, "how come you're down here?"

Conrad smells Wilhelm's ammoniac morning breath. He stares at the pastor, waiting silently.

"Conrad, what're you doing?" the pastor asks nasally. His pink face registers befuddlement while his bleary blue eyes are wide, questioning. Then a hint of suspicion crosses his features. Conrad smells the pastor's fear.

Conrad thinks the old guy's been a good guardian and has tried to do the right thing. But the stealth, sneaking down the stairs, the religious incantations . . . just like years ago: the basement, the dank coldness of it, the cruelty, the ugly secret he'd held for so long before finally revealing it to Nicole DuPont.

"I have to leave," Conrad says.

"Leave?"

The fear odor is stronger now, filling Conrad's nostrils.

"Yes. You won't be seeing me anymore."

"What do you mean, son? I don't understand."

"The time has come."

"The time for what, Conrad?" Wilhelm asks, shaking his head; he looks perplexed. Then his tongue flicks out; he licks his lower lip and blinks rapidly. His eyes widen when he notices the screwdriver partly tucked under Conrad's forearm.

The fear odor intensifies.

"I'm sorry, Pastor. This isn't going to be pleasant, and I ask your forgiveness."

"Forgiveness? For what, Conrad?"

"For this."

Conrad lunges at Wilhelm—panther-quick—and in a swift, slamming thrust, plunges the screwdriver into the pastor's chest. The tool's hilt thumps heavily against Wilhelm's breastbone mid-sternum. The shaft pierces it and sinks deeply into his heart.

A gasp erupts from Wilhelm's throat. His eyes bulge and their whites go bloodshot red. For a half second, he stands there, as though suspended in stupefied shock. His knees buckle with the impact; he begins sinking slowly downward.

Conrad catches him midfall and lowers him slowly to the kitchen floor. He pats the pastor's head gently, almost lovingly.

"Shh . . . Shh . . . Father," Conrad whispers. "I know you'll forgive me."

He sets the pastor on his back, rests his arms at his sides, and crouches beside him. He straightens the pastor's mussed hair and pats his face gently.

"It'll be over soon, Father."

Conrad slides the screwdriver shaft out from Wilhelm's chest and steps back.

A tube of blood jets upward in a fountain surge from the hole in the pastor's chest—the crimson stream shoots upward with each beat of his dying heart. Wilhelm's eyes roll back and up; he grimaces as a pencil-thin blood burst gushes into the air. It spurts with each heartbeat, pulses more rapidly as the beat quickens—faster, then faster still with less height—as his heart weakens to a diminished pumping. Blood spills onto the pastor's bathrobe, each blood rush lessening in height and pressure as his heart quivers, and then there's a thready dribble. Less and less and less, waning steadily, and finally it puddles in a bubbling pool on his chest, seeps down on the pastor's bathrobe, then everywhere, dripping and spreading as a thickening red paste on the kitchen floor.

The pastor lets out a throaty gurgle; spittle forms on his quivering lips. Then there's a sibilant dying sigh. The air goes out of him. Crouching, Conrad places his fingers to the pastor's neck and feels for a pulse.

There's nothing. The skin is flaccid, getting mottled, losing color.

A minute later the pastor is drained. He's gone.

Conrad turns on the sink water, washes his hands and the screwdriver, dries the tool with a kitchen towel, and drops it in the day pack along with the folding knife, chisel, electrician's tape, and hanger wire. He leaves the pack and toolbox on the counter. Opening a kitchen drawer, he removes an eight-inch boning knife—razor-sharp, a Wenger—precision forged in Switzerland. They make the Swiss Army Knife and a fine line of hunting knives, too. Conrad bounds quickly to the stairway, moving along the edge so there's no creaking as he makes his way to the still-open bedroom door.

Martha Wilhelm is asleep on her back. Her mouth is open; her uvula flutters with each strident intake of air. Her pinkish cheeks puff with each exhalation. There's a low-level whistle as exhaled air passes raucously through her clogged nose and pursed lips. It's the way his adoptive mother struggled for breath during her last cancer-ridden days. Martha's chalky-white arms lie above the bedcovers, tight against her torso. Gazing at those sticklike arms, Conrad is reminded of his adoptive mother's cadaverous arms at the end of her life—her wasting body consumed by the malignant cells seeding her organs. He recalls she did nothing to protect him, thinks of her conspiracy of silence with his adoptive father, and he suddenly realizes Martha—snoring in her sleep—looks and sounds like a slumbering pig. A withering, cancerous pig—devoid of feelings for human suffering, emptied of soul.

Conrad lifts the pastor's pillow, sets it over Martha's face, and in a swift motion, runs the boning knife across her throat and slices deeply—feels the blade scrape across the spinal bones at the back of her neck—and as the blood spurt begins, he presses the pillow over her face and neck, stifling the pumping flow. Her body jumps in a sleeping spasm and she begins bleeding out. A guttural air blast erupts from her severed trachea; the cut ends of her windpipe flutter amid the bloody soak beneath the pillow.

Soon the pillow is drenched in a crimson flood. It seeps downward and oozes onto the sheets beside her severed head. Her life's blood pumps from her carotids and soaks into the mattress as the bedroom air turns fetid from Martha's emptied bowels.

Conrad drops the knife onto the bed and scrambles downstairs. At the kitchen sink, he washes his hands and then dries them.

Conrad knows he has time. So he thinks about everything since he's been at Whitehall and how he fooled them all—even that bloodhound son of a bitch Grayson.

There was the whole deal with Risperdal. In the hospital, Conrad read Kaplan & Sadock's *Comprehensive Textbook of*

Psychiatry and the *Physicians' Desk Reference*. They were quite illuminating. To combat his craziness, his so-called delusion about Megan, Douglas, and the kid, they gave him Risperdal each morning—*liquid medication* in orange juice—so it couldn't be cheeked like a pill. Tasted like piss. If you didn't swallow the cocktail, a gang of huge male aides would pin you down and jab a needle in your ass.

It was injectable sanity. In the ass—another rape, a mind-fuck.

Conrad read all about Risperdal—in the library and online using Don Compton's laptop. The Fairfield County chess champ. Ha! He let Conrad use it each evening after the shrinks went home.

After oral administration, peak plasma concentration takes one hour, according to Kaplan and Sadock. *One hour*. So, after drinking the stuff, he had time to get to the bathroom, shove a finger down his throat, and hurl—upchuck the medication-laced juice. Maybe a tenth of a milligram was absorbed through his stomach lining.

After a month, they changed the medication to pill form. Easy to cheek, then spit into the toilet followed by a quick flush—and he hasn't swallowed any since he's been at Whitehall. That crap messes with serotonin and dopamine levels in the brain—just like what Nicole DuPont said at the competency hearing.

But he's avoided state-mandated sanity.

It's been a long, tough chess game. And his main opponent has been John Grayson—a worthy adversary. Nicole DuPont helped ease the way.

If there's one thing he's thankful for, it's that Don Compton taught him to play chess. And Conrad has studied the game carefully. Chess has its opening moves, its middle game, and the endgame. And Conrad used a conservative opening strategy—like the low-key Réti Opening as opposed to the aggressive Latvian Gambit. The opening strategy sets up your opponent's expectations. Grayson's a smart guy, and he has backup—the entire PSRB. It was important for Conrad to outmaneuver them one move at a time, to slowly execute his strategy.

And it's been an eighteen-month trek to redemption, to restoration of sanity.

Conrad realizes his thoughts are racing—from past to present, streaming wildly over the days of his life and the ugliness of the past—and he finds himself laughing and nearly crying at the same time.

Thirty-eight

Conrad picks up his day pack and goes to the Shaker-style console near the side door. The keys to the pastor's Chevy sit beside an antique brass lamp on the console. He grabs them.

Conrad knows the moment he leaves the house, the ankle bracelet will be out of the receiver's range. An alarm signal will be set off. The hospital and police will be contacted within seconds. And that bloodhound Grayson will orchestrate a search. Conrad realizes he'll have only a narrow window of time before the sheriff and his posse come for him.

Severing the bracelet will also send a signal. Conrad's certain Grayson's arranged for a GPS tracking device somewhere in the pastor's car. There's probably one in Martha's, too, if he's right about Grayson, and he's sure he's got the guy doped out. He's a sneaky son of a bitch. Most likely the device is behind a bumper or in a wheel well, but there's no time to do a thorough search once he sets off the monitoring signal. So Conrad thinks of the alternative he's devised. It takes just a touch of creativity to outflank Grayson.

He opens the folding knife and severs the ankle bracelet.

Now he must move quickly.

He rushes out the side door, unlocks the pastor's Impala, jumps in, and starts the engine.

He figures he'll have a five-minute head start. Maybe more, if he's lucky.

Grayson sits at the maple breakfast room table in his Stratford home. He's wearing jeans, a sweatshirt, and his Jordan 1 Flight basketball sneakers, and he's ready to begin his Saturday. His gym bag's packed. At ten, he'll meet Phil, Matt, and Jeff down at the Y; they'll shoot a few hoops, and afterward they'll go out for breakfast at Danny's Diner.

Right now, Ellen and the kids are asleep, so he'll down a mug of freshly made coffee and go through the *New York Times* online. He unplugs his laptop from the wall socket; it's charged up with four hours of battery life. He boots up and tries to recall when he last bought a newspaper, when he actually *held* a real paper in his hands. *The world's definitely changing.*

He's about to scroll down the front page when his cell phone trills.

He looks at the readout. The message says, "Alarm."

The circuit's been broken at the Wilhelm house. It's 7:59 in the morning. There's no way Wilhelm would be going anywhere with Conrad Wilson this early. Wilhelm's never failed to call in when they go to the mall or to Dunkin' Donuts, to church or a local restaurant. Something's definitely wrong.

It's a breakaway from the receiving device. Holy shit!

Grayson thoughts race as he hits the speed dial on his cell for the Wilhelm home.

Six rings, then comes the answering machine's outgoing message.

Wilson's snuck out and left the house. Or maybe he's tampered with the ankle bracelet. The pastor and his wife must be sleeping. But wouldn't they hear the phone? After six rings? Grayson assumes they have a bedside telephone, but there's no answer.

Grayson snaps his cell shut.

He turns to the laptop, types "SkyCam" into the address bar, hits "Enter."

A menu comes up; he types in his user name and password.

A map of Bridgeport loads in quickly. He has good Wi-Fi reception in the house.

A red dot pulses every two seconds.

Wilhelm's car—the blue Chevy Impala—is moving along Main Street in downtown Bridgeport. The GPS device behind the front bumper pinpoints the vehicle and denotes it's the Impala, not Mrs. Wilhelm's Ford. The device is accurate within twelve inches of the car's location. It's moving at a good clip; it looks like it's heading toward Route 8—a north-south highway.

Holding the still-open laptop, Grayson grabs his cell phone and car keys and heads into the garage. A quick press on the remote and the garage door slides up. He suddenly realizes he'd better call the police.

He dials 911 on his cell and gets a high-pitched sound. No signal, not here in the garage.

He jumps out of the car and stands on the driveway blacktop. He again dials 911.

"Stratford Police, Emergency."

"Officer, this is Dr. John Grayson, medical director of Whitehall Hospital. An insane criminal is on the loose. His name's Conrad Wilson, and he's very dangerous. He's escaped."

"From the asylum in Ansonia?"

"He's on a weekend pass with his guardian, Pastor Daniel Wilhelm. But he's escaped from the Wilhelm house in Bridgeport."

"Where in Bridgeport?"

"Twenty-five Hancock Avenue. And the pastor may be hurt."

"Any idea where this Wilson is now?"

"Yes. I'm tracking him on a GPS. He's in Bridgeport heading onto Route 8. And you'd better have the Bridgeport PD check the pastor's house and chase down that car. Wilson's driving a blue

2001 Chevy Impala, Connecticut tag 919 WKR."

The dispatcher repeats the car's description and plate number.

"Right now he's getting onto Route 8, heading north . . . toward Trumbull. He's heading toward the home of Adrian Douglas and his wife at 22 Hickory Hill Lane in Trumbull. So contact the Trumbull police and send then there."

"A 2001 blue Chevy Impala heading north on Route 8."

"Yes. Trumbull's his destination . . . 22 Hickory Hill Lane."

"We're on it. We'll contact the Bridgeport PD and the Trumbull PD," says the dispatcher.

Grayson gives his address and cell number to the cop, then snaps his phone shut. Breathless, his pulse pounding, he dashes back to the car and jumps inside. He leans to his right, unlocks the glove compartment and opens the inside partition. It's right there: a Walther PK380 pistol—fully loaded. He's had it since he was mugged at knifepoint in a Bridgeport parking lot one winter night three years ago. He'd come out of the correctional facility after examining an inmate when the mugger—who'd been hiding behind his parked Volvo—put the knife to his throat and demanded money.

Grayson opens his cell phone, scrolls down his contacts and stops at "Douglas, Adrian." It's Adrian's cell number. He jumps out of the car, runs to the front of the garage, and hits the speed-dial button. He hears four rings and then he's switched to voice mail. The outgoing message is in Adrian's voice.

"Adrian," Grayson says. "It's John Grayson. Conrad Wilson's escaped. He's in Bridgeport heading toward Trumbull . . . I'm sure he's headed for your house. When you get this message, call the police. I gotta go."

Grayson snaps the phone shut, whirls, and heads for the car. He realizes his hands are shaking and his legs feel weak.

He turns the key in the Volvo's ignition; the engine purrs to life. He's about to back out when he realizes Gary's bicycle is lying on its side, blocking his path. He jumps out of the car, grabs the bike, and tosses it aside.

Returning to the car, he throws it into reverse and backs down the driveway. He makes a broken U-turn, pounds the gas pedal, burns rubber, and races away. He speeds through the Stratford streets, and a few turns later he's on the main drag, Boston Avenue, heading westbound. Most of the stores are still shuttered; a few are opening for the Saturday-morning trade.

Behind him, the sun has risen in the morning sky; the streets haven't yet filled with Saturday traffic. He roars down the avenue, every few moments glancing at the laptop on the seat beside him.

Wilson's now on Route 8, heading north where it merges into Route 25. Yes, he's headed to Trumbull. Grayson's certain he's headed for Adrian and Megan's house.

Grayson realizes he's hitting sixty. Trees and streets hurtle by as the car's engine growls and its tires hammer on the asphalt road. He's gripping the steering wheel so tightly his fingers ache. His heart pounds and his pulse sprints furiously. At the intersection of Boston Avenue and Route 25, he brakes hard, turns right, and fishtails. The Volvo swerves toward a Burger King parking lot. He steers into the skid, then yanks the wheel and straightens the car. He peels out and then cruises onto Route 25 toward Trumbull.

Grayson glances at the laptop: the red light blinks steadily. Yes, Wilson's going to Trumbull. If Grayson recalls, they bought a small ranch house in Trumbull awhile back, soon after Wilson's trial. Does Wilson realize he's being tracked?

Thirty-nine

Conrad sees a sign at the side of the road.

WELCOME TO TRUMBULL

ESTABLISHED 1725

He cruises north, careful now not to speed. If he's pulled over by a cop, it's bye-bye, baby. Game over. He hears a siren in the distance and lowers the window and listens carefully. It's headed in his direction. Yup, Grayson's called it in. He's one smart fucker, that shrink.

Just gotta keep going. If the cops're coming, it'll be a race to the finish line. After that, it'll be checkmate.

On the left side of White Plains Road, he sees a mammoth corporate park—a cluster of ultramodern office buildings with glass facades shimmering in the morning light. The surrounding trees reflect off their mirrorlike veneers. A sprawling parking lot fronts the buildings where a few dozen cars are parked. A hapless group of corporate drones are working their bedraggled asses off on a Saturday morning. Perfect.

He barrels into the parking area and heads toward the cars. He pulls to a stop near the rear row, turns the ignition off, and jumps out with his day pack.

In a crouch, he slinks over the blacktop and darts between cars, looking for one that'll fit the bill. He's gotta find a gas-guzzler from 2004 or earlier. The newer models have "kill switches," so hotwiring them's a major hassle. You could get a world-class shock just trying. An older heap won't have a state-of-the-art alarm and has a simpler door lock mechanism.

A beige 2000 Ford Taurus sits right there. Perfect. He peers in the passenger-side window. No sign of an alarm system. Of course, you never know. *But life's filled with unknowns*, thinks Conrad.

He opens his day pack, grabs the chisel, wedges it between the rubber insulation and metal edge of the passenger-side window, forces the handle toward the car, and gets good leverage. There's a groan as the door separates from the frame, leaving a quarter inch of space between the door and weather-stripping. He slides the hanger wire in, angles it down to the door lock lever and presses. The electrical tape makes for good friction; there's no slippage. The lever depresses. There's a snapping sound as the passenger's door unlocks. He opens it.

No alarm.

He leans across and presses the master unlock button on the driver's side: all locks snap open. He scampers around the Taurus, flings open the driver's-side door, jumps in and tosses his day pack onto the passenger seat. He knows he's gotta move fast.

Grayson comes to the intersection of Route 25 and White Plains Road. He suddenly realizes his pulse is totally amped; it's going so fast, he feels fluttering, as though there's a bird in his chest. His arms feel like jelly; his hands go weak. He slows to thirty. Jesus, this is a goddamned freak-out.

He glances at the laptop. Wilson's been heading northeast on White Plains Road. Now it looks like he's slowing down. Grayson catches another glimpse of the screen. The dot blinks in place, maybe a mile away. Grayson estimates he's a minute behind Wilson. He's gotta be on the lookout for a blue Impala.

Suddenly, the dot stops moving and blinks in place; then

there's a blurred blip.

The dot vanishes.

Grayson realizes what's happened: Wilson's stopped the car.

The GPS tracker is motion-activated. It turns off when the car stops. The tracking device is useless. Grayson pulls the Volvo onto the shoulder of the road. He turns on the flashers. His thoughts streak to the possibilities facing him.

The last signal was at the Trumbull Corporate Park, a group of office buildings. Wilson may've gone into one. But which one? There are five buildings. No doubt the Impala's parked out front. But why would Wilson go there?

Another possibility strikes Grayson: he might have lost Wilson because of poor wireless transmission. He could be in a dead zone. It happens all the time in the wireless world. He can test it by hitting the speed dial on his cell phone—see if he gets a connection. In fact, he'll call 911. It occurs to Grayson that in his rush to notify the police about Wilson's escape, he didn't call the Trumbull police directly—he'd depended on the Stratford Police dispatcher. Maybe he should call the Trumbull cops directly, since he's in their town right now.

He fishes in his pocket, no phone. He pats himself down but can't find it. He looks on the seat near the laptop and then beneath it: not there. He bends over and looks on the floor and then in the glove compartment. There're only the registration, insurance card, and pistol. He again slaps his pockets and then reaches beneath the car seat. There's nothing.

He must have dropped the phone in the garage. He was in such a rush, he wasn't thinking, No cell phone and no option. He can't call anyone.

Conrad opens the day pack and removes the screwdriver, the folding knife, and the electrician's tape. He quickly undoes the screws from the plastic access cover beneath the Taurus's steering wheel.

Two red wires are there—the power supply for the ignition switch. He pulls them down; with the knife, he strips away an inch of insulation from the end of each wire. He twists the ends together, wraps them with tape, and leaves bare a small section of joined copper above the taped ends. The wires dangle in a V-shaped configuration.

No time to lose. The cops are only minutes away. He hears a siren's whine—closer now.

The ignition wire is covered with brown insulation. He strips away a half inch and touches the stripped wire to the bare copper of the intertwined red wires. Contact.

The engine whirrs and then turns over, running smoothly.

A fusillade of thoughts rushes through Grayson's mind.

Am I in a dead zone? Is Wilson in a dead zone? And if he's stopped the car, where has he gone? What's Wilson doing in an office building?

Grayson looks at the laptop. He decides to hit a different Web site.

With weak fingers, he types "VeriPoint" into the address bar and hits "Enter."

It *must* be a dead zone: the laptop's loading slowly. It registers nearly zero millibytes per second.

He throws the Volvo into "Drive," hits the gas, and hurtles onto the road with his blinker lights still flashing. Now he hears sirens approaching.

Grayson speeds ahead a quarter mile. He brakes and pulls onto the shoulder with the blinkers still flashing. The corporate park is nearby. He glances at the laptop.

The laptop loads in—quickly.

Conrad pulls out of the parking lot and swerves onto White Plains Road. He heads south, the opposite direction he drove to get here. He brings the Taurus up to sixty.

Cruising along, he passes a stalled silver Volvo sitting on the shoulder of the northbound side of the road; its blinker lights are flashing. Poor fucker's car has conked out. Those are the breaks.

He heads toward the Merritt Parkway.

Conrad's sure there's a GPS device in the pastor's Impala, most likely behind a bumper. It's just stuck in there, like a wad of bubble gum on a shoe sole. How else would the cops know he's here? He knows they're zeroing in on him because back at that corporate park, he heard sirens coming closer. A GPS—Grayson's doing. He's one smart shrink. It was a good move to dump the Impala in Trumbull—a solid diversion.

No matter what, the monitoring company knows he's gone—probably notified Grayson and the cops—and they're looking for a blue Impala in Trumbull. Good luck, Charlie.

Soon he's on the 49S entrance ramp to the Merritt. This early on a Saturday morning, the parkway's nearly deserted. Conrad cruises at a steady sixty-five, heading west along the two-lane, tree-lined highway. The sun's risen and it'll be a beautiful day—and he's gonna do what needs to be done.

He drives steadily past Easton, heading toward Eastport.

Forty

Megan stands at the stove, warming Philip's formula. Marlee is upstairs watching him, while she's downstairs preparing his bottle.

After Philip is fed, Adrian will be back from his morning run, and he'll take over while she prepares the kids' stuff to bring to Erin and Bob's place. In fact, she'll telephone Erin and find out if she wants Megan to bring a fresh baguette they can share at dinner. In another minute, the pot of water will be at a boil; it'll make the Similac too hot. Hearing a thump from upstairs, Megan goes to the foot of the stairway.

"Marlee, honey, are you watching your brother?"

"Yes, Mom. I'm just bouncing a ball."

"Okay. I'll be up in a minute."

Back at the stove, she picks up the bottle and squeezes a drop of formula onto her wrist. It's a bit too hot, so she'll let it cool for a few minutes.

Megan hears the mudroom door open; there's a shuffling sound, barely audible.

"Adrian, honey?" she calls, turning off the stove jet. "You said you want to call your mother early today. It might be a good time now, before we get busy with the kids."

The door into the kitchen clicks open.

"Adrian, when I finish feeding Philip, I'll call Erin and—" She turns.

And sees Conrad.

A shock wave of fear blasts through Megan. It's so sudden and violent, her body pitches backward and slams against the kitchen counter. She freezes in place as waves of fear jangle through her.

Conrad is huge, so muscular, his bulging shirt seems ready to tear at its seams. He's in a half crouch, arms spread to cut her off if she bolts. His face is red, contorted with rage. That purple forehead vein of his bulges and seems to throb. His eyes are insane-looking globes of blue-gray ice, and a guttural snort erupts from his throat. He looks like a beast.

He moves closer, and his lips are wet with spittle so thick it looks like the foam of a mad dog's mouth. It's animal madness in the guise of a human being.

Megan's thoughts flood in a mind rush: the night he took a knife to Marlee, the locker room, the elevator—it's a heated broth of confusion and fear, and she wants to run. But she can't, not here, not with the kids at home and not with her legs so weak and rubbery. Volts of panic burst through her, sending shock waves of inertia to every part of her body.

Conrad's lips move—he's saying something—but Megan hears only the blood rush in her ears. Her hands are like jelly, and she's frozen with terror.

He nears her and reaches out.

In a mindless blur, Megan—somehow galvanized—hurls the pot of near-boiling water in his face. Conrad blinks and says nothing as his mouth twists into a grimace of pain. He blinks a few times, shakes his head, and moves in.

Megan sprints around the butcher-block island.

Conrad—his face crimson and blistering, the skin curdling—circles the island. His movements are feline, like a lion stalking prey through the veld.

Megan cries out, but it's garbled. Her heart slams like a

piston; her muscles quiver; every nerve ending in her body fires frantically.

He lunges for her, but Megan scrambles away. She gropes for something and her hand slaps onto the kitchen counter, her eyes steadily on him. Plates rattle and shatter onto the floor.

He circles the island. The skin on his face bubbles; his eyes are reddened, puffy.

Megan finds it behind her: a slicing knife is in her hand. She circles away from him.

"I'll cut you, you son of a bitch," she hears herself shriek.

He lunges toward her.

She lashes out. The knife slices through the air. Misses.

He draws back and circles the other way.

Something changes in Megan. Suddenly, she feels no fear. Instead, a flush of rage—like white heat—sears through her. She waves the knife—left, right—feints, ready to thrust or slice.

He lurches to her left and comes at her from the right.

She lashes out and the knife slices the back of his hand. Blood seeps from a severed vein, oozes and drips to the floor and spatters in crimson bursts.

He smiles, disregards the seep and drip of blood, stares at her, and feints again.

She slashes and misses.

"You knew I'd come back and catch you both . . ."

Megan backs away as Conrad lunges in each direction. God, he's so fast, shifting from one angle to another. With her free hand, she slaps again at the counter, grabs a frying pan, and flings it. It whips through the air and smashes into the refrigerator.

"Mommy!" Marlee shrieks from upstairs.

"Stay where you are, honey! Don't come down!"

"What's happening?" Marlee screams.

Conrad's eyes dart toward the stairway and quickly back to Megan. With melting skin hanging from his face, he circles the island.

Megan slashes; he jumps back. She thrusts and he quickly sidesteps the blade.

In an instant, he clamps a huge hand on her wrist and yanks her arm with such force it feels like it's ripping from its shoulder socket. Then he twists her arm and the knife clatters to the floor.

He clutches her arm and a fistful of hair. Everything swirls as Megan is hurled across the kitchen. Air bursts from her lungs as her back slams into the pantry door. The impact leaves her breathless, and she crumples to the floor.

"Mommy!" she hears Marlee cry.

Megan struggles to breathe. She gasps, and through a haze, sees Conrad above her. She hears Marlee shriek again—a horrified yelp, closer now—and Megan tries to tell Marlee to run, but she can't get air, can't get a word out. A hoarse, guttural sound erupts from her throat, nothing sensible. Her lungs feel like they've collapsed. She tries to get to her feet, but she's weak and dizzy, and Conrad's heavy boot thuds into her belly. It feels like her guts rupture. Nausea rises in a sickening eddy. She retches, gags, and chokes, and the room dims. Things seem far away as Conrad's knee thumps onto her chest and crushing pressure pins her to the floor.

Conrad grabs the knife.

Coming through the kitchen door, Adrian hears a deep thump.

His insides jump when he sees Megan on the floor, her features twisted in agony.

Conrad Wilson straddles her, clutching a raised knife.

Adrian moves quickly, but it feels like a languid flow of time. He hurtles toward Conrad. The knife flashes like a sliver of light, and he sees Conrad's melting face—purple, blistered, contorted. He hears Marlee shriek as Megan retches and the knife plummets down in a lethal arc.

Adrian's sneakers grip the tiles; he feels momentum build as he hurtles across the kitchen, and he senses the impending impact as he closes in on Conrad. He feels the power-packed spring in his legs as he bursts forward, but it feels like a freeze frame stoppage—as though he's plowing through some viscous substance, glue, or mucilage. Yet it's only a fraction of a second. He slams into Conrad, hurling him to the floor. Conrad lands on his back with a deep thud. Adrian tumbles on top of him.

Conrad pushes up; his power is incredible. Adrian leaps to his feet as Conrad rises from a crouch. Adrian rears back and swings from his hip with all his weight, his fist slams into Conrad's jaw. Conrad's head snaps back. He grunts from the force of the blow, yet stays on his feet. Even in that adrenaline-fueled moment, Adrian wonders how the man could withstand such a punch. Conrad moves forward. Adrian's other fist shoots out; he gut punches Conrad, landing a heavy blow to his midsection. Air whooshes from Conrad's lungs, and the knife slips to the floor. But Conrad stays on his feet.

Adrian lunges, but in a catlike move, Conrad sidesteps him, grabs Adrian's torso, and clamps his arms around Adrian. Conrad's hands lock, then squeeze. It's a viselike bear hug, constricting like a python's embrace. Adrian's ribs and spine compress and his face fills with blood. It feels swollen, like it'll explode. His chest feels too small for his lungs and heart; Conrad's grip tightens. Adrian can't get air; he can't expand his chest to breathe.

His knee plunges into Conrad's groin, but Conrad holds on, and suddenly Adrian is hoisted up and hurled back, and he tumbles through the air; the kitchen spins and he hits the floor. Bouncing like a discarded doll, the back of his head cracks onto the tile floor. There's an explosion of pain and white lights burst in his eyes.

Conrad looms over him.

Adrian's head clears; he kicks and thrusts his feet at Conrad, but it makes no difference. Conrad drops down—his knees crash into Adrian's chest and Adrian's breastbone feels crushed. Conrad straddles him, and his hand clamps onto Adrian's windpipe. Adrian is pinned, choking, as desperate gurgles ripple from his throat.

Conrad has the knife.

Adrian bucks his hips. Conrad pitches up and then comes down, still straddling him.

Adrian clutches Conrad's wrist and stops the knife thrust. The blade quivers as each man pushes. The knife sinks slowly toward Adrian.

Adrian tries to roll to the side, but he can't. Conrad is too heavy, far too powerful. His weight is overwhelming. Conrad's free hand curls into a fist as he drives a punch to Adrian's temple, but Adrian turns his head so the blow only grazes him, slamming his skull against the floor. A shower of lights bursts in his eyes, but Adrian holds on.

Adrian lurches sideways as the knife plunges down and pierces his left arm, near the shoulder. A lancing pain sears though his biceps and digs deeply. A shocklike sensation—like a blue light—shoots through his flesh. His arm spasms, then flops helplessly at his side. Adrian retches and fights the urge to vomit.

The blade rises—a lethal steel sliver in Conrad's fist.

Adrian hears Megan shriek, then groan; he hears Marlee scream. Adrian sees blood, smells its coppery odor, sees it ooze and drip—Conrad's blood, his own—flowing, seeping everywhere, on and around them; it's a slippery puddle in which they writhe on the floor; and Adrian feels Conrad's power, smells his breath, sees his scalded face, sees the blisters on his flesh, sees a huge vein pulsing on Conrad's forehead, sees mucous dripping from his nose, and sees the bubbling spittle on his lips and the wild look in his blood-reddened eyes. In that moment, the craziest thoughts swarm through Adrian's mind. His brain is afire with the instinct to survive, to avoid that abyss, the endless darkness, and he knows for certain he should have blown Conrad away that night in the cemetery on Bald Hill. He should have squeezed the trigger, shot out his brains and taken his life, wasted him—it would have been so easy—but he hadn't. And this is what it's come to, at this moment in their home, with Marlee screaming and Megan groaning. Adrian thinks she'll somehow save him—she'll grab a kitchen knife and thrust it into Conrad's neck, then twist it and slice through his carotid. She'll stab and slice, spraying his blood everywhere. But deep in Adrian's mind, he realizes Megan is semiconscious on the floor and Marlee's still shrieking, even as the knife begins its final plunge, and Adrian realizes he's weak and draining. He's sucking air, losing the struggle. In that split second of suspended time, Adrian realizes it's over. Everything he's ever known is coming to an end—the way it did for Dad in those final deathly seconds thirty-four years ago. Adrian knows he's dying, and he accepts that life will leave him. There are no more thoughts, no revelations, and nothing passes before his eyes—no backlit tunnel or white light or dreamy images, or visions, or illusions. It's not a misty, ethereal experience. It's Marlee screaming—the very last thing he'll ever hear. There's Conrad above him, grunting, his face contorted with hatred and looking like a wild animal, as the knife plummets. And in that fateful moment, Adrian hears an ear-shattering roar and sees Conrad's right eye burst open, as his face and head explode in a red, foam-filled blowback of blood, bone, and brains.

Police are everywhere, burly guys in blue. Sirens whoop insanely. Cops swarm through the house. Cameras click and whirr; flashes burst brightly in the kitchen; there's a blurred circus of movement and noise; it's all confusing. Adrian hears Megan trying to console Marlee, whose shrieking continues. Amid the tumult, Adrian hears men talking: cops, a fireman, and EMTs. He hears radio static, crackling, buzzing, and then more sirens. So many people, so much movement, everything seems to tumble and spin out of control. He's not really certain where he is, but it must be home because he can hear Megan and Marlee, even though they're far away.

Adrian lies on something soft. It moves a bit, and he realizes the EMT guys have him on a gurney; they're rolling him out to an ambulance. "You'll be okay, Doc," one says. "It's a nick to the brachial artery. You lost a lot of blood, but we're getting plenty of normal saline into you, and they'll hook you up in the ER."

"I feel so sleepy. Whadya give me?"

"Just a shot to mellow things out."

Adrian peers up through a haze and sees the IV bag hanging from a pole and a pulse oximeter on his index finger. He hears more voices, all blending now, and then more cameras click and it's all fuzzy. His lips feel thick. His tongue, too. It seems to flop in his mouth, and it's tough to get words out, so he's mumbling something, slurring his words, and everything drifts lazily. And now he's swaying gently. He's certain the EMT guys shot him up with morphine, maybe Demerol. It's like a kiss to the brain.

Suddenly, Megan's there and plants her moist lips on his. She whispers, "I love you."

He says something but isn't sure what it is. He thinks he reaches for her and feels her hand. He's being wheeled through the mudroom, then the garage, where he sees the rafters above, past the snow shovels, rakes, and weed whacker and out to the ambulance. The morning air hits him like a shock. His eyes tear. Everything is blurred and the gurney's rolling. Megan walks beside it and pulls a blanket up beneath his chin.

"How're the kids?" he asks thickly. Suddenly things spin, and yes, he's starting to drift down some foggy trail. Meandering now, just wandering, he isn't sure where. He knows his eyelids are fluttering—a sure sign of stupor, going to another world—and he can no longer feel his hands. Things are going dim, and the world wafts away. Soon he'll be somewhere else, if he's not there already.

He thinks he hears Megan say something, but he can't make it out. There's the fragrance of her hair, the feel of her skin as she bends over him and kisses him again. It's a soft, warm, moist feeling, her lips on his. She's incredibly delicious—unmistakably Megan. Like no other woman ever in his life.

"Love you," he slurs, and he closes his eyes and then opens them, and of all things, there's Mulvaney's huge, lined face—the granite jaw, those weathered Irish features—and Mulvaney's smiling at him through a rolling fog bank. It feels like he's somewhere in the English moors because everything's hazy, like in a dream.

Mulvaney says something, but it's indistinct. Adrian feels the gurney rising, and then he's in the ambulance. The gurney wheels collapse as he slides into the compartment. It smells antiseptic, like an OR. He feels Megan stroke his forehead. She pulls the blanket up again.

Patty's still talking, but his voice is fading.

Adrian's slipping away, just drifting somewhere, even as he's inside this ambulance—yes, that's where he is—and there's a keening sound as the siren wails and then he's hovering. He feels Megan next to him, hears Marlee, too, and it's so peaceful. He could stay this way forever.

Mulvaney goes into the living room.

"You get his statement?" he asks Harwood.

"Yeah, Chief. Got it all," Harwood says and pockets his digital voice recorder.

Mulvaney plops down in an armchair and then says, "How ya

doin', Doc?"

"I'm okay," Grayson replies, feeling an ache deep in his bones.

"Rough day, huh?"

Grayson nods, takes a deep breath and shakes his head wearily.

"That's some powerful piece; it packs quite a punch."

"It's registered. I have a permit."

"I know. A Walther 380. One of the best."

Mulvaney waits and then says, "You know the guardian and his wife are dead."

"Captain Harwood told me." Grayson shakes his head again and sighs. "It's a shame. The pastor was a good man . . . had a view of life that's hard to hold in this insane world. He had hope for humanity."

"How 'bout you, Doc? As a shrink, you see good and evil all the time, like I do. Is there any hope for us crazy sons of bitches?"

Grayson leans his tall frame forward and sets his forearms on his thighs as a wave of crushing fatigue plows through him. He peers at Mulvaney and says, "I wonder about humanity . . . I wonder and worry."

"Ya don't think kindness and love'll save us, Doc?"

Grayson smiles weakly and says, "Chief, I don't fucking know."

"Fair enough," Mulvaney says with a nod. He clasps his hands together. "Tell me somethin', Doc. How'd you know to come here?"

"To tell you the truth, Chief, I never knew that Dr. Douglas and Megan moved to Eastport. I thought they still lived in Trumbull, and I tracked Wilson there with the GPS."

"I got it, Doc. But the pastor's car was left in Trumbull. The tracking unit inside the bumper was useless. So how'd you know to get over here?"

"I never trusted Wilson—ever."

"So you had the monitoring bracelet on the guy and the GPS in the car."

"Right."

"But once he dumped the car in Trumbull, how'd ya know he'd come here?"

"I tracked him."

"How'd ya do that?"

"I didn't think we had enough safeguards. Whenever Wilson went on a pass, I insisted on examining his day pack before he brought it back to the ward. I told the pastor we didn't want inmates bringing in contraband. So while I had the thing, I had a lightweight GPS unit sewn into the lining. It weighs only a few ounces. Once the car's tracking device deactivated, I logged on to the Web site for the unit in the backpack."

"Clever," Mulvaney says. "Triple redundancy."

"That's right."

"Well, Doc, ya saved some lives today."

"But two innocent people are dead. The system failed completely."

"But *you* succeeded."

"If you want to call it success, Chief. It's a stain on the legal and psychiatric communities, and the Department of Corrections, too. We all failed, if you ask me."

"I'm not askin', Doc. I'm just sayin' you're a hero. You saved the life of the guy who saved *my* life. And his wife's life. Probably the kids', too."

Grayson wonders how it all came to this. Then he looks into Mulvaney's eyes. "Hey, Chief, you weren't at Wilson's trial, were you?"

"Na, I gotta run a police force."

"I still think about what he said on the stand."

"Yeah? What's that?"

"The DA asked Wilson if he wanted the jury to understand his version of the truth . . . about Adrian and Megan, and the little girl, Marlee . . . you know, Wilson's crazy belief that she's Adrian's kid."

"Yeah?"

"And Conrad said the jury didn't matter, that nothing matters."

"And?"

"He said, 'You can even kill me. It doesn't matter. My soul is dead.'" Grayson looks at Mulvaney. "He called it soul murder."

Mulvaney gets up and sets a huge paw on Grayson's shoulder. "Yeah, well, now the bastard's dead . . . and may his dead soul rest in peace."

Forty-one

"It's great to see ya lookin' so good," Mulvaney says as he dumps a third teaspoonful of sugar into his coffee, adds cream, and stirs the brew. He and Adrian sit in a vinyl booth across a Formica-topped table at Rory's, a roadhouse known best for its huge fire-grilled burgers—juicy half pounders made of ground chuck and sirloin, served with a heaping batch of french fries. The place is thronged by a clamorous lunchtime crowd. Patrons are bellied up three deep at the bar, talking, laughing, guzzling mugs of draft beer. Some people chomp burgers at the bar, while others down a liquid lunch. The clatter of cutlery, dishes, kitchen noise, and the hum of conversation fill the air.

"I know it isn't Starbucks," Mulvaney says with a shrug, "but the food's good. I come here all the time. Oh, and the tab's on me today."

"Thanks, Patty. Who needs Starbucks?" Adrian is aware that once again, when he's with Mulvaney, he feels enveloped in a protective shield—and it's not because the big guy's a police chief. It's a father-son kind of thing, and Adrian senses it's just as gratifying for the chief as it is for him. Mulvaney has no kids, and each has become for the other what was never to be had, or was lost early in life.

Mulvaney sips his coffee. "So tell me, when ya getting back to crackin' chests?"

"Tomorrow. Four weeks is enough time off, and I'm ready. The arm feels like new, and I've been exercising it."

"Ya gonna save some more lives, huh?"

"I'm gonna try."

Adrian pauses and looks at Mulvaney's ruddy complexion. "You're looking good, Patty. How's the diet?"

"Marge keeps an eagle eye on me, but to tell ya the truth, I gotta splurge now and then. That's why I come here—for the burgers. A little fat once in a blue moon won't kill me, right? If she ever asks what I order, tell her it's tuna on whole wheat," Mulvaney says with a wink.

Adrian nods, knowing Mulvaney loves this little conspiratorial exchange.

"How're Megan and the kids?"

"Between dealing with Marlee's trauma, nursing me, and taking care of Philip, Megan's been busy. She's getting back to work next week . . . part-time. We've arranged for someone to care for Philip since Erin's gone back to work, too."

"Ah, modern married life," Mulvaney says. "Marge and I'll never understand this day-care crap."

"It's a different world now, Patty."

"Yeah, I'm just an old fart."

"But you're *my* old fart, and it's always good to be with you, Patty."

The waitress, standing at another table, spies Mulvaney, smiles and nods. He gives her a wave. It's obvious Mulvaney visits quite often for his lunchtime splurges.

"So like I said, Adrian, Grayson's testifying at the Public Health Commission. He's pushin' for some reforms in the Mental Hygiene Laws."

"Maybe something good'll come out of all this."

"I hope so. We don't wanna see another situation like Wilson's."

Mulvaney's cell phone goes off. He looks at the screen and

puts it to his ear.

"What's up, Ed?"

His eyebrows rise and he says, "Who's the vic?" Listening again, his eyes widen. "Really? *Here*? In Eastport?" He shoots a glance at Adrian; Mulvaney's eyes seem to say, *Wait until you hear this . . .*

Adrian feels his muscles tighten. *Vic? What the hell's going on? A murder?*

Mulvaney listens intently, shakes his head, and says, "Conrad Wilson? Jesus!" His index finger rises, a clear signal that something's up—something relating to Adrian and Megan.

Adrian's entire body tenses. *Conrad Wilson? Vic? What the hell's going on?*

"No kiddin'?" Mulvaney says. He listens again, glances at Adrian, and shakes his head. "Son of a bitch," Patty says. "That bastard leaves a wake of destruction wherever he goes."

A jangling sensation rips through Adrian. Through the lunchtime crowd, he hears his pulse pounding in his ears. His face feels hot and his throat constricts.

Conrad Wilson? The bastard's dead. What the hell's going on?

"Twenty-two Middle Brook Road, got it," Mulvaney says. "You call the ME yet?"

There's a pause as Mulvaney listens again, shakes his head and sighs.

"All right. I'm sure Doc Sandler'll be there soon."

Mulvaney listens for a moment and then says, "About ten minutes." He nods and says, "No kiddin'." He's about to close the phone but adds, "Listen, Ed, do me a favor. Call Dr. John Grayson at Whitehall Institute in Ansonia."

Mulvaney snaps the cell phone shut. "Lunch is over, Adrian," he says. "It's police business." He pushes away from the table and says, "Actually, you might wanna come along and see for yourself."

"Why?" Adrian's stomach gurgles, and it isn't because he's

hungry.

"I'll tell you in the car."

"Hello, Chief," the pert, ponytailed waitress says with her pad and pencil at the ready. "What'll it be, a burger, medium rare with fries, extra pickles, then apple pie à la mode?"

"Not today, Cheryl," Mulvaney says, standing. He drops two dollar bills onto the table, grabs his coat, and says, "Let's go Adrian."

Twenty-two Middle Brook Road is a modest brick house set back from the leafy, sycamore-lined sidewalk. Unlike other dwellings on the street, no bikes or toys are scattered about the lawn. Nothing signals that kids live there. Two police cruisers are parked in front of the place; one has its lights flashing. Neighbors—mostly women with young kids and strollers—stand on the sidewalk. Adrian sees two police officers talking at the open front door.

As Adrian and Mulvaney get out of the chief's car, a green Buick Regal parks in front of them. A distinguished-looking older man with a shock of wavy white hair gets out of the car; he's carrying a leather satchel. "That's the ME," says Mulvaney.

"How ya doin', Harry?"

"Fine, Patrick. And you?" They shake hands.

"I'm great. Harry, this is Dr. Adrian Douglas. Adrian, Dr. Harry Sandler, medical examiner."

"You're a cardiovascular surgeon at Eastport General, right?" Sandler says as they shake hands. "You operated on my brother-in-law, Steve Burnham."

"I remember him," Adrian says. "He's a professor of economics at Yale."

"That's right, and he's doing great, thanks to you."

"Give him my regards," Adrian says.

They walk into the house through the open front door.

"Down here, Chief," Harwood says, pointing to a stairwell.

Through an arched entrance to the living room, Adrian sees a police officer and a dark-haired woman in her forties. She sits on a sofa, elbows on her knees, head buried in her hands. Sobbing, she never looks up. The place is furnished in Early American style, very colonial looking. Curled up asleep on a rocking chair is an orange tabby housecat.

"That the older sister?" Mulvaney asks Harwood.

"You got it, Chief. She decided to come home for lunch to check things out."

Adrian follows Harwood, Mulvaney, and Sandler down a narrow wooden stairway to an unfinished basement. A bare lightbulb illuminates the gray cinder-block walls and rough cement floor. A furnace and water heater are located on one side of the room. A sump pump is in the corner.

Adrian estimates the basement ceiling's about eight feet high. Wooden floor planks above are supported by thick, rough-hewn joists. Cast-iron and copper pipes crisscross the ceiling, along with rubber-coated wires intertwined among them. Aluminum air ducts sprout from the furnace, pierce the basement ceiling and lead to different rooms of the house. It's forced-air heating. A dark crawl space is behind the furnace.

A repulsive odor permeates the dimly lit basement. Adrian thinks it's the stench of excrement, urine, dust, and mold mixed with damp masonry. Actually, he thinks, it's the reek of abject misery. It catches at the back of his throat. Mulvaney pulls out a handkerchief and covers his nose. Harwood gags. Sandler has no reaction.

Hanging from an overhead pipe by a thick, braided rope is the limp, nightgown-clad body of Nicole DuPont. Her bare feet droop downward in death, her toes only inches from the basement floor. Her feet are purple and swollen. Body fluids have leaked downward and collected in her lower limbs. Her roped neck is arched and stretched at an obscene angle. Her nose is angled up; the nostrils look like dark ovoid caves. Purple bruising permeates the neck skin beneath the rope. Her face is bluish, with lividly swollen lips and protruding tongue. Her eyes are vacant, bulging, partly rolled up into her head. A short wooden stool lies off to the side.

"A horrible death," murmurs Sandler. "She knocked the stool over. It was too short a fall to break the neck, so she just dangled and was strangled to death. It took awhile," he mutters. "The cyanotic face and feces are a giveaway. It's like she was garroted from behind . . . slowly."

Sandler reaches out and touches Nicole's wrist. "Cold as ice. She's been dead for a while," he says. "It takes time for the feet to swell . . . maybe five or six hours. Must've hung herself early this morning."

"After the sister left for work," Mulvaney says.

"That's the way most suicides go . . . when the victim's alone," Sandler says.

Harwood heads for the stairs.

The body sways after Sandler's touch. Adrian recalls Nicole at the competency hearing and trial, her passion, her confidence, her incredible vitality, and her knowledge—medical and legal—and her potent sensuality. Now she's limp, lifeless—extinguished.

My God! Adrian thinks. What could have gone so wrong that she now hangs like a gutted animal in a slaughterhouse? Flaccid, swaying at a rope's end in a dank basement. Life's so strange, so fucking crazy.

In the dull glow of the sixty-watt bulb, Adrian regards Nicole's diaphanous nightgown, the silky down on her arms, the painted toenails, and the chalky pale—now ghostly—cast of her skin. Though he's seen many dead bodies—in hospitals, operating rooms, morgues, and the dissection room in medical school—Adrian's never seen a suicide victim. It hits him like a fist in the chest.

Two more cops tramp down the stairway. One turns back and retches at the stench. The other covers his nose, turns away, and heads upstairs.

"Eastport cops aren't used to this," Mulvaney says. "They shoulda served in New Haven."

"When the forensic unit gets here, we'll take her down and process the body," Sandler says.

"Chief," calls Harwood from atop the stairs. "The note's upstairs. It's printed out and it's on the computer. Her sister found it, then found the body downstairs."

They stomp up the stairs. Nearing the study, Adrian sees John Grayson enter the house. He has that dark stubble; his eyes are red, bleary. From his haggard, ashen look, it's clear that Harwood told Grayson about Nicole DuPont's suicide.

"Sorry about this," Mulvaney says to Grayson.

Grayson nods.

"The body's in the basement," Mulvaney says. "You wanna see it?"

Grayson shakes his head. He sees Adrian. They shake hands silently.

"I've been worried about her," Grayson says. "She took medical leave from Whitehall two weeks ago, seemed really depressed. It got so bad, she left her place in Hamden and moved in here with her sister."

"Any idea why?" Mulvaney asks.

"No. She was really withdrawn these last few weeks. I tried to get her to talk about it, but she wouldn't."

"There's a suicide note in the den," says Mulvaney.

A schoolhouse clock in the hallway lets out Westminster chimes and bongs twice. It's two o'clock in the afternoon.

In the den, Mulvaney nods to an officer standing at the

computer. A sheet of paper rests on the keyboard. Mulvaney begins reading.

"It's on the monitor, too," says the officer.

"May I?" Grayson asks.

"Sure," Mulvaney says. "Just touch the side of the mouse; nothing else."

Grayson sits in the computer chair and touches the mouse. The screen reveals a single-spaced typed letter.

My dear Nina:

I'm truly sorry for any pain I've caused you, my beloved sister, and others.

My life is no longer worth living. This is the only way to right the wrongs that I've done. This is the only choice left. My life is an abysmal failure.

Please contact John Grayson at Whitehall and tell him how much I regret my role in what happened. He was right about Conrad Wilson. I was wrong. I was convinced Conrad's sanity was restored. I became his advocate. It should never have been my role. I was so forceful and so wrong.

Conrad and I had a physical relationship in my office when we met for his counseling sessions. I crossed that boundary and violated everything I held dear. I loved him and thought he loved me. I never saw through his lies and deceit. I convinced myself we would move to Colorado and live together. I even applied for a medical license there.

I lost all perspective. I no longer saw Conrad as a madman. I didn't let myself see that his only goal was to leave Whitehall so he could exact revenge on Megan Haggarty and Adrian Douglas.

I'm responsible for what happened. I coached Conrad and told him about the MMPI. I warned him about the cross-referenced questions, so he memorized them as he went along and never gave contradictory answers. He outwitted the test and appeared normal. It was all an act. Because I loved him, I was blinded, even deluded by love.

Because of me, Pastor Wilhelm and his wife are dead.

Because of me, Adrian Douglas and Megan Haggarty almost died, and their children were put at terrible risk. I don't know if their daughter, Marlee, will ever get over what she saw happen. Or if she'll ever erase seeing John Grayson forced to kill Conrad in their home.

I betrayed my colleagues, my profession, everyone. I thought Conrad loved me, and I was as mad as he was. I caused terrible pain and suffering. I cannot go on.

My dearest Nina, everything I have is yours, especially my love.

Nicole

Grayson shakes his head and peers up at Adrian. "Remember what I said about delusions?"

"They never go away."

"She loved that crazy bastard," Mulvaney says. "Maybe love's mad, huh?"

"Early on, probably," Grayson says. "You know, the whole falling in love thing, before you get to know the real-life person."

"You think it's delusional?" Adrian asks.

"Maybe it is."

"You think *she* was crazy?" Mulvaney asks.

"Falling for Conrad Wilson was madness," Grayson says.

"But was *she* crazy?"

"*Killing* herself was crazy," Grayson says.

"Is *love* mad?" Adrian asks.

"Do you remember first falling in love?"

"Sure," Adrian says.

"Maybe it's temporary loss of sanity," Mulvaney says.

"Do we ever see a lover realistically . . . in a completely sane way?" Grayson asks. His eyes look bleary.

"I'm crazy about my wife," Mulvaney says. "How 'bout you, Adrian. You *mad* about Megan?"

"Absolutely," Adrian says, thinking how he wants—more than anything in the world—to go home to the people he loves. Call it absurd, call it madness, or even crazy.

Soon Marlee will be home from school, and she'll ask him with those eyes of hers, wide and inquiring—as she always does—to help with her homework. It's a ritual by now, almost a little game they play. Like when they play checkers; and now she's learning chess. He teaches her and she catches on to everything very quickly. He loves it, and Marlee knows he does. She adores it, too. It's part of their being together, sharing; it's part of being a family.

And for the rest of the day, into the evening and night, he'll be with them—with Megan, Marlee, and Philip—and while the next day's surgeries will be at the back of his mind, as they should be, the most important part of his life is being with them, spending time with the three beings on this earth who are so precious to him. It's impossible to find words to express his feelings.

Adrian knows he wants always to be with them—the people who make everything worthwhile, who give his life substance and meaning, who fill his life with possibility, who've kept his soul alive and about whom he's crazy and without whom Adrian knows he'd go mad.

And he thinks to himself, *so what if love is a form of madness? That's just the way it is. I'm lucky to love and be loved. I'm the luckiest guy in the world.*

Afterthought

The interface between psychiatry and the law has always been murky.

The cases and principles of law cited in *Love Gone Mad* are all true. They depict the medicolegal quandaries occurring frequently in American courtrooms. Of course, neither psychiatry nor the law can address the conundrum of the soul. What exactly is a "soul"? Is it the capacity for human empathy, for feelings, understanding, caring, and loving?[1] Or does it have some higher, even religious implication?

A novel usually depicts conflict and feelings: love, jealousy, hatred, revenge, greed, lust, and others. In living our lives, we often face dilemmas—legal and otherwise—as complicated as the human condition.

---

[1] Dr. Leonard Shengold, in his book *Soul Murder: The Effects of Childhood Abuse and Deprivation,* noted the phrase *a soul murder* was first used by playwrights Henrik Ibsen and August Strindberg to describe the destruction of the love of life in another human being.

Acknowledgments

As I've said before, no novel is a product of its author alone. Many people contributed their time and effort to reading and making suggestions, thereby improving the manuscript. They were my brain trust—my partners in creativity—and were indispensable to my writing efforts. I cannot thank them enough.

Deepest thanks to Kristen Weber for showing me the way of the novel. She devoted time, energy, and enthusiasm to this project.

Relatives and friends graciously devoted their time and talent to reading the manuscript at various stages and made valuable suggestions. They include Claire Copen, Rob Copen, Marty Isler and Natalie Isler, Helen Kaufman and Phil Kaufman, Arthur Kotch and Jill Kotch, and Barry Nathanson and Susan Nathanson. Their suggestions, criticisms, and comments were marks of friendship and vastly improved what I'd written. They cared enough to provide me with honest feedback, which was crucial to the novel.

Other people, both living and dead, made their own (most unknowingly) contributions to my knowledge base and authorial efforts. They include Dick Simons, Bill Console, Warren Tanenbaum, Charles Darwin, Edgar Rice Burroughs, Clarence Darrow, Sigmund Freud, Zane Grey, the Grimm Brothers, Edith Hamilton and a vast array of Greek myths, Homer, Herodotus,

Aeschylus, Sophocles, Jim Kjelgaard, John R. Tunis, Jack London, Edgar Allen Poe, and William MacLeod Raine.

Equally important to the writing of the novel and its eventual execution were Melissa Danaczko, Bruce Glaser, Sharon Goldinger, Kristen Havens, Lynda Ling, Penina Lopez, Pam Miller, Leonard Shengold, Liz Lauer, Tracy Minsky, Meryl Moss, and a cadre of writers, artists, physicians, attorneys, and educators of every kind.

My brilliant wife, Linda, tirelessly read different versions of the manuscript and made all the difference in the world to the final outcome. She's a source of courage, inspiration, and love.

About the Author

After graduating from NYU with a degree in business administration, Mark Rubinstein served in the US Army as a field medic tending to paratroopers of the Eighty-Second Airborne Division. After discharge from the army, he gained admission to medical school. He became a physician and then took a psychiatric residency, becoming involved in forensic psychiatry and testifying in trials as an expert witness.

He became an attending psychiatrist at New York Presbyterian Hospital and a clinical assistant professor of psychiatry at Cornell University Medical School, teaching psychiatric residents, psychologists, and social workers while practicing psychiatry.

Before turning to fiction, he coauthored five nonfiction, self-help books for the general public. His first novel, *Mad Dog House*, was published by Thunder Lake Press in 2012.

He is a contributor to *Psychology Today* and a blogger for the *Huffington Post*. He lives in Connecticut and is working on other novels.

Preview of *Mad Dog Justice*

Chapter 1

Danny Burns sits at his office desk and rubs his forehead. His temples throb. It's another headache beginning, and this one's going to be a bone-crusher. Doc Gordon says it's tension, because he can't find a thing wrong—physically. It feels like a vise is clamping down on his skull.

"So what's troubling you?" Doc Gordon asked.

"Nothin', Doc . . . absolutely nothin'."

"Well, these are classic tension headaches."

Tension, worry, and aggravation: they're permanent fixtures in his life, ever since what went down ten months ago.

It's nearly eight o'clock on this frigid February night. The office is sepulchral. The only sound is the occasional whooshing of tires as cars pass by on McLean Avenue, two stories below. The windowpane rattles as a gust of wind whips against it. Danny reminds himself to talk to the landlord about the thermal pane replacements he said he'd install. *Yeah, don't hold your breath,* Dan thinks. *Leave it to Donovan and it'll never get done.* The building's owner is too busy flipping properties all over Yonkers.

Danny gazes at his laptop screen and then at the papers on his desk. The April 15 tax deadline is only two months away, and he's got a ton of work. Even though most clients have their returns filed electronically, the majority don't use the worksheet Danny provides them. They mail him hand-scrawled notes and figures—a jumble of jottings along with heaps of documentation. He and his assistants spend more time sorting through the junk than actually entering data into the computer. They're all billable hours, but it's mostly crap that could be done by a monkey. He thinks it might be wise to hire another part-time assistant. If he does, it'll set a personal record for employing temporary help.

Danny knows the reasons he's needed additional assistance these last few months: he hasn't been focused on work. Sometimes he just zones out like he's floating in space. God Almighty, he used to zero in on things like a laser beam. "Detail Dan" was what Angela would jokingly call him. But for the past ten months, he's been lucky if he remembered to slip into his pants in the morning. And Angela's noticed it big-time.

"You're not listening to a word I say," she calls after him as he wanders through the house, looking for his wallet or car keys, which always seem to be misplaced. "You're in another world," she mutters as he retraces his steps for the third time, searching for his watch or cell phone.

"Angela, I'm late and I need my cell phone."

"I swear, Danny, you're out of it these days. You were never this way . . . not till last May or June. What's happened to you?"

Dan's thoughts are interrupted by a nerve-jangling blast of sound that sends him lurching forward. It's the telephone. He picks up the receiver.

"Daniel Burns . . ." he says, trying to sound professional.

"Danny, when are you coming home?"

"Angela, honey . . . I have a ton of work."

"*Daniel . . .*"

She uses his formal name only when she's really annoyed, totally pissed. She picked it up from Ma, years ago. But nowadays, she uses *Daniel* way too often. It annoys him, but why start an argument? It'll just bring on another headache.

"You're always late and you're always at the office. I swear, if I didn't know better, I'd think you had a girlfriend."

"Oh, Angela . . . please stop this nonsense."

"I can't. You've been *living* at the office. You used to rush home so we'd have dinner together at six, as a family. Now you're a ghost."

Ghost. The word sends a shiver through him. And it runs the risk of throwing his lungs into a full-blown asthmatic attack. *Ghost*. It was Grange's moniker, and it reminds him of that horrific night in the woods with Roddy and Kenny.

"What's happening with you? Can you tell me something . . . *anything*?"

"I've been working on some personal deals for Jack Sobin—for John Harris, too. It's gotten very complicated and I—"

"Oh, c'mon. You've always hired people a few months before tax time. You never stayed at the office this late. I'll bet you're there alone, right?"

"Look—"

"Am I right? You're there alone. No help?"

"I know, but—"

"Danny, what's going on?"

"Whaddaya mean?"

"It's not because of tax time. It's been almost a year since I had the *real* Danny . . . *my* Danny."

"C'mon, Angie. You're exaggerating."

"No, I'm not. Since you guys got rid of that restaurant, you've changed."

"I don't know what you mean."

"You've been jumpy. And remote."

"Remote?"

"Yes, *remote*. As though you're not really here with me and the kids anymore. And Tracy says it's the same with Roddy. She sometimes sees him with this faraway look in his eyes. What's with you two?"

"I don't know what you're talking about."

But he does; he knows precisely what she means. Since that night upstate, it feels like he's been living in the arctic tundra—alone and in a whiteout.

"Yes, you do. You know *exactly* what I mean."

Danny's about to protest, but he knows Angela's right. She's nobody's fool, and she reads him like a fortune cookie. He closes his eyes and sighs.

"Oh, Dan . . . can't you tell me what's bothering you? We've never kept things from each other . . ."

A feeling of futility seeps through Danny. How can he tell Angela that he and Roddy live every day wondering if the guillotine's blade will drop? They worry the Jersey mob or the Russian Brotherhood or Grange's shadowy associates will slither out from beneath a rock and come gunning for them.

And how can he ever tell Angela about that night near that isolated pond with the peeping frogs, the lanterns, and the crickets—the night that changed their lives forever?

Jesus, this is torture, Danny thinks. He and Roddy will never escape the monster they created by going into business with Kenny Egan, now rotting in the swampy soil an hour from where he, Angie, and the kids live in Tuckahoe.

"Listen, Angela . . ."

"Don't give me that *Listen, Angela . . .*"

Dan wants to object to Angela's characterizations, but he knows it'll be little more than some feeble protestation. And the frailty of his denial will only deepen Angela's conviction that something's wrong—very wrong. He's about to say something—anything that will cut short this mind-numbing discussion—when Dan hears something near the office door. Is it a creaking sound? It could be someone walking across the outer office's wooden floor. Or maybe it's the wind rattling the windowpanes and he's hearing it from down the corridor.

Still holding the receiver in his hand, Dan peers at the partially opened office door. Angela says something, but it's merely a swirl of chatter tumbling in his right ear. Dan's mind spins; there are no real thoughts, just a sense of *something*—a primal awareness of danger. He definitely hears something in the corridor, next to the small conference room to the right of his office. It's nearly obscured by the rush of wind rattling the windowpane.

Danny feels the hairs on his wrist standing as voltage sears through his nerve endings.

Angela's voice seeps through the telephone, but it's just meaningless sound pouring from the receiver.

"Wait, honey," he says, craning his neck, but he sees nothing. Holding the phone receiver to his right ear, he says, "I'll be home soon."

There's movement—it's in his peripheral vision, a blur—and in the moment it takes to realize it, Danny hears the office door swing open. He's starts to swivel the chair; he squints and tries to focus on the door. He feels his body tense; a strange sound comes from the doorway—like the muffled pop of a cork being pulled from a wine bottle. In that moment, just as he turns the chair, Danny's right hand and the telephone receiver explode in a shocklike blast. Shards of plastic slash his ear and face, and a searing sensation tears at the back of his head. The hand pain is so intense, it's blinding.

Danny is thrust back violently; the chair nearly topples over. His body tightens in paralytic fear. There's another cork popping, and something slams into his chest—his lungs feel like they're imploding as he and the chair pitch backward.

The overhead lights swirl, and Danny realizes he's lying on the floor. He hears something to his right—furniture moving or a cabinet opening—he can't be sure. The room grows fuzzy.

His breath comes in shallow bursts, and he hears a sucking sound from his chest. His mouth goes dry. He feels bone-crushing pain in his hand. He opens his eyes. The room pinwheels and he slaps his left hand to the floor, as if to steady himself in a whirlpool's vortex. The room sways like a huge sea swell and then whirls. Everything is bleached, turns brilliantly white, and his insides shudder as though something crawls through his chest. Danny's in a haze, and things get foggy, as the strangest thought streaks through his mind. *Jesus, sweet Jesus . . . I deserve this.*

The chest pain recedes. The room swirls again—it's a merry-go-round—then everything dims and grows cold. He shivers. It all seems muted and distant, and he suddenly feels he's floating in a void.

Then comes darkness.